PEOPLE of THE BOOK
(עם הספר)
A Decade of Jewish Science Fiction & Fantasy

OTHER BOOKS BY RACHEL SWIRSKY

How the World Became Quiet (forthcoming)
Through the Drowsy Dark

OTHER BOOKS BY SEAN WALLACE

Bandersnatch (with Paul Tremblay)
Best New Fantasy
Fantasy (with Paul Tremblay)
Horror: The Best of the Year (with John Gregory Betancourt)
Japanese Dreams
The Mammmoth Book of Steampunk (forthcoming)
Phantom (with Paul Tremblay)
Realms: The First Year of Clarkesworld Magazine (with Nick Mamatas)
Realms 2: The Second Year of Clarkesworld Magazine (with Nick Mamatas)
Weird Tales: The 21st Century (with Stephen H. Segal)
Worlds of Fantasy: The Best of Fantasy Magazine (with Cat Rambo)

PEOPLE OF THE BOOK
(עם הספר)
A Decade of Jewish
Science Fiction & Fantasy

edited by
Rachel Swirsky
& Sean Wallace

PRIME BOOKS

People of the Book: A Decade of Jewish Science Fiction & Fantasy
(עם הספר)

Prime Books
www.prime-books.com

For more information, contact Prime Books.

ISBN: 978-1-60701-238-2

To Sandy Swirsky and Lyle Merithew, the best parents ever to serve
Chinese food on Christmas Eve.

To Cordelia and Natalie, and my wife: *Ikh hob dikh tsufil lib.*

Acknowledgements

Thanks to all of the people who helped us put this book together by giving advice, pointing us toward great stories and great authors, digging up contact information, occasionally assisting us with correspondence, and even taking the time to discuss philosophy and history when we had questions.

Our profound thanks to Sonya Taaffe for her labor, recommendations, and insight, most particularly for her inspiring reading of "The Problem with Susan." Thanks to Charles Tan for building a database to help us scour the Internet, to Gordon Van Gelder for connecting us with excellent stories and authors from *The Magazine of Fantasy and Science Fiction*, to Lavie Tidhar for his thoughts on Jewish science fiction and fantasy authors outside the United States, to Boris Sidyuk for connecting us with authors outside the U.S., and to Jeannelle Ferreira for her early aid and support. We also owe special thanks to Ann VanderMeer for agreeing to provide us with an introduction.

Many people helped us find stories via email, forums, blogs, and our Internet database. Some recommended stories directly; others helped us by boosting the signal. We extend our thanks to all of them, including this partial list: Saladin Ahmed, Camille Alexa, Nathan Blumenfield, Leah Bobet, Stephanie Burgis, Doug "Dougals" Burke, Michael A. Burstein, Douglas Cohen, Cathy Dalek, Leah Cypress, A. M. Dellamonica, Wendy Delmater, Michele Lee, Shira Lipkin, Nick Mamatas, Deirdre Saoirse Moen, Ben Phillips, Gillian Pollack, Tim Pratt, Benjamin Rosenbaum, Lawrence Schimel, Diana Sherman, Felicity Shoulders, Steven Silver, Roger Silverstein, Katherine Sparrow, Jonathan Strahan, Dave Thompson, and A.C. Wise.

PEOPLE OF THE BOOK

Introduction

Ann VanderMeer

In the beginning there was the story. And the story was without form or expression. Then the writer infused the story with life. The writer said, let there be a tale so wondrous that all will want to read it. The writer wrote the story and saw that it was good.

Okay, so I am taking liberties here with the book of Genesis. However without the story there would be no book, no People of the Book either. The Bible is often recognized as the story of the Jewish people. Throughout history we have used stories to educate, to amuse, to frighten and to soothe ourselves—to survive and to pass the words on to the next generation.

There is the Written Law (The Torah) and the Oral Law (The Talmud). But what are these ancient writings, really, except stories we tell ourselves?

The Oral Law is the commentary on the Written Law. It's filled with tales to help illustrate and explain the laws in the Torah. In some cases it fills in the gaps and shows us how to live our lives. So the stories have a specific purpose—to enlighten. As the legend goes, the Torah was given to the Jewish people because they promised to pass it on to their children. And the Torah was to be accessible to scholar and layman alike.

At my synagogue in Tallahassee we have four Torah scrolls. On Erev Yom Kippur during the Kol Nidre service each one is held lovingly by a congregant who has been honored with this assignment. One year I was given this honor. As I stood on the *bimah* holding this Torah scroll that originated from Europe over one hundred years ago on this holiest of nights, I couldn't help but feel all the souls that came before me. All the people who had held, read from and touched this scroll. The ones who listened as the Baal Torah chanted from it. I felt connected to all of them, and it was the words in the scroll that brought us together across all time and space.

For so many years the Jew has traditionally felt like an outsider and has striven to belong. We try to take on the culture of the people around us, try to assimilate; however, we can't help but feel pride and belonging with the all the generations that came before us. We seek to blend in, and yet still wanting to stand out. And as much as we try to escape ourselves and our history, we're drawn back to it—by the stories.

At the same time as we want to acknowledge the stories we grew up with, we also want to create our own, and thus add to our history. We strive to re-imagine ourselves. In these pages you will find fantastical realms that are not that much different in type from the ones we grew up with in the Torah or Talmud.

In the Torah you will find giants who mate with human women. A sea monster, an enormous bird and a huge mammal that will become our feast in the World to Come. A man with a speech impediment turns a staff into a snake and later parts the Red Sea after he has brought ten plagues onto the Egyptians. Manna falls from heaven, tasting exactly like whatever food you desire. And how about a burning bush that is never consumed?

There are angels and demons, their existence made more believable by the details of their written lives. Almost every book of the Torah contains references to angels and they are mentioned all through the Jewish prayer book. And the most important prayer of all, the Amidah (also known as the Shmoneh Esreh—the eighteen blessings, because there is magic in numbers), portrays bringing the dead back to life. The prophets—seeing into the future and foreseeing all kinds of doom and gloom for the Israelites. And just take a glance at the writings of Ezekiel, where he describes the Divine Chariot and a creature with four faces. If that's not fantastical, then I don't know what is.

By comparison, *The People of the Book* features transformation, from an angel to a demon, from a statue to a weapon. Redemption, as a boy comes to terms with the death of his older brother and his brother's ghost. Guilt, when a young man cannot carry the burden his forefathers place on him as he is called upon to protect our legacy to ensure our future. Yearning, as a family in war-torn Europe dreams of a better future. Desire, as a wife figures out how she really sees herself and what she really wants. Fear, as we hide from who we are and the true nature of *golems*. Wonder, when a young boy finds magic in his family's belongings. Relief, when we finally know we're safe.

These stories allow us to identify with, although briefly, so many different characters and places, they entertain us and they give us comfort.

And yet, the tales in this anthology often have a melancholic tinge, similar in tone to the minor keys of our musical liturgy. We don't want to be too comfortable, too happy. Because that might bring some bad luck onto us, might tempt the evil eye.

As I read these tales I can almost hear the cantor singing Kol Nidre. And I am drawn to the words (and worlds) written here. I feel a connection to these fictional souls just as I did that night in the synagogue, holding the Torah scroll. We're not the only people of the Book, but we are a people of the book. I hope you enjoy these stories chosen by Rachel Swirsky and Sean Wallace as much as I did. Perhaps you'll hear your own music. *L'chaim!*

Burning Beard:
The Dreams and Visions
of Joseph ben Jacob,
Lord Viceroy of Egypt

Rachel Pollack

"There was a young Hebrew in the prison, a slave of the captain
of the guard. We told him our dreams and he interpreted them."

Genesis, 41,12

"Why did you repay good with evil? This is the cup from which my
lord drinks, and which he uses for divination."

Genesis, 44,5

"If A Man Sees Himself In A Dream
—killing an ox.
Good. It means the removal of the dreamer's enemies.
—writing on a palette.
Good. It means the establishment of the dreamer's office.
—uncovering his backside.
Bad. It means the dreamer will become an orphan.

Excerpts from Egyptian Dream Book
(found on recto, or back side of a papyrus
from the Nineteenth Dynasty.

In the last month of his life, when his runaway liver has all but eaten his body,
Lord Joseph orders his slave to set his flimsy frame upright, like the sacred
pillar of the God Osiris in the annual festival of rebirth. Joseph has other things
on his mind, however, than his journey to the next world. He has his servant
dress him as a Phoenician trader, and then two bearers carry him alone to the
dream house behind the temple of Thoth, God of magic, science, writing, celestial navigation, swindlers, gamblers, and dreams. Joseph braces himself against

the red column on the outside of the building, then enters with as firm a step as he can. The two interpreters who come to him strike him as hacks, their beards unkempt, their hair dirty, their makeup cracked and sloppy, and their long coats—

It hardly matters that the coats are torn in places, bare in others. Just the sight of those swirls of color floods Joseph's heart with memory. He sees his childhood dream as if he has just woken up from it. The court magicians in their magnificent coats lined up before Pharaoh. The Burning Beard and his brother shouting their demands. The sticks that changed into snakes. And he remembers the coat his mother made for him, the start of all his troubles. And the way he screamed when Judah and Gad tore it off him and drenched it in the blood of some poor ibex they'd caught in one of their traps.

Startled, Joseph realizes the interpreters are speaking to him. "Sir," they say, "how may we serve you?"

"As you see," Joseph says, "I am an old man, on the edge of death. Lately my dreams have troubled me. And where better to seek answers than in Luxor, so renowned for dreamers?" The two smile. Joseph says, "Of course, I would have preferred the interpretations of your famous Joseph—" He watches them wince. "—but I am only a merchant, and I am sure Lord Joseph speaks only to princes."

The younger of the two, a man about thirty with slicked down hair says, "Well, he's sick, you know. And there are those who say the Pharaoh's publicity people exaggerate his powers." He adds, with a wave of his hand, "One lucky guess, years ago . . . "

"Tell me," Joseph says, his voice lower, "is he really a Hebrew? I've heard that, but I find it hard to believe."

In a voice even lower, the young one says, "Not only a Hebrew, but a slave. It's true. They plucked him out of prison."

Joseph feigns shock and a slight disgust. "Egypt is certainly more sophisticated than Phoenicia," he says. "In Tyre our slaves sweat for us, not the other way around."

The other stares at the stone-cut floor. "Yes," he says. "Well, the Viceroy is old, and things change."

Quickly, the older one says, "Why don't you tell us your dreams?"

"Lately, they've been very—I guess vivid is the best word. Just last night I dreamed I was sailing all alone down a river."

"Ah, good," the older one says. "A sign of wealth to come."

"It had better come soon, or I won't have much use for it. But to continue—I climbed the mast—"

"Wonderful. Your God will bear you aloft with renewed health and good fortune."

Joseph notices their eyes on the purse he carries on his belt. He goes on, "When I came down I became very hungry and ate the first thing I saw, which only afterwards I realized was the offal of animals. I haven't dared to tell anyone of this. Surely this is some omen of destruction."

"Oh no," the younger one jumps in. "In fact, it ensures prosperity."

"Really?" Joseph says. "Then what a lucky dream. Every turn a good omen." He smiles, remembering the fun he had making up the silly dream out of their lists. But the smile fades. He says, "Maybe you can do another one. Actually, this dream has come to me several times in my life." They nod. Joseph knows that the dream books place great emphasis on recurrence. After all, he thinks, if a dream is important enough to come back, maybe the interpreters can charge double.

He closes his eyes for a moment, sighs. When he looks at them again he sees them through a yellow haze of sickness. He begins, "I dream of a man. Very large and frightening. Strangely, his beard appears all on fire."

He can see them race through their catalogues in their minds. Finally the old one says, "Umm, good. It means you will achieve authority in your home."

Joseph says, "But the man is not me."

The young one says, "That doesn't matter."

"I see. Then I'll continue. This man, who dresses as a shepherd but was once a prince, appears before Pharaoh. He demands that Pharaoh surrender to him a vast horde of Pharaoh's subjects." He pauses, but now there is no answer. They look confused. Joseph continues "When the mob follow the man he promises them paradise, but instead leads them into the desert."

"A bad sign?" the old one says tentatively.

Joseph says, "They clamor for food, of course, but instead he leaves them to climb a mountain. And there, in the clouds, he writes a book. He writes it on stone and sheepskin. The history of the world, he calls it. The history and all its laws."

Now there is silence. "Can you help me?" Joseph says. "Should I fear or hope?" The two just stand there. Finally, so tired he can hardly move, Joseph drops the purse on a painted stone table and leaves the temple.

Ten-year-old Joseph wants to open a school for diviners. "Prophecy, dreams interpreted, plan for the future," his announcements will say. And under a portrait of him, "Lord Joseph, Reader and Advisor." Reuben, his oldest brother, shakes his head in disgust. Small flecks of mud fly out of his beard and into Poppa Jacob's lentils. Reuben says, "What does that mean, reader and advisor? Since when do you know how to read?"

Joseph blushes. "I'm going to learn," he says. Over Reuben's laugh he adds quickly, "Anyway, when I see the future, that's a kind of reading. The dreams and the pictures I see in the wine. That's just like reading."

Reuben snorts his disgust. To their father he says, "If you'd make him do some decent work he wouldn't act this way."

Rachel is about to say something but Joseph looks at her with his please-mother-I-can-handle-this-myself look. He says, "Divining is work. Didn't that Phoenician woman give me a basket of pomegranates for finding her cat?"

Under his breath, Reuben mutters, "*Rotten* pomegranates. And why would anyone want a cat, for Yah's sake?"

But Joseph ignores him. He can see he's got the old man's attention. "And we can sell things," he adds. "Open a shop."

"A shop?" Jacob says. His nostrils flare slightly in alarm.

"Sure," Joseph says, not noticing his mother's signal to stop. "When people study with me they'll need equipment. Colored coats, cups to pour the wine, even books. I can write instruction books. 'The Interpretation of Dreams.' That's when I learn to read, of course."

Jacob spits on the rug, an act that makes Rachel turn her face. "We are not merchants," he says. "Damnit, maybe your brothers are right." He ignores his wife's stagy whisper, "Half brothers," and goes on, "Maybe you need to get your fingers in some sheep, slap some mud on that pretty face of yours."

Before Joseph can make it worse Rachel covers his mouth and pulls him outside.

Over the laughter of the brothers, Judah yells, "Goodbye, *Lord* Joseph. See you in the sheep dung!"

Rachel makes sure Joseph wraps his coat around him against the desert's bite. Even under the thin light of the stars, the waves of color flicker as if alive. What wonderful dreams this boy has, she thinks. She remembers the morning he demanded the coat. Needed it for his work, he said. Leah's brats tried to stop it being made, of course, but Rachel won. Just like always. She says, "Those loud-mouths. How dare they laugh at you? You *are* a lord. A true prince compared to them."

But Joseph pays her no attention. Instead, he stares at the planets, Venus and Jupiter, as bright as fire, hanging from the skin of a half-dead Moon. Images fall from them, as if from holes in the storage house of night.

He sees a lion, a great beast, except it changes, becomes a cub, its fur a wave of light. Seraphs come down, those fake men with the leathery wings that Joseph's father saw in his dream climbing up and down that ladder to heaven and never thought to shout at them "Why don't you just fly?" The seraphs place a crown like a baby sun on the lion's head. And then they just fly away, as if they have done their job. No, Joseph wants to scream at them, *don't leave me*. For already he can see them. The wild dogs. They climb up from holes in the Earth, they cover the lion, tear holes in his skin, spit into his eyes.

Joseph slams his own eyes with the heels of his hands. The trick works, for suddenly he becomes aware of his mother beside him, her worry a bright mark on her face as she wipes a drop of spit from his open mouth. Vaguely, he pushes her hand away. Now the tail comes, he thinks. The bit of clean information after the torrent of pictures. Just as his brothers begin to leave their father's grand tent, it hits Joseph, so hard he staggers backward. They want to kill him. If they could, they would tie him to a rock and slit him open, the way his great-grandfather Abraham tried to kill Grandpa Isaac, and even struggled against the—seraph?—that held his hand and shouted in his ear to stop, stop, it was over, Yah had changed His mind. And yet, in all the terror, Joseph can't help but smirk, for he realizes something further. Reuben, Reuben, will stop them.

"What are you laughing at?" Reuben says as he marches past, and it's all Joseph can do not to really laugh, for it almost doesn't matter, scary as it is. He knows something about them that they don't even know themselves. And doesn't that make him their lord?

Mostly Joseph divines from dreams, but sometimes the cup shows him what he needs to know. His mother gave him the cup when he was five. She'd ordered it made two years before, when their travels took them past the old woman who kept the kiln outside Luz. Rachel had had her own dream of how it should look, with rainbow swirls in the glaze, and four knobs of different colors. It took a long time but she made Jacob wait, despite the older boys' complaints, until the potter finished it. And then Rachel put it aside until the ceremony by the fire, when Joseph's first haircut would turn him from a wild animal (one who secretly still sucked at his mother) into a human. Rachel couldn't attend—yet another boys' only event—but they came and told her what happened—how he whooped it up, jumping and waving his arms like a cross between a monkey and a bat, how his hair made the fire flare so that Jacob had to yank the child back to keep him from getting scorched. And then how Joseph quieted when his father gave him the cup, how he purred over it like a girl, how his father poured the wine. But instead of drinking Joseph just stared at it, stared and made a noise like a nightmare, and might have flung it away if Jacob hadn't grabbed hold of him (a salvation Jacob later regretted) and forced him to drink the wine so they could end the ceremony.

It took Rachel a long time to get Joseph to tell her what he'd seen. Darkness, he said finally. Darkness over all the world, thicker than smoke. And a hand in the dark sky, a finger outstretched, reaching, reaching, stroking invisible foreheads. He heard cries, he said, shrieks and wails in the blackness. Then light came—and everywhere, in every home, from palace to shack, women held their dead children against their bodies. "I'm not going to die, am I?" Joseph asked her.

"No, no, darling, it's not for you, it's for someone else. The bad people. Don't worry, sweetie, it's not for you." Joseph cried and cried while his mother held him and kissed the torn remnants of his hair.

As much as they make fun of him, as much as they complain to Jacob about his airs and his lack of work, the brothers will sometimes sneak into his tent, after they think everyone has fallen asleep. "Can you find my staff?" they'll say, or "Who's this Ugarit girl Pop's got lined up for me? Is she good looking? Can she keep her mouth shut?" The wives come even more often, scurrying along the path as if anyone who saw them would mistake them for rabbits. "Tell me it's going to be a boy," they say. "Please, he'll kill me if it's another girl," as if the diviner can control something like that, as if events are at the mercy of the diviner, and not the other way around.

At first, Joseph soaks in their secret devotions. When Zebulon ridicules him, Joseph looks him in the eye, as if to say, "Put on a good show, big brother, because you know and I know what you think about after dark, under your sheepskin." Or maybe he'll just finger the colored stone Zeb gave him as a bribe not to say anything. But after awhile he wishes they'd leave him alone. He even pretends to sleep, but they just grab him by the shoulder. Worst of all are the ones who offer themselves to him, not just the wives, but sometimes the brothers too, pretending it's something Joseph is longing for. Do they do it just to reward him, or because they really desire him, or because they think of it as some kind of magic that will change a bad prediction? Joseph tries to find the answer in his cup, or a dream, but the wine and the night remain as blank as his brothers' faces. He can see the fate of entire tribes but not the motives of his own brothers. Maybe there are no motives. Maybe people do things for no reason at all.

And Joseph himself? Why does he do it? Just to know things other people don't? To make himself better than his brothers? Because he can? Because he can't stop himself? As a child he loves the excitement, that lick of fire that sometimes becomes a whip. Later, especially the last days in Egypt, he wishes it would end. His body can't take the shock, his mind can't take the knowledge. He prays, he sacrifices goats stolen from the palace herd and smuggled into the desert. No use. The visions keep coming, wanted or not.

Only near the very end of his life does he get an answer. The half burnt goat sends up a shimmer of light that Joseph stares at, hypnotized, so that he doesn't hear the desert roar, or see the swirl of sand that marks a storm until it literally slaps him in the face. He cowers down and covers himself as best he can, and wonders if he will die here so that no one will ever find his body. Maybe his family will think Yah just sucked him up into heaven, too impatient to wait for

Joseph to die. In the midst of it all, he hears it. The Voice. An actual voice! High pitched, somewhere between a man and a woman, it shouts at him out of the whirlwind. **"Do you think I do this for *you*? I opened secrets for you because I *needed* you. I will close them when I close them!"**

The fact is, Joseph is no fool. By his final years, he's known for a long time that Yah has used him. He doesn't like that this bothers him, but it does. A messenger, he tells himself. A filler. A bridge between his father and the other one, the Burning Beard. He knows exactly what people will think over the millennia. Jacob will get ranked as the last patriarch (the only real patriarch, Joseph thinks, the only one to pump out enough boys to found a nation), the other one the Great Leader. And Joseph? A clever bureaucrat. A nice guy who lured his family to Egypt and left them there to get into trouble.

He considers writing his own story. "The Life of Joseph ben Jacob, Lord Viceroy of Egypt." But what good would it do? A fire would incinerate the papyrus, or a desert lion would claw it to shreds, or maybe a freak flood would wash away the hieroglyphs. By whatever means, Yah would make sure no one would ever see it. The Beard is the writer, after all. God's scribe.

Some things Joseph knows from the ripples and colors of the wine. Others require a dream. He first sees the man he calls "the Beard" in a dream. Joseph is eight, a spindly brat with a squeaky voice. He's had a bad evening, swatted by Simeon for a trick he'd played on Levi. In despair that no one loves him, he drinks down a whole cup of wine from the flask his mother has given him. The cup falls with a thud on the dirt floor of his tent as he instantly falls down asleep.

At first, he sees only the flame. It fills his dream like floodwaters hitting a dry riverbed. Finally, Joseph and the fire separate so that he can see it as a blaze on a man's face. No, not the face, the beard. The man has thick eyebrows and thin hair, and sad eyes, and a beard bushier than Reuben's, except the beard is on fire! The flames roar all about the face and neck, yet somehow never seem to hurt him. They don't even seem to consume anything, his beard always stays the same. Later in life, in countless dreams, Joseph will study this man and the inferno on his face. He will wonder if maybe the fire is an illusion—the man's a master magician, after all—or a trick of the desert light (except it looks the same inside Pharaoh's palace). And he will wonder why no one ever seems to notice it, not the Pharaoh, not the Beard's self-serving brother, not the whiny mob that follows him through the desert. In that first time, however, the fiery beard scares him so much he can only hide in the corner of his dream, hardly even aware that the man stands on a dark mountain scorched by lightning, and talks to the clouds.

✡

Joseph doesn't like this man. He doesn't like his haughty pretension of modesty, the I'm-just-a-poor-shepherd routine. He detests the man's willingness to slaughter hordes of his own people just for the sake of discipline. He dislikes his speeches that go on for hours and hours, in that thick slurry voice, always with the same message, obey, obey, obey. Joseph distrusts the man's total lack of humor, his equal lack of respect for women. Can't he see that his sister controls the waters, so that without her to make the rocks sweat they would all die of thirst? As far as Joseph can tell, the mob would have done a lot better if they had followed the sister and not the Beard. Joseph thinks of her as his proper heir as leader of the Hebrews. But then, he has to admit, he always did like women better.

Most of all, Joseph detests the Beard's penchant for self-punishment. The way he lies down in the dirt, cutting his face on the pebbles, the way he'll swear off sex but won't give his wife permission to take anyone else. And what about his hunger strikes that go on for days and days, as if Yah can't stand the smell of food on a man's breath? It might not bother Joseph so much if the man wasn't such a role model for his people. *Joseph's* people. Doesn't the man know that Joseph saved his family—the mob's ancestors, after all—and all of Egypt from starvation just a few generations before? It was Joseph who explained Pharaoh's dream of the seven fat cows and the seven lean ones, Joseph who took over Egypt's food storage systems during the seven good years, building up the stocks for the seven years of famine. It was Joseph who took in his family and fed them so the tribes could survive. Doesn't the Beard know all this? He claims to know everything, doesn't he? The man who talks to Yah. How dare he denounce food? How *dare* he?

Some dreams come so quickly they seem to pounce on him the moment he closes his eyes. Others lie in wait all night until they seize him just before he plans to wake up. The dream of the coat comes that way. Joseph has fidgeted in his sleep for hours, flinging out his arm as if trying to push something away. And then at dawn, just as Reuben and Judah and Issachar and Zebulon are gulping down stony bread on their way to the sheep, their little brother dreams once more of the Burning Beard. He sees the Beard stride into the biggest room Joseph has ever seen. Stone columns thicker than Jacob's ancient ram hold up a roof higher than the Moon. The Beard comes with his brother, who has slicked down his hair and oiled his beard, and wears a silver plate around his neck, obviously more aware than the Beard of how you dress when you appear before a king. Or maybe the Beard has deliberately crafted his appearance, his torn muddy robe, his matted hair, as either contempt for the Pharaoh or a declaration of his own humility. "Look at me, I'm just a country bumpkin, a simple shepherd on an errand for God." Later, in other dreams, Joseph will learn just how staged this act is from the man who grew up as Pharaoh's adopted son.

Now, however, the dreaming boy knows only the gleam of the throne room and the scowl of the invader.

The brothers speak together. Though Joseph cannot follow any of it (he will not learn Egyptian for another twenty years) he understands that the Beard has something wrong with his speech so that silver-plate needs to interpret for him. Whatever they say, it certainly bothers the king, who shouts at them and holds up some gold bauble like a protection against the evil eye. The Beard says something to his brother, who strangely throws his shepherd's staff on the floor. Have they surrendered? But no, it's a trick, and a pretty good one, because the stick surrenders its rigidity and becomes a snake!

Asleep, Joseph still shivers under his sheepskin. The king, however, shouts something at one of his toadies who then rushes away, to return a moment later with a whole squad of magicians in the most amazing coats Joseph has ever seen. For Joseph the rest of the dream slides by in a blur—the king's magicians turn their sticks into snakes too only to have silver-plate's snake gobble them up like a basket of honeycakes—because he cannot take his dream eyes off those coats. Panels of linen overlaid with braids of wool, every piece a different color, and hung with charms and talismans of stone and metal. *I want that*, the dream Joseph thinks to himself, and "I've got to have that" he says out loud the moment he wakes up.

He begins his campaign that very day, whining and posturing and even refusing to eat (later, he will blame the Beard for this fasting, as if his dreams infected him) until he wins over first his mother and then at last his father. With Jacob on his side, Joseph can ignore the complaints of his brothers, who claim it makes Joseph look like "a hittite whore."

Joseph doesn't try for the talismans. Jacob probably could afford it, but Joseph knows his limits. Besides, it's the coat he cares about, all the colors, even more swirls than his cup of dreams. The day he gets it he struts all about the camp, the sides of it held open like the fan of a peacock—or maybe like a foolish baboon who does not know enough to protect his chest from his enemies.

That same night, Joseph dreams of the coat soaked in blood.

Joseph's dream power comes from his mother. "All power comes from mothers," Rachel tells him, and thereby sets aside the story Jacob likes, that Yah taught dream interpretation to Adam, who taught it to Seth, who taught it to Noah, whose animals dreamed every night on the boat, only to lose the knack when they walked down the ramp back onto the sodden earth. "Listen to me," Rachel whispers, "you think great men like Adam spent their time with dreams? It was Eve. And she didn't learn it from God, she learned it from the serpent. She bit into the apple and snipped off the head of a worm. And that's when people started to dream."

✡

Joseph's worst moment comes in prison. He sits on his tailbone with his legs drawn up and his arms around his knees, trying to let as little of his body as possible touch the mud and slime of the floor. He's tried so hard, it's so unfair. No matter what terrible tricks Yah played on him—his brothers' hatred, his coat taken from him and streaked with blood—he's done his best, he's accepted it, really he has. And now this! And all because he tried to do something right. When your master's wife wants to screw you you're supposed to say no, right? Isn't that what Yah teaches (not that it's ever stopped Jacob, but that's not the point). And instead of a reward he has to sit in garbage and eat worse.

Something touches Joseph's sleeve. He screams and jerks back, certain it's a rat. But when he opens his eyes he sees two men not much older than himself. They wear linen and their hair is curled, signs they've fallen from a high place. "Please," one says. "You're the Hebrew who interprets dreams, aren't you? Will you help us? Please?"

"No," Joseph says. "Go away, leave me alone." And yet, he feels a certain tug of pleasure that his reputation as Potiphar's dream speaker has followed him into hell. He tries to ignore them, but they just stand there, looking so desperate, that finally he says "Oh all right. Tell me your dreams."

The one who goes first announces that he was Pharaoh's chief wine steward before the court gossips slid him into jail. He tells Joseph, "In my dream I saw— I was in a garden. It was nighttime, I think. I looked up high and saw three branches. They began to bud. Blossoms shot forth. There were three ripe grapes. Suddenly, Pharaoh's cup was in my hand. Or maybe it was there before, I'm not sure. I squeezed the grapes in my hand. I poured the juice into the cup. I gave it to Pharaoh. He was just there and I gave it to him and he drank it."

Joseph rolls his eyes. This is not exactly a great mystery, he thinks. He says, "All right, here's the meaning. In three days Pharaoh will lift up your head. He will examine your case and restore you to your office. You'll be safe from this filth and back in the palace. Congratulations."

The man claps his hands. "Blessed Mother Isis!" he cries. "Thank you!" He bends down to kiss Joseph's knees but Joseph pulls his legs even closer to his chest.

"Just promise me something," Joseph says. "When you're back pouring wine for Pharaoh, remember me? Tell him I don't deserve this."

"Oh yes," the man says, and claps his hands again.

"Now me," the other one says. He kneels down before Joseph and says, "In my dream I'm walking in the street behind the palace. There are three baskets on top of my head. Two of them are filled with white bread, but the one on top holds all the lovely things I bake for Pharaoh. Cakes shaped like Horus, a spelt bun like the belly of Hathor. Just as I'm thinking about how much the king will like them, birds come and pluck them away." He laughs, as if he's told a joke. "Right out of the basket. Now," he says, "tell me the meaning."

Joseph stares at him. He stares and stares at the man's eager face. Why has Yah done this to me, he thinks, but even that last shred of self-pity drains out of him, washed away in horror at such pathetic innocence.

"Go on, go on," the man insists.

Can he fake it? Joseph wonders. He tries to think of some story but his mind jams. He can't escape. Yah has set the truth on him like a pack of dogs. In a cracked whisper he says, "In three days Pharaoh shall lift your head from your shoulders. He will hang you from a tree and the birds will eat your body."

The baker doesn't scream, only makes a noise deep in his chest. "Oh Gods," he says, "help me. Help me, please."

Joseph is stunned. No anger, no hate. No demands to change it or make it go away or even to think again. Just that trust. Without thought, Joseph wraps his arms around the man like a mother. "I'm sorry," he says, "I'm so sorry."

Joseph will stay two years in the prison before Pharaoh will dream a dream not found anywhere in the catalogues, and his wine steward, hearing of lean cows and fat cows, will remember the man he had promised not to forget. In all those months, Joseph will think of that empty promise only three or four times. But he will see the face of the baker every morning, before he opens his eyes.

People at court sometimes joke about the Viceroy's clay cup. Childish, they call it. Primitive. Hebrew. Visitors from Kush or Mesopotamia look shocked when they see him raise it in honor of Pharaoh's health. Their advance men, whose job it is to know all the gossip, whisper to them that Lord Joseph uses this cup to divine the future. Perhaps he sees visions in the wine, they say. Or perhaps— these are the views of the more scientifically minded—some impurity in the clay flakes off into the liquid and induces heightened states of awareness. The visitors shake their heads. That's all well and good, they say. He saved Egypt from famine, after all. But why does he drink from it in public?

During long dinners the Viceroy, like other men, will sometimes pause to swirl his barley wine, or else just stare blankly into his cup. At such times, all conversation, all breathing, stops, until Lord Joseph once more lifts up his eyes and makes some bland comment.

The princes, the courtiers, and the slaves all agree. The God Thoth visits Joseph at night, when together they discuss the secrets of the universe. A bright light leaks under the door of the Viceroy's bedchamber, and sometimes an alert slave will hear the flutter of Thoth's wings. And sometimes, they say, Thoth himself becomes the student, silent with wonder as Joseph teaches him secrets beyond the knowledge of Gods.

✡

The boy Joseph curls himself up in the pit where his brothers have thrown him. Frozen in the desert night without his coat, he clutches the one treasure they didn't take from him, the cup his mother gave him, which he keeps always in a pouch on a cord around his waist. What will it be? A lion, a scorpion, a snake? Instead, before Judah and Simeon come back to sell him as a slave, a deep sleep takes him. He does not know it, but Yah has covered him with a foul smell that will drive away the beasts, for now is the time to dream. Joseph sees himself standing before a dark sky, with his arms out and his face lifted. A crown appears on his head. The crown becomes light, pure light that spreads through his body—his forehead, his mouth, his shoulders, all the way to his fingertips, light that streams out of him, through his heart and his lungs, even his entrails, if he shits he shits light, his penis ejaculates light, the muscles and bones of his legs pure light, his toes on fire with light. Joseph tries to cry out, but light rivers from his mouth.

And then it shatters. Broken light, broken Joseph splashes through the world, becomes darkness, becomes dust, becomes bodies and rock, light encased in darkness and bodies. And letters. Letters that fall from the sky, like drops of black flame.

Joseph wakes to the hands of the slave traders dragging him up from the dirt.

Does the Beard dream? Does the fire on his face allow him even to sleep? Or does he spend so much time chatting with Yah, punishing slackers, and writing, writing, writing, that he looks at dreams, and even the future, as a hobby for children and weak minds? After all, what does the Beard care about the future? He has his book. For him, time ends with the final letter.

When his brothers bully him, when they throw mud on his coat or trip him so he falls on pebbles sharp enough to splash his coat with blood, Joseph just wants to get back at them. In Jacob's tent one night he decides to make up a prophecy. "Listen, everybody," he announces, "I had a dream. Last night. A really good one." They roll their eyes or make faces but no one stops him. They don't want to believe in him, but they do. "Here it is," he says gleefully. "All of us were out in the fields binding sheaves. We stepped back from them, but my sheaf stood upright and all yours bowed down to it." He smiles. "What do you think?"

Silence. No one wants to look at anyone. At last, Reuben says, "Since when do you ever go out and bind sheaves?" Inside their laughter, Joseph hears the whisper of fear.

That night, a dream comes to him. The Sun, the Moon, and eleven stars all bow down to him. He wakes up more scared than elated. He should keep it to himself, he knows. He's already got them mad, who knows what they'll do if he pushes this one at them. He pours some water into his cup from the gourd his mother's handmaids fill for him. Before he can drink, however, he sees in the bubbles everything that will follow—how the dream will provoke his brothers, how he will become a slave in Egypt, how he will rise to viceroy so that his family and in fact all Egypt will bow to him. It will not last, he sees. Their descendants will all become slaves, only to get free once more and stumble through the desert for forty years, *forty years*, before they can get back to their homeland. The vision doesn't last. Startled, he spills the water, and the details spill from his brain. And yet he knows now that everything leads to something else, that all his actions serve some secret purpose known only to Yah. Is it all just tricks, then? Do Yah's schemes ever come to an end?

He can stop it, he knows. All he has to do is never tell anyone the dream. Doesn't Grandpa Isaac claim God gives all of us free will? (He remembers his father whisper, "All except my brother Esau. He's too stupid.") If Joseph just keeps silent, the whole routine can never get started.

That afternoon, Zebulon kicks him and he blurts out, "You think you're so strong? I dreamed that the Sun and Moon and eleven stars all bowed down to me. That's right, eleven. What do you think of that?"

Joseph is old now, facing the blank door of death. He has blessed his children and his grandchildren and their children. Soon, he knows, the embalmers will suck out his brains, squirt the "blood of Thoth" into his body, wrap him in bandages, and encase him in stone. He wonders—if his descendants really do leave Egypt, will they find him and drag him along with them?

At the foot of his bed lies a wool and linen coat painted in swirls of color. Joseph has no idea how it got there. By the size of it it looks made for a boy, or maybe a shrunken old man. Next to the bed, on a little stand, sits his cup, as bright as the coat. He has told his slave to fill it with wine, though Joseph knows he lacks the strength to lift it, let alone pour it down his throat.

When he dies, will he see Rachel and Jacob? Or has he waited so long they've grown impatient and wandered off somewhere where he will never find them? He is alone now. The doctors and the magicians, his family, his servants, he's ordered them all away, and to his surprise they have listened. He wants more than anything to stay awake, so he can feel his soul, his *ka*, as the Egyptians call it, rattle around inside his body until it finds the way out. He tells himself that he's read all the papyruses, the "books of the dead," and wants to find out for himself. But he knows the real reason to stay awake. He doesn't want any more dreams. As always, however, Yah makes His own plans.

In his dream, Joseph sees the Burning Beard one more time. With his face even more of a blaze than usual, he and his brother accost Pharaoh in the early morning, when Pharaoh goes down to wash in the Nile. Joseph watches them argue, but all he can hear is a roar. Now the brother raises his staff, he strikes the water—and the Nile turns to blood! Joseph shouts but does not wake up. All over Egypt, he sees, water has turned to blood, not just the river but the streams and the reservoirs and even the wells. For days it goes on, with the old, the young, and the weak dying of thirst. Finally the water returns.

Only—frogs return with it. The entire Nile swarms with them. Soon they cover people's tables, their food, their bodies. And still more horrors follow. The brother strikes the dust and lice spring forth. Wild beasts roar in from the desert.

Joseph twists in agony, but Yah will not release him. He sees both brothers take fistfuls of furnace ash and throw them into the sky. A wind blows the ash over all the people of Egypt, and where it touches the skin, boils erupt. Now the Beard lifts his arms to the sky and hail kills every creature unfortunate enough to be standing outside. As if he has not done enough he spreads his hands at night and calls up an east wind to bring swarms of locusts. They eat whatever crops the hail has left standing. *No,* Joseph cries. *I saved these people from famine. Don't do this.* He can only watch as the Beard lifts his hand and pulls down three days of darkness.

And then—and then—when the darkness lifts, the first born of every woman and animal, from Pharaoh's wives and handmaids to the simplest farm slave who could never affect political decisions in any way, even the cows and the sheep and the chickens, the first born of every one of them falls down dead.

Just at the moment of waking up, Joseph sees that the finger of death has spared certain houses, those marked with a smear of lamb's blood. The Hebrews. Yah and the Beard have saved the Hebrews. Joseph's people. But aren't the Egyptians Joseph's people as well? And didn't he bring the Hebrews to Egypt? If all this carnage comes because the Hebrews have lived in Egypt, *is it all Joseph's fault?*

He wakes up choking. For the first time in days his eyes find the strength to weep. He wishes he could get up and kneel by the bed, but since he cannot he prays on his back. "Please," he whispers. "I have never asked You for anything. Not really. Now I am begging You. Make me wrong. Make this one dream false. Make all my powers a lie. Take my gift and wipe it from the world. Do anything, *anything,* but please, *please, make me wrong.*"

But he knows it will not happen. He is Joseph ben Jacob, Lord Viceroy of dreams. And he has never made a wrong prediction in his life.

How the Little Rabbi Grew

Eliot Fintushel

Rabbi Shlomo Beser was born with a caul, a shiny membrane that covered his head. It came to his maiden Aunt Dora that the child must have mystical capabilities, and she was right. At the age of two, Rabbi Shlomo recited all of the holy names of God as listed in the Book of Brilliance. He also recited several names that had never been written down. Everyone knew them to be true names, because on hearing them the cabalists, old wise ones, could not conceal their amazement. As one, they bowed their heads and mumbled, *"Bar'chu uvaruch sh'moh!"*: Blessed be the name.

These were names entrusted through nods and whispers by graybeards to graybeards in the secret room in the basement of the synagogue. No mortal man would have related such matters to a child. It was quite clear that Shlomo Beser had had commerce with angels.

At three Rabbi Shlomo delivered a new testament in Hebrew and Aramaic. Aunt Dora, ignorant of the holy tongues, transliterated everything syllable for syllable into English script, with a smattering of Cyrillic; to the end of her life she confused the two alphabets, one from her old country, one from her new. Dora was no maven. The old cabalists locked Rabbi Shlomo's testament away. Not even the most learned and holy among them could look upon it without fainting or going mad for half a day, and the more a man understood of it, the worse it went for him.

All this happened in Schuylertown, New York, a town not far from Albany, in a small immigrant Jewish community. The Jews there only knew one another. They must remain pure, so the old wise ones urged them, in the service of God Almighty. They stayed strange together while the world changed. They even imagined, in their ignorance, that the city of Albany was some sort of large orphanage, as in the Hebrew, *al b'nai*, which means, for the children's sake.

Rabbi Shlomo's father and mother were ordinary people. They worked when the old wise ones told them to work and they rested when they told them to rest. He was a cabinet maker of slight means and no religious inclination. She was a woman of few words and fewer thoughts. She had thick arms and liked to sleep. Shlomo was their only child; still, they treated him like a stray dog who had followed them home and stayed on. They were not unkind to him.

The little rabbi grew faster. By his fifth birthday, Rabbi Shlomo Beser completed his formal studies under the tutelage of the wise and holy ones. Perhaps, if I may be so bold, it was like Jesus receiving the baptism of John in the stories of the Christians: Shlomo was a pious and respectful little pupil, but he knew everything before the old wise ones ever said it. Grumble as they might, they had no choice, at last, but to defer to him and call him "rabbi."

That year he enunciated new mysteries by the light of which all present were given to understand that the great Rabbi Akiva himself had been mistaken: the Chanukah candles must be lit for eight nights in diminishing number, as against the practice, universal among Jews since the argument of Rabbi Akiva, of increasing them, one to eight. Even the old cabalists with their forked beards and black hats could find in Shlomo's words not a cranny in which to wedge the slightest objection. Thenceforth the Jews of Schuylertown lit their Chanukah candles eight down to one.

There was a hill he liked to climb. It wasn't a mountain. He could see mountains from it, however, the Adirondacks, capped with snow like the embroidered white cloth over the *afikomen*, the *matzoh* for hiding on Passover. He would climb this hill each Sunday afternoon if it didn't rain or snow, beardless little rabbi in his black coat and hat, to talk with God. His father and mother let him. Aunt Dora used to walk him from home to the bottom of the hill and wait. She would read romance novels sometimes, and sometimes she would nap or nibble HiHo crackers or whistle, while Rabbi Shlomo talked with God.

When he returned from talking with God, she would bow her head and say, "How did it go, Rabbi?" or else, "What news, Shloimy? Is it anything?"

And the child would tell her stories. When he was six, Rabbi Shlomo told her how the Almighty had described to him the exact circumstances of the creation. She listened cross-legged on an old blue quilt she had spread across the couchgrass, and he sat on his knees at the edge of the quilt, half on and half off. If it was cold they would wrap themselves together in the blue quilt, all comfy, like two buns in a broiler, a big one and a little.

He told her what angels and how many and of what color hair and eyes had stood at the Blessed One's right side and what and how many and of what coloration had stood at the Blessed One's left when he separated the light from the dark and called it *yom echad*, "one day." Her brows would arch and her mouth would open as he told her what happened to the seeds of the apple of which Adam and Eve had eaten, and the last words of Methuselah.

No fly would come near. No bird would twitter. If the sun was out, a cloud would come and shade them while the rabbi spoke and vanish as soon as he fell silent. Aunt Dora would sit and listen, and the little rabbi would sit nearby and speak until she begged him to stop.

That's how it was. She always asked, and he always told her everything. His words flowed like lemon tea steaming from the cozy, too hot, too hot, delicious to smell, but terrible at last: she covered her face, her ears. Out of mercy, he would stop. But next time she had to ask him again. Who could help it? Others asked too, of course, but Rabbi Shlomo told them only lesser things. He reserved the deepest mysteries for Dora's ears alone. If it is not disrespectful to say so, perhaps he loved her.

The little rabbi grew fast, and the older he got, the faster he grew. He grew in his mind and in his heart and in other subtle ways, but in stature, for a long time, he stayed small. Dora took care of Shlomo as one would take care of a child. After all, he was a child: count his years—just six.

The town was abuzz with all these strange doings. People lowered their heads before Rabbi Shlomo when they passed him on the street, all but the old cabalists themselves, who would raise their chins as an example to the people, for are not all men equal before the Almighty? But the townspeople started to importune the little rabbi in preference to the old wise ones with spiritual questions and with questions of Jewish law. Whoever managed to get past Dora received the most wonderful answers imaginable. Answers that could change a person's life or open his heart to a happiness the like of which he had not felt for fifteen or twenty years.

This was bad enough, but when the learned and holy men, the cabalists of Schuylertown, heard about the things that happened on Dora's quilt, they became very jealous indeed. They sent Dora a note in English: come and see us at such and such a time in the basement of the synagogue. That is where the holy ones liked to pore over their ancient texts in secret, where yellowed pages crumbled under their thumbs, reading by reading, year by year, turning to dust. For an ordinary person to be permitted to enter their little room was a remarkable thing.

They said, "Tell us everything your nephew Rabbi Shlomo says. He is learned in holy matters but simple in the ways of the world. We old wise ones want to keep watch over him in case his insights should lead him to a place his child's heart cannot yet understand, and he should fall."

She said, "Learned sirs, I watch over him."

They said, "When the prodigy Reb Menachem Ben Levi was a boy of seventeen, the Evil One opened the Book of Life before him in a dream. He ran to the book to cipher out its wonders, burying his face in the sacred script, and the Evil One shut it on him, snuffing out his life. He never woke. Had he not been talking in his sleep, we would never know this. And if his mother, a common woman, who heard it all, had had the wisdom to intercede, Reb Menachem would have lived. What further insights and glories we might have gained from Reb Menachem then!

"You are a common person like that mother of Reb Menachem's. Will you let little Rabbi Shlomo die because of you, when we old wise ones have the power to see and save? Will you not give us access?"

"Tell me what to do."

"Remember and write down every word. Leave the writings in a tube in a hole we will show you in the west wall of the synagogue. We old wise ones will examine these words, and, if need be, protect him. Tell him nothing of this. He is young."

As always, Dora and Shlomo walked. Shlomo climbed his hill and spoke with God. She read and napped and nibbled and whistled, and then he came back from God, and he spoke, and she listened, until she had to say, "No more." He kissed her on the cheek then, and she bowed her head and felt guilty, because she was hiding something.

All the way home, Dora repeated in her mind the wonders and the terrors of which the little rabbi had told her. After he kissed her goodbye and closed the door of his father's house, Dora would turn on her heel and run like the wind. She ran home to write everything down. She mixed Cyrillic and English letters, as always, and she even invented signs or drew little pictures when she was stuck. Then she spindled the paper tightly, tightly, ran to the synagogue, went round to the west wall, looking left and looking right, and she put it in the tube in the old wise ones' hole.

Rabbi Shlomo acted the same as always, always the same. He didn't seem to notice a thing. If anything, he trusted her more. He sat in Dora's lap. He played with the curls of her hair, little rabbi, while he revealed great mysteries. He closed his eyes and leaned his head against her breast, so that she could feel his words vibrate in her bosom as well as hear them with her ears.

Sometimes she thought, "I am betraying him." Sometimes she thought, "I am keeping him safe." The thoughts went round and round in Dora's heart, like a rope that tightened and wrung out tears.

Once, Rabbi Shlomo said, "Aunt Dora, why are you crying? Have I done something to hurt you?"

"No, Shloimy, it's only how wonderful the things are that you tell me. That, or dust in my eye."

"Shall I stop speaking now?"

"Maybe that would be better."

Once, as they walked home, he said, "Why do your lips move, Aunt Dora? What are you saying to yourself?"

"Oh, I have to buy some groceries, and I don't want to forget my list."

"Write it down as soon as you get home, why don't you?"

"Yes, Shloimy, that's what I'll do."

This went on for a long time. Shlomo turned seven, and Shlomo turned eight. The little rabbi grew faster in the latter year than in the former. Faster and faster he grew, in his mind and in his heart and in other subtle ways, but in stature he stayed small. He told her, and Dora wrote, of the shapes of the branches of the Tree of Knowledge of Good and Evil, and of what hung on every branch, what budded, what bloomed, and what fell.

Following his words, she recorded eighty-seven righteous acts that no one had ever heard of, enlarging the traditional list of six hundred thirteen mitzvot to an even seven hundred. She wrote down the words that Moses had uttered to part the sea, and she drew a picture of the mystical gesture that accompanied them.

It all went into the old wise men's hole. At the butcher's or the fish market or the rear of the synagogue on *shabbos*, they would nod to her sometimes, she thought, but apart from that, they never said a word, no, not so much as a thank-you or a grunt. Even the nods might have been nothing, after all. They might have been little bows for the prayers that the wise men prayed in their minds. The old wise ones, everyone knew, were always praying in their minds.

Shlomo turned nine, and Shlomo turned ten. The little rabbi grew faster and faster. As with his erudition and his spiritual life, so with some of his other qualities, though in stature he stayed small. It was as if Rabbi Shlomo's Earth turned faster than the ordinary one, and his seasons were shorter, and his sight finer and quicker in proportion. At nine and a half his voice changed, and he started to grow a beard. In other respects he seemed a child. He was respectful as a good child is. He lived in his father's house.

One Sunday morning, sunny but cold, some of the old wise ones went to Dora in the back yard of Shlomo's father's house. She was hanging up the little rabbi's *tzitzit*, the ritual undergarment with sacred embroidery and tiny fringes, to dry. She loved to do it, for love of the boy. She heard the crunch of the old ones' black leather shoes on the driveway gravel. She never lifted her head. She saw their black pants, spattered with mud, and the hems of their serious black coats. She dropped her clothespins. She picked them up again. She said, "Oh, I'm sorry."

One of them said, "Dora, you are a good woman, but you are making a mistake by not telling us everything."

"Oh, no, Your Reverences, I write down all he says."

They were quiet for a moment. She saw shoes shift and tap. Then the same old wise one said, "You end too soon. If there are reasonings, they trail off, and we can't see where they are leading. If there are words and spells that want to be spoken or gestures that want to be made, they are always lacking a crucial last step. We can't get them to do anything."

Another wise one broke in and said in a high-pitched voice, "We could help the people. We could do much good. Rabbi Loew of Prague, it is said, made a man out of mud with such words, and it saved the people from a terrible pogrom. That is nothing to what we might accomplish by the mysteries that Rabbi Shlomo enunciates. But they are incomplete."

Dora said, "Learned sirs, I can't help it. I'm a simple woman. I listen as long as I can listen. When Shloimy starts in to naming the deeper mysteries and untying the holy knots where no one has ever fit a finger, why, my heart goes numb, my skin bristles, I shake and shiver, day becomes night, night becomes day, and I don't know what I am.

"Have Your Reverences ever opened up and finished reading the testament our Shloimy spoke when he was three? I wrote that one down completely, despite my shattered nerves, in tongues of which I understood not one single syllable. I had to sleep three days running to get over that one. Didn't that testament make you reel, even you wise ones, so that you had to lock it up? Shloimy was only three when he gave us that one. How can you expect to fare better with something new, even if I should survive the listening to it and the writing of it after?"

The first old wise one thundered, "You let us worry about that, Dora. Your Shloimy isn't the only soul God speaks to. We old wise ones listen to Him constantly. That the Almighty has chosen the little rabbi as his confidante in certain small matters doesn't make us nobodies, you know. We have most of it with or without little Shloimy. There's just a thing or two we want to clarify, as we've told you.

"If you can't inconvenience yourself for the work of God, if you can't put up with a case of nerves or a chill up the spine or two, what good are you to anybody? Do you think you're doing Rabbi Shlomo a service by withholding things from us, his protectors?

"We've been talking about this. We are of a mind to send Shlomo to Al B'nai to be taken care of properly. His mother and father won't object. There's only you, and you haven't any rights."

Dora saw by their shadows that all the old wise ones were nodding. A breeze picked up; Shlomo's *tzitzit* whipped back and forth on the clothesline at her back. The fringes tickled her neck.

"I'll do everything just as you say. I'll listen to the end. I'll write down all of it. Only, please, Your Holinesses, no more talk of Al B'nai. I couldn't stand to be parted from my little Shloimy."

The old wise one with the high-pitched voice said, "Especially write down more exactly how to part the sea. That would be something to know."

That very day Dora accompanied Shlomo to his hill. He held her hand as they walked there. He liked to do that sometimes. They smiled at each other but hardly spoke.

The little rabbi seemed to grow beside her as they walked, like a carrot top in a cup on the windowsill, visibly, hour on hour, or like the moon climbing up from the horizon, higher by the second. She seemed to feel her forearm move like a clock hand as they walked and as Shlomo grew, his hand in hers rising higher, because he was taller and taller.

As always, the little rabbi climbed up to have his talk with God. As always, Dora waited. But today she could neither read nor nap nor nibble nor whistle. Sometimes she sat and sometimes she stood and sometimes she paced or kicked stones. She spread out the quilt, and she folded it up again. Then she spread it again. Then she folded it again.

She said to herself, "Who am I to doubt the holy learned ones? I am here for my Shloimy. I am here for those wise ones. It's all God's work, one and the same. What I said I'd do, I'll do."

Rabbi Shlomo came down the hill. He seemed older than before.

"What news, Shloimy? Is it anything?" The quilt, which she had gathered under her arm again, Dora spread again. She sat, and the little rabbi sat close beside her. He leaned his head upon her shoulder and spoke now into Dora's ear and now below. His lips brushed the hollow of Dora's ear, and he planted his words in her mind. His lips brushed the delicate skin under Dora's collarbone, and his words penetrated her heart.

He spoke of the Garden of Eden, how the Creator, Blessed be He, had pulled the rib from Adam as he slept. Rabbi Shlomo took Dora's hand—she didn't understand at first, because she was busy trying to engrave this phrase and that phrase into her memory—and he slipped it along his *tzitzit* to the spot where a man's missing rib had been, close to his heart. He held her hand there as he spoke. She felt his voice tremble through her fingers from his heart to her own.

All too soon Rabbi Shlomo came to the point where Dora would have said, stop. Of itself her brow furrowed and arched so, she thought it might turn to an angel and fly up into heaven. He was speaking of the taste of the fruit of the Tree of Knowledge of Good and Evil, how it lingered on Eve's tongue long after the serpent had gone.

The little rabbi grew.

He spoke, and she listened. She never said, stop, and he never paused to hear if she would say so. As revelation piled on revelation, ecstasy on ecstasy, Dora's heart fluttered, then pounded; her blood turned to hummingbirds, and her skin became the sky. In her mind, it was like the time, if there was one, before *yom echad*, when there was neither firmament above nor firmament below.

She forgot to remember it, to write it down later. He spoke with his heart, anyway, as much as with his tongue, through her hand as much as to her ear. How could a person write such things in English, in Cyrillic, or even in the holy alphabet of Hebrew or Aramaic? She forgot who the old wise ones were. She forgot who she herself might be, or if there was somewhere a little rabbi named Shlomo or a place called Schuylertown.

It was as if God was speaking to Dora directly, just as He spoke to Shloimy. He had such a big voice, the Almighty, that there was no room in the world left for the listener. She became a part of God's voice, and she knew what He said not by listening, but because she was part of the saying of it.

She gasped once, and in between the one word and His next, God seemed to breathe. During that breath, as quick as a wing flutter, Dora was Dora, and she saw Shlomo beside her. The little rabbi was growing fast. He was growing old. Across his face a million waters streamed, so it appeared to her. Some of them streamed into Dora.

She gasped a second time, and the little rabbi was all skin and bones. What clothes stayed on him hung like cobwebs from an old rafter. The white of his bones showed at the cheeks, the forehead, the chin, and one hip, bare above loose pants. His fingers were bones. She wanted to say, stop. But she listened on.

She awoke shivering. She was sitting under a tree, all bundled up in her quilt. It was dark. She thought she saw Shlomo lying nearby on a patch of barren dirt. When she touched him, though, it was not he—what she touched crumbled at once to ashes.

"Wicked creature!" someone shouted from the dark. "You never planned to do what the old wise ones said to do. You deceived us."

Another said, "You distrusted us, your teachers and counselors. You think we meant to harm him? Woe unto you, deluded girl!"

She heard their boots crunch the frosted grass. They came nearer. "Where have you sent him? Where is he hiding? It won't help, you know. We'll find him and send him to Al B'nai. It's all over between you and your Shloimy, unless . . . "

They let her tremble for a moment, halfway between terror and hope, as they thought; then another old wise one picked up the thread: "Unless you tell us everything. Did you listen to the end this time?"

She nodded.

Dora began to tell them the wonders and the terrors that God Almighty had secreted in her heart through the little rabbi. She chanted and she sang. Her eyes filled with tears. She did not know what words she spoke. But the more she spoke the darker and angrier old wise ones grew.

"Are you playing with us now? Do you think us fools?"

"Why do Your Reverences say that?" she asked. "Have I done something disrespectful?"

"Don't you know what words you have been saying? *Yisgadal, v'yiskadash sh'may rabah* . . . Glorify and sanctify His Great Name . . . "

"The Mourner's Kaddish!" she exclaimed. "The prayer for the dead!"

"Of course! Of course! Everybody knows that. That's child's stuff. We want to know mysteries, hidden things, not this cheap prattle."

"Reverend sirs, my little rabbi, my Shloimy, was born and he lived and he died. This Kaddish, the simple praise of God, which He has put in my heart to sing, is the highest of His mysteries. That's the last thing Shloimy learned and the last thing that he taught me. But it's as if all the world had suddenly turned to gold, and so, because everybody had piles of it, no one valued gold any more. Still, gold is gold, sirs. No mystery is deeper than the simple praise of God."

Then the old wise ones were ashamed. They knew that what she said was true, just as they had known that all the little rabbi's words had been true. There was that much gold in the old wise ones' hearts that it would shame them to lie about this.

As well as they could manage it, they gathered the dust that had been the little rabbi, and they buried him and prayed over him and placed a marble stone there. Dora tended it all her days. She sang the Kaddish each year on the day of Shlomo's death. It was all the Hebrew that Dora ever knew—*Yisgadal, v'yiskadash sh'may rabah . . .*—and the little rabbi had taught it to her, he and God Almighty.

Geddarien

✡

Rose Lemberg

Zelig's grandfather liked to smoke with his window half open, even though winter's breath melted on the old parquet. When the snow on the streets turned as porous and yellow as a matzo ball, a pigeon flew into the room. It hid under the chaise, there to await compliments or perhaps bread crumbs.

Zelig asked, "Do you think the pigeon would like some cake?"

Grandfather examined the offering from the lofty height of his chaise: a piece of honey cake on Zelig's outstretched palm. "A good one like that, he will want."

The boy clambered onto the chaise and wormed his way under the blanket, close to the old man's legs. Grandfather smelled comfortably of chicken soup, hand-rolled *papirosen*, violin rosin. Outside the window the abandoned cathedral still sputtered pigeons into the darkening square, and a neighboring house obstructed the rest of the view.

Grandfather said, "Do you know what Geddarien is?"

Zelig flattened a piece of cake and dropped it into a crack between the chaise and the wall. Moments later, he heard hesitant crooning from below. "No, grandfather. What's Geddarien?"

The old man closed his heavy eyelids. "These cities like ours, my boy, they have a life of their own. And sometimes, you should know," he whispered, "the city dances." Grandfather's eyes opened again: watery gray with a thin grid of red, like railroad tracks across a thawing country. "Could you bring it to me? My *fiddele*?"

"Grandmother says it will only make you upset." But he threw the rest of his cake under the chaise and jumped off. In the small polished wardrobe, the battered black case was buried under an avalanche of hats. Not so long ago Grandfather used to go out, dandy like a pigeon in his gray pin-striped suit and a fedora; but these days he could not even properly hold the instrument. His grumpy nephew Yankel now came to give Zelig music lessons.

Grandfather opened the creaky case, and inside it the old violin glowed, waiting for touch. "Your *fiddele*, now," the old man said, "is only a quarter-fiddle, and newly made. But soon you will graduate to one-half, and then to full." He stroked the large fiddle's neck with his fingers. "To this one. My father played it, and his grandfather, too." He took up the cake of rosin from the case, moved it slowly along the horse-hairs in the bow.

Zelig felt the sounds this movement created, a music of honey sap upon wind, melting the heart into his bones. "Grandfather, what of Geddarien?"

"Ah. Geddarien, there's a story." The old man smiled sadly. "The houses in this city, they do not meet. They are fixed in their places. But once in a hundred years they come all together, the living houses, and they dance." He put the bow back into the case and took up the violin; his fingers shook. "And they need music then, so they call us, the musicians. My father played at Geddarien once, and I was there as well, you see, with my quarter-fiddle, and my big sister Bronya with her trombone. And my father had this violin in its case and I held to the handle right here," Grandfather put Zelig's hand on the worn leather, "and he took Bronya's hand, and off we went. Oh, Zelig, the music was nothing I have ever heard. The houses, my *yingele* . . . I have seen Sankta Maria spread her gray marble hands and dance, and the old Blackstone house, and this little library I used to go to, and the Town Hall—very fond of waltzing, they all seemed."

Grandmother entered the room from the kitchen, carrying a steaming cup of cocoa on a tray. "You are not telling that old tale again, are you, Grandfather?" She shook her head and placed the tray in the old man's lap.

"And what's the harm in it, grandmother?" The old man blew the thin film of milk off the top of his cocoa, closed one eye and took a cautious sip.

"There are things going on in the world more important than old stories. The war will come here . . . Yankel's wife says they are going to move away."

"Oh, the war," Grandfather said, not impressed. "It's going to be just like the last time. They won't harm us. Our languages, they are almost the same, yes?" The old man took another gulp, and boasted, "I played my *fiddele* to the generals of three different armies!" He paused, contemplative. A soft crooning voice came from under the bed, and grandmother tilted her head in suspicion. "Yankel isn't going to leave this city if you paid him. He too is waiting for Geddarien. Missed the last one . . . . What are you doing? No, no . . . "

Grandmother bent laboriously, and looked under the chaise. "*Oy vey z mir!* An airborne rat in my house! Are you out of your mind?" She brought the broom from the kitchen and waged war on the poor bird.

A cube of sugar sat upon the kitchen table, a small shining king adored by three musicians, two old and one young. This summer the war had reached the city of Luriberg. "This war's nothing at all like the last time," Yankel grumbled; but grandfather shook his head and smiled, sipping his unsweetened tea. "You see, Zeligel, war is like this, that you drink your tea looking at the *tsuker*. It feels as sweet, melting in your mouth, but it doesn't go anywhere." He winked, and

Zelig smiled back, his hands busy sewing a blue star onto the old man's second-best jacket.

Yankel fidgeted in his chair. "Are you *mishigene*? Haven't you seen the loons marching in their uniforms and their eyes all steely, not caring, not seeing . . . "

"What are they, not people?" Grandfather shrugged. "They'll take off their uniforms and they will have parties. They'll want music. Just like the last time. I don't remember his name, that big guy who married. And a *groiser* bandit he was . . . remember?"

"They all were *banditn*." Yankel stared at his hands.

Grandfather turned to Zelig. "Yankel and I had played them the wedding music, the *freilakhs*, so jolly they gave us a big piece of lard to eat." The old man fingered the sugar cube and looked plaintively at Grandmother, busy at the stove.

"Stolen from some peasants, no doubt." Yankel murmured.

"You weren't supposed to eat it, old man." Grandmother peered into a bubbling blue pot. Potato steam rose above it, reminding Zelig of the times when he had a stuffy nose and she made him lean over this very pot, and covered his head with a towel, and told him to breathe in, deep, deep, my Zeligel, *neshumele*, my little soul.

"What did you want, for us to starve? We were hungry. We ate it all night."

"It was good lard," Yankel sighed, "with plenty of garlic."

Grandmother fished out a potato and banged the plate down onto the table in front of her husband. "Well, here. No lard. No butter. We're lucky to have the *kartof'l*."

The potato broke on the plate, yellow and mealy, puffing out sweet healing steam. Grandfather dug into the salt-cellar. He rubbed the salt between his fingers, and it made a secret sound, like a door opening in the night, like the smallest movement of bow against strings. Zelig looked up, and his grandfather said, "Do you hear it?"

"Yes," Zelig whispered.

Yankel said, "Hear what?"

"How can anyone be upset," Grandfather said, "when the whole world makes music?"

Grandmother slammed the lid and sat down heavily. Before the war, her blue pot was magic; it cooked 'pigeon rolls,' cabbage with filling of meat and rice; and twice a year, *gefilte* fish . . .

Yankel said, "I will tell you how. Yesterday they made some *yiddn* kneel by the Opera theatre, in the street, just like that, and the passers-by pointed fingers and laughed. That's what those blue stars mean. Now I am asking you, is that right?"

"What did the Opera theatre have to say?" Grandfather's eyes sparkled in the dim light.

"Nothing. What could she say?"

"That's not right," said Grandfather.

When the snow curdled again on the ledge of Grandfather's window, they came to make all the *yiddn* move to the ghetto. Grandmother did not want to go. She did not want to leave her blue pot. You can take the pot, they said. She said in the other room there was a big cardboard box of her old theatre dresses, smelling of must and love letters and music sheets. You cannot take the box, they said. You don't understand, she said, I played the oldest daughter of Tevye the Milkman . . .

They shot her in the belly.

In the ghetto they lived in a single room: Zelig and Grandfather, Yankel and his wife. The windows had no curtains. Steely wind wailed outside, and the horse-chestnut scraped its frozen fingers on the glass. The neighbors came to whisper of all the old people who had disappeared; a woman with bruises for eyes said they had all the grandparents shot on Peltewna street because they couldn't work, and please hide your grandpa, it's a miracle he's still alive. She brought them a blanket that smelled of heart medicine and cinnamon, an old woman's smell.

There were only two beds; Zelig and grandfather huddled in one, and sometimes in the night they'd pretend not to hear each other cry. In the evenings grandfather made Zelig take out the old violin and play *doinas*. The *fiddele* wept in his hands, in an old man's voice, in a boy's voice, in its own voice; it sang of a *shtetl*, the girl with the loud voice betrothed to a rich man, that girl who fell for a fiddler, and how one night they ran away on a bumpy road in an old cart drawn by a horse that loved to eat sugar. Some evenings Yankel would play second fiddle, his fingers stiff from working in the construction sites in the cold.

When snow started turning to sleet on its way to the ground, Zelig'sdoinas became livelier. Yankel listened, frowning. "Soon you will want to play wedding *freilakhs*, boy, shame on my gray hairs. Have you been to any weddings of late?" No, even funerals now were haphazard affairs, and hushed.

The winter exhaled the last snowy breath and died. The horse chestnut plastered its newly hatched leaves on the window outside, and the neighboring house sent pigeons to clap their wings when the fiddling was done. Yankel's wife brought out her stash of tea to celebrate the spring, but there was no table to sit around, and the magical sugar cube was lost.

One late afternoon Yankel's wife did not come home. There was a party at one of the uniformed big shots' place and you can play waltzes, they said to Yankel. They turned to Zelig too, but Yankel said, quickly, "This boy is my student. He's good for nothing, something horrible."

The door closed.

"Grandfather," Zelig asked, "why didn't he want me to go?"

The old man spoke with eyes closed. "Some things, my Zeligel, your eyes are too young to see."

Darkness fell, but neither Yankel nor his wife returned, and the neighbors came by to whisper, whisper, whisper, until it was past time for bed.

"Wake up!" Grandfather was shaking him.

Zelig murmured, "Is Yankel back yet?" Thin music waved in the air, an outmoded waltz melody that made his feet want to move. "Is it Yankel?"

"No, give a look!" The old man pointed. Lights flickered through the dark chestnut leaves outside the window. He put his feet down. The floor shook slightly, as if invisible dancers were whirling on the unpolished parquet. "Another bombing . . . "

"No, silly. It is Geddarien!" Joy melted in Grandfather's voice like raspberry syrup in tea. "Now, quick, you must help me dress." Grandfather looked alive, for the first time in months, as if miracles bubbled right under the surface of his wrinkled face. Zelig swallowed a lump in his throat. They would have to brave the dark streets, chasing . . . looking for something that wasn't quite there. He grimaced when he thought of returning, and Grandfather's face parched and empty like the bruised-eye woman's. Better not to think about it.

He helped the old man pull the pants over his white *kaltsones*, and then the shirt, the suspenders, the jacket . . . "Hurry, Zeligel, please, take the violin." Grandfather slid from the bed into Zelig's waiting arms; "how good that you've grown so tall," but in truth it was Grandfather who had become little, little and white like the sugar. They were almost to the door when grandfather slapped his forehead. "My hat! The city will not approve otherwise." Zelig topped the old man's white head with the Fedora, and arm in arm they made slow progress down the stairs. Nobody was awake. Outside the front door, the drain pipe dripped with the memory of rain, and an echo of music beckoned them further into the empty streets. There was no electricity in the ghetto at night, and yet the lanterns gave off flickering blue warmth. "Gas," the old man said, "Just like in the old days. We must find us a living house . . . "

Zelig soon understood what this meant when a three-storied gray building stepped out of the street's row. It stomped and pranced on the cobblestones, as if impatient to be gone. Zelig rubbed his eyes with the back of the hand that held the case; it swung awkwardly in front of his nose. Grandfather took off his hat and bowed.

"Good evening, Mendel's house!"

The dark double doors swung open, and Zelig, still disbelieving, helped grandfather in. The hallway was covered with murals, and the boy's young eyes made out pale figures, a bride with a rooster for a crown and two leaping sheep. The stairway shook and danced. Grandfather urged Zelig up to the roof, where parasite maples grew through rain-painted tiles. "Play, Zeligel," grandfather said, and the boy took the warm fiddle out of its case. He adjusted the pegs and lowered his chin to the chinrest. The polished blackness of it creaked gently under his face, and with his ear so close, he heard the sound of the still strings waiting for music. Mendel's house moved, and the bow flew up in his hands, and lured the melody out of the night into the polished planes of the fiddle. The house jumped over the ghetto's border, broke into a gallop on the sleeping streets, leaving behind it a trail of plaster.

They found the city's Geddarien in the Market square. The arrangement of streets has been discarded, and houses large and small whirled round, embracing their dancing partners with hands of stone and glass. And there, by the dried-up fountain, two human musicians sent silver and feathered honey into the night: a young cellist whom Zelig did not recognize, and grandfather's friend Velvl with his clarinet. "Finally!" Velvl cried, "We need violins . . . " Zelig sat grandfather down on the fountain's edge. He smiled and swung his bow, and the waltz poured from under his fingers.

All round them the bright Market Square kept unfolding, a dance-floor for hundreds of houses, for churches and bakeries, palaces, libraries, humble gray-stones with their windows a-flapping, revealing inside sleeping figures tucked into their beds. The stone dancers moved one two three, one two three, one two three, and they whirled and they turned, swinging trees from the rooftops, and pigeons kept balance pretending to sleep, but they secretly flapped one two three, one two three, and in Zelig's hands music was magic.

The golden spiral of the waltz died down, and through the wild thumping of blood in his ears Zelig heard Grandfather speaking to someone. "It is too soon, my city, my Luriberg. I know. I counted. I wasn't supposed to live long enough to see another Geddarien."

"I am afraid . . . " someone said, making words into old-fashioned shapes, "that soon there won't be any musicians left, and what kind of Geddarien is it without music?" The speaker was a warm glow wrapped around the Council Tower, and its face was the shining face of an ancient clock. "When Zbigniew rode up this hill to lay my first stone, reb Lurie was riding behind him with a fiddle in his hands." The city itself was speaking through the tower, Zelig felt; Luriberg's face wavered, as if concealing tears. "I wanted a dance, one last dance from my yiddn musicians before they're all gone."

Other houses came closer now. Good riddance, one said, and another one added, the *yiddn* people are pigeons, thieving and dirty, and the Opera theatre said no, the music is too fine to die, but a sharp-roofed one said, there'll be music without them. Other houses wanted more waltzing and why did you stop, we don't care what kind of people they are for as long as the dancing continues.

Grandfather said, "Where is my Yankel?"

"He is not well enough to play here," said the city, "but if you want, I can invite him."

Grandfather said. "Please . . . He waited all of his life."

A black building approached, its stones finely chiseled; it was crowned by a lion that stepped on a book. Zelig inclined his head to the famous Blackstone house, and he thought that it nodded back at him, but the building did not speak. The Council Tower that was the city swung its doors wide, and the musicians waited in silence. The houses shuffled their feet.

Then a voice cried out on the tower's doorstep. Yankel's face was a *doina* that stopped in mid-wail. He could not walk properly. His left hand that used to hug the fiddle's neck so tenderly now hung useless at his side, and his good right hand was empty.

"Yankele, what's with you?" Grandfather pushed Zelig gently in the ribs, and the boy ran up to Yankel and helped him wobble over and sit by the old man.

"You want to know? Then I will tell you. They took all these people to kill . . . " He took a gurgling breath and leaned over, put his face in his hands. "They made me play 'Hava Nagila'."

Grandfather pulled him close. "Your wife?"

It was some time before Yankel whispered, "Yes."

The cellist crouched and took Yankel's good hand. "Have you seen my girl there? My Gita?" No, the fiddler whispered. She might still be all right.

Luriberg's light dimmed. "Can we please have the last of the music?"

"Everything's gone." Yankel said. "We need to run. There's nowhere to run."

The Blackstone House edged closer; its lion spoke. "I can guide you to a place of safety."

"I know what you have in mind," the city said, "But they must not go yet. I have waited for eighty years."

The cellist said, "Well, I am not going, not without my *libe*. Later we'll try to escape together."

The clarinet—Velvl—said, "I also will stay. Whatever happens, happens."

Grandfather said, "I will stay if you let my Zelig go."

"You're too old to play," the city replied, "and what kind of dancing is it without the fiddle?"

"You'll see."

The boy knelt by the old man and put his hands on grandfather's cheeks. "How can I ever leave you?" It seemed that the old man was melting under his hands, his wrinkled warm skin insubstantial like a memory.

"You must go," Grandfather said. "This *fiddele* wants to meet your grand-children."

"Come with us then. Yankel's going, and you . . . "

"I cannot."

"Please. I will help you . . . " But Zelig wasn't sure he knew how. Grandfa-ther seemed translucent, and his shadow merged with the fountain's water that spilled over to become a modest a river that ran through the Market Square. Strange, Zelig thought that the fountain was dry before.

Grandfather's eyes crinkled. "It's all right. I want to play again, here in my shining gray city."

The doors of the Blackstone house wavered. Yankel hauled himself up somehow and grabbed Zelig by the hand. "Come on, come on, come on."

Zelig got up, then leaned over and kissed grandfather's wet cheek." But how will you play without an instrument?"

The old man's lips turned up. "Oh, like this." He brought his palms sharply together, and announced, *"Patsch Tants!"*

The doors of the Blackstone House swung gently behind them. Outside, the clarinet swirled into the lantern-lit night, and the houses stomped their stones in tune with the music of grandfather's soft white hands.

Blackstone house was a respectable building once, a palace of commerce; he had traveled wide between Luriberg and other free living cities. In his rooms he kept shells and dark wooden commodes inlaid with mother-of-pearl; mermaids looked coquettishly out of aged oil paintings. Blackstone opened all doors wide, and swung his stairs down. "Underneath me," he said, "there are roadways of old wood and brick that lead south and west to the land by the sea. Always take right turns until a living city speaks to you from above. If you do not hear her voice, do not go up."

"Thank you, Blackstone," Zelig bowed, but Yankel was strangely docile, not complaining, not even frowning. Slowly they descended the stairs. The catacombs under Blackstone were dry and warm, and the brick floor felt reassuring beneath their feet; the walls sported a dark-red paint splashed with little gold dots. After three right turns the brick began to lose shape and the paint on the walls to chip; there were other hours and turns, and clean water that seeped through the ancient floor-slabs and pooled in the cracks as they walked. "Enough of this," Yankel suddenly said, and Zelig made him sit on the drier stones by the wall. The fiddler was out of breath, if not out of words.

"I was wrong to drag us down here. There's no point in walking further. There's nothing here. We're as good as dead. Everybody's dead."

Zelig sighed. "Well, Grandfather is still in Geddarien . . . "

Yankel looked at him strangely. "He is gone, my boy. There never was a

Geddarien. I came back to the room and found you both . . . He died of starvation. White and empty."

"No, Geddarien really happened." Grandmother had died, but grandfather was still there, where the houses whirled in the last waltz; Zelig could hear them inside his violin case if he brought it close to his ear. Like a shell that caught the whole ocean inside it the violin caught the city, and if he were to play it again, the houses would spill from under his fingers and dance. "Geddarien is here, Yankel. All here inside."

The fiddler petted him on the head. "You are delirious with hunger. Perhaps tomorrow we'll have some *mazl* and find us a *bisele* to eat." He bent his legs awkwardly, as if they were soft and filled with rags. "I don't know where this tunnel leads," he whispered, "I do not remember how we got here . . . "

"I do," Zelig said. He put a hand on Yankel's forehead. It felt furnace-red, but still real. "You should try to sleep."

He curled on the cold tiles himself, but rest did not come. He cradled the violin case and listened to Yankel's kettle-thin snores, and after a while it seemed to him that he heard music come from inside the black case, a slow and sweet melody that covered his back in grandfather's gray pin-striped jacket, and grandmother's face leaned over and whispered to him, *shluf, mayn kind*, and he sank into the goose-down of sleep.

In the morning Yankel was cold to the touch and did not wake, no matter how much Zelig shook him. He just sat there with his face all sharp and his mouth open, revealing teeth. Zelig put both hands on the wet wall just above Yankel's head, and brought himself up somehow, fearful to touch the cold flesh. Zelig's feet came to life then and carried him away, away, further down the tunnel.

A rat darted between his legs and tripped him, and he fell face first into the dirt. He lay there for a while, empty of feelings, empty of himself. *He died of starvation. White and empty.* He should have at least covered Yankel's face and said *shma*. But he could not go back. Yankel was . . . no longer human. And what if he lost his way? No, no . . . but he hugged the black fiddle-case tightly and backed out into a crawl, then clambered to his feet. The water still seeped on the floor, and he traced it back, hoping that back was back, hoping that he had not taken turns.

A tiny drumming sound grew alongside him, like chubby old fingers on glass, like rain on a coffin. He would here die, too, somewhere underneath living cities too large and important to bow down and take a look. He heard tiny squeaks now; and suddenly Yankel swam back into view, still propped against the wall, but now his half-solid form was surrounded by diners. Rats. Dozens of them, hundreds, with naked pink tails and shifting, beady eyes. Zelig could not even muster a scream; the horrors boiled over in his heart. He opened his case. The fiddle was cold under his cheek. It played nameless dances, the music of might-have-beens. It licked sounds from the semi-transparent red candy of childhood, it scraped on the residue of loss; it vibrated along the frosted windows of winters, tip-toed over rooftops to glide the bow over the moon.

The rats were gone. Zelig's soul poured viscous and heavy, back into his hollow clothes. The boy put the fiddle back home and said *shma* for Yankel, but his voice rang inhuman after the fiddle's.

The corridor stretched before the boy again; endless, lightless. He put his right hand on the damp wall and walked where it guided.

Days later—or was it weeks? months?—he heard a voice, a gentle voice from above. *Caro mio, não percas a esperança.* A woman was speaking. Was that the city? Her voice of stone mingled with salt water in his eyes, and Zelig walked on blinded, trailing fingers over the wall. Light blinked uncertainly; he dragged his eyelids open. A square of sunlight spread its promise on the floor by his feet.

"Here you are!"

Zelig tilted his head up. The movement made him suddenly dizzy. A girl's face peered through the grating. "The city sent me to look for you." Zelig sheltered his eyes against unfamiliar sun, but he could not make out her features. The girl shouted to someone, "Boruch! Borya! Come here quick!" He heard the long scrape of the grate being moved. He wanted to say something, anything, but could not draw a breath. The world tilted.

When he came to, he was sitting on a small piece of cloth under a white awning, overlooking the ocean. Everything was full of sound; in the harbor, ships spoke to each other in a language of metal and rope, and the breeze played a lazy melody tilting small boats in the water. Gulls and pigeons strutted on the pier, waiting for pieces of bread, pieces such as he held in his hand. He bit into his bread hastily, afraid that the world was unstable yet; but it was real enough.

"And a good day to you." The girl that had found him now sat by his side. She was older, maybe sixteen, seventeen; she had a nose like a potato, and laughing brown eyes. The most beautiful girl in the world, he thought, but said nothing, his mouth full of bread. "I am Reyzl, and this is my brother Borya." The youth beside her had the same face, only sadder and thinner somehow. "Is that your fiddle?"

"Yes," he said." I am Zelig. From Luriberg. Where are you from?"

"Oh. Malin." Into Zelig's confused eyes she added, "It's a small town near the border. We've never been to Luriberg, but we heard . . . "

"How did you escape?" Zelig asked, a bit more harshly than he intended.

"Malin's *kosciol* sheltered us. Her name is Sankta Elzbeta."

Zelig gulped. "A church saved you?"

"Yes, us and some others. We hid in the basement. Malin is a small town, you see. Only four living buildings. Luriberg, now, Luriberg must be so big. I heard that once every hundred years there is a thing called Geddarien . . . "

Zelig interrupted, his mouth dry. "How many *yiddn* survived in Malin?"

"More than half, I think. Two hundred are here now, waiting to sail to America."

The serious boy spoke up for the first time. "How many survived in Luriberg?"

"I . . . I don't know about anyone else."

Reyzl frowned fiercely, and said, "Well, you're coming with us, of course. I play the clarinet, by the way, and my brother is a fiddler like you."

Borya said. "I lost my fiddle . . . "

"Maybe it's for the best," Reyzl said, "It's not good for you to play. He gets too excited, you see, and he has a bad heart," she explained to Zelig.

" . . . but I can sew pants."

"Our grandfather went to America once," Reyzl said, "he came back, said it was a poor country. He brought back a sewing machine and he taught us."

"I will work hard and buy me a new fiddle."

Reyzl sighed. "But who knows if they even need musicians there . . . "

"What are they, not people?" Zelig shrugged. "Everybody wants music." Even the people who kill do, he thought, yes, even the stone-clad cities.

"Everybody wants pants," Borya said. "That's for sure."

"Would you like to play a bit now?"

Zelig nodded. "Of course! Anything but 'Hava Nagila'." When he saw Borya's haunted expression he added quickly, "I can show you this melody. 'Patsch Tants' for clarinet and hands."

He took Borya's palms between his own to teach him his grandfather's music.

The Wings of Meister Wilhelm

Theodora Goss

My mother wanted me to play the piano. She had grown up in Boston, among the brownstones and the cobbled streets, in the hush of rooms where dust settled slowly, in the sunlight filtering through lace curtains, over the leaves of spider-plants and aspidistras. She had learned to play the piano sitting on a mahogany stool with a rotating top, her back straight, hair braided into decorous loops, knees covered by layers of summer gauze. Her fingers had moved with elegant patience over the keys. A lady, she told me, always looked graceful on a piano stool.

I did try. But my knees, covered mostly by scars from wading in the river by the Beauforts' and then falling into the blackberry bushes, sprawled and banged—into the bench, into the piano, into Mr. Henry, the Episcopal Church organist, who drew in the corners of his mouth when he saw me, forming a pink oval of distaste. No matter how often my mother brushed my hair, I ran my fingers through it so that I looked like an animated mop, and to her dismay I never sat up straight, stooping over the keys until I resembled, she said, "that dreadful creature from Victor Hugo—the hunchback of Notre Dame."

I suppose she took my failure as a sign of her own. When she married my father, the son of a North Carolina tobacco farmer, she left Boston and the house by the Common that the Winslows had inhabited since the Revolution. She arrived as a bride in Ashton expecting to be welcomed into a red brick mansion fronted by white columns and shaded by magnolias, perhaps a bit singed from the war her grandfather the General had won for the Union. Instead, she found herself in a house with only a front parlor, its white paint flaking, flanked by a set of ragged tulip poplars. My father rode off every morning to the tobacco fields that lay around the foundations of the red brick mansion, its remaining bricks still blackened from the fires of the Union army and covered through the summer with twining purple vetch.

A month after my first piano lesson with Mr. Henry, we were invited to a dinner party at the Beauforts'. At the bottom left corner of the invitation was written, "Violin Recital."

"Adeline Beaufort is so original," said my mother over her toast and eggs, the morning we received the invitation. "Imagine. Who in Balfour County plays the violin?" Her voice indicated the amused tolerance extended to Adeline Beaufort, who had once been Adeline Ashton, of the Ashtons who had given their name to the town.

Hannah began to disassemble the chafing dish. "I hear she's paying some foreign man to play for her. He arrived from Raleigh last week. He's staying at Slater's."

"Real-ly?" said my mother, lengthening the word as she said it to express the notion that Adeline Beaufort, who lived in the one red brick mansion in Ashton, fronted by white columns and shaded by magnolias, should know better than to allow some paid performer staying at Slater's, with its sagging porch and mixed-color clientele, to play at her dinner party.

My father pushed back his chair. "Well, it'll be a nice change from that damned organist." He was already in his work shirt and jodhpurs.

"Language, Cullen," said my mother.

"Rose doesn't mind my damns, does she?" He stopped as he passed and leaned down to kiss the top of my head.

I decided then that I would grow up just like my father. I would wear a blue shirt and leather boots up to my knees, and damn anything I pleased. I looked like him already, although the sandy hair so thick that no brush could tame it, the strong jaw and freckled nose that made him a handsome man made me a very plain girl indeed. I did not need to look in a mirror to realize my plainness. It was there, in my mother's perpetual look of disappointment, as though I were, to her, a symbol of the town with its unpaved streets where passing carriages kicked up dust in the summer, and the dull green of the tobacco fields stretching away to the mountains.

After breakfast I ran to the Beauforts' to find Emma. The two of us had been friends since our first year at Ashton Ladies' Academy. Together we had broken our dolls in intentional accidents, smuggled books like *Gulliver's Travels* out of the Ashton library, and devised secret codes that revealed exactly what we thought of the older girls at our school, who were already putting their hair up and chattering about beaux. I found her in the orchard below the house, stealing green apples. It was only the middle of June, and they were just beginning to be tinged with their eventual red.

"Aren't you bad," I said when I saw her. "You know those will only make you sick."

"I can't help it," she said, looking doleful. The expression did not suit her. Emma reminded me of the china doll Aunt Winslow had given me two summers ago, on my twelfth birthday. She had chestnut hair and blue eyes that always looked newly painted, above cheeks as smooth and white as porcelain, now round with the apple pieces she had stuffed into them. "Mama thinks I've grown too plump, so Callie won't let me have more than toast and an egg for breakfast, and no sugar for my coffee. I get so hungry afterward!"

"Well, I'll steal you some bread and jam later if you'll tell me about the violin player from Slater's."

We walked to the cottage below the orchard, so close to the river at the bottom of the Beauforts' back garden that it flooded each spring. Emma felt above the low doorway, found the key we always kept there, and let us both in. The cottage had been used, as long as we could remember, for storing old furniture. It was filled with dressers gaping where their drawers had once been and chairs whose caned seats had long ago rotted through. We sat on a sofa whose springs sagged under its faded green upholstery, Emma munching her apple and me munching another although I knew it would give me a stomach-ache that afternoon.

"His name is Johann Wilhelm," she finally said through a mouthful of apple. "He's German, I think. He played the violin in Raleigh, and Aunt Otway heard him there, and said he was coming down here, and that we might want him to play for us. That's all I know."

"So why is he staying at Slater's?"

"I dunno. I guess he must be poor."

"My mother said your mother was original for having someone from Slater's play at her house."

"Yeah? Well, your mother's a snobby Yankee."

I kicked Emma, and she kicked back, and then we had a regular kicking battle. Finally, I had to thump her on the back when she choked on an apple from laughing too hard. I was laughing too hard as well. We were only fourteen, but we were old enough to understand certain truths about the universe, and we both knew that mothers were ridiculous.

In the week that followed, I almost forgot about the scandalous violinist. I was too busy protesting against the dress Hannah was sewing for me to wear at the party, which was as uncomfortable as dresses were in those days of boning and horsehair.

"I'll tear it to bits before I wear it to the party," I said.

"Then you'll go in your nightgown, Miss Rose, because I'm not sewing you another party dress, that's for sure. And don't you sass your mother about it, either." Hannah put a pin in her mouth and muttered, "She's a good woman, who's done more for the colored folk in this town than some I could name. Now stand still or I'll stick you with this pin, see if I don't."

I shrugged to show my displeasure, and was stuck.

✡

On the night of the party, after dinner off the Sèvres service that Judge Beaufort had ordered from Raleigh, we gathered in the back parlor, where chairs had been arranged in a circle around the piano. In front of the piano stood a man, not much taller than I was. Gray hair hung down to his collar, and his face seemed to be covered with wrinkles, which made him look like a dried-apple doll I had played with one autumn until its head was stolen by a squirrel. In his left hand he carried a violin.

"Come on, girl, sit by your papa," said my father. We sat beside him although it placed Emma by Mr. Henry, who was complaining to Amelia Ashton, the town beauty, about the new custom of hiring paid performers.

The violinist waited while the dinner guests told each other to hush and be quiet. Then, when even the hushing had stopped, he said "Ladies and gentlemen," bowed to the audience, and lifted his violin.

He began with a simple melody, like a bird singing on a tree branch in spring. Then came a series of notes, and then another, and I imagined the tree branch swaying in a rising wind, with the bird clinging to it. Then clouds rolled in, gray and filled with rain, and wind lashed the tree branch, so that the bird launched itself into the storm. It soared through turbulence, among the roiling clouds, sometimes enveloped in mist, sometimes with sunlight flashing on its wings, singing in fear of the storm, in defiance of it, in triumph. As this frenzy rose from the strings of the violin, which I thought must snap at any moment, the violinist began to sway, twisting with the force of the music as though he were the bird itself. Then, just as the music seemed almost unbearable, rain fell in a shower of notes, and the storm subsided. The bird returned to the branch and resumed its melody, then even it grew still. The violinist lifted his bow, and we sat in silence.

I sagged against my father, wondering if I had breathed since the music had started.

The violinist said "Thank you, ladies and gentlemen." The dinner guests clapped. He bowed again, drank from a glass of water Callie had placed for him on the piano, and walked out of the room.

"Papa," I whispered, "Can I learn to play the violin?"

"Sure, sweetheart," he whispered back. "As long as your mother says you can."

It took an absolute refusal to touch the piano, and a hunger strike lasting through breakfast and dinner, to secure my violin lessons.

"You really are the most obstinate girl, Rose," said my mother. "If I had been anything like you, my father would have made me stay in my room all day."

"I'll stay in my room all day, but I won't eat, not even if you bring me moldy bread that's been gnawed by rats," I said.

"As though we had rats! And there's no need for that. You'll have your lessons with Meister Wilhelm."

"With what?"

"Johann Wilhelm studied music at a European university. In Berlin, I think, or was it Paris? You'll call him Meister Wilhelm. That means *master* in German. And don't expect him to put up with your willfulness. I'm sure he's accustomed to European children, who are polite and always do as they're told."

"I'm not a child."

"Real-ly?" she said with an unpleasant smile, stretching the word out as long as she had when questioning Adeline Beaufort's social arrangements. "Then stop behaving like one."

"Well," I said, nervous under that smile, "should I go down to Slater's for my lessons?" The thought of entering the disreputable boarding house was as attractive as it was frightening.

"Certainly not. The Beauforts are going to rent him their cottage while he stays in Ashton. You'll have your lessons there."

Meister Wilhelm looked even smaller than I remembered, when he opened the cottage door in answer to my knock. He wore a white smock covered with smudges where he had rubbed up against something dusty. From its hem hung a cobweb.

"Ah, come in, Fraulein," he said. "You must forgive me. This is no place to receive a young lady, with the dust and the dirt everywhere—and on myself also."

I looked around the cottage. It had changed little since the day Emma and I had eaten green apples on the sagging sofa, although a folded blanket now lay on the sofa, and I realized with surprise that the violinist must sleep there, on the broken springs. The furniture had been pushed farther toward the wall, leaving space in the center of the room for a large table cracked down the middle that had been banished from the Beauforts' dining room for at least a generation. On it were scattered pieces of bamboo, yards of unbleached canvas, tools I did not recognize, a roll of twine, a pot of glue with the handle of a brush sticking out of it, and a stack of papers written over in faded ink.

I did not know what to say, so I twisted the apron Hannah had made me wear between my fingers. My palms felt unpleasantly damp.

Meister Wilhelm peered at me from beneath gray eyebrows that seemed too thick for his face. "Your mother tells me you would like to play the violin?"

I nodded.

"And why the violin? It is not a graceful instrument. A young lady will not look attractive, playing Bach or Corelli. Would you not prefer the piano, or perhaps the harp?"

I shook my head, twisting the apron more tightly.

"No?" He frowned and leaned forward, as though to look at me more closely.

"Then perhaps you are not one of those young ladies who cares only what the gentlemen think of her figure? Perhaps you truly wish to be a musician."

I scrunched damp fabric between my palms. I scarcely understood my motives for wanting to play the violin, but I wanted to be as honest with him as I could. "I don't think so. Mr. Henry says I have no musical talent at all. It's just that when I saw you playing the violin—at the Beauforts' dinner party, you know—it sounded, well, like you'd gone somewhere else while you were playing. Somewhere with a bird on a tree, and then a storm came. And I wanted to go there too." What a stupid thing to have said. He was going to think I was a complete idiot.

Meister Wilhelm leaned back against the table and rubbed the side of his nose with one finger. "It is perceptive of you to see a bird on a tree and a storm in my music. I call it Der Sturmvogel, the Stormbird. So you want to go somewhere else, Fraulein Rose. Where exactly is it you want to go?"

"I don't know." My words sounded angry. He did think I was an idiot, then. "Are you going to teach me to play the violin or not?"

He smiled, as though enjoying my discomfiture. "Of course I will teach you. Are not your kind parents paying me? Paying me well, so that I can buy food for myself, and pay for this bamboo, which has been brought from California, and glue, for the pot there, she is empty? But I am glad to hear, Fraulein, that you have a good reason for wanting to learn the violin. In this world, we all of us need somewhere else to go." From the top of one of the dressers, Meister Wilhelm lifted a violin. "Come," he said. "I will show you how to hold the instrument between your chin and shoulder."

"Is this your violin?" I asked.

"No, Fraulein. My violin, she was made by a man named Antonio Stradivari. Some day, if you are diligent, perhaps you shall play her."

I learned, that day, how to hold the violin and the bow, like holding a bird in your hands, with delicate firmness. The first time I put the bow to the strings I was startled by the sound, like a crow with a head cold, nothing like the tones Meister Wilhelm had drawn out of his instrument in the Beauforts' parlor.

"That will get better with time," he told me. "I think we have had enough for today, no?"

I nodded and put the violin down on the sofa. The fingers of my right hand were cramped, and the fingers of my left hand were crisscrossed with red lines where I had been holding the strings.

On a table by the sofa stood a photograph of a man with a beard and mustache, in a silver frame. "Who is this?" I asked.

"That is—was—a very good friend of mine, Herr Otto Lilienthal."

"Is he dead?" The question was rude, but my curiosity was stronger than any scruples I had with regard to politeness.

"Yes. He died last year." Meister Wilhelm lifted the violin from the sofa and put it back on top of the dresser.

"Was he ill?" This was ruder yet, and I dared to ask only because Meister Wilhelm now had his back to me, and I could not see his face.

"*Nein.* He fell from the sky, from a glider."

"A glider!" I sounded like a squawking violin myself. "That's what you're making with all that bamboo and twine and stuff. But this can't be all of it. Where do you keep the longer pieces? I know—in Slater's barn. From there you can take it to Slocumb's Bluff, where you can jump off the big rock." Then I frowned. "You know that's awfully dangerous."

Meister Wilhelm turned to face me. His smile was at once amused and sad.

"You are an excellent detective, *kleine* Rose. Someday you will learn that everything worth doing is dangerous."

Near the end of July, Emma left for Raleigh, escorted by her father, to spend a month with her Aunt Otway. Since I had no one to play with, I spent more time at the cottage with Meister Wilhelm, scraping away at the violin with ineffective ardor and bothering him while he built intricate structures of bamboo and twine.

One morning, as I was preparing to leave the house, still at least an hour before my scheduled lesson with the violinist, I heard two voices in the parlor. I crept down the hall to the doorway and listened.

"You're so fortunate to have a child like Emma," said my mother. "I really don't know what to do with Elizabeth Rose."

"Well, Eleanor, she's an obstinate girl, I won't deny that," said a voice I recognized as belonging to Adeline Beaufort. "It's a pity Cullen's so lax with her. You ought to send her to Boston for a year or two. Your sister Winslow would know how to improve a young girl's manners."

"I supposed you're right, Adeline. If she were pretty, that might be some excuse, but as it is . . . Well, you're lucky with your Emma, that's all."

I had heard enough. I ran out of the house, and ran stumbling down the street to the cottage by the river. I pounded on the door. No answer. Meister Wilhelm must still be at Slater's barn. I tried the doorknob, but the cottage was locked. I reached to the top of the door frame, pulled down the key, and let myself in. I banged the door shut behind me, threw myself onto the sagging sofa, and pressed my face into its faded upholstery.

Emma and I had discussed the possibility that our mothers did not love us. We had never expected it to be true.

The broken springs of the sofa creaked beneath me as I sobbed. I was the bird clinging to the tree branch, the tree bending and shaking in the storm Meister Wilhelm had played on his violin, and the storm itself, wanting to break things apart, to tear up roots and crack branches. At last my sobs subsided, and I lay with my cheek on the damp upholstery, staring at the maimed furniture standing against the cottage walls.

Slowly I realized that my left hip was lying on a hard edge. I pushed myself up and, looking under me, saw a book with a green leather cover. I opened it. The frontispiece was a photograph of a tired-looking man labeled "Lord Rutherford, Mountaineer." On the title page was written, "The Island of Orillion: Its History and Inhabitants, by Lord Rutherford." I turned the page. Beneath the words "A Brief History of Orillion" I read, "The Island of Orillion achieved levitation on the twenty-third day of June, the year of our Lord one thousand seven hundred and thirty-six."

I do not know how long I read. I did not hear when Meister Wilhelm entered the cottage.

"I see you have come early today," he said.

I looked up from a corner of the sofa, into which I had curled myself. Since I felt ashamed of having entered the cottage while he was away, ashamed of having read his book without asking, what I said sounded accusatory. "So that's why you're building a glider. You want to go to Orillion."

He sat down on the other end of the sofa. "And how much have you learned of Orillion, *liebling*?"

He was not angry with me then. This time, my voice sounded penitent. "Well, I know about the painters and musicians and poets who were kicked out of Spain by that Inquisition person, Torque-something, when Columbus left to discover America. How did they find the island in that storm, after everyone thought they had drowned? And when the pirate came—Blackbeard or Bluebeard or whatever—how did they make it fly? Was it magic?"

"Magic, or a science we do not yet understand, which to us resembles magic," said Meister Wilhelm.

"Is that why they built all those towers on the tops of the houses, and put bells in them—to warn everyone if another pirate was coming?"

Meister Wilhelm smiled. "I see you've read the first chapter."

"I was just starting the second when you came in. About how Lord Rutherford fell and broke his leg on a mountain in the Alps, and he thought he was going to die when he heard the bells, all ringing together. I thought they were warning bells?"

"Orillion has not been attacked in so long that the bells are only rung once a day, when the sun rises."

"All of them together? That must make an awful racket."

"Ah, no, *liebling*. Remember that the citizens of Orillion are artists, the children and grandchildren of artists. Those bells are tuned by the greatest musicians of Orillion, so that when they are rung, no matter in what order, the sound produced is a great harmony. From possible disorder, the bells of Orillion create musical order. But I think one chapter is enough for you today."

At that moment I realized something. "That's how Otto Lilienwhatever died, didn't he? He was trying to get to Orillion."

Meister Wilhelm looked down at the dusty floor of the cottage. "You are right, in a sense, Rose. Otto was trying to test a new theory of flight that he thought would someday allow him to reach Orillion. He knew there was risk—it was the highest flight he had yet attempted. Before he went into the sky for the last time, he sent me that book, and all of his papers. 'If I do not reach Orillion, Johann,' he wrote to me, 'I depend upon you to reach it.' It had been our dream since he discovered Lord Rutherford's book at university. That is why I have come to America. During the three years he lived on Orillion, Lord Rutherford charted the island's movements. In July, it would have been to the north, over your city of Raleigh. I tried to finish my glider there, but was not able to complete it in time. So I came here, following the island—or rather, Lord Rutherford's charts."

"Will you complete it in time now?"

"I do not know. The island moves slowly, but it will remain over this area only during the first two weeks of August." He stood and walked to the table, then touched the yards of canvas scattered over it. "I have completed the frame of the glider, but the cloth for the wings—there is much sewing still to be done."

"I'll help you."

"You, *liebling*?" He looked at me with amusement. "You are very generous. But for this cloth, the stitches must be very small, like so." He brought over a piece of canvas and showed me his handiwork.

I smiled a superior smile. "Oh, I can make them even smaller than that, don't worry." When Aunt Winslow had visited two summers ago, she had insisted on teaching me to sew. "A lady always looks elegant holding a needle," she had said. I had spent hours sitting in the parlor making a set of clothes for the china doll she had given me, which I had broken as soon as she left. In consequence, I could make stitches a spider would be proud of.

"Very well," said Meister Wilhelm, handing me two pieces of canvas that had been half-joined with an intricate, overlapping seam. "Show me how you would finish this, and I will tell you if it is good enough."

I crossed my legs and settled back into the sofa with the pieces of canvas, waxed thread and a needle, and a pair of scissors. He took *The Island of Orillion* from where I had left it on the sofa and placed it back on the shelf where he kept the few books he owned, between *The Empire of the Air* and *Maimonides: Seine Philosophie*. Then he sat on a chair with a broken back, one of his knees crossed over the other. Draping another piece of canvas over the raised knee, he leaned down so he could see the seam he was sewing in the dim light that came through the dirty windows. I stared at him sewing like that, as though he were now the hunchback of Notre Dame.

"You know," I said, "if you're nearsighted you ought to buy a pair of spectacles."

"Ah, I had a very good pair from Germany," he answered without looking up from his work. "They were broken just before I left Raleigh. Since then, I have not been able to afford another."

I sewed in silence for a moment. Then I said, "Why do you want to go to Orillion, anyway? Do you think—things will be better there?"

His fingers continued to swoop down to the canvas, up from the canvas, like birds. "The citizens of Orillion are artists. I would like to play my Sturmvogel for them. I think they would understand it, as you do." Then he looked up and stared at the windows of the cottage, as though seeing beyond them to the hills around Ashton, to the mountains rising blue behind the hills. "I do not know if human beings are better anywhere. But I like to think, *liebling*, that in this sad world of ours, those who create do not destroy so often."

After the day on which I had discovered *The Island of Orillion*, when my lessons had been forgotten, Meister Wilhelm insisted that I continue practicing the violin, in spite of my protest that it took time away from constructing the glider. "If no learning, then no sewing—and no reading," he would say. After an hour of valiant effort on the instrument, I was allowed to sit with him, stitching triangles of canvas into bat-shaped wings. And then, if any time remained before dinner, I was allowed to read one, and never more than one, chapter of Lord Rutherford's book.

In spite of our sewing, the glider was not ready to be launched until the first week of August was nearly over. Once the pieces of canvas were sewn together, they had to be stretched over and attached to the bamboo frame, and then covered with three layers of wax, each of which required a day and a night to dry.

But finally, one morning before dawn, I crept down our creaking stairs and then out through the kitchen door, which was never locked. I ran through the silent streets of Ashton to Slater's barn and helped Meister Wilhelm carry the glider up the slope of the back pasture to Slocumb's Bluff, whose rock face rose above the waving grass. I had assumed we would carry the glider to the top of the bluff, where the winds from the rock face were strongest. But Meister Wilhelm called for me to halt halfway up, at a plateau formed by large, flat slabs of granite. There we set down the glider. In the gray light, it looked like a great black moth against the stones.

"Why aren't we going to the top?" I asked.

He looked over the edge of the plateau. Beyond the slope of the pasture lay the streets and houses of Ashton, as small as a dolls' town. Beyond them, a strip of yellow had appeared on the hilltops to the east. "That rock, he is high. I will die if the glider falls from such a height. Here we are not so high."

I stared at him in astonishment. "Do you think you could fall?" Such a possibility had never occurred to me.

"Others have," he answered, adjusting the strap that held a wooden case to his chest. He was taking his violin with him.

"Oh," I said, remembering the picture of Otto Lilienthal. Of course what had happened to Lilienthal could happen to him. I had simply never associated the idea of death with anyone I knew. I clenched and unclenched my hands.

"Help me to put on the glider," said Meister Wilhelm.

I held the glider at an angle as he crouched under it, fastened its strap over his chest, above the strap that held the violin case, and fitted his arms into the armrests.

"Rose," he said suddenly, "listen."

I listened, and heard nothing but the wind as it blew against the face of the bluff.

"You mean the wind?" I said.

"No, no," he answered, his voice high with excitement. "Not the wind. Don't you hear them? The bells, first one, then ten, and now a hundred, playing together."

I turned my head from side to side, trying to hear what he was hearing. I looked up at the sky, where the growing yellow was pushing away the gray. Nothing.

"Rose." He looked at me, his face both kind and solemn. In the horizontal light, his wrinkles seemed carved into his face, so that he looked like a part of the bluff. "I would like you to have my books, and my picture of Otto, and the violin on which you learned to play. I have nothing else to leave anyone in the world. And I leave you my gratitude, *liebling*. You have been to me a good friend."

He smiled at me, but turned away as he smiled. He walked back from the edge of the plateau and stood, poised with one foot behind the other, like a runner on a track. Then he sprang forward and began to sprint, more swiftly than I thought he could have, the great wings of the glider flapping awkwardly with each step.

He took one final leap, over the edge of the plateau, into the air. The great wings caught the sunlight, and the contraption of waxed canvas fastened on a bamboo frame became a moth covered with gold dust. It soared, wings outstretched, on the winds that blew up from the face of the bluff, and then out over the pasture, higher and farther into the golden regions of the sky.

My heart lifted within me, as when I had first heard Meister Wilhelm play the violin. What if I had heard no bells? Surely Orillion was there, and he would fly up above its houses of white stucco with their belltowers. The citizens of Orillion would watch this miracle, a man like a bird, soaring over them, and welcome him with glad shouts.

The right wing of the glider dipped. Suddenly it was spiraling down, at first slowly and then faster, like a maple seed falling, falling, to the pasture.

I heard a thin shriek, and realized it had come from my own throat. I ran as quickly as I could down the side of the bluff.

When I reached the glider, it was lying in an area of broken grass, the tip of its right wing twisted like an injured bird. Meister Wilhelm's legs stuck out from beneath it.

I lifted one side of the glider, afraid of what I might see underneath. How had Otto Lilienthal looked when he was found, crushed by his fall from the sky?

But I saw no blood, no intestines splattered over the grass—

—just Meister Wilhelm, with his right arm tangled in a broken armrest and twisted under him at an uncomfortable angle.

"Rose," he said in a weak voice. "Rose, is my violin safe?"

I lifted the glider off him, reaching under him to undo the strap across his chest. He rolled over on his back, the broken armrest still dangling from his arm. The violin case was intact.

"Are you going to die?" I asked, kneeling beside him, grass tickling my legs through my stockings. I could feel tears running down my nose, down to my neck, and wetting the collar of my dress.

"No, Rose," he said with a sigh, his fingers caressing the case as though making absolutely sure it was unbroken. "I think my arm is sprained, that is all. The glider acted like a helicopter and brought me down slowly. It saved my life." He pushed himself up with his left arm. "Is it much damaged?"

I rubbed the back of my hands over my face to wipe away tears.

"No. Just one corner of the wing."

"Good," he said. "Then it can be fixed quickly."

"You mean you're going to try this again?" I stared at him as though he had told me he was about to hang himself from the beam of Slater's barn.

With his left hand, he brushed back his hair, which had blown over his cheeks and forehead. "I have only one more week, Rose. And then the island will be gone."

Together we managed to carry the glider back to Slater's barn, and I snuck back into the house for breakfast.

Later that day, I sat on the broken chair in the cottage while Meister Wilhelm lay on the sofa with a bandage around his right wrist.

"So, what's wrong with your arm?" I asked.

"I think the wrist, it is broken. And there is much pain. But no more breaks."

His face looked pale and old against the green upholstery. I crossed my arms and looked at him accusingly. "I didn't hear any bells."

He tried to smile, but grimaced instead, as though the effort were painful. "I have been a musician for many years. It is natural for me to hear things that you are not yet capable of hearing."

"Well, I didn't see anything either."

"No, Rose. You would see nothing. Through the science—or the magic—of its inhabitants, the bottom of the island always appears the same color as the sky."

Was that true? Or was he just a crazy old man, trying to kill himself in an especially crazy way? I kicked the chair leg, wishing that he had never come to Ashton, wishing that I had never heard of Orillion, if it was going to be a lie. I stood up and walked over to the photograph of Otto Lilienthal.

"You know," I said, my voice sounding angry, "it would be safer to go up in a balloon instead of a glider. At a fair in Brickleford last year, I saw an acrobat go up under a balloon and perform all kinds of tricks hanging from a wooden bar."

"Yes, you are right, it would be safer. I spent many years in my own country studying with Count von Zeppelin, the great balloonist. But your acrobat, he cannot tell the balloon where to go, can he?"

"No." I turned to face him again. "But at least he doesn't fall out of the sky and almost kill himself."

He turned away from me and stared up at the ceiling. "But your idea is a good one, Rose. I must consider what it is I did wrong. Will you bring me those papers upon the table?"

I walked over to the table, lifted the stack of papers, and brought it over to the sofa. "What is this, anyway?" I asked.

Meister Wilhelm took the stack from me with his left hand. "These are the papers my friend Otto left me." He looked at the paper on top of the stack. "And this is the letter he wrote to me before he died." Awkwardly, he placed the stack beside him on the sofa and lifted the letter to his nearsighted eyes.

"Let me read it to you," I said. "You'll make yourself blind doing that."

"You are generous, Rose," he said, "but I do not think you read German, eh?"

I shook my head.

"Then I will read it to you, or rather translate. Perhaps you will see in it another idea, like she of the balloon, that might help us. Or perhaps I will see in it something that I have not seen before."

He read the letter slowly, translating as he went, sometimes stumbling over words for which he did not know the English equivalent. It was nothing like the letters Emma and I were writing to each other while she stayed in Raleigh. There was no discussion of daily events, of the doings of family.

Instead, Otto Lilienthal had written about the papers he was leaving for his friend, which discussed his theories. He wrote admiringly of Besnier, the first to create a functional glider. He discussed the mistakes of Mouillard and Le Bris, and the difficulties of controlling a glider's flight. He praised Cayley, whose glider had achieved lift, and lamented Pénaud, who became so dispirited by his failures that he locked his papers into a coffin and committed suicide. Finally he wrote of his own ideas, their merits and drawbacks, and of how he had attempted to solve the two challenges of the glider, lift and lateral stability. He had solved the problem of lift early in his career. Now he would try to solve the other.

The letter ended, "My dear Johann, remember how we dreamed of gliding through the air, like the storks in our native Pomerania. I expect to succeed. But if I fail, do you continue my efforts. Surely one with your gifts will succeed, where I cannot. Always remember that you are a violinist." When he had finished the letter, Meister Wilhelm passed his hand, still holding a sheet of paper, over his eyes.

I looked away, out of the dirty window of the cottage. Then I asked, because curiosity had once again triumphed over politeness, "Why did he tell you to remember that you're a violinist?"

Meister Wilhelm answered in a tired voice, "He wanted to encourage me. To tell me, remember that you are worthy to mingle with the citizens of Orillion, to make music for them before the Monument of the Muse at the center of the city. He wanted—"

Suddenly he sat up, inadvertently putting his weight on his right hand. His face creased in pain, and he crumpled back against the seat of the sofa. But he said, in a voice filled with wonder, "No. I have been stupid. Always remember, Rose, that we cannot find the right answers until we ask the right questions. Tell me, what did the glider do just before it fell?"

I stared at him, puzzled. "It dipped to the right."

He waved his left forefinger in the air, as though to punctuate his point. "Because it lacked lateral stability!"

I continued to look puzzled.

He waved his finger again, at me this time. "That is the problem Otto was trying to solve."

I sat back down. "Yes, well he didn't solve it, did he?"

The finger waved once again, more frantically this time. "He solved it in principle. He knew that lateral stability is created with the legs, just as lift is controlled with the position of the body in the armrests. His final flight must have been intended to test which position would provide the greatest amount of control." Meister Wilhelm sat, pulling himself up this time with his left hand. "After his death, I lamented that Otto could never tell me his theory. But he has told me, and I was too stupid to see it!" He rose and began pacing, back and forth as he spoke, over the floor of the cottage. "I have been keeping my legs still, trying not to upset the glider's balance. Otto was telling me that I must use my body like a violinist, that I must not stay still, but respond to the rhythm of the wind, as I respond to the rhythm of music. He thought I would understand."

He turned to me. "Rose, we must begin to repair the glider tomorrow. And then, I will fly it again. But this time I will fly from the top of Slocumb's Bluff, where the winds are strongest. And I will become one with the winds, with the great music that they will play through me."

"Like the Stormbird," I said.

His face, so recently filled with pain, was now filled with hope. "Yes, Rose. Like Der Sturmvogel."

Several days later, when I returned for dinner after a morning spent with Meister Wilhelm, Hannah handed me a letter from Emma.

"Did the post come early?" I asked.

"No, child. Judge Beaufort came back from Raleigh and brought it himself. He was smoking in the parlor with your papa, and I'm gonna have to shake out them parlor curtains. So you get along, and don't bother me, hear?"

I walked up the stairs to my room and lay on top of the counterpane to read Emma's letter. "Dear Rose," it began. "Aunt Otway, who's been showing me an embroidery stitch, asks what I'm going to write." That meant her letter would be read. "Father is returning suddenly to Ashton, but I will remain here until school begins in September." She had told me she was returning at the end of August. And Emma never called Judge Beaufort "Father." Was she trying to show off for Aunt Otway? Under the F in "Father" was a spot of ink, and I noticed that Emma's handwriting was unusually spotty. Under the b and second e in "embroidery," for instance. "Be" what? The letters over the remaining spots spelled "careful." What did Emma mean? The rest of her letter described a visit to the Museum of Art.

Just then, my mother entered the room. "Rose," she said. Her voice was gentler than I had ever heard it. She sat down on the edge of my bed. "I'm afraid you can't continue your lessons with Meister Wilhelm."

I started at her in disbelief. "You don't want me to have anything I care about, do you? Because you hate me. You've hated me since I was born. I'll tell Papa, and he'll let me have my violin lessons, you'll see!"

She rose, and her voice was no longer gentle. "Very well, Elizabeth. Tell your father, exactly as you wish. Until he comes home from the Beauforts', however, you are to remain in this room." She walked out, closing the door with an implacable click behind her.

Was this what Emma had been trying to warn me about? Had she known that my mother would forbid me from continuing my lessons? But how could she have known, in Raleigh?

As the hours crept by, I stared at the ceiling and thought about what I had read in Lord Rutherford's book. I imagined the slave ship that had been wrecked in a storm, and the cries of the drowning slaves. How they must have wondered, to see Orillion descending from the sky, to walk through its city of stucco houses surrounded by rose gardens. How the captain must have cursed when he was imprisoned by the citizens of Orillion, and later imprisoned by the English as a madman. He had raved until the end of his life about an island in the clouds.

Hannah brought my dinner, saying to me as she set it down, "Ham sandwiches, Miss Rose. You always liked them, didn't you?" I didn't answer. I imagined myself walking between the belltowers of the city, to the Academy of Art. I would sit on the steps, beneath a frieze of the great poets from Sappho to Shakespeare, and listen to Meister Wilhelm playing his violin by the Monument of the Muse, the strains of his Sturmvogel drifting over the surface of the lake.

After it had grown dark, I heard the bang of the front door and the sound of voices. They came up the stairs, and as they passed my door I heard one word—"violin." Then the voices receded down the hall.

I opened my door, cautiously looking down the hall and then toward the staircase. I saw a light under the door of my father's study and no signs of my mother or Hannah.

Closing my bedroom door carefully behind me, I crept down the hall, stepping close to the wall where the floorboards were less likely to creak. I stopped by the door of the study and listened. The voices inside were raised, and I could hear them easily.

"To think that I let a damned Jew put his dirty fingers on my daughter." That was my father's voice. My knees suddenly felt strange, and I had to steady them with my hands. The hallway seemed to sway around me.

"We took care of him pretty good in Raleigh." That was a voice I did not recognize. "After Reverend Yancey made sure he was sacked from the orchestra, Mr. Empie and I visited him to get the money for all that bamboo he'd ordered on credit. He told us he hadn't got the money. So we reminded him of what was due to decent Christian folk, didn't we, Mr. Empie?"

"All right, Mr. Biggs," said another voice I had not heard before. "There was no need to break the man's spectacles."

"So I shook him a little," said Mr. Biggs. "Serves him right, I say."

"What's done is done," said a voice I knew to be Judge Beaufort's. "The issue before us is, what are we to do now? He has been living on my property, in close proximity to my family, for more than a month. He has been educating Mr.

Caldwell's daughter, filling her head with who knows what dangerous ideas. Clearly he must be taken care of. Gentlemen, I'm open for suggestions."

"Burn his house down," said Mr. Biggs. "That's what we do when niggers get uppity in Raleigh."

"You forget, Mr. Biggs," said Judge Beaufort, "that his house is my house. And as the elected judge of this town, I will allow no violence that is not condoned by law."

"Than act like a damned judge, Edward," said my father, with anger in his voice. "He's defaulted on a debt. Let him practice his mumbo jumbo in the courthouse jail for a few days. Then you can send him on to Raleigh with Mr. Biggs and Mr. Empie. Just get him away from my daughter!"

There was silence, then the sound of footsteps, as though someone were pacing back and forth over the floor, and then a clink and gurgle, as though a decanter had been opened and liquid were tumbling into a glass.

"All right, gentlemen," said Judge Beaufort. I leaned closer to the door even though I could hear his voice perfectly well. "First thing tomorrow morning, we get this Wilhelm and take him to the courthouse. Mr. Empie, Mr. Biggs, I depend on you to assist us."

"Oh, I'll be there all right," said Mr. Biggs. "Me and Bessie." I head a metallic click.

My father spoke again. "Put that away, sir. I'll have no loaded firearms in my home."

"He'll put it away," said Mr. Empie. "Come on, Biggs, be sensible, man. Judge Beaufort, if I could have a touch more of that whiskey?"

I crept back down the hall with a sick feeling in my stomach, as though I had eaten a dozen green apples. So this was what Emma had warned me about. I wanted to lie down on my bed and sob, with the counterpane pulled over my head to muffle the sounds. I wanted to punch the pillows until feathers floated around the room. But as I reached my door, I realized there was something else I must do. I must warn Meister Wilhelm.

I crept down the stairs. As I entered the kitchen, lit only by the embers in the stove, I saw a figure sitting at the kitchen table. It was my mother, writing a note, with a leather wallet on the table beside her.

She looked up as I entered, and I could see, even in the dim light from the stove, that her face was puffed with crying. We stared at each other for a moment. Then she rose. "What are you doing down here?" she asked.

I was so startled that all I could say was, "I heard them in the study."

My mother stuffed the note she had been writing into the wallet, and held it toward me.

"I was waiting until they were drunk, and would not miss me," she said. "But they think you're already asleep, Rose. Run and give this to Meister Wilhelm."

I took the wallet from her. She reached out, hesitantly, to smooth down my mop of hair, but I turned and opened the kitchen door. I walked through the back garden, picking my way through the tomato plants, and ran down the streets of Ashton, trying not to twist my ankles on invisible stones.

When I reached the cottage, I knocked quietly but persistently on the door. After a few minutes I heard a muffled grumbling, and then a bang and a word that sounded like an oath. The door opened, and there stood Meister Wilhelm, in a white nightshirt and nightcap, like a ghost floating in the darkness. I slipped past him into the cabin, tossed the wallet on the table, where it landed with a clink of coins, and said, "You have to get out of here, as soon as you can. And there's a note from my mother."

He lit a candle, and by its light I saw his face, half-asleep and half-incredulous, as though he believed I were part of some strange dream. But he read the note. Then he turned to me and said, "Rose, I hesitate to ask of you, but will you help me one final time?"

I nodded eagerly. "You go south to Brickleford, and I'll tell them you've gone north to Raleigh."

He smiled at me. "Very heroic of you, but I cannot leave my glider, can I? Mr. Empie would find it and take it apart for its fine bamboo, and then I would be left with what? An oddly shaped parachute. No, Rose, I am asking you to help me carry the glider to Slocumb's Bluff."

"What do you mean?" I asked. "Are you going to fly it again?"

"My final flight, in which I either succeed, or— But have no fear, *liebling*. This time I will succeed."

"But what about the wing?" I asked.

"I finished the repairs this afternoon, and would have told you about it tomorrow, or rather today, since my pocket watch on the table here, she tells me it is after midnight. Well, Rose, will you help me?"

I nodded. "We'd better go now though, in case that Mr. Biggs decides to burn down the cottage after all."

"Burn down—? There are human beings in this world, Rose, who do not deserve the name. Come, then. Let us go."

The wind tugged at the glider as we carried it up past the plateau where it had begun its last flight, toward the top of Slocumb's Bluff. In the darkness it seemed an animated thing, as though it wanted to fly over the edge of the bluff, away into the night. A little below the top of the bluff, we set it down beneath a grove of pine trees, where no wind came. We sat down on a carpet of needles to wait for dawn.

Through the long, dark hours, Meister Wilhelm told me about his childhood in Pomerania and his days at the university. Although it was August, the top of the bluff was chilly, and I often wished for a coat to pull over my dress. At last, however, the edges of the sky looked brighter, and we stood, shaking out our cold, cramped legs.

"This morning I am an old man, *liebling*," said Meister Wilhelm, buckling the strap of the violin case around his chest. "I do not remember feeling this stiff, even after a night in the Black Forest. Perhaps I am too old, now, to fly as Otto would have me."

I looked at the town. In the brightening stillness, four small shapes were moving toward Judge Beaufort's house. "Well then, you'd better go down to the courthouse and give yourself up, because they're about to find out that you're not at the cottage."

Meister Wilhelm put his hand on my shoulder. "It is good that you have clear eyes, Rose. Help me to put on the glider."

I helped him lift the glider to his back and strap it around his chest, as I had done the week before. The four shapes below us were now moving from Judge Beaufort's house toward Slater's barn.

Meister Wilhelm looked at me sadly. "We have already said our goodbye, have we not? Perhaps we do not need to say it again." He smiled. "Or perhaps we will meet, someday, in Orillion."

I said, suddenly feeling lonelier than I had ever felt before, "I don't have a glider."

But he had already turned away, as though he were no longer thinking of me. He walked out from under the shelter of the trees and to the top of the bluff, where the wind lifted his gray hair into a nimbus around his head.

"Well, what are you waiting for?" I asked, raising my voice so he could hear it over the wind. Four shapes were making their way toward us, up the slope above Slater's barn.

"The sun, Rose," he answered. "She is not yet risen." He paused, as though listening, then added, "Do you know what day this is? It is the ninth of August, the day that my friend Otto died, exactly one year ago."

And then the edge of the sun rose over the horizon. As I had seen him do once before, Meister Wilhelm crouched into the stance of a runner. Then he sprang forward and sprinted toward the edge of the bluff. With a leap over the edge, he was riding on the wind, up, up, the wings of the glider outspread like the wings of a moth. But this time those wings did not rise stiffly. They turned and soared, as thought the wind were their natural element. Beneath them, Meister Wilhelm was twisting in intricate contortions, as though playing an invisible violin. Then the first rays of the sun were upon him, and he seemed a man of gold, flying on golden wings.

And then, I heard them. First one, then ten, then a hundred—the bells of Orillion, sounding in wild cacophony, in celestial harmony. I stood at the top of Slocumb's Bluff, the wind blowing cold through my dress, my chin lifted to the sky, where the bells of Orillion were ringing and ringing, and a golden man flying on golden wings was a speck rapidly disappearing into the blue.

"Rose! What in heaven's name are you doing here?" I turned to see my father climbing over the top of the bluff, with Judge Beaufort and two men, no doubt Mr. Biggs and Mr. Empie, puffing behind. I looked into his handsome face, which in its contours so closely resembled mine, so that looking at him was like looking into a mirror. And I answered, "Watching the dawn."

I managed to remove *The Island of Orillion* and the wallet containing my mother's note from the cottage before Mr. Empie returned to claim Meister Wilhelm's possessions in payment for his bamboo. They lie beside me now on my desk, as I write.

After my father died from what the Episcopal minister called "the demon Drink," I was sent to school in Boston because, as Aunt Winslow told my mother, "Rose may never marry, so she might as well do something useful." When I returned for Emma's wedding to James Balfour, who had joined his uncle's law practice in Raleigh, I read in the Herald that the Wrights had flown an airplane among the dunes near Kitty Hawk, on the winds rising from the Atlantic. As I arranged her veil, which had been handed down through generations of Ashton women and made her look even more like a china doll, except for the caramel in her right cheek, I wondered if they had been searching for Orillion.

And then, I did not leave Ashton again for a long time. One day, as I set the beef tea and toast that were all my mother could eat, with the cancer eating her from the inside like a serpent, on her bedside table, she opened her eyes and said, "I've left you all the money."

I took her hand, which had grown so thin that blue veins seemed to cover it like a net, and said, "I'm going to buy an airplane. There's a man in Brickleford who can teach me how to fly." She looked at me as though I had just come home from the river by the Beauforts', my mouth stained with blackberries and my stockings covered with mud. She said, "You always were a troublesome child." Then she closed her eyes for the last time.

I have stored the airplane in Slocumb's barn, which still stands behind the remains of the boarding house. Sometimes I think, perhaps Orillion has changed its course since Lord Rutherford heard its bells echoing from the mountains. Perhaps now that airplanes are becoming common, it has found a way of disguising itself completely and can no longer be found. I do not know.

I read Emma's letters from Washington, in which she complains about the tedium of being a congressman's wife and warns about a war in Europe. Even without a code, they transmit the words *be careful* to the world. Then I pick up the wallet, still filled a crumbling note and a handful of coins. And I consult Lord Rutherford's charts.

The Dybbuk in Love

✡

Sonya Taaffe

And then there are souls, troubled and dark, without a home or a resting place, and these attempt to enter the body of another person, and even these are trying to ascend.
— Tony Kushner, *A Dybbuk or Between Two Worlds*

Sunset through the clouds, air full of ozone and the sweet aftertaste of fallen rain, and she walked home from the bus stop through gleaming, deserted streets, the first time with Brendan.

Side by side all the way back from the library, they had talked quietly, about unimportant things like teaching kindergarten and accounting and the books in Clare's leather-bottomed backpack, while the sky spilled over with rain and the bus wipers squeaked back and forth across the flooding windshield. Arteries and tributaries of water crawled along along the glass as they moved slowly through traffic, in washes of red and green; the downpour sounded like slow fire kindling everywhere a raindrop hit, matchstrike and conflagration. Against Brendan's knee where it had shed rain all over his khakis, the vast blackboard-colored folds of his umbrella stuck out struts at odd angles: he had offered its shelter to Clare on the library's neoclassical steps, and again when they got down from the bus in the last fading scatter between storm and breaking sun, though she had refused him both times. Now they were crossing a street crowded only with puddles, and Clare looked down between her feet to mark their reflections. No shadows, in this diffuse light; no certainty. Brendan's eyes were whitened blue as old denim, a pale mismatch for the heavy leaves of his hair that he wore drawn back into a fox-colored ponytail; she watched them, and listened carefully to his voice, and prayed to be proven wrong.

The sky had turned a washed-out gold, full of haze, luminous, blinded; unreal as an overexposed photograph, dissolving into a grainy blur of light. Up and down the street, windows that had not been thrown open to the cooling, clearing air were opaque with reflection, blank alabaster slates, like the broken hollows in the asphalt that had filled up and rippled only as Clare and Brendan passed. Rain-slicked still, the gutters and the pavement shone: filmed with light, paved with gold; *goldene medine*. Words she could have bitten from her tongue even for thinking them, because they might so easily not have been hers. *Sheyn vi gold iz zi geven, di grine . . .* No one's cousin, only child of only children: a spare-boned girl, eyes half a shade lighter than her hazelnut hair hacked short and pushed behind her ears; denim coat that buttoned almost to her knees and a scar across her left eyebrow where a stainless steel ring had been. Her sneakers had worn down to soles flat as ballet slippers, laces mostly unraveled into grit and no-color fuzz. She tilted her head up to Brendan and said back reasonably, "If you think I should be reading Gershon Winkler to half a dozen five-year-olds, you can come in and explain their nightmares to their parents."

His prehistoric umbrella was swung up over his shoulder, cheerful parody of Gene Kelly; she had noticed him in the stacks, rust-tawny hair and suit jackets, before he came up to her this afternoon at the circulation desk and asked why she was always taking out children's books. "I don't see why they'd have nightmares."

"This is why you're the number-cruncher."

For the first time, she saw his mouth warm in a laugh, almost soundless as though he feared someone might interrupt and catch him at it. "Clare," he said, and stopped. The laughter stayed trapped in small places in his face, the lines around his eyes and the angles of his gingery brows, his lips still crooked slightly to his surprise, her teasing, the conversation that might fork and feather out like crystal into somewhere unexpected. "Clare," he said again, gently. A chill pulsed down her bones. "Will you let me come to you?"

The color of his eyes had not changed, neither their depth nor their focus; his voice was as relaxed and nasal as the first time he had spoken to her in the library. But he was looking through his eyes now, not with them: panes of stonewashed stained glass, and she said, dead-end recognition, "Menachem." Something like ice and brandy sunfished up into her throat, sluice and burn past her heart; she put it from her, as she had weeks ago put away her surprise. Wondering for how long this time, she gave her greeting to this new face. "I was wondering when you'd turn up."

"Constellations follow the Pole Star; I follow you." All his sly chivalry in those words, in this earnest head-cold tenor; her mouth tugged itself traitorously up at the corners, and she wanted to slap Brendan's tender, deadpan face until she jarred him loose. If she could have pulled the long hair and faintly freckled cheekbones aside, stripped down through layers of flesh and facade to the teardrop spirit beneath, she might have done it. But nothing would force him out save a full exorcism, candles and *shofar* blasts and perhaps not even those, and she did not know a rabbi and a *minyan* that would not call her crazy. With Brendan's mouth, less an accent than the remembered heft and clamber of another language nudging up underneath this one, he was saying, "There's rain in your hair," and even that spare statement was light and wondering.

She stepped backward, one foot up onto the curb and the other above a grate where a page of draggled newspaper had twisted and stuck. Where the clouds threaded away, the sky was like parchment, backlit; summer twilight would leave this glow lingering below the clouds long after Clare had left Brendan standing in the middle of this rain-glazed street and walked home to her apartment alone, in solitude where no one would surface in a stranger's eyes and speak to her. "Leave him alone. It's not—do you understand this? It's not fair. To him." Easy enough to tell, once she knew what to look for. Brendan's acquaintance gaze would never track each of her movements with such ardent attention, even her frustration, his inability or refusal to understand that she slammed up against each time: that the world was not made of marionettes and masks, living costumes for a rootless dead man. "To any of them. People always ask me, afterward. They know something happened. So I'm supposed to tell them, *Oh, yeah, a freethinker from the Pale who died of typhus in 1906 just walked through your head, don't mind him . . . ?*" Too absurd a scenario to lay out straight and she clenched her teeth on the knowledge; he kept her smiles like cheating cards up his sleeve. Or perhaps not cheats at all, face-up on the table and nothing at stake but what he had told her, and that might have been worse. "Some comforter you are."

Some things, a century of death and drifting had not worn away. Menachem's wince was a flicker of heat lightning at the back of Brendan's eyes. But he laughed, still with more sound than the accountant, and shrugged; a complicated movement with the umbrella still braced over his shoulder, jounced behind his head like an eclipse. The puddles were drying out from under their feet, mirrors evaporating into the light-soaked air. His voice was less wistful than wry, fading toward farewell. "I'd never seen you in this light before."

She said, more gently than she had thought, "I know. Neither has Brendan. You have to go."

"I would be with you always, if I could. Through grave-dirt, through ashes, through all the angels of Paradise and all the demons of the Other Side, Clare Tcheresky. When I saw you, I knew you for my beloved, the other half of my *neshome*," a quick spill of words in the language that he had given up before he died, in this country of tenements and music halls and tea-rooms, before Clare's great-grandparents had married or even met. " . . . years, I wondered sometimes if this was Gehenna, if I was wrong. The things I have seen, Clare, waiting for you." Brendan's face was distant with the pain of strange memories, atrocities he had never witnessed and laments he had never heard. Within him, Menachem Schuyler, twenty-seven years old and dead for more than three times that, smiled like a snapped bone and said, "You don't need me. But if I could, I would be your comfort. I would cleave to you like God."

Clare closed her eyes, unable to look anymore at his eyes that were not his eyes, his face that was not his face, his borrowed flesh that she would never touch, even in anger, even to comfort. When she opened them again, only Brendan would meet her gaze: denim-eyed, fox-haired, essential and oblivious; already knitting up the gap in their conversation, muscles and tendons forgetting the movements they had not consciously made, the same collage and patches she had seen over and over throughout this long, haunted month. She whispered, before Brendan could hear her, "I know," and did not know if he took the words with him when he disappeared, swifter than an eddy of smoke or the mimicry of a reflection, her *dybbuk*.

Sunlight fell through the plate-glass windows onto shelves of pale wood, bright covers and spines, and the tune danced like dust motes and photons, *Shtey dir oyf, mayn gelibter, mayn sheyner, un kum dir,* hummed under Clare's breath as she wrapped up paperbacks of Susan Cooper and Laurence Yep for the fair-haired woman who had come in to buy a birthday present for her nine-year-old daughter, an early and voracious reader. Four days through intermittent showers, a half-moon swelled above the skyline for the midpoint of the month. Still Clare stayed too cautious to relax, dreams like an old reel of film run out and flapping in her mind. Yesterday's rain had left the sky blue as morning glories when she looked up between the buildings, soft with heat: no puddles underfoot to play tricks of light and shadow as she walked from her stop to The Story Corner, and no Brendan by her side. No Menachem today, like a wick sputtering into light behind the woman's lipsticked smile: nothing yet, and that meant nothing.

Always there when she forgot to look for him, until she was looking all the time; courting her with apologies, with history, with fits and starts and fragments of song. *Friling, nem tsu mayn troyer. Oy, dortn, dortn.* Because of him, Clare had read Aleichem and Singer and Ansky at night in her apartment, piecing together the intricacies of past and possession, what might lie on the other side of a mirror and what might kindle up from the embers of a deathbed desire. Like the song she played over and over again, nine-of-hearts piano and Jill Tracy's voice of dry-sliding silk—*and I'm engaged, and I'm enraged, and I'm enchanted with this little bit of magic I've been shown* . . . Sometimes, when she gave him time enough for the loan of lips and tongue to tell a story, he shared tales of Lilith and Ketev Mriri, *mazzikim* like smoke stains and tricksters who could swindle even Ashmedai, even Metatron. The names of his parents, Zvi and Tsippe. His three sisters who had read Shaykevitsh while their brother read Zola in translation. *You are the only living soul who remembers them now.* Confidences bound to chains between them, a cat's-cradle of need and amazement, amusement and nuisance, and she still should have met him a cemetery. Even a wedding, seven blessings and the glass stamped underfoot like a reminder of every broken thing, would have suited him more than the subway crush of a hot summer's night, coming home from the fireworks: announcements too garbled to make out in the rattle and rush of darkness past the windows and Clare jammed up against an ESL advertisement and a black woman with the face of an aging Persian cat, sure she had lost her mind. But if she had, then so had every second person she had met since the Fourth of July; so had the universe, to let him slip through.

You are why I am here. She tried not to believe him.

Two or three weeks ago, on a day terrible enough to have come right out of one of the picture books The Story Corner sold—alarm that never went off until she had already woken up and yelled at the placid stoplight-red numerals, humid drizzle and buses running late and her coffee slopped all over her hand—he had slid underneath the day's itinerary that Lila Nicoille was reeling off to her, and said something quiet, meaningless, comforting, and for once she thought he and his name were well matched. He could not slide an arm around her shoulders, no brief brush of solidarity from a ghost; but the words were as strong as a handclasp, unasked and given for no more reason than that she needed them. Then Lila had faltered to a halt, her greenish eyes as blurred and surfacing as though she had been shaken awake from dreaming sleep, and Clare felt only cold where she had imagined Menachem's fingers slotted between hers, nothing in her palm but the ashes of another momentary bridge.

No way to explain to Lila, to this woman with sleek blond braids, what about Clare Tcheresky made the world waver like uneasy sleep, *déjà vu*, like a ghost walking over memories' grave. No way to explain to Brendan, though she had seen him once in the stacks and once walking down the other side of a rush-hour street and his business card lay like a cue on her windowsill at home, why she would not meet him again—give another person's body and soul over to this wandering stranger, to satisfy her curiosity? She could only withdraw, stay alone, and try not wonder too much about what would happen when the school year began. If one of her new class suddenly raised a small head and said in a bird-pipe of a voice, not *Miss T.*, but *Clare*— There were things she thought she would not forgive him for, no matter how lovestruck, how fascinating, and she did not want to find out what they were.

Across the counter, the woman had fallen silent. A glitter moved across her eyes, and Clare snapped her head up, tensing already for the words that would drive him back.

"Is everything all right?"

That was not Menachem's language, nor Menachem looking back in puzzlement and the faintest rim of suspicion: the woman had only blinked. Her eyes were marked out like a leopard's with mascara, even to the tear-line at the inner corners. Like picture frames for her warmly brown irises; like glasses, which

Clare did not know if Menachem had worn. Brendan wore contact lenses. Her eyes were going to hell: staring at small print all day, screens and receipts, staring into strangers' eyes. "Yes," she said, clumsy syllable like a weight against her teeth, tongue-twister misunderstanding, and slid the package of books over into the manicured hands. When the woman had gone, aloud to the gilt-slanting light and the soft white noise of the fan in the back: "Only looking for the truth." Clare pushed her sliding hair back behind her ears; her laugh was little more than a sharpness of air, a puff to blow away ghosts and wishful thinking. *Shtey dir oyf. Extraordinary.*

That night she dreamed of him, once, when the velour air cooled enough for sleep and there were fewer cars honking in the streetlit haze under her window: that she stepped between slender, scarred-black birches into the cemetery where they had not met, and walked among the graves grown up like trees of granite and sawed-off memories, like stumps. Spade-leafed ivy clustered over the weather-blotched stone, delicately rampant tendrils picking through names that the years had all but rubbed out. When Clare pushed leaves aside, scraped softly with a thumbnail at gray-green blooms of lichen, she still could not read who lay beneath her feet; not in this retrograde alphabet, though the dates, in five thousands, were clear. The sky was pewter overcast, pooled dully above the horizon of the trees, and the wind that came through the rustling edges of forest smelled like autumn already turning in cool earth and shortening days.

"Clare," he said behind her, a voice she had never heard, and she turned knowing who she would see.

If anything, she had still expected a character from old photographs and Yiddish literature, a sallow *yeshiva* student in his scholar's black and white fringes, a prayer for every occasion calligraphed onto his tongue and no more experience of women than the first, promised glimpse of his arranged bride. Bowed over pages so crowded with commentary upon commentary that the candlelight could scarcely find room to dance pale among the flickering letters, nights spent with the smells of burned-down wax and feather ticking, dreaming of angels that climbed up and down ropes of prayer, demons that drifted like an incense of malice down the darkened wind. But he had studied seams and treadles as intently as Bereshis or Vayikra, taken trains that trailed cinders like an eye-stinging banner and read yellow-backed novels in the tired evenings, and Paradise had not opened for him like a text of immeasurable light when he died, dry-throated and feverish and stranded in a land farther from anything he recognized than even his ancestors had wandered in exile.

He was not tall; he wore a dark overcoat, a gray-striped scarf hanging over his shoulders like an improvised *tallis*, and wire-rimmed glasses that slid the nowhere light over themselves like a pair of vacant portholes until he reached up and removed them in a gesture like the slight, deliberate tip of a hat: not the movement of a stranger, and it made her smile. Bare-headed, he had wiry hair the color of stained cherrywood, tousled, the same color as his down-slanting brows; all his face gathered forward, bones like promontories and chisel slips. His eyes were no particular color that Clare could discern. Among the cracked and moss-freckled headstones, he stood quietly and waited for her; he did not look like a dead man, cloudy with light slipping around the edges of whatever otherworld had torn open to let him through, like a shroud-tangled *Totentanz* refugee with black holes for eyes and his heart gone to dust decades ago, and she wondered what she was seeing. Memories patched like old cloth, maybe, self sewed back together with fear and stubbornness and the blind, grappling desire for life. She did not think he was as truthful as a phonograph recording, a daguerreotype in sepia and silver, more like a poem or a painting; slantwise. He might have been thinking the same, for all the care his eyes took over her— puzzling out her accuracy, her details and her blind spots, the flawed mirrors of her eyes from the inside. What did the dreams of the living look like, from the vantage point of the dead?

Then there was half a step between them, though she was not sure which of them had moved: both, or neither, as the cemetery bent and ebbed around them. The trees were a spilling line of ink, camouflage shadows bleeding into the low sky. With his glasses off, he looked disproportionately vulnerable, lenses less for sight than defense against whomever might look too closely. If she moved close, gazed into his colorless eyes, past the etched-glass shields of the irises and through the pupils, what she might read in the darkness there . . . "Menachem," she murmured, and his name caught at the back of her throat. So ordinary her voice shook, "Put your glasses back on."

For a moment he had the sweet, dazzled smile of the scholar she had pictured, staggered by the newly met face beneath the veil that he lifted and folded back carefully, making sure this was his bride and no other, and then he laughed. The sound was not seminary laughter. "Clare, *oy*—" One stride into the wind that blew her hair up about them, dreamcatcher weave on the overcast air, and she felt him solid in her arms: breastbone against breastbone hard enough to jar her teeth through the buffers of cloth and coat, arms around her shoulders in a flinging afterthought; his delight like a spark flying, the crackling miracle of contact, and she hugged him back. He smelled like sweat, printer's ink and starched cloth, the powdery bark and fluttering leaves of the birch trees that she had walked through to meet him. Desire, wonder, curiosity; Clare roped her arms around his back, her chin in the hollow of his shoulder and his wild hair soft and scratching down the side of her neck, and held him fast. Embracing so tightly there was no way to breathe, no space for air, not even vacuum between them, like two halves of the universe body-slammed together and sealed, cleaving—

The wind rose as though the sky had been wrenched away. Clare shouted as a gust punched into her from behind, invisible boulder growling like something starved and let suddenly off its chain, snapped the scarf from around Menachem's neck and flung it at her throat like a wool garrote and it hurt hard as rope, all the whirlwind tearing at them, tearing loose. Thrown aside hard enough that her shoulder hurt from the deadweight jolt of keeping hold of one of his hands, arms jerked straight like cable and she heard a seam in his coat rip, she watched his face go liquid with terror: whatever a dead soul had to fear from a dream. The headstones were folding forward under the wind, peeling back, papery as dry leaves; names and dates and stars of David blown past her in fragments, bits of marble like a scarring handful of rain, even the flat, plate-silver sky starting to bulge and billow like a liquid surface, a mercury upheaval. When he cried out her name, the sound vanished in a smear of chalk-and-charcoal branches and granite that shed letters like rain.His glasses had evaporated like soap bubbles, not even a circle of dampness left behind. He was sliding away into landscape beneath her fingers.

His eyes were the color of nothing, void, before any word was spoken and any light dawned. When she blinked awake, sweat dried to riverbeds of salt on her naked skin, heart like something caged inside her chest and wanting out, even the close darkness of her bedroom felt bright in comparison. Still she wished she could have held him a moment longer, who had clung to her like a lifeline or a holy book; and she wondered, as she watched the sun melt up through the skyline's cracks and pool like burning honey in the streets below, whether she should have let go first.

Six days gone like flashpaper in the heat as August hurtled toward autumn, and she had seen nothing of him, not in strangers or dreams. The cemetery was there behind her eyes when she submerged into sleep, unclipped grass and birches like a palisade of ghosts, but never Menachem; the dreamscape held no more weight than any other random fire of neurons, brainstem spattering off images while her body tossed and settled under sheets that crumpled to her skin when she woke. She was already beginning to forget his articulate, unfamiliar face, the crispness of his hair and the rhythms of his voice, cadences of another place and time. Once or twice she even caught herself, in The Story Corner's little closet of a bathroom, looking over her reflected shoulder for his movements deep in the mirror's silver-backed skim. Dream as exorcism, wonder-worker subconscious: it should have been so easy.

Preparing for classes, she sorted away books for the year, old paperwork and child psychologies and mnemonic abecedaries, stacking her library returns next to the Japanese ivy until she could take them back. Air that smelled of sun and cement came in warm drifts through the open windows, propped up permanently now that Clare's air conditioner sat out on the sidewalk between a dented Maytag and ripening trash bags, found art for the garbage collectors; music from some neighbor's stereo system like an argument through the wall, bass beats thumping out of sync with The Verve's melancholy guitars and hanging piano chords, "Weeping Willow" set on loop while she worked. Comfort music, and the smile her mouth moved into surprised her; faded as the phrase's edge turned inward.

Off the top of the nearest pile, she picked up one of the books from the library afternoon with Brendan, considering weight in her hand before she opened it—blue ballpoint underlinings here and there, scrawled notes in the margins, some student's academic graffiti—and read aloud, *"There is heaven and there is earth and there are uncountable worlds throughout the universe but nowhere, anywhere is there a resting place for me."* It might have been an incantation, save that Menachem did not answer; save that it was not meant for him. Her voice jarred against the rich layers of sound, the dissonant backbeat from next door. Self-consciously, she put the book down, paranoiac's glance around her apartment's shelves and off-white walls as though some observant gaze might be clinging in the corners like dust bunnies or spirits.

Brendan's card was still bleaching on the windowsill, almost two weeks' fine fuzz of dust collected on the stiff paper, black ink slightly raised to her fingertips when she picked it up and the penciled address on the back dented in, to compensate. Swatches of late-morning light, amber diluted through a sieve of clouds, moved over her hands and wrists as she leaned over the straight-backed chair to her laptop; paused the music, *Beside me,* pulled up her e-mail and started to type.

Full evening down over the skyscrapers, a milky orange pollution of light low in the sky like a revenant of sunset, by the time her doorbell buzzed; Brendan looked almost as startled standing in her doorway as she felt opening the door to him, so many days later than it should have been. Out of his suits and ties, gray T-shirt with some university crest and slogan across the chest and a worn-out blue windbreaker instead, he might have passed for one of the students that she had walked past a few hours ago at the library, younger and less seamless, Menachem without his glasses. Some shy welcome handed back and forth between them, too much space between replies, unhandy as an arranged date; he was still smiling, bright strands of hair streaked across his forehead with sweat and four flights of stairs, and Clare gestured him into the apartment with a wave that almost became a handshake, a panoramic introduction instead.

As she stepped past him to lock up the door, deadbolt snap and she always had to bump the door hard with her hip, she caught the odd half-movement he made toward her, slight stoop and lean, arrested: as if he had been expecting something more, an embrace or a kiss, Judas peck on the cheek before she led him in to the sacrifice. But he was no Messiah, anointed in the line of David; there were no terrors and wonders attendant upon him, only halogen and shaded lamplight as he looked absently across her bookshelves, the stacks of CDs glittering on either side of her laptop, back at Clare coming in from the little hallway and she thought her heartbeat was louder than her bare feet on the floor.

Shnirele, perele, gilderne fon: Chasidic tune she had not learned from Menachem, nothing he would ever have chanted and swayed to in his lifetime. She wanted to blame him anyway, as it ran through her head; nonsense accompaniment to her voice raised over the burr of the little fan on the bare-boards floor of her bedroom, behind the door half swung shut and her name in street-vendor's dragon lettering over the lintel. "I didn't see you when I took the books back this afternoon."

"Believe it or not," he answered, "I don't spend that much time at the library. Just that week, really. I needed some statistics." Wary camaraderie, testing whether they could simply pick up where they had left off or whether this was a different conversation altogether, if that mattered, "I guess I just got lucky."

She had to smile at that, at him, dodging any reply as he picked up a paper-back of *The Day Jimmy's Boa Ate the Wash* and flipped through the meticulous, ridiculous illustrations. Lights peppered the night outside her window, street-lights and storefront glare and windows flicked to sudden brightness or snapped off to black, binary markers for each private life; sixty-watt eyes opening and closing, as on the wings of the Angel of Death. There was a tightness in her throat that she swallowed, that did not ease. Hands on the chair's slatted back, she observed, "You don't have your umbrella."

Not quite an apology, waiting to see where these lines were leading, "No."

"It was a really scary umbrella."

The same near-silent laugh that she remembered, before Brendan said dryly, "Thank you," and she thought in one burning second that he should have known better than to come here. On her threshold, he should have shied away, not stepped across the scuffed hardwood strip and almost knocked one worn oxford against the nearest milk crate of paperbacks: some twitch of memory, pole stars and shrugging with his arms full of umbrella, should have warned him off. Never mind that Clare had known no one who had flashbacks from Mena-chem, leftover remains of possession like an acid trip. She rarely saw again those people whom he had put on and taken off, unless she could not avoid them. Strangers made briefly familiar and not themselves, their secret that she carried and they might never guess: she never dared. If Brendan had any recollection of a *dybbuk* swimming like smoke in his blood, he should have run from Clare's apartment as though she were fire or radiation, a daughter of Lilith beckoning from beyond his reflection, trawling for his soul. But he was standing next to her desk, perusing children's books in the sticky breeze through the windows, and Clare did not want to know what he remembered from ten days ago, whether he remembered anything; and why he was still here, if he did.

Before she could find out, she called softly, "Brendan," and when he glanced up from Dr. Seuss, no catch in her throat this time, "Menachem Schuyler."

Bewilderment rose in Brendan's face, but no following curiosity. The *dybbuk* was there instead.

Always before, he had stepped sideways into being when Clare was not looking; now she kept her eyes on Brendan and saw how Menachem moved into him, like a tide, an inhalation, filling him out; rounding into life beneath his skin, his flesh gravid with remembrance. His features did not press up through Brendan's, skull underneath the face's mask of meat, but all its expressions were abruptly his own. She held on to the dog-eared, dreaming memory of his face seen under a tarnished-metal sky, and said quietly, inadequate sound for all of what lay between them, "Hey."

Menachem said, "I dreamed of you."

A sharp, stupid pang closed off her throat for a moment. He had always taken the world for granted, for his own. Half rebuttal, half curiosity, "The dead don't dream."

"The dead have nothing to do *but* dream."

"Don't make me feel sorry for you." Barely six weeks and already she might have known him all her life, to order him around so dryly and familiarly: childhood friends, an old married couple, and her next sentence stopped. Menachem was watching her through frayed-blue eyes, taller in a stranger's bones than she had dreamed him. Brendan stood with *Fox in Socks* in his hand and was not Brendan, and she had made him so. She had always known that there was too little room in the world.

No other way, no reassurance in that knowledge, and she said finally, "I dreamed of you," and shook her head, as though she were the one possessed; nothing loosened, nothing realigned. "He'll never speak to me again," as lightly as though it did not matter at all, another possibility chopped short as starkly as a life by fever and louse-nipped chills; shove friendship under the earth and leave it there, a picture book for a headstone, an umbrella laid like flowers over the grave. "I liked him."

He put down the book that Brendan had picked up, soft slap of hardcover cardboard against desktop, like a fingersnap. His voice was pinched off somewhere in his nose, hushed and sympathetic; no comfort, and perhaps none intended. "I know."

"Our parents never promised us to each other, Menachem," the name like the flick of a rein, the way his gaze pulled instantly to hers, a handful of jumbled letters to make him animate and rapt. "No pact before we were born. There's no rabbinical court in this world that will rule you my destined bridegroom. This isn't Ansky, this isn't even Tony Kushner. I can't write a good ending for this . . . " Too easily, she could recollect the particular scent of him, salt and iron gall and cigarette-paper flakes of bark, as she took a breath that still left her chest tight; barely a flavor in the warm night air, the phantom of a familiar smell. Halfway across the room, Brendan would have smelled like a newer century, Head & Shoulders rather than yellow soap, no chalk smudges on the shoulders of his coat. She said, inconsequentially, "I wasn't sure you'd come."

"You called me." A thousand declarations she had heard from him before, promises as impossible and persistent as his presence; now he said only, "I wouldn't stay away." Then he smiled, as she had never yet seen Brendan smile and now never would, and added, "I've never seen your apartment before. You have so many books, my sisters would have needed a month to get through them all," and Clare hurt too much to know what for.

"Don't." Cars were honking in the street below her window, hoarse voices raised in argument; maybe shouting would have been simpler than this whisper that backed up in her throat, fell past her lips softer than tears. "I can't look at these faces anymore. I'm trying to imagine what you look like, looking out, but there's nothing to see. You're here; you're not *here*. There's no one I can—find."

His voice was as soft, breath over Brendan's vocal cords; the faint rise of a question waiting to be rebuffed. "But you held me."

"In a dream." She made a small sound, too barbed for a laugh. "Forget everyone else, I can't even keep you out of my head."

He blinked. Faint shadows on the walls changed as he took one step toward her, stopped himself, stranded in the middle of the room away from shelves, desk, doorways, Clare; apart. "I didn't come to you," Menachem said carefully. With great gentleness, no cards on the table, "You came to me."

Clare stared at him. He stared back, Brendan's eyebrows tilted uncertainly, hesitant. Maybe she should have felt punched in the stomach, floor knocked out from under her feet; but there was no shock, only an empty place opening up where words should have been, blank as rain-blinded glass. Denial was automatic in her mouth, *That can't be true*, but she was not sure that she knew what *true* looked like anymore. He had never lied to her. She had always been waiting for him to try.

Brendan's hand lifted, folded its fingers suddenly closed and his mouth pulled to one side in the wry sketch of a smile; Menachem, she realized, had been reaching to adjust his glasses, a nervous habit more than ninety years too late. "When I'm not . . . with you," he started, choosing words as delicately as stepping stones, laying out for a living soul the mechanics of possession, occupancy, that they never discussed, "it's what I said, Clare, it's dreaming. Or it's a nightmare. For a soul to be without a body, without a world . . . I don't think I even believed in souls when I was alive," and this shrug she remembered from an afternoon of fading storm-light and streets cobbled with rain. "But I am not alive. And maybe I know better, maybe I know nothing; I know that I was in the place like a snuffed-out candle, where angels take no notice and even demons have better things to do, and you were there. In a graveyard, but there. With me.

"Clare, if there's one thing I want in this world, in any world, it's not to have died—I wanted so much more life, isn't that what all the dead say?" If she should have assented, argued, she had no idea; she listened, and did not look away. "But I would have died an old man before I ever met you. I wonder if that would have made you happier."

Clare smiled a little, though it was not a joke. *Do you love me?* Four words tangible and thorny enough on her tongue that for a moment she thought she had actually asked them, the chill and sting of sweat across her body in the seconds before he answered, and a high school musical flashed through her mind instead. Golde's squawk of disbelief, *Do I what?* and the scathing dismissal of her advisor in college, *took Tevye and made him into a chorus line—tra-la-la-la-la, pogroms ain't that bad!* One of her own great-grandfathers had lost a brother in a maelstrom of shouting students and iron-shod hooves, taken a saber cut across his temple that he carried like a badge through two marriages, past quarantine in Holland and all the way to his New Jersey grave. Those same politics had no more than grazed Menachem, set him alight with ideas, left him for the angel of tenement bedclothes to destroy. Broken branches on the Tree of Life. She wondered if it looked like a birch sometimes.

He was close enough now that if she reached out her arms, she could have held him as in dreams, in the flesh. He had kept the distance between them; she had moved, bare heel down onto the varnished pine as hard as onto folded cloth and something inside that crunched, snapped, would cut if carelessly unwrapped. Menachem was silent, no dares or teasing, cleverness proffered to coax her into laughter, her smiles that had paved the way for him in this alien, unpromised land; quiet, as he had been in rare moments when she saw through more layers than that day's borrowed skin, as he had waited in the cemetery that existed nowhere but the fragile regions of dream. She could send him away now and he would never return, she knew this as though it had been inscribed on the inside of her skin, precise and fiery hand engraving on the level of cells and DNA, deep as belief. She needed no name holier than his own, nothing more mystic than the will not to want; and wherever the soul of Menachem ben Zvi v'Tsippe fled, it would be none of Clare Tcheresky's concern.

She said, knowing it had never been the turning point, this decision made long ago and the dream only its signatory, smoke from the fire that was every soul, "I should never have touched you."

Menachem's cheerful slyness moved over Brendan's lines and freckles, resettled into a twist of sadness around the corners of his smile. Perhaps he had said these words before, perhaps never; no matter. "You still haven't."

This step she could not take back; the glass broken once and for all. "Then come here," Clare said, "come to me." As softly as though the words might summon a storm, make one of them vanish like a drying tear, she whispered, *"Dortn vel ikh gebn mayn libshaft tsu dir,"* and turned her hand palm-up.

Brendan's fingers did not close around hers, the *dybbuk* like an armature within his body, moving him; if he had reached to embrace her, she would have stepped back and screamed like a siren and maybe never stopped. But behind the pupiled lenses of his eyes, a color that was no color swirled, faded, bloomed outward and Brendan fell to his knees, painful double-barreled smack of bone against flooring and she would have reached out to catch him, but nothingness still spilled from him in streams and veils, flesh on flesh too easy a betrayal, and she had only room for one in her arms right now. Like trying to gather an armful of smoke, overflowing, reaching out to pull down a cloud: all vision and no weight. No chill against her skin, nothing like body heat, only the steady bleed that she watched disappear when it touched her outstretched arms, her fingers spread wide and her unguarded chest and throat, one skein even drifting against her face so that she saw through it, for less time than it took her to release the breath she had held, into a dull gleam of clouds and pewter, a crumble of ambiguous darkness like soot. Tattered glimpses of what lay between dreams, those of the living and those of the dead, and she would never close her eyes on only one world again. On hands and knees now, Brendan coughed, hoarse and racking, and his body jerked as though all its muscles were climbing away from one another under skin and cotton and nylon; taran-tella of sinew and flesh that chattered Clare's teeth, fingers buried in a lightning bolt and not enough sense to pull away, but the last nothing haze was soaking into her hand and gone.

Dimly, through sheetrock and posters, she heard music starting up, the same electronic slam from this afternoon. After all the buildup, what a finish: walking three apartments down the corridor whose doors were all painted the same monotonous sage-green as the banisters and stairs that cored the building, and walking back again without ever asking them to turn down the noise, the endless party that always seemed to be happening behind 5G's door once the sun went down; one ordinary night, with *dybbuk*. Her head felt no different, if dizzy, her fingers flexed and folded like her own; only someone might have hung lead weights from all her joints when she was not looking, so that she sat down abruptly on the floor beside Brendan, one hand out behind her for balance and the back of her knuckles brushed against the rumpled sleeve of his windbreaker. No danger, now. When she looked over and down at his long, sprawled form, merciful blackout or the next best thing, Clare realized that she was still looking for the little giveaways of gaze and movement and inhabitance, tell-tale pointers to the presence beneath his skin. She had never considered what it might be like to look for them in herself.

She parted her lips to speak Menachem's name, closed them instead. Beside her, Brendan stirred and groaned, "Oh, God," a vague mush of syllables and sense; his face was pressed against her floor, his eyes still shut. Gently, she touched his shoulder and said his name, as odd to the taste as Menachem's might not have been. Still she tried to sort through her thoughts, to find what she would say when he opened his eyes, what comfort or acceptable explanation, this last time with Brendan.

The last few days of the month, as the fragile rind of feather-white moon and the stars she could not see for the city's horizon glow pronounced; coincidence of lunar and Gregorian calendars, and some of the nights had begun to turn cold. Clare had hauled an old quilt from the top shelf of her bedroom closet, periwinkle-blue cloth from her childhood washed down to the color of skimmed milk, and occasionally woke to a sky as wind-scoured and palely electric as autumn. The day before yesterday, she had worked her last shift at The Story Corner, said goodbye to Lila until next summer and turned a small percentage of her paycheck into an Eric Kimmel splurge; some of the stories too old to read to her class in a couple of weeks, most for herself, tradition and innovation wound together as neatly as the braided wax of a candle, an egg-glazed plait of bread. Cross-legged on her bed, she read two retellings of Hershel Ostropolier aloud to the little pool of lamplight that made slate-colored shadows where the quilt rucked up, yellow and steadier than any dancing flame. She had lit a candle on the windowsill when the sun set, but it had burned down to the bottom of the glass; wax and ashes melted there.

When she leaned over to lay the book down on the jackstraw heap accumulating near the head of her bed, her shadow distorted to follow, sliding bars of dark that teased the corners of her vision, and she made a butterfly shape with her hands against the nearest wall. Out in the other room, *Blood on the Tracks* had finished and *Highway 61 Revisited* come on, Dylan's voice wailing right beside his harmonica, "Like a Rolling Stone." Homeless, nameless, roving: Clare had never been any of these things, but she knew something of how they felt; and she sang along as best as she could find the melody while she stripped off her clothes, black-and-white Dresden Dolls T-shirt and cutoff jeans, unremarkable underwear and socks all tossed into the same milk crate in the far corner, and stood for a moment in the lamp's frank shine before turning back the covers. Another chill night, wind like silver foil over the roofs, and she would have welcomed some warmth beside her as she tucked her feet up between the cool sheets; but she had chosen, she might sleep cold for the rest of her life, and she was not sorry.

If she pressed her face into the pillow, she could imagine a scent that did not belong to her own hair and skin, her soap that left an aftertaste of vanilla: slight as a well-handled thought, the slipping tug of reminiscence, a memory or a blessing. *Zichrono liv'rachah.* But her eyes were already losing focus, the Hebrew wandering off in her head toward smudges of free association and waking dream; Clare turned over on her side, arm crooked under the pillow under her head, and said softly into the shadow-streaked air, *"Zise khaloymes."*

A murmur in her ear that no outsider would ever pick up, lover's tinnitus with the accent of a vanished world, Menachem said back in the same language, "Sweet dreams."

Together they reached out and turned off the light.

> My life gets lost inside of you.
> —Jill Tracy, "Hour After Hour"

Fidelity: A Primer

Michael Blumlein

I. Born Torn

Lydell called me with the news that he was torn. This, of course, was no news at all. Lydell has been torn since birth. This time it had to do with his sons, Max and Ernest. The boys were twins, and still *in utero*. Lydell couldn't decide whether to have them circumcised or not.

He'd done the leg-work. When it came to so deeply personal a matter, he was nothing if not thorough. Uncircumcised men, he had found, did have a slightly higher incidence of infection, but the infections were usually trivial and easily treated. Balanitis, where the foreskin became red and inflamed, was uncommon. Phimosis, where the inflammation led to scarring, trapping the penis in its hood and making erections and intercourse painful (if not impossible), was likewise rare.

Circumcision, by contrast, was a uniformly traumatic event. What effect this trauma had was debatable, although the preponderance of evidence suggested long-lasting and not entirely beneficial *sequelae*. After all, such a grisly and disfiguring procedure at so young and tender an age. At any age. Was this absolutely necessary for a man to be a man? Some thought not.

As to the issue of pleasure, there seemed little question. The greater the amount of intact skin, the greater the concentration of nerves. The greater the concentration of nerves, the better the sensation. And while sensation itself did not guarantee pleasure, there was certainly the chance that it might.

On the other hand was tradition. Lydell was a Jew. Jews were circumcised. Judith, his wife, thought the boys might think it slightly odd if they were not. But she could see the advantage in it, most notably the avoidance of unnecessary pain and trauma. If pressed, she would probably have cast her vote with letting the poor things' tiny penises be, but in the end, she deferred to her husband, who not only had a penis but strong views as to its proper handling and use.

Lydell consulted a rabbi, who advised him to search his soul. He suggested he remember his parentage and lineage, and if he still had doubts after that, to take a good hard look in the mirror. In addition, he referred him to the Old

Testament, First Kings, Chapter 3, which spoke of King Solomon, the great and illustrious Jewish leader, who, when faced with two women, each claiming to be the mother of the same infant, advised them to share the baby by cutting it in two. The false mother agreed, the true one did not, and thus was the question of motherhood decided.

Lydell pondered the well-known tale. On the face of it, the message seemed clear enough: be clever, be insightful, value life (and love) above possessions. But the lesson seemed difficult to generalize, and Lydell sensed a deeper meaning that was far from transparent. He puzzled it day and night, up until the very hour of the boys' birth.

They came out strapping and healthy, with dark, curly hair, brown eyes, and flattened little baby faces. Identical faces, at that. Identical bodies. They were, in fact, identical twins.

It was a transformative event for Lydell. Both the birth and the fact that they were identical. A light seemed to shine from above (it was a sunny day). Suddenly, the path was clear. Ernest and Max, Max and Ernest: the very sameness of the children held the key to the solution. An individual was a precious thing—perhaps the most precious thing in the world. Just as the true mother would not permit her only child to be split asunder, so Lydell would not allow his two sons to grow up indistinguishable from one another. They were unique, and thus would be uniquely set apart.

One would be circumcised (this fell to Max). The other (Ernest) would not.

Judith took issue with this, strong issue, but Lydell would not be deterred. He was resolute, and she had little choice but go along. She soothed herself (or tried) with the belief that somehow, somewhere, he knew best. The penis was his territory: she kept telling herself this. It was her mantra during this difficult and trying time. The penis was his.

II. Poolside, Where A Stone Tossed Years Before Creates a Ripple

He had a lingering medical problem. She had a difficult marriage. They met at the pool where their children were taking swimming lessons.

Her eyes were large and compassionate.

His hair was to his shoulders.

He wore a silver bracelet and held his wrist coquettishly.

She favored skirts that brushed the floor.

They sat on a wooden bench with their backs to the wall, watching the children swim. They spoke without turning, like spies. Pointed observations delivered in a glancing, off-handed way.

She was a devoted mother.

He was a solicitous father.

He had a daughter. She, two sons.

The swimming lessons lasted thirty minutes. To him this was never quite enough. He worked alone and felt the need for contact. He wanted more.

She was often distracted by her sons, delighted by their antics and their progress. She would clap for them and call out her encouragement.

He sensed in some small way that she was using them as a buffer, or a baffle, to deflect his interest in her and hers in him, to disrupt their fledgling chemistry.

They spoke about their jobs. About their children's schools. About religion. She was Jewish. They spoke about the Holocaust. She decried the lingering hatred. Decried and understood it. She was interested, in theory, in forgiveness.

He listened to her closely and attentively, often nodding his agreement. He showed his sympathy and understanding, smelled her hormones, won her trust.

At the end of the lessons they parted without ceremony, sometimes without so much as a word. She wrapped her sons in towels and escorted them to the dressing room, waiting outside the door until they were done. He did the same for his daughter. Afterwards, there was candy and then the walk to the car. Often the five of them walked together, though they rarely talked. The kids weren't interested, and the grown-ups had had their time together. Half an hour, session done.

III. Brain Work

His name was Wade. He'd been married twenty years. There was a family history of mental illness, notably depression (a grandmother) and manic-depression (a great aunt). Another grandmother suffered from feelings of inferiority. Wade's father had a number of compulsions, none incapacitating, while his mother, heroic in so many ways, lived with the anxieties and minor hysterias typical of a woman of thwarted ambition with too much time on her hands.

Wade himself, like his great aunt, was a victim of mood swings. A year previously, after a brief bout of mania followed by a much longer one of despair, he started taking medication.

It was a good year for medication. Sales were booming, and three of the top ten drugs on the market were specifically designed to treat disturbances of mood. This represented an enormous advance from the days of his great aunt, who had to make do with electric shock (it served her well), insulin shock (not so well), and prolonged hospitalizations.

Wade tried Prozac, but it left him feeling muzzy-headed, about as animated as a stone. He tried Zoloft, with the same effect. Paxil likewise left him feeling like a zombie, and in addition, it robbed him of his sex drive.

He was too young to go without sex. At forty-six, he felt he was still too young to be a zombie. So he stopped the medication.

Eli Lilly called him. Pfizer called him. SmithKline Beecham called him, too. They sympathized with his problem. Sacrifice was difficult. No man should have to give up his manhood. But likewise, no man, particularly no American man, should have to be depressed.

Ironically, after stopping the pills, he got better. He was no longer victimized by sudden bouts of mania, nor was he paralyzed by depression. He was able to work, to care for his daughter and be a decent husband to his wife. He was sane again, and functional, in all ways except one. He remained impotent.

This happens, said his doctor. Give it time. This happens, said Lilly, Pfizer, and Beecham. Read the small print. We regret the inconvenience. We're working on a cure.

Months went by, and he didn't recover. His penis didn't get hard, not even in the morning when his bladder was full. His penis, poor thing, rarely stirred.

IV. Virtue and Necessity

Judith had no intention of having an affair. She believed in the sanctity of marriage, most especially her own. That said, her husband had of late been going through one of those times of his. One of those intense and trying times of self-intoxication, when he couldn't see beyond himself, couldn't think or talk about anything but him.

Judith did her best to show compassion, but in truth, she was tired of his histrionics. Ten years of marriage, eight since the boys were born, had taken their toll. She wanted a man, not another child to care for.

Men were useful, or they could be—vaguely, she remembered this. They had that male way about them, that male sense of entitlement and self, that male look and feel. In theory, there was much to recommend a man.

She wanted one.

V. In Heat

The pool was by the ocean. Cypress trees and sand dunes ringed the parking lot. Across the street in one direction was a golf course. In another was the city zoo.

Often, when walking to their cars, they'd hear a high-pitched keening sound. A peacock's cry, perhaps an animal in heat. Or a golfer in extremis.

She was a businesswoman. She organized trade conventions.

He was a cartoonist. He made his living with ink and pen.

He had a fey and predatory nature.

She had a sixth sense.

Their conversations were never casual.

She was in a book group, all women. Why all women? he asked, to get her talking about her womanhood. To be among women.

It's safer, she said. The whole sexual thing. And women have a way of talking. They have an understanding.

They see beneath the surface.

They share the same complaints.

What complaints, he asked.

She smiled. So many.

For three months they met. They never touched, not once. Sat an inch apart, backs to the wall, sweaty and sticky in the steamy equatorial heat of the pool. The children were their safety net. The children and their marriages, their loyalties, their loves, their pacts.

VI. Setting the Record Straight

I'd like to clear my chest. Bear with me on this. I've known several Judiths in my life. One was a belly dancer. Another was a lawyer. The one who stands out the most was a red-headed woman, big boned and brassy, out of Nebraska. Married a man name of Chan, Sam Chan, an acupuncturist. The two of them emigrated to Argentina, where they set up practice. As far as I know, none of these Judiths ever worked on conventions, or for that matter, had twins. But it's possible. I just can't say for sure.

As for Lydell, the only Lydell I remember with certainty was a football player, and I may be wrong about that. It might have been basketball, and come to think of it, the name was Lyell, not Lydell.

On the other hand, this guy Wade, this is a guy I know. And I have to say, my opinion of him is not high. I met him at the pool—Judith introduced us—and we ended up seeing each other a few times on the side. So what I know about him is firsthand information. It's gospel. Same goes for his wife, a helluva nice lady name of Flora, whom I also had the chance to meet. What she sees in a guy like this is beyond me. The man's a charmer, no question, especially with the ladies. But the fact is, he only delivers what he himself decides to. What and when. That's the type of guy he is.

His whole purpose in coming on to Judith was to save his marriage. That's how he justified it. It was the impotence thing—he just couldn't stand not being able to get a hard-on. It was a humiliation to him, he said. A humiliation and a disgrace.

He and Flora had tried everything. The pills, the pumps, the injections, the talk. He'd been to a prostitute. And hypnotism, he'd tried that. Now he was trying a married woman.

He didn't plan to take it all the way, even if she wanted to. He had his limits, or so he said. It was the idea of it, the titillation. The journey, not the destination. The hunt.

It was a noble purpose, I suppose. To save a marriage. (Although to hear Flora tell it, she was getting by all right. She was, by nature, independent, and had her work to occupy her. She also kept a plastic dildo in her bedside table to use in time of need.)

A noble purpose, but ignobly executed. The man was using Judith. That's what I can't stomach.

Then again, she was using him.

VII. A Somewhat Tortured Logic

The boys had a pet rat named Snowflake. She was a gentle, friendly rat, with a white coat and a long pink tail. At the age of a year Snowflake developed a tumor in her side. It was small at first, the size of a grape, but it grew rapidly. By six months it was the size and consistency of a ripe plum. They took her to a vet, who diagnosed a lipoma, in other words, a big ball of fat. This was good news in the sense that it wasn't cancer. Less good was the two-hundred dollar fee to have it excised.

Lydell felt the surgery unwarranted. Snowflake was a rat, and rats could be had for pennies. Beyond the issue of cost was the deeper question of value, the life lesson about man and the natural world. In Lydell's view, intervention was far too often man's way with nature. And it didn't have to be. There was much to be said for watchfulness, for letting the world weave its intricate and beautiful web without disrupting its threads prematurely, if ever.

There was also the issue of anthropocentrism. Judging the rat unhappy in its current condition was so quintessentially human a gesture, so human an assumption, that it could easily be a mistake. Perhaps, the creature was content with its burden. Perhaps, it didn't care.

The question of consciousness came up: did the rat notice that it was different from other rats? Was it even aware of the mass?

After some discussion, it was agreed that the rat did, in fact, notice. There was really no ignoring a lump that size. But whether it cared, whether its level of consciousness included a sense of dissatisfaction with the ways things were and a desire to change them—this was uncertain. Snowflake had such a genial temperament to begin with. Even when the mass, after being dragged along the floor of the cage for months on end, became infected, her demeanor didn't noticeably change. Perhaps she slowed down a bit, but then she had never been much interested in speed. And being a rat of good breeding and character, qualities the boys learned about in detail, she wasn't the type to complain.

The tumor grew. At a subsequent visit the vet was frankly amazed. "This animal should have been dead months ago," he exclaimed, a comment notable, if not for its thoughtlessness, then certainly for its ambiguity. The boys were left to ponder just what exactly he meant.

Max, a child of fledgling polemical tendencies, assumed he meant that without the operation Snowflake would be better off dead. He didn't want her to die, and he argued with his father to intervene. He invoked the rights of animals, the concept of *tzedakah* (charitable deeds, from a charitable heart), the universality of souls. A canny, verbally precocious boy, he presented his case eloquently (albeit unsuccessfully). In this he made his father proud.

Ernest was more deliberate, more reserved. He was cautious in expressing his opinions and shied from conflict. On the surface he accepted his father's dictum. The rat would live its life, then die. But underneath the surface he knew differently. Underneath, his mind was rife with visionary landscapes and dreams. If Snowflake should have been dead but wasn't, then clearly she had powers hitherto unimagined. He'd read about such beings—entities, they were called—in comic books; he'd seen them on TV. Alien entities. Invincible, ineffable, immortal ones.

Snowflake was no ordinary rat. Each day she lived and beat the odds was proof of this. She was something different. Something special. Something more.

He therefore didn't worry what would happen. Snowflake would take care of that herself. Consequently, there was no reason to argue with his father. On the contrary, he agreed with him. Leave the rat alone.

Judith, meanwhile, fumed.

She agreed that a rat was a rat, but this particular rat, their rat, was a pet. Pets were family, and family needed to be looked after. She thought what Lydell was doing, what he was teaching, was stingy, gratuitous, and cruel.

And insufferable. And sadistic. And Nazi-Darwinistic (she got to him with that). And, quite frankly, obscene.

He got her back one night. Got her bad. He was talking about the money they were saving by letting nature take its course. Then he dropped the bomb.

He wanted to use it to get Ernest circumcised.

Ernest at this point was eight.

Judith said, No way.

Lydell pleaded his point. He admitted to having made a mistake.

Live with it, she said.

He couldn't.—I look at him and think, how can this be a Jew?

—He's a Jew if he wants to be. If you let him.

—I'm ashamed of myself. I set him apart. I thought I knew best, but I didn't.

—You want to atone? Leave him alone. Practice what you preach.

—Let's ask him, said Lydell.

Her eyes flashed.—Don't you dare.

VIII. Idealism! Temptation! Restraint!

She had long fingers, hazelnut eyes, and a passion for people.

He had a soft mouth and a way with words.

She missed the freedom and excitement of her younger days.

He dressed for the occasions. Wore his brightest colors. Worked for her attention.

She saw in him a respite. A way station on the arduous and lifelong path of marriage. She was going through a period of reflection, a taking account of her life. She was recalling what had been put aside, what dream of self, what vision. Retracing her past to its fork points: the choice to marry, to have a career, to be a mother. And prior to that, the choice to end the wildness and anarchy of a protracted adolescence, the choice to grow up and follow the rules. To be a solid citizen. To practice self-respect and love.

Which she intended to continue.

Being an honorable woman. With honorable desires.

She never littered. She never spat. She wouldn't cheat.

A woman of conviction, she had her limits, too.

He favored irregularly shaped panels as opposed to the traditional squares. He also liked to experiment with sequencing and placement. Linear cartooning was too constrained for his taste. Too contrived. If he was going to the trouble of drawing all those pictures, he wanted people to look at them, not skim past them as if they were the written word.

He had Ideas. He spoke of a modern aesthetic. Commitment to craft and to Art with a capital A. He was passionate, which tempered his pomposity.

She was drawn to him.

He thrilled at the game they were playing.

He also had qualms.

He meant no harm.

She was flattered by his attention. Interested in his ideas. At one time she herself had painted.

Aha, he chortled. A kindred spirit!

Hardly that, was her reply. A hobbyist, at best. But nothing at all since the boys were born. She missed the creativity of it, the tactile pleasure of brush in hand, the fun. Not that she couldn't live without. Obviously, she could. And furthermore, she didn't believe in regrets.

He agreed. Regrets were useless.

Yes, she said. Completely useless.

Utterly, he added with finality.

At that they ceased to speak, meditating silently on the uselessness of regret.

They were so determined to be friends. It was their stated purpose. A male and female friendship. Their creed.

Mirabile dictu! Such lofty ideals! Such audacity. Intimacy without jeopardy. Freedom of expression. Pleasure without pain.

IX. Further Revelations

How do I know these things? Word gets around. These are my friends.

If you believe Wade, what he was doing was for a good cause. If you ask me, Flora let him get away with too much. But she saw it differently. She, after all, had to live with his mood swings, and he'd been free of them for nearly a year. She wasn't about to upset that particular apple cart. Her philosophy was fairly straightforward: if a man wanted to hang himself, so be it. The tighter the leash, the greater the chance it would break.

Judith, quite simply, was filling a need. When you're with someone like Lydell for as long as she was, someone with his capacity for self-absorption, you can't help but have periods of longing. Periods when you feel yourself shriveling for lack of companionship. Periods of self-doubt when you wonder if anyone hears you or sees you at all.

Judith fought these feelings. She had work, which helped. She had her children. And now she had a new companion, someone who wanted her around, someone who looked at her and listened.

It was a flirtation of ideas, she told herself. A flirtation of interests. A flirtation of spirit and, therefore, of necessity.

Flirtation, she felt, did not preclude fidelity. On the contrary. Fidelity depended on respect, and it was self-respect that made her flirt. God, she knew, helped those who helped themselves. It was up to her to make her presence known.

X. The Scholar Finds a Way

Sabbath Day. Lydell wears a *yarmulke* pinned to his head and a many-fringed *tallit* around his hefty shoulders. In his anguish and his fervor he has turned to the Bible. The Book of First Samuel, Chapter 18, wherein David slays two hundred Philistine men and brings their foreskins to King Saul (who had only requested a hundred) as dowry for his daughter Michal's hand in marriage. What King Saul wants with so many foreskins, what he does with them, is not mentioned. Lydell can only speculate. Reading the Holy Scriptures has him in a barbaric, morbidly Old Testament mood.

King Saul might have made a tapestry of them, sewn together with the finest threads.

Or a flag, a battle standard to be borne against the heathen armies.

A patchwork quilt.

A bridal veil.

A blanket for his wives.

While fresh, he could have used them as grafts for poorly healing wounds.

Once dried, as snack food for the troops, like pemmican.

Or party favors.

Or rewards for jobs well done.

Yahweh, God in Heaven, God of Lydell's father and his father's father, is an angry God. He is a spiteful God, a savage God, a vengeful God. But He is a smart and clever God, too.

Lydell has one more thought. One that King Solomon, son of David and grandson of Saul, might have approved of. Solomon with whom he feels kinship, Solomon the wise and understanding, Solomon the just. Solomon who in his later years forsook his religion for that of his wives. Solomon who, smitten with love, turned from Judaism to the pagan faith.

A foreskin can be re-attached. Not one cut off in a fly-infested battlefield and carried for days by camel in a rank and grimy sack, but a fresh one, a hygienically-removed one, a pretty pink virginal one. There are doctors, cosmetologists, who will do anything for a price. If Lydell can't get his son into the fold, he can join him on the outside. It would be an act of atonement. A day to remember. A *yom kippur*.

XI. Visions of Grandeur

He wanted to touch her. He wanted to run his hand down the crease in her buttocks. Smell her, lick her, slather his body with her tart and liquidy self.

He thrilled at the thought of it, the temptation.

He wondered if this was the mania. If it was, he could wash his hands of responsibility. You couldn't blame a person for being ill.

Besides, he was serving Flora.

Patient, loving, flint-eyed Flora. Faithful Flora, who gave him all the slack he needed.

XII. Onan the Barbarian

It was Flora, incidentally, who alerted me to a recent survey of Net users that found ten times as many synonyms for male, as compared to female, masturbation. She was doing research for a book on gender and technology. While not particularly surprised at the disparity, she did find it rather offensive. She was also somewhat dismayed.

Religion, politics, and humor were common themes among the more than two hundred male-oriented entries, although a good number seemed chosen solely on the basis of alliteration or rhyme. As for women, the themes ranged from the pedestrian to the sweepingly grandiose, from the biblical to the sublime. Among the examples: "doing my nails," "parting the Red Sea," "surfing the channel," and "flicking the bean." And, of course, that old metaphysical standby, "nulling the void."

Flora makes a good point. The list, while notable, is decidedly short. Is this because women masturbate less than men? A common belief, but one that is unsupported by the data. Is it because they talk about it less? Again, the data say no. Could it be that they simply overlooked the poll?

Or have we been silenced? (We, I say, for I take this quite personally—an injustice to one is an injustice to all). Shamefully silenced, I might add, our lips sewn together by the threads of inequity, our tongues disenfranchised from the very words we would use to express our self-love.

We may not "tease the weasel," we keepers of the flame. (Why on Earth would we ever do that?) We may not "tug the slug" or "pump the python." Nor, routinely, do we "bop the bishop" or "make the bald man puke." But listen. We surely burp the baby, we toss the salad, we choke the chicken, we pop the cork, and at least every few weeks we whip up a batch of instant pudding. And yes, oh yes, we do sometimes have sex with someone we love.

We've been silenced, I say! Robbed of speech (if not thought), cheated in all the ways we have always been cheated.

Tickling the taco. Brushing the beaver. Making soup. Rolling the dough.

Is this what they think we do all day? Imagine. It's outrageous.

We are more than homebodies. More than domestics. More than mothers and whores.

We need to rise up. The time has come to null the void and give these words a second meaning, a meaning more powerful and self-fulfilling than staying home to surf the channel or idly flick the bean. We can brush the beaver later, ladies. The void needs nulling now.

We need to be creative. On behalf of Flora and everyone else who has ever felt the yoke of inequality, I incite you: soar above your own Mt. Baldy. Be irreverent. Be enticing. Pound the peanut. Pick the peony. Wave to Dr. Kitty. Laugh out loud.

Send your words and phrases, your ditties and your doggerel, your witty little euphemisms and inventions, your unchained melodies to me. Send them quickly. Send them to my website. Everyone's a poet.

Send them now.

✡

XIII. Underwaterworld

The children were diving for hoops. Slapping the water, struggling downward to the bottom of the pool, then splashing to the surface like puppies.

—I'm happy with my choices, she said. All in all.

—I'm happy we met, he said.

She waved to one of her sons, who had succeeded in getting a ring.

—No? he asked.

—Yes, she said.

—Outside of my wife I've never had an intimate female friend, he said.

She waved to her other son, who was poised on the edge of the pool, building up the nerve to leap.

—You're a beautiful woman.

—Don't, she said.

—I'm only observing.

She fell silent.

He told her not to worry. He was impotent.

This interested her.

He thought it might. Not entirely impotent, he added. Lately, he'd been having signs of life.

She changed the subject.

The book group had been reading Dante. She told him of a dream she had.

—We were pilloried outside the gates of Macy's.

—The gates?

—The gates, the doors. Whatever. You on one side, me on the other.

—Which store?

It was an irrelevant question, but somehow he made it seem otherwise.

—The one in Stonestown.

—Busy day?

—Very. We were naked.

—How embarrassing.

—Yes. Exceedingly.

—What was our crime?

—Swimming.

—Swimming naked?

—No, just swimming.

—That's it?

—Yes.

—Swimming's no crime.

—It wasn't the swimming, she said. It was the fun.

✡

XIV. The Art of Compromise

Judith had been thinking. Maybe Lydell was right. Not that Ernest should be circumcised, but that he at least should be talked to. Presented with the options. Sounded out.

She spoke to him alone one day after school. He was in his room, playing with his pet. Or rather stroking her fur and comforting her. The tumor was now enormous. The days of the entity known as Snowflake, at least on Earth, were clearly numbered.

Ernest, unlike his brother Max, was not a verbal child. He came across as rather distant. But he never missed a word that was said. He absorbed and processed everything. His mind was as facile as anyone's, and his inner world was deep.

He listened patiently to his mother, and when she finished, surprised her by saying he wanted to have the circumcision done. She asked him why.

—Because, he said.

She pressed him.—Because why?

He hesitated a moment.—Because I deserve it.

It was an ambiguous statement, and one that begged for an explanation. First, however, she reiterated that in her eyes, in everyone's eyes, he was fine—he was perfect—just the way he was.

—I want to be like everybody else, he said.

—The world's a big place. Everybody's different.

—I don't want to be.

Her heart went out to him.—I understand, she said.

He asked if it would hurt. She said it would. He said he didn't want anyone to know.

— Not Max?

He didn't mean Max.

—I'll have to tell your father, she said.

—Let's surprise him, said Ernest.

—I don't think he'd like that.

—It's my choice, isn't that what you said?

—To a point, said his mother.

—It's private, he said. Between you and me. Like between you and that man.

—What man?

Ernest averted his eyes.—You know.

XV. The Sweet Embraceable

You can put yourself in someone else's shoes, you can even get inside their shirt and pants, but it doesn't mean you know them. It's guesswork who they are and what they're thinking and feeling. Guesswork and maybe intuition. As an outsider, you do your level best, but you never really know.

It's what they say and do, not think. If a guy says he's faithful, despite the fact he's getting hard-ons plotting how to get some chick in bed, he's faithful. If a woman says she's faithful, despite the fact she's sitting squarely on the fence, she's faithful.

If they don't touch, they're faithful. If they don't think, they're dead.

The two of them didn't touch. I mentioned that already. Not at the pool or anywhere else. Not once.

Wait a minute. I forgot. They did touch. But only once.

It happened in a neighborhood cafe. They had a date, a nighttime assignation. The kids were tucked at home in bed.

The swimming lessons had been over for several weeks. They'd spoken once by phone but hadn't seen each other. He was carrying a briefcase in one hand. With the other he touched her palm in greeting. Lightly, like a whisper, or a veil. Imperceptibly, she caught her breath. She let the contact linger.

He said,—I've been thinking of you.

She said,—Did you get my letter?

—No, he said.

They took a table in the corner, ordered coffee and dessert.

—I've started to paint again, she said.

—How wonderful, he replied.

—Watercolors. I used to paint with them a lot.

—What made you start again? he asked.

—You, she said.

His penis stirred.

—I've given myself two hours a week. Not much, but it's a start.

—A start is all you need.

—I told you in the letter. I'm surprised you didn't get it.

—You could have called, he said.

She had wanted to. But in the wanting knew she shouldn't.

He said,—I've been painting, too. Drawing really. Cartoons. Of us.

Her heart sped up. She got a little nervous. "Us" had never been mentioned before. "Us" to her meant husband and wife.

—I'd like to see them.

He told her they were pornographic. He'd brought them with him.

—I think they'll turn you on, he said.

She hesitated.—Well then, maybe not.

—They do me, he added.

He could have said "you," not "they." He had before, or almost.

Then again, he could have brought a carriage drawn by horses. He could have brought a slipper.

She had to smile. How uninvited certain thoughts were. How willful.

—Do you do drawings of your wife? she asked.

The question gave him pause.—On occasion. Why do you ask?

—Cartoons? Pornographic ones?

The motive behind the question now seemed clear. He shrugged.

—I don't want anyone getting hurt, she said.

—No one's been hurt, he said. And then,—I don't either.

She wanted to see the pictures. Itched to see them.

Equally, she was determined not to compromise her marriage. Not to act dishonorably. She wondered what behavior this allowed.

She felt torn.

He said,—I'm sorry. I didn't mean to cause you grief.

He said,—I didn't mean to tempt you.

He was wearing silver that night. A silver chain around his neck. A silver earring. A silver bracelet, the same he'd worn the day that they first met.

He had washed his hair in chamomile shampoo. He had used a scented body soap.

He said,—I'm wrong. I have been tempting you.

She felt the truth in this.—Why?

—To see how far you'll go. To test your limits.

—Why?

—Because I don't trust mine.

—And mine you do? She didn't know whether to be flattered or insulted.—You're daring me to be unfaithful? Is that it?

—No, he said. I'm daring you not to be.

How puerile, she thought. How unappealing and crude.

He didn't care for her. She saw this plainly now. Nor did she care for him.

It came as something of a revelation. As did what followed: they cared for each other equally.

How remarkable, she thought. How apposite.

—Show me the pictures, she said.

He took a folder from his briefcase and handed it to her. His penis, which had defervesced, showed signs of life.

She stuffed the folder in her purse.—I'll look at them later.

—They're yours, he said. Keep them. Look at them whenever.

It was the last they were to see of each other. Both knew it.

She wanted to give him something in return.

—A hug, he suggested.

She thought it over. Rising, she pulled on her coat.

—I'll say no to that, she said.

He had risen also, expectantly. Now he felt cheated, and incomplete.

—Take it home, she said.

—Take what home?

—That impulse. That hug. Take it home and give it to your wife.

These were her parting words.

Upon thinking them over, he found, astonishingly, that they were exactly what he wanted to hear.

XVI. The Gift of the Magi

Solomon was wise, but he wasn't all wise. Lydell was crazy, but his motives were pure.

He had the operation. He did it in secret. While he was healing, he dressed and undressed in private. To forestall questions and minimize discomfort, he slept with his back to his wife.

Judith assumed she was being punished for her philandering. Never mind that she had resisted, that she in the end had proved stalwart and faithful. Adultery was as much of the mind as of the body. Her husband might not know the details, but he had doubtlessly suffered. Had the roles been reversed, she would have suffered, too.

She swallowed her pride one night and asked his forgiveness.

—For what? he replied.

—For being so uninvolved, she said, thinking it best to break the truth to him slowly, by degrees.—So distant.

Lydell was nonplussed.—For that I should be asking yours.

She asked what he meant.

It was he who had been remote, he said, impossibly, insupportably so. Remote and self-absorbed. But all that was going to change.

—Are you going to touch me? she asked.

—There's a reason I haven't.

—I know, but are you?

—Yes, he said. Oh yes. Most definitely.

—Anytime soon?

He gave her a smile.—I have a surprise, he said, with a look that made her just the tiniest bit nervous.

They were in the bedroom. Ernest, who was still a little sore from his own procedure, was watching TV in the room next door. She'd been wondering how to break the news to her husband. Maybe now was the time.

—I have one, too.

—How perfect, he said.

That would not have been her word for it. Bracing herself, she told him about Ernest.

He was stunned. Thinking what the hell, she told him secret number two: she'd had Snowflake put to sleep.

Before, he would have gotten angry, possibly furious, but now he simply nodded. As if to say, of course, how fitting. As if he finally understood. Moments later, having recovered his voice, he told her—and showed her—what he himself had done.

—Love made me do it, he said, bemused, contrite. And then,—I'm a fool.

—No, you're not, she said. No more than me.

They both were fools. And both, she felt, deserved a place of honor in their marriage.

She hugged him close. He hugged her back.

—It doesn't hurt, he said.

She was glad of this.

—It feels nice, he said.

She felt the same.

XVII. The 17 Questions

How is a story told? With flesh and blood people, and a beginning, middle and end.

How is it held together? Imperfectly.

With what is it held? Epoxy and wire and glue, balls of string, strings of words, paste.

For whom is it told? The willing.

To what value? Submission.

At what price? An hour's worth of television.

Is there a purpose? Yes.

What is the purpose? The purpose is hidden.

What are the prominent symbols? The foreskin stands for the natural world and the untrammeled innocence of man. The circumcised penis is lost innocence, civilization. The skullcap is the foreskin re-found.

Are there other metaphors? Yes. The pool is the Garden of Eden. The rat is Fate. The multiple short chapters represent our fragmented world. The varying voices are false prophets. The title, Fidelity, is the name of a bank.

Can we read this story in parts, at separate sittings? It is inadvisable. Like foreplay, there is a cumulative effect.

Why all the sexual references? This is biblical.

What happens to Judith and Lydell? Both are strengthened by their trials and tribulations. Judith lands a lucrative business contract. She and her book group tackle *The Prologemena to a Future Metaphysics* by Immanuel Kant. Lydell visits Israel. In a bizarre case of mistaken identity, he is abducted by a group of Palestinian freedom fighters, then later released.

And the boys? Max becomes a lawyer. Ernest, a veterinarian.

What about Wade? Wade is currently back on drugs and doing quite well.

And the rat? She lives in Heaven.

And the moral? Life and death are ruled by Nature,

Foolishness and faith, by man.

Between the God of Moses and Temptation,

You do the best you can.

Niels Bohr and the Sleeping Dane

✡

Jonathon Sullivan

The Gestapo had imposed curfews and roadblocks for the first time since the occupation of Denmark. They stopped our train at Helgoland, where the tidy streets of Copenhagen blend into the sparse woods and open gray sky of coastal Zealand. An SS captain and two men with short rifles clambered into our car. They demanded papers from every passenger, and I knew that by nightfall my father and I would be on another train, bound for darkness.

The man who sat across from us was also a Jew, but he would not go to the camps with us. Niels Henrik David Bohr would remain in Denmark, or perhaps he would be sent to Berlin. But he would be no less a prisoner.

The black uniforms and burnished weapons cut into the reality of the railcar like nightmares. You could hear the shared thought of everyone aboard: Not here. Not in Copenhagen. There's some mistake.

The Danes had lived with a monster in their house for two years, and they had learned to ignore it. The monster looked like them. It seemed to be house-broken. It kept out of sight, hiding under the bed while Denmark slept. But finally, inevitably, the monster had emerged, and it was ravenous.

Looking for us.

The SS captain was a handsome young man, square-jawed and blue-eyed, Hitler's Aryan ideal in the flesh. But his pale complexion reminded me of a wax doll. His ink-black uniform, with its red armband and skull insignia—the regalia of death—enhanced his pallor. In his eyes I saw the deep hunger that drives a man to devour his fellows. He evaluated the passengers, his head cranking from side to side with each click of his black leather boots, as if clock-work connected his legs to his neck.

He stopped a few rows away from us, to examine a young couple. Speaking in curt, inflected Danish, he demanded their papers. The man, a swarthy fellow with curly black hair, rummaged nervously in a satchel.

The captain put up his hand. "That's all right," he said. "It won't be necessary."

The man nodded with relief.

"You are Juden, yes?" The captain smiled.

One of the most vivid memories of my life is how the air on the bus changed at that moment, suddenly cloying and and thick. A smell of quiet panic, like sweat and rotten meat.

The young man blanched. "I am a Danish citizen," he said, voice quavering.

The officer's expression was not so much a smile as a gash cut into his face. "You are a subject of the German Reich," he said. He made a command with his fingers: on your feet. The young man stood, and he and his wife were led off the bus. The woman carried an infant bundled in blue wool.

I have often wondered what became of that family. Did they die at There-sienstadt? Dachau? Auschwitz? I still have nightmares about the look in that young woman's eyes.

The captain approached us. His gaze settled on me for a moment, then passed to my father.

The Danish resistance had told us we must pass for everyday people. Papa had retorted that we were people, every day, but he hadn't really argued. He had shaved that majestic, iron-gray beard, trading his broad-brimmed black hat and dark coat for the dress of a goy.

Papa had strange gifts. But I could not imagine he would deceive the pale Hauptsturmführer. My father's essence would shine through the rumpled khaki trousers and thick sweater of green wool, and any fool would see him as a rabbi of the Hassidim.

Who could look at my father and fail to see what he was? Until the day I die, his will be the human face of Yahweh: fierce but serene, severe but kind, deeply etched with sadness and humor, encompassing the mystery of opposites that are one. Brilliant, forceful Chockhmahand dark, gentle Binah united in Tiferet, the living heart of Israel that is the center of the universe. No man who met my father, Jew or Gentile, failed to be awed by him. Least of all me.

When he saw Papa, the Hauptsturmführer frowned.

Papa said, "Good morning."

The captain nodded, his frown slowly unwinding. "Good morning. Heil Hitler."

He quickly looked away from Papa's eyes, and next gave a cursory glance to the brother and sister seated next to us. With their light brown hair and sullen expressions, the two teenagers could not possibly have looked more generically and ethnically Danish. They were, in fact, armed members of the threadbare Danish resistance. They didn't get a second look.

The captain turned to scrutinize the three people in the seat facing ours. A frumpy man with unruly red hair pretended to look out the window. Hans Nielsen was the father of the two young partisans. Next to him sat an elegant woman in her mid-fifties, with a slender neck and fine Nordic features.

Beside her, directly across from me, sat the father of the modern atom.

Bohr had a paunch, but he was still a lanky man, with that characteristic Danish angularity and length of bone. His brown suit fit him with a balanced, casual elegance. His features had sagged beneath the weight of the occupation, the constant threat from the Nazis who circled him like hyenas, waiting for him to go too far in his vocal defense of Danish culture against the Reich. Thick-lipped, balding, and aged—he should have been ugly. But the intelligence was there, quiet and profound, like clean water pouring out of a rocky cave. I like to think that, even if I had not known him as the man who had resurrected the corpse of Rutherford's atom and made it dance to the strange music of Planck and Einstein, I would have loved him the moment I saw him.

"Herr Doktor Bohr!" The captain's cruel smile returned. "What a relief. We've been very concerned about you."

Hans, the frumpy man at the window, forced himself to look, a film of defeat in his eyes. The two young partisans next to Papa stared at the floor. I thought of the weapons beneath their coats. In their stillness I could sense a gathering, desperate violence.

Bohr sighed, looked up at the Gestapo captain with calm resignation, and took his wife's hand. He started to get up.

"You are mistaken, sir," Papa said.

I wanted to scream at him: No! This creature has already passed us over and now you beg for his attention!

I was nineteen years old. I had followed Bohr's career for half my life, with something bordering on worship. A terrible miracle of circumstance had finally brought me into his presence. But at that moment his life meant nothing next to my own. Niels Bohr was already a prisoner of the Third Reich—nothing could stop that now, save some desperate stupidity from Hans and his children. Papa's action could only put us on a boxcar to Theresienstadt.

The Gestapo captain gave Papa another nervous glare. "What did you say?"

"I said you are mistaken. This is my brother-in-law, Karl Gervuld. This woman is my sister, Frieda."

The captain's features hardened, but Papa's stare held him prisoner. "This man's face is known throughout the world," he said, uncertainty creeping into his voice. "This man is Niels Bohr and he will be taken into protective custody."

"Take a closer look," Papa said.

The captain obeyed: Bohr was unmistakable. He shook his head, frowning. "I'm . . . quite sure . . ."

It won't work, Papa. You're killing us.

"Look at me."

The captain turned. Confusion and fear grew in his eyes.

"This is my brother-in-law, Karl Gervuld." Papa's belly tensed in and out beneath his sweater. I could almost see the power surging between Papa's Tiferet and the captain's Yesod.

"It would be embarrassing if you presented him to your superiors as some-body he is not. You wouldn't want to be embarrassed!"

"I . . . "

"This is my brother-in-law, Karl Gervuld."

The captain licked his lips. "I should see his papers. Yours too."

The young man next to Papa reached into his coat, tensing for action. I thought of the last time Papa had tried this. My mother had died anyway.

"That won't be necessary," Papa said. "This is my brother-in-law, Karl Gervuld."

By now, everyone was staring at Papa, except for the two SS men checking papers a few rows up. Bohr himself was transfixed by the motion of Papa's belly, pumping in and out like a bellows. The partisans watched like mystified chil-dren. And I could see from the young captain's face that Papa's eyes had become the center of his universe.

The German's jaw slackened, then snapped shut. His glassy eyes came back into focus. His hand went to rest on his holster, and I knew that Papa had failed again.

But the captain turned away, and did not look at us again. He swaggered back the way he had come, hand at his holster in a posture of Prussian authority. He ordered his men off the train, and moments later we were clattering up the Zealand coast toward Elsinore.

Nobody spoke for a long time. I stared at my knees, running the episode over and over.

Eight years earlier, Papa's power had failed to save Mama from the brown-shirts. But even before that I had begun to doubt whether I could follow his path to knowledge.

I looked over at him. He sat with eyes half-closed, as if he were drunk.

No. I refused to regret my decisions. I refused to feel guilty for taking my own path. But for not having the courage to tell him . . . for that I could feel guilty. And I did.

"Sir?" Bohr reached over to touch Papa's knee. "We're grateful for . . . what-ever it was you did. I thought for sure we would . . . " He shook his head. His wife managed a thin smile. She had not let go of her husband's arm.

Papa put out his hand to shake with Bohr and his wife. "I'm Itzak Goldblum. My son, David."

"My wife, Margrethe. Oh. I'm, uh . . . "

"Yes, I know." Papa shrugged. "But you certainly look like my brother-in-law Karl."

Bohr's eyes twinkled. "Do you have a brother-in-law?"

Papa smiled at Margrethe. "I don't even have a sister."

The Bohrs laughed. Niels looked over at me and smiled. "Nice to meet you, David."

I shook that noble hand and gawked at him, trying to think of something to say.

"Forgive him," Papa said. "If his brain were working now, he'd tell you that he's a great admirer of yours."

Bohr nodded. "Well . . . I'm honored." A polite dismissal of the schoolboy. He turned back to Papa. "I have to ask you. What did you do to that Gestapo man?"

"Barely a man," Papa said, shrugging. "A real man I could not have managed. He was more of a *golem*."

Bohr frowned. "I beg your pardon?"

"A *golem*. A fairy-tale monster, yes? An empty creature of wood or clay that can be filled with the will of another. A strong man cannot be manipulated so easily. But a *golem* . . . "

Margrethe leaned forward to listen. The two partisans were whispering with their father. Bohr shifted in his seat to retrieve a pipe from his pocket. "A *golem*."

"A man like that," Papa said, "is empty. You just have to know how to fill him. Dress him up in an imposing uniform, fill his head with grand ideas, and point him at a target. The poor Germans."

Bohr, tamping tobacco into the bowl, shook his head. "The poor Germans?"

Papa shrugged. "They've become a nation of *golem*. To make a *golem* of clay is a sin, a mortal sin. To make a *golem* of a man, is that any better? Perhaps God will punish me, although I didn't create that creature. Hitler has tapped into the unconscious, the world of dreams."

Bohr lit his pipe. "You sound like Herr Doktor Freud."

Papa reached up to stroke his beard, found it missing, scratched his chin. "Yes. Well, there's little that's new in Freud, except for the words."

Bohr took exception, and they got into a friendly argument over whether Freud was a scientist or metaphysician. It was exhilarating to watch the two most important men in my life joust and find each other worthy. And maddening, because I wasn't part of it. I could quote every word Bohr had ever published, almost verbatim. But for now I was just the boy.

By the time we passed the low hills of Klampenborg, halfway to Elsinore, I was seething. Papa was doing it deliberately. Another ploy to keep me in his world. Out of Bohr's. Almost before I could read, Papa had taught me that numbers were God's brick and mortar. To his lasting chagrin, I'd followed that teaching in a different direction than he'd intended. While he sought mystery and beauty in the Torah and Sefir Yetzirah, I had found my own truth in the writings of Bohr and Dirac, Heisenberg and Born.

"Of course," Papa said as the argument wound down, "I'm just an old rabbi. There's nothing I can point to and say: There's my proof. Herr Freud, he's in the same boat. But a man like you, you can put a handle on wisdom, no?"

Bohr shook his head. "I'm not sure what you mean."

Papa looked up, begging the roof for patience. "He's not sure what I mean! You are the man who discovered the atoms, no?"

Bohr shifted uncomfortably.

Hans leaned forward, over Margrethe's lap. "Not everybody on this god-damn train is known to us," he said. "I know the cat's out of the bag, but you could still keep it down to a dull roar."

He sat back and shook his head at his two children.

"He didn't discover the atom," I told Papa in a whisper. "He described the atom, in terms of Planck's quantized energy."

"Ahhh," Papa said. "A description."

"A description," I said, "that predicts atomic spectra, including the Zeeman perturbations, to the nanometer. A description that rescues the Rutherford atom from its own angular momentum. A description that explains the periodic table with a few quantum numbers."

Bohr shrugged. "An imperfect description," he said. But he was smiling at me.

"Ah! Numbers!" Papa shook his finger in affirmation. "Yes, I knew it would come down to numbers."

Bohr's grin widened. "Why is that?"

"Because everything does! My tradition also describes the universe with numbers."

"I am half-Jewish, you know," Bohr said. "In middle school, I dabbled in the Kabbalah."

"And what did you learn from dabbling in the Kabbalah?" Papa looked at Bohr, but I knew he was speaking to me.

Bohr shrugged. "Not much."

"Not much, because you dabbled! But in science you did not dabble. There you gave your all, and you learned a great deal. Am I wrong?"

"I suppose that's true." Bohr's pipe unfurled an aromatic veil that hid his expression from me.

"My son, he dabbles in everything," Papa said. "He dabbles in physics. He dabbles in the Talmud and the Zohar. Any more dabbling, he ends up a *nebbish*."

The conversation aborted. There was only the clattering of the tracks and the whispers of the partisans. Bohr puffed at his pipe and pretended to look at his feet.

It was Margrethe who saved me. Margrethe Bohr, who challenged me with her steely Nordic eyes and a look on her face . . . a look she might have given her own son Kristian, had she not lost him in an accident. A look my mother might have given me, had my father not lost her to the brownshirts. The secret message on her face was one of empathy, but not pity. A tiny nod and a curl of her lips that said: Are you going to let these two old men dismiss you like that? Fight!

"I never dabble," I said. "Not in Kabbalah. Not in physics."

Bohr fidgeted. Papa waved a dismissive hand and snorted.

I reached into my coat for the only scrap of paper I had: the letter from Cambridge. I unfolded it and turned it over quickly, so Papa could not read it. I set it on my knee, blank side up, and began to sketch out the Tree of Life: ten Holy Sefirot connected by twenty-two paths.

"My father," I said, "is an international authority on the Zohar and Sefir Yetzirah. In his last book, The Song of Adam Kadmon, he says, 'The Sefirot are not things.' "

Bohr, whose old friend Heisenberg had once said the same of atoms, sat up and looked at my drawing.

"The Sefirot, the ten nodes of existence, are numbers—like everything else," I said. "As my father writes, they are musical notes sung by God. Thus, vibrations. Vibration implies frequency. Frequency implies energy. The Sefirot are the 'quantum numbers,' if you'll forgive me, that describe all creation."

Bohr smiled. The expression was indulgent, but not patronizing. And I had his attention.

"The right branch of the Tree is creative, impulsive, masculine, positive. The left is receptive, nurturing, feminine, negative. The duality reconciles in the middle trunk, the synthesis of opposites that drives all creation. The Tree is a map of the Universe."

Bohr shook his head, but he kept listening.

I kept scribbling. "For example, in Adam Kadmon my father maps the Tree onto human physiology. Catabolism, motor processes and the sympathetic nervous system appear on the right—all the functions that involve action, the release of energy. Anabolism, sensory processes and parasympathetic activity map to the left side." Then I pointed with my pen at Tiferet, the Sefirot in the center of the Tree, the one that connected to all the others.

"The heart?" Bohr offered.

"Ah, he sees!" Papa said.

I shook my head. "No, I don't think that's right."

"What?" Papa leaned over to look at my drawing. "Mishegos! Of course it's right!"

I hesitated, but then I caught Margrethe out of the corner of my eye again.

"No," I said, and continued scribbling. "The heart is a circulatory organ. It belongs at Nezah, on the lower left trunk. No, Tiferet is Beauty, the thing created. Balance, integration, essence."

"And so," Bohr asked, "what is the Tiferet of human physiology, young David?"

I flushed under Papa's withering glare. "The central nervous system," I said, and wrote it in. "The brain and spinal cord."

Bohr's pipe had gone cold from neglect. Papa chewed on his lower lip and stared at my drawing.

"We can also map the atom," I said. Across the top of the page I wrote n, l, m, s. "These are the four quantum numbers that underlie the structure of matter. Shell, subshell, magnetic, spin. But to describe matter, we also need to describe the electric force that binds electrons to the nucleus, and the force that holds the nucleus together. We need mass and charge . . . "

I kept talking, kept scribbling, my hands and brain working together in a storm of delight.

When I finished, Papa shook his head. "Huh. My son a *knaker*. Mr. Big Shot."

A smile grew on Bohr's thick lips, and he took the paper from my hand, so he didn't have to look at it upside-down. I was afraid Papa would read the other side.

"This is really quite beautiful," Bohr said.

Papa stared at me, and my delight intertwined with my dread. I had not told him of the scholarship I had won to study physics at Cambridge, recently announced in the Letters. I had avoided confronting him by telling myself it didn't matter. We had lost everything in Germany. Everything. Now Denmark was a mess, and if the resistance couldn't get us across the Elsinore Sound and into Sweden I might never go to university at all. So I willed myself to stop worrying about it, to bask in that perfect moment when the two men I loved and admired most looked at me with new eyes and nodded their heads with wonder and respect.

Bohr studied my drawing for a long time. I don't think he wanted to give it back.

Hans had made arrangements with the engineer, who stopped the train a kilometer shy of Elsinore Station. Seventeen Jews, including the Bohrs, disembarked at this unscheduled stop. Hans and his children led us to a nearby bus stand. There we caught a ride to Kronborg Castle, where Claudius had murdered Hamlet's father and Hamlet had murdered Claudius.

The fortress of stone and timber overlooks the Elsinore Sound at its narrowest point. From this vantage, Denmark had once imposed her will on all naval traffic through the Baltic. But Danish power had long since ebbed, and Kronborg Castle, with its wide moats and towers topped with spires of bluing copper, had become a museum. The Nazis had not closed the castle, just as they had not interfered in most aspects of Danish life—until now.

The bus pulled up to a wide bridge of wood and iron, half a kilometer from the castle. Our party joined a dozen sightseers who had already gathered around a tour guide. She was a plump woman with thick glasses and the bearing of a schoolmistress. While she collected the tour fee she lectured us in a nasal, singsong voice. Stay with me. The tour must end on time, because of the curfew. No photos. Don't touch.

Hans stood behind Papa and me. "She is our contact," he told us. "But you stay with me, not her, understand? Just before the tour enters the courtyard we split off and go to the old stables."

He moved on, whispering into other ears, including Bohr's. Hans's son and daughter stood on either side of the group, scanning the area.

My gaze kept wandering past the gorgeous mass of the castle, across the gray waters of the Sound, to the swelling of land on the other side.

Sweden. Neutral Sweden.

Our guide led us through a wooden gate and over a cobblestone footpath to the castle, lecturing all the way. Somebody built this in that year, over there was the residence of so-and-so. As we approached Kronborg, the majesty of the structure became more imposing, and for a moment I forgot our peril. I had seen my share of German castles—outside our home town of Heidelberg sits a seventeenth-century ruin of lichened stone. But Kronborg was huge, well-preserved, and graceful. The sun broke through the clouds, and I craned my neck to watch the spires rise into the bright sky. It was a perfect moment. I looked over at Papa, and he smiled.

We crossed the moat, our feet drumming the ancient drawbridge like the hooves of cattle. The guide continued her jabbering, leading us into a broad cobblestone courtyard, with a grand fountain at the center. I was sorry I wouldn't get to see more. But now Hans gave us a grim nod over his shoulder. As the rest of the group filtered into the sunlit courtyard, the Jews split off and took their own path into hiding.

As usual, I thought.

Hans and his children led us down a narrow path that ran along the outer moat and into the abandoned stables, a labyrinth of rotting wood set into the castle's eastern wall. There was no lighting here, and as we followed Hans into a maze of abandoned stalls my mood darkened.

Soon we were deep within the entrails of the castle. Hans led us through a broad wooden door and down a narrow staircase. We emerged into utter darkness.

A yellow flicker from his electric torch cut into the black like a firefly, moving crazily through the void. Then the light of a candle mounted on the wall began to etch out our surroundings. Hans lit two more, illuminating a place of despair.

"Looks like a dungeon," Papa said, and everybody turned to frown at him. Papa was always willing to say things people would rather not hear.

"Catacombs," Hans said. "But the dungeons aren't far."

The chamber was oppressively small. Rough stone curved just overhead, damp and ugly. Bohr had to stoop. Gravel and dirt crunched beneath our feet. The walls were abrasive and bare—even lichen refused to grow in this place.

But one creature did dwell here. Seated on a throne of rock against one wall, an eight-foot-tall Viking slept with his chin on his chest, a broadsword across his knees. The statue of gray stone was exquisite and menacing. Even in repose, the warrior's features were implacable and noble. His legs were as thick as my torso. He wore a simple helmet and a tunic of mail, but his thick arms were bare. A massive shield sat propped against his thigh.

"Why do they keep this down here?" I asked Hans. "It's beautiful."

"Holger Danske sleeps here," he said matter-of-factly, as if I were an idiot.

"Well, now we know, don't we?" Papa said.

"We'll be here a few hours," Hans said, settling into a dark corner. "Try to rest. You especially, Doktor Bohr. Sweden is just a way station for you."

"I understand," Bohr said, and like everybody else he began searching for a stretch of wall. He removed his coat and spread it over the dirt so Margrethe could sit. He lit his pipe, and the sweet aroma was a great improvement. Some in our group whispered among themselves, but the close walls of the catacomb magnified every sound, and so for a long time there was only silence and, finally, the sound of Hans's snoring.

I, too, was exhausted. I sat beside Papa in the gravel beneath the stone warrior. Soon I joined Holger Danske in sleep.

I dreamed of my father's bookstore, in the Jewish quarter of Heidelberg. The brownshirts had come. One stood out front to trumpet his epithets, wearing sandwich boards that said *Warning! Germans Don't Buy From Jews!* While I tended the shop, four men came inside to ransack the shelves and break the windows. They beat me with fists and clubs, doubling me over with pain and shame. My parents came down the stairs from our apartment. My mother screamed and rushed to my side. The leader pushed her away, called her a whore.

The other three brownshirts converged on Papa, but they stepped back without laying a hand on him. He transfixed them with those dark eyes full of power, his belly rippling beneath his coat.

"You need to go now," he said, and they turned away.

But the leader had his own iron, his own malignant strength. He was too deep or too shallow for Papa's power to fill him. He cursed at his men, mocking them. He struck with his club, and Papa crumpled to the floor. Like cowardly dogs emboldened by blood, the others took his example. While they beat Papa, the leader kicked me in the face. As I lay choking on my own blood, he seized my mother by her hair and dragged her toward the street.

To be met at the doorway by Neils Henrik David Bohr. The Bohr I knew from books and photos. The young, gangly Bohr who had gone to England in 1911 to change the world.

He held up his atom of spinning orbitals, vibrating with latent energy. His fingers broke it apart, and released a brilliance that blinded the Nazis and dispelled them like a vapor.

When the brilliance faded, only Papa and I remained. My mother was gone.

The catacomb was dark enough to nourish the dream a few minutes into waking. Papa had taught me to cling to my dreams and interrogate them—they were wisdom from Yesod, or even from Da'at, and not to be discarded without examination.

My eyes adjusted slowly. Bohr and my father sat together at the stone feet of Holger Danske. Their low voices echoed off the walls.

"I promise," Bohr was saying. "I did my best work at Cambridge. And I still have friends there. It won't be difficult."

His words intertwined with my dream, a good fit. But not difficult? If the resistance managed to get Bohr to England, his task would be difficult in the extreme.

It was no secret that Bohr might be instrumental in splitting the atom for the Allies—if Heisenberg didn't beat him to it. My father's path might lead to wisdom, and a sort of ineffable power. But Bohr's path, the path I had chosen, led to a more reliable power, the kind of power that might rescue humanity from the grip of the Axis.

My father, bloody and helpless, splayed on the floor with his tattered books. Bohr at the doorway, splitting his atom to dispel evil.

The dream faded. Neither path would bring Mama back to me.

"He's awake," Papa said. "Welcome back! Better you shouldn't sleep, if you're going to be so fitful."

I went to sit with them. Everybody else sat quietly, except the two young partisans who stood at the entrance to the catacomb, smoking. Hans had abandoned his corner.

Bohr followed my gaze. "He left at nightfall, to check the area. He should be returning soon."

I nodded, rubbing the sleep from my eyes. A long silence ensued. I realized I had interrupted something.

Papa looked up at Holger Danske.

"My son is right. It's a strange thing to find in such a place."

"This is where he belongs," Bohr said. "Holger Danske is our national hero. The Sleeping Dane, we call him. This statue was put here in 1911, just before I went to England. The Sleeping Dane fought many battles for Denmark abroad.

But eventually he grew weary of war. He came back to Elsinore, and fell asleep on this spot." Bohr lit his pipe again, and I smiled. He seemed unable to speak without a pipe in his hand.

"They say he is the final defender of Denmark. When invaders come, the Sleeping Dane will awaken to save us." Bohr gave Papa a fatalistic smile. "But still he sleeps. So much for legends."

Papa looked up at Holger Danske for a long time. Finally he said: "You're wrong, Doktor Bohr. The Sleeping Dane is awake."

Bohr shook his head, bemused.

"The occupation has been almost painless up to now." Papa scratched at his bare chin. "You Danes have had it easy. The Germans pretend to respect your neutrality, and you pretend you still have something to respect."

Bohr frowned, then nodded. "Yes, I'm afraid so."

"But since the rumors started two days ago, that the Nazis would round us up like cattle, what have you seen? The King's government refuses to cooperate and resigns in protest. The newspapers speak out against the Nazis, when they would do better to keep silent. The Danish people take us in to hide us from the Gestapo. Hans and his children risk their lives to smuggle us to Sweden. The Sleeping Dane is awake, Herr Doktor Bohr. You should be proud of your people."

Bohr stared at Holger Danske. His chin quivered, and again I sensed how heavily the occupation had weighed on him.

He put out his arm to clasp Papa's shoulder. "I'm glad we met, Rabbi."

Hans emerged from the shadows. He looked grim. "I need everyone's attention."

Everybody stirred, groaning at the cold in their muscles.

"The Gestapo is on the castle grounds," Hans said.

Muttered fear echoed through the catacomb. Margrethe put her hands over her mouth. Bohr went to put his arms around her.

Hans waved us into quiet. "Unless more are on the way, it's unlikely they'll find us before the rendezvous. It's a small detail—our friend from this morning and a half-dozen troops. But in half an hour we'll have to cross five hundred meters of open ground under a full moon down to the beach. We'll be exposed. If we're lucky, they'll still be searching the castle proper."

"How did they know?" somebody asked.

"Considering what happened this morning," Hans said, "we're lucky we made it this far. We hadn't anticipated the search at Helgoland. I suspect the Hauptsturmführer came to his senses." He looked over at us.

Papa shrugged. "I should solve all your problems? Nobody's perfect."

Hans managed a grim smile, then disappeared with his son. His daughter stayed with us. She produced a Luger and checked the chamber and magazine. We watched her with mute terror.

Papa withdrew a bundle of cloth from the pocket of his wrinkled khakis. As he unfolded it, I saw what it was: his *tallis*. He wrapped the prayer shawl over his shoulders.

"Hear, O Israel." Barely a whisper, but in that awful place it still carried my father's power.

We all went to him, all except the girl.

"Hear, O Israel. The Lord Our God, the Lord is One . . . " As my father intoned the Shema, and repeated it twice, my heart slowed and my terror ebbed. I looked at the others, saw the calm seep into their faces.

Such power. No, I had made the right choice. I knew: I did not have my father's gifts.

Hans reappeared, alone. His forehead glistened with effort and fear. "More SS have arrived," he said. "They're dispersing over the castle grounds."

Silence.

"I'll go," Bohr said.

Hans frowned, licking his lips. He was thinking about it.

"They're looking for me," Bohr said. "As far as they know, it's just Margrethe and I. If we surrender, perhaps they'll leave."

The rest of us voiced our protest, but Bohr held up his hands. "They won't harm us!" he said. "Margrethe is . . . Aryan, and I'm only half-Jewish. And I'm valuable. They think they can use me."

"Which is exactly why it won't do," Hans said. "And it doesn't solve the problem of getting the rest of us down to the shore. No, thank you, Doktor."

Bohr shook his head. I thought he would weep.

"My son is watching for the boat," Hans said. "When he gets the signal from the Sound, we'll just have to run for it. Stretch your muscles."

He lit a cigarette and turned away from us. I saw his daughter ask a question with her eyes.

Hans shook his head. This was no time for lies.

We weren't going to make it.

As the group gathered at the opening of the catacomb, I went to join Papa. He stood apart from the rest, at the foot of the Sleeping Dane, fingering his *tallis*.

My decision didn't matter now. This path, that path. Telling him the truth would only hurt him, gaining nothing.

I looked over at Bohr, standing with the others, Margrethe's face in his chest. And then at my father, praying silently.

The truth gains nothing? The thought struck from within, like the stinging shame of a well-deserved slap. For Bohr, for my father, there had never been anything but truth.

"There's something I have to tell you, Papa," I said, pushing against the words. "Important."

He spread his arms and rolled his eyes at the ceiling. "*Gevalt!* Important, he says!" His voice dropped into a coarse whisper. "The Nazi wolves are at the door and they'll be tearing out our throats any minute! We need to talk about something else?"

"Yes. Because the wolves are at the door, and we may not have another chance. Don't make this harder for me, Papa."

His face settled into its true nature, kind and sad. "You would not be a Rabbi. You would not study the word of God."

I took a deep breath. "Not as you do, no."

"No. You would go to Cambridge and study the word of Bohr under your fancy scholarship."

My heart skipped. "You knew?"

"Am I a *schmuck*? Of course I knew! I knew about Cambridge, I knew about the scholarship, I knew about the paper you published in the contest from the fancy journal to win the scholarship." He half-closed his eyes, as when he recited scripture. "*Correlating Experimental Lithium Spectra with Bohr Model Predictions of Valence Angular Momenta* by David Goldblum." He managed a smile. "Such language! Yes, I knew."

I gaped at him.

"What I did not know," he said, "was when you would work up the courage to tell me, or whether you'd just elope with your books and go *shlepping* off into the night!" He gave me an affectionate slap on the cheek.

"It doesn't look like I'll be *shlepping* anywhere," I said.

"I'm afraid you're right. But you told me anyway, and you didn't have to. You faced me like a man. As a man."

I took a deep, shuddering breath. "You're not angry? Disappointed?"

Again he questioned the roof. "If he's so smart, Lord, how can he be such a *putz*?" He glowered at me. "Of course I'm angry and disappointed! What, you think I'm not paying attention? Just because my son makes his own decisions doesn't mean I have to be happy about them!"

Hans's son appeared at the opening, breathing hard. "The SS are moving this way," he said. "The boat hasn't signaled yet, but I can see her moving up the Sound. We can't wait."

"Let's move," Hans said.

Papa took my face in his hands and kissed me. "You are my gift to the world," he said. "Now . . . let's run for our lives."

The next few moments were a blur of jostling bodies, cold rock, and black fear. By the time we emerged from the stables, the moonlight that washed over the castle grounds seemed like midday brilliance. The ground sloped gently, 500 meters to the water. A fishing boat waited just offshore.

"Do you see it?" Hans asked us. "There are dinghies waiting on the beach.

At my signal, run as fast as you can, and don't stop. No matter what happens, you keep running."

I took Papa's hand.

"No," he said. "Better not. I'll try to keep up. Do as the man says."

"Now!"

We sprinted into the night like terrified deer. I took Papa's arm again, but he twisted away and pushed me. My fear took over then, my legs pumping away at the turf like pistons.

We covered perhaps two hundred meters, spreading out in a panicky Gaussian distribution before the first shouts, the first gunshots, the first blood. Hans's daughter fell in front of me, her lower back bursting into a dark spray of gore. I stopped to help her up, but her limbs were flaccid. When I saw her eyes, I knew she was dead. More shots rang out, and I saw others fall.

I stumbled back to my feet, and looked over my shoulder for Papa. He should have been behind me, but by now I was the last straggler.

"David!" A strong hand seized my arm and spun me around.

It was Bohr. He had come back for me.

"What are you doing, boy? Run!"

"Where's my father?" I cried.

More gunshots, closer. We turned, and saw at least ten SS running toward us across the green. There were more assembling on the walls above the moat.

"Halt! Halt!"

We turned to run, but the ground at our feet boiled under a rain of bullets, and we cowered with our hands in the air.

"Niels!" Margrethe's voice came from direction of the shore, where the others were piling into dinghies.

"Damn," Bohr muttered, and raised his hands a little higher.

It was over. Because of me.

The sporadic pop-pop-pop of gunfire erupted into a hailstorm. I expected to die at that moment. Instead I heard shouting. Screams. Terror and confusion. From the SS troops.

Bohr and I turned to look, our hands still in the air.

The Sleeping Dane was awake.

He still had the color of stone, but his massive limbs were supple with life. The arc of his broadsword passed through two SS men, cleaving them at the waist. The sword continued its orbit, swinging overhead and then dropping vertically, biting through a soldier's helmet to split him like firewood. In the moonlight I saw the Hauptsturmführer step forward to empty his sidearm into the Dane's chest. Holger Danske swung his shield, and the captain fell into a misshapen heap twenty yards away.

More SS spilled onto the field. Their rifles might as well have been quarterstaffs.

The Dane stood rooted to one spot, legs spread wide like the roots of an oak. But the sword never ceased swinging, like an electron switching between orbitals— horizontal, vertical, oblique. Body parts and blood spread over the ground. And still the SS kept coming.

I caught sight of Papa, at the opening of the stables beneath the east wall, his *tallis* hanging from his shoulders, arms stretching into the night, waving about to animate the limbs of Holger Danske. I screamed at him, but he could not have heard me over the din of gunfire.

And then he died, as a black bird spread its liquid wings across his chest. But his *golem* kept cutting and killing, fully roused to bloodlust.

"He's gone," Bohr said. "Come on!"

I couldn't move. I couldn't breathe.

"David."

I couldn't even wail.

"David!" Bohr shook me so hard that I bit my tongue. "Come on!"

The gunfire ceased as the remaining SS finally retreated. We ran to the shoreline and splashed into the icy water of the Sound. We had to swim a few yards to catch up to one of the dinghies. The others dragged us out of the water and somebody wrapped his jacket about my wet shoulders. My teeth chattered, and it was good to be numb with cold, nothing but cold.

They pulled us aboard the fishing boat a few minutes later. I stood alone, still shivering. I saw Hans and his boy fall to their knees, embracing each other with quiet grief. Margrethe was in Bohr's arms, shaking with relief and rage. My fellow Jews stood at the railing and wailed for those who had fallen.

As the boat turned her prow toward Sweden, I went aft for a last look at Kronborg castle. The Dane stood in the moonlight with carnage at his feet. His shoulders slumped. The tip of his sword dragged in the dirt. Weariness seeped into his stoney flesh. He shuffled toward the stables. Before he stooped into the darkness, he lay aside his shield and went down on one knee. He draped Papa's body over a massive shoulder. Then Holger Danske took up his shield and returned to his rest.

Presently I realized that Bohr and Margrethe were standing next to me. They didn't say anything trite or useless. Margrethe took my hand.

"Your father made arrangements with me," Bohr said. For a moment he could not speak. "Just in case. I have an audience with the King of Sweden tomorrow. After that, they will put me on a plane to England. You'll come with me."

I shook my head.

"Your father told me the scholarship would pay your tuition," he said. "But you'll need room and board. A good advisor. Many other things. It won't be difficult. I have friends at Cambridge. He made me promise."

It was only then that I wept, my hands tearing at the damp fabric of my shirt. Margrethe took me into her arms, as a mother might.

As I write this, I have at hand the drawing I made for my Papa and Niels Bohr, sixty years ago. It is yellowed and cracked from age and over-handling. Today, as on many days, I have taken it out to consult it, to make refinements, to seek inspiration, or simply to remember.

Beneath the drawing sits a recent letter from the Nobel Academy, congratulating me for the work I did in the seventies on the topological analysis of 10-dimensional quantum-observer interfaces. In recent years, the neuroscientists have appropriated that work, as part of a fundamental new theory of consciousness. My father's gift to the world.

Soon I will return to Sweden for the first time since that night. I will go by way of Denmark, to visit the one who sleeps beneath Kronborg Castle. In Stockholm I will shake hands with a King. For a few moments the world will be mine. The world will listen.

When I speak, it will not be of physics, or Kabbalah, or the nobility of science, or the power of faith. I will speak of my father, Rabbi Itzak Josef Goldblum, and my other father, Niels Henrik David Bohr. I will speak of my debt to them, and how my life and work have been nothing, nothing but my effort to be worthy of them both.

The Tsar's Dragon

Jane Yolen & Adam Stemple

The dragons were harrowing the provinces again. They did that whenever the Tsar was upset with the Jews. He would go down to their barns himself with a big golden key and unlock the stalls. Made a big show of it.

"Go!" he would cry out pompously, flinging his arm upward, outward, though, having no sense of direction, he usually pointed towards Moscow. That would have been a disaster if the dragons were equally dense. But of course they are not.

So they took off, the sky darkening as their vee formation covered a great swath of the heavens. And as they went, everyone below recited the old rhyme, "Bane of Dragons":

Fire above, fire below,
Pray to hit my neighbor.

Well, it rhymes in the dialect.

Of course, the Jews were all safe, having seeded their *shtetls* with a new kind of drachometer—an early-warning device that only they could have invented. The Tsar should have listened to me when I told him to gather the Jewish scientists in one place and force them to work for him. Away from their families, their friends. Use them to rid ourselves of the rest. But no, once again I was not heeded.

So deep inside their burrows, the Jews—safe as houses—were drinking *schnapps* and tea in glasses with glass handles . . . which always seems an odd combination to me, but then, I am not Jewish, not even seven times down the line, which one must prove in order to work for the Tsar.

Balked of their natural prey, the dragons took once more to raking the provinces with fire. This time, it cost us a really fine opera house, built in the last century and fully gilded, plus a splendid spa with indoor plumbing, and two lanes of Caterina the Great houses, plus the servants therein. Thank the good Lord it was summer—all the hoi plus all the polloi were at their summer dachas and missed the fun. The smoke, though, hung over the towns for days, like a bad odor.

I pointed all this out this to His Royal Graciousness High Buttinsky, but carefully, of course. I know that I'm not irreplaceable. No one is. Even Tsars, as we all found out much later. And I wanted my head to remain on my shoulders. At least until my new wife wore me out.

Bowing low, I said, "Do you remember, gracious one, what I said concerning the Jewish scientists?"

The Tsar stroked his beard, shook his head, mumbled a few words to the mad magician who danced attendance on the Tsaritsa, and left abruptly to plan his next pogrom. It would have as little effect as the last. But he was always trying.

Very trying.

Have I mentioned how much Tsar Nicholas is constantly upset with the Jews?

Now the mad magician and I had this in common: we did not think highly of the Tsar's wits. Or his wishes and wants. This did not, of course, stop us from cashing his chits and living at court and finding new young wives at every opportunity, our own and other men's. But where we differed was that Old Raspy thought that he knew a thing or three about dragons. And in that—as it turned out—he was terribly, horribly wrong.

Some twelve feet below the frozen Russian surface, two men sat smoking their cigarettes and drinking peach *schnapps* next to a blue-and-white-tiled stove. The tiles had once been the best to be had from a store—now long gone—in the Crimea, but in the half-lit burrow, the men did not care about the chips and chinks and runnels on them. Nor would they have cared if the stove were still residing upstairs in the house's summer kitchen. They were more concerned with other things now, like dragons, like peach *schnapps*, like the state of the country.

One man was tall, gangly, and humped over because of frequent stays in the burrow, not just to escape the dragons either. He had a long beard, gray as a shovelhead. With the amount of talking he tended to do, he looked as if he were digging up an entire nation. Which, of course, he was.

The other was short, compact, even compressed, with a carefully cultivated beard and sad eyes.

The taller of the two threw another piece of wood into the stove's maw. The heat from the blue tiles immediately cranked up, but there was no smoke, due to the venting system, which piped the smoke straight up through ten feet of hard-packed dirt, then, two feet before the surface, through a triple-branching system that neatly divided the smoke so that when it came into contact with the cold air, it was no more than a wisp. Warm enough for wolves to seek the three streams out, but as they scattered when there were dragons or Cossacks attacking the villages, the smoke never actually gave away the positions of the burrows.

"You ever notice," the taller man, Bronstein, began, "that every time we ask the Tsar to stop a war—"

"He kills us," the other, Borutsch, finished for him, his beard jumping. "Lots of us." Bronstein nodded in agreement and seemed ready to go on, but Borutsch didn't even pause for breath. "When he went after Japan, we told him, 'It's a tiny island with nothing worth having. Let the little delusional, we're-descended-from-the-sun-god-and-you-aren't bastards *keep* it. Russia is big enough. Why add eighteen square miles of nothing but volcanoes and rice?' "

Bronstein took off the oval eyeglasses that matched his pinched face so well and idly smeared dust from one side of the lenses to the other. "Well, what I mean to say is—"

"And this latest! His high mucky-muck Franz falls over dead drunk in Sarajevo and never wakes up again, and all of a sudden Germany is a rabid dog biting everyone within reach." Borutsch gnashed his teeth at several imaginary targets, setting his long beard flopping so wildly that he was in danger of sticking it in his own eye. "But why should we care? Let Germany have France. They let that midget monster loose on us a century ago; they can get a taste of their own borscht now."

"Yes, well—" But Borutsch was not to be stopped.

"How big a country does one man need? What is he going to do with it? His dragons have torched more than half of it, and his 'Fists' have stripped the other half clean of anything of value."

"Wood and grain," Bronstein managed to interject. *The only things worth more than the dragons themselves,* he thought. *Wood in the winter and grain in the spring—the only two seasons Russia gets. The nine aggregate days that made up summer and fall didn't really count.*

"Yes. So he sends us to fight and die for a country we don't own and that's worth nothing anyway, and if we happen to survive, he sends us off to Siberia to freeze our dumplings off! And if we *complain*?" Borutsch pointed his finger at Bronstein, thumb straight. "Ka-pow!"

Bronstein waited to see if the older man was going to go on, but he was frowning into his *schnapps* now, as if it had disagreed with something he'd just said.

"Yes, well, that's what I wanted to talk to you about, Pinches."

Borutsch looked up, his eyes sorrowful and just slightly bleary from drink.

"I've got an idea," Bronstein said.

Borutsch's lips curled upward in a quiet smile, but his eyes remained sad. "You always do, Lev. You always do."

The mad monk was not so mad as people thought. Calculating, yes. Manipulative, yes. Seductive, definitely.

He stared speculatively at himself in a gilded mirror in the queen's apartments. His eyes were almost gold.

Like a dragon's, he thought.

He was wrong. The dragons' eyes were coal black. Shroud black. Except for the dragon queen. *Hers* were green. Ocean green, black underwater green, with a lighter, almost foamy green color in the center. But then the mad monk had never actually been down to see the dragons in their stalls, or talked to their stall boys. He didn't dare.

If there was one thing that frightened Rasputin, it was dragons. There had been a prophecy about it. And as calculating a man as he was, he was also a man of powerful beliefs. Peasant beliefs.

He who fools with dragons
Will himself be withered in their flames.

It is even stronger in the original Siberian.

Not that you can find anyone who speaks Siberian here in the center of the Empire, the monk thought. *Which is where I belong. In the center.* He'd long known that he was made for greater things than scraping a thin living from the Siberian tundra, like his parents.

Or dying in the cold waters of the Tura, like my siblings.

Shaking off these black thoughts, he made a quick kiss at his image in the mirror.

"Now *there's* an enchanting man!" he said aloud.

His own face always did much to cheer him—as well as cheer the ladies of the court.

"Father Grigori," said a light, breathy child's voice in the vicinity of his hip. "Pick me up."

The mad monk was not so mad as to refuse the order of the Tsar's only son. The boy might be ill, sometimes desperately so. But one day soon, he would be Tsar. The stars foretold it. And the Lord God—who spoke to Father Grigori in his dreams of fire and ice—had foretold it as well.

"As you wish and for my pleasure," he said, bending down and picking the child in his arms. He bore him carefully, knowing that if he pressed too hard, bruises the size and color of fresh beets would form and not fade for weeks.

The boy looked up at him fondly, and said, "Let's go see Mama," and Father Grigori's mouth broke into a wolfish grin.

"Yes, let's," he said. "As you wish and for *my* pleasure." He practically danced down the long hall with the child.

So having been balked once again of my chance to persuade the Tsar of the foolishness of his plans, I thought to go back to my apartment and visit with my young wife. We had met not a year earlier at the *Bal Blanc*, she in virginal white, her perfect shoulders bare, diamonds circling that perfect neck like a barrier. I was so thoroughly enchanted, I married again, less than a year after my last wife's death. It was only much later that I discovered the diamonds were her sister's. It was only much, much later that she discovered how little money *I* actually have.

Now, early afternoon, she might be napping. Or she might be entertaining. I hoped she would be available and not with some of her admirers. The problem with taking someone so young to wife is getting one's turn with her. Nights, of course, she is always mine, but who knows what she is doing during the day.

Suddenly realizing that I didn't *want* to know, I turned abruptly on my heel, my new boots on the tiled floor making a squealing noise that was not unlike the sound a sow makes in labor. I have watched many of them at my summer farm.

I'd made a decision, and I made it quickly. It's one of the things the Tsar likes about me since he has so many ditherers around him. Old men, old aristos, who cannot come down on one side or another of any question. Much like the Tsar. I think it's in the bloodlines, along with the many diseases. Inbreeding, you know.

This was my decision: I would go down to the stalls and visit the dragons. See if I could figure them out. There is a strange, dark intelligence there. Or maybe not exactly intelligence as we humans understand it, more like cunning. If only we could harness that as well as we have harnessed their loyalty—from centuries of captivity and a long leash. Much like the Cossacks actually. With a bit of luck, I might figure out this harrowing business. The Tsar might finally make me a Count. New blood might appeal to him. He'd listen to my plans. Then my young wife, Ninotchka, would be available in the afternoons, too. I strode down the hallway smiling. Making decisions always lifts my spirit. I breathed more deeply; my blood began to race. I felt fifty years old again.

It was then that I saw the mad monk, halfway down the hall and coming toward me, carrying the young prince. He's the only one who dares do that without soft lambs'-wool blankets. That child's skin is like old china. It can be smashed by the slightest touch.

"Father Grigori," I said, my hand to my brow in salute. He may be just a *muzhik* by birth, he may be as mad as they say he is, but I would be madder still to neglect the obeisance he demands. He has the ear of the young Tsar. And the young Tsar's mother, Alexandra. Maybe more than just her *ear*, if you believed the rumors.

He glanced at me, my name ashes in his mouth. He never uses my title. Then he smiled, that soft, sensual smile that drives the women wild, though to me it looks like a serpent's smile. "Commend me to your young wife."

It was then that I knew what I had only feared before. My own Ninotchka had fallen under his spell. I would have to kill him. Alone or with others. For Ninotchka's sake, as well as my own.

But how?

The answer, I felt, was down in the stalls with the dragons. So, down I went.

You always smell the dragons long before you see them. It is a ripe musk, fills the nostrils, tastes like old boots. But it's not without its seductions. It is the smell of power, a smell I could get used to.

The door squalled when I opened it, and the dragons set up a yowling to match, expecting to be fed. Dragons are always hungry. It has to do with the hot breath, and needing fuel, or so I'd been told.

I grabbed a handful of cow brains out of a nearby bucket and flung it into the closest stall.

There was a quick rustling of their giant bat wings—three or four dragons share a stall because it calms them down. I wiped my hands on the towel hung on the peg for just that purpose. I would need to wash before going back to my apartment, or Ninotchka would never let me touch her tonight.

The Tsar's dragons were slimmer and more snakelike than the Great Khan's dragons from whom they'd been bred. They were black, like eels. Their long faces, framed with ropy hair, always looked as if they were about to speak in some Nubian's tongue. One expected Araby to issue forth instead of curls of smoke.

I gazed into the eyes of the largest one, careful not to look down or away, nor to show fear. Fear only excites them. *Prey* show fear. His eyes were dark, like the Crimea in winter, and I felt as if I swam in them. Then I sensed that I was starting to drown. Down and down I went, my eyes wide open, my mouth filled with the ashy water—when suddenly I saw the future breaststroking towards me: hot fires, buildings in flames. The Russias were burning. St. Petersburg and Moscow buried in ash. The gold leaf of the turrets on Anichkov Palace and Ouspensky Cathedral peeling away in the heat.

"Enough!" I said, hauling myself away, finding the surface, breaking the spell. "I will not be guiled by your animal magic."

The dragon turned away and nuzzled the last of the cow brains at his feet.

I'd been wrong. There'd be no help from these creatures. And I'd be no help for them.

The dragons finally gone, the drachometer signaled the all clear, a sound like cicadas sighing. Bronstein and Borutsch crawled out of the burrows and into a morning still thick with dragon smoke. The two squinted and coughed and nodded to the other folks who were emerging besmirched and bleary from their own warrens.

No one exchanged smiles; they were alive and unharmed, but houses had been burned, businesses ruined, fields scorched through the snow. A stand of fine old white birch trees, after which the town was named, were now charred and blackened stumps. And perhaps the next time, the drachometers would fail and there would be no warning. It was always a possibility. Drek *happens,* as the rabbis liked to say.

The *babuschkas* were not so full of bile, but they were realists, too, as they told of the old times before the drachometers, when Tsars with names like "Great" and "Terrible" savaged the lands with their dragons and their armies. The Jews had been nearly wiped out then, and only the invention of the first drachometer—a primitive device by today's standards—had saved them. Borutsch's old grandmother often said, "We live in the better times."

"Better than *what*?" he would tease.

Hearing the old women's stories, the children shuddered at the wanton destruction while the young men scoffed and made chest-puffed proclamations of what they would or wouldn't have done had they been faced with sudden, fiery death from above.

But not Bronstein. He'd always listened intently to the stories and tried to imagine what it was like in the far-off days when you had no time to get safely underground and you had to face the dragons in the open: flame, tooth, and claw against man's feeble flesh. Because he realized something that the other young men seemed not to: technologies fail, or other technologies supplant them, and the contraption you count on one day can be useless the next. *In this, the rabbis are right*, he thought. Drek *really does happen.* There was only one thing you could really count on, and it certainly wasn't a sheep-sized gadget that ran on magnetism and magic and honked like a bull elk in rut when a dragon came within ten miles.

It was power.

Those who have it stand on the backs of those who don't, and no amount of invention or intelligence could raise a person from one to the other. No, to get power you had to grab it by force. And to hold it, you had to use even more force.

We Jews, Bronstein thought, as he led Borutsch out of town, *are unaccustomed to force.* Then, frowning, *Except when it's used against us.*

As they climbed the hills outside the *shtetl*, both men began to breathe heavily, their breath frosting like dragon smoke in the chill December air. Borutsch shed his outer coat. Bronstein loosened his collar. They walked on. Entering the forest at midday, they moved easily through the massive cedars and spruce, grown so tall as to choke out the undergrowth and even keep the snow from falling beneath them.

Bronstein led confidently, despite seeming to follow no trail. Each time he came here, he took a different route. But it didn't matter. He was as attuned to what he sought as a drachometer to the wings of dragons.

If someone with the Tsar's ear discovers my machinations before I am ready . . .

The results were too dire to consider.

Signaling a halt in a small clearing, he pointed to a fallen log. "Sit," he said, then pulled a loaf of bread from beneath his coat and handed it to Borutsch. "Eat," he said to the older man. "I go to see we aren't followed."

"If I'd known the journey was goin' to be so long, I would have brought more *schnapps*."

Bronstein smiled and reached into his other coat pocket, revealing a flask. "I'll take it with me to ensure you'll wait."

"Be safe, then," Borutsch mumbled through a mouthful of bread.

Bronstein was not only safe, but quick as well, merely trotting back to the forest's edge and peering down the slope. He could see the *shtetl*, still swathed in smoke, and, beyond it, the thin strips of burning grain fields. There was no one working the fields at this time of year, though it was little enough they got from the harvest even when they did. The Tsar's *kruks*—the "Fists" that Borutsch had mentioned—took the lion's share and the lamb's as well, leaving them with barely enough to starve on. It was the same with the peasants, only the Tsar did not set his dragons on them.

Seeing nobody climbing the slope after them, Bronstein turned back to the forest.

From field to forest, he thought. *Grain to wood.*

"Up," he said as he reentered the clearing and tossed the flask to Botrutsch. "We are almost there."

Bronstein moved quickly now, and Borutsch struggled a bit to keep up. But as Bronstein had said, they were almost there.

They came upon a brook running swift and shallow through snowy banks. Bronstein turned downstream and paralleled it, stopping finally at an old pine tree that had been split by lightning long ago. He paced off thirty steps south, away from the stream, then turned sharply and took another thirty. Flinging himself to the ground, he began pawing through a pile of old leaves and pine needles.

"Grain and wood, Borutsch," Bronstein said. "Two of the three things that give power in this land." He'd cleared away the leaves and needles now and was digging through the cold dirt. The ground should have been frozen and resisting, but it broke easily beneath his fingers. "However, to get either one, you need the third." Stopping his digging, he beckoned Borutsch over.

Borutsch shambled over and stared into the shallow hole Bronstein had dug. "Oh, Lev," he said, his voice somewhere between awe and terror.

Inside the shallow depression, red-shelled and glowing softly with internal heat, lay a dozen giant eggs. Dragon's eggs.

"There's more," Bronstein said.

Borutsch tore his gaze from the eggs and looked around. Clumps of leaves and needles that had appeared part of the landscape before, now looked suspiciously handmade. Borutsch didn't bother to count them, but there were many.

"Oh, Lev," he said again. "You're going to burn the whole world."

The monk carried the child into his mother's apartments. The guards knew better than to block his way. They whispered to one another when he could not hear him, calling him "Devil's Spawn," and "Antichrist" and other names. But always in a whisper, and always in dialect, and always when he was long gone.

Rasputin went through the door, carrying the sleeping child.

The five ladies-in-waiting scattered before him like does before a wolfhound. Their high, giggly voices made him smile. Made him remember the Khlysts, with their orgiastic whippings. What he would give for a small cat-o'-nine-tails right now! He gazed at the back of the youngest lady, hardly more than a girl, her long neck bent over, swanlike, white, inviting. "Tell your mistress I have brought her son, and he is well, if sleeping."

They danced to his bidding, as they always did, disappearing one at a time through the door into the Tsaritsa's inner rooms, the door snicking quietly shut on the last of them.

After a moment, Alexandra came through the same door by herself, her plain face softened by the sight of the child in the monk's arms.

"You see," he told her, "the child only needs sleep and to be left alone, not be poked by so many doctors. Empress, you must *not* let them at him so." He felt deep in his heart that he alone could heal the child. He knew that the Tsaritsa felt the same.

He handed her the boy, and she took the child from him, the way a peasant woman would take up her child, with great affection and no fear. Too many upper-class women left the raising of their children to other people. The monk admired the Tsaritsa, even loved her, but desired her not at all, no matter what others might say. He knew that she was totally devoted to the Tsar, that handsome, stupid, lucky man. Smiling down at her, he said, "Call on me again, Matushka, Mother of the Russian People. I am always at your service." He bowed deeply, his black robe puddling at his feet, and gave her the dragon smile.

She did not notice but tucked the boy away in the bed, not letting a single one of her ladies help her.

As Rasputin backed away, he instinctively admired the Tsaritsa's form. She was not overly slim like her daughters, nor plump—*zaftik*, as the Jews would say. Her hair was piled atop her head like a dragon's nest, revealing a strong neck and the briefest glimpse of a surprisingly broad back.

Some peasant stock in her lineage somewhere? he thought, then quickly brushed the ungracious thought aside. *Not all of us have to raise ourselves from the dirt to God's grace. Some are given it at birth.*

The rest of her form was disguised by draping linens and silks, as the current fashion demanded, but the monk knew that her waist was capable of being cinched quite tight in the fashions of other times. Her eyes, the monk also knew, were ever so slightly drooping, disguising her stern nature and stubborn resolve—especially when caring for her only son.

She turned those eyes on him now. "Yes, Father Grigori? Do you require something of me?"

The monk blinked twice rapidly, realizing he'd been staring and that perhaps "desiring her not at all" was overstating things a touch.

"Only to implore you once more to keep the bloodsuckers away," he managed to say, covering his brief awkwardness with a bow. The Tsaritsa nodded, and the monk shuffled quickly out of the chamber.

Where is the girl with the swan's neck? he thought. *I should like to take these unworthy feelings out on her.* He rubbed his hands together, marveling at how smooth his palms had become during his time at court. *Perhaps it is not too late to find a whip.*

"Where did you get them? Where did they come from? What do you plan for them?" Borutsch's voice trembled slightly on the last phrase.

Bronstein felt a sudden urge to slap Borutsch. He'd had no idea his friend was so woman-nervous.

"Quiet yourself. We approach the *shtetl*."

Borutsch didn't answer, but took another quick sip of the *schnapps*.

"And if you say anything about . . . about what I have just showed you . . . anything at all . . . "

Bronstein's voice trailed off, but there was a hard edge to it, like nothing Borutsch had ever heard from him before. He took another sip of the *schnapps*, almost emptying the flask.

"I'll not speak of it, Lev," he said quietly. He tried for the *schnapps* again, but sloshed it over his shirtfront as Bronstein grabbed him roughly by the shoulders.

"You won't!" Bronstein almost hissed. His eyes seemed to gleam. "I swear to you, Borutsch. If you do . . . "

Borutsch bristled and shook himself free. "Who would I tell? And who would believe an old Jew like me? An old Jew with fewer friends in this world every day." He peered up at Bronstein and saw the manic light slowly dim in his eyes. But suddenly Borutsch realized that he feared his friend more than he feared any dragon. It was a sobering thought.

"I . . . I am sorry, Pinches." Bronstein took off his glasses. Forest dirt was smeared on the lenses. He wiped them slowly on his shirt. "I don't know what came over me."

"They say that caring for dragons can make you *think* like one. Make you think that choosing anything but flame and ruin is a weakness."

Shaking his head, Bronstein said, "No, it's not that. This world is untenable. We cannot wait upon change. Change must be brought about. And change does not happen easily." He frowned. "Or peacefully."

Borutsch took a deep breath before speaking. What he had to say seemed to sigh out of him. "The passage of time is not peaceful? And yet nothing can stand before it. Not men, not mountains. Not the hardest rock, if a river is allowed to flow across it for long enough."

"You make a good, if overeloquent point." Bronstein sighed. "But *he* would disagree."

Borutsch frowned as if the *schnapps* had turned sour in his mouth. "*He* is not here."

"But he will return. When the dragons hatch . . . "

Borutsch looked stunned. "You have shown him the eggs, too?"

Shaking his head, Bronstein said, "Of course, I have shown him the eggs."

"*If* they hatch, Lev. Do you know what this means?"

"Don't be an idiot. Of course I know what this means. And they will hatch. And I will train them."

Neither one of them had spoken above a whisper, as all the Jews of the area had long been schooled in keeping their voices down. But these were sharp, harsh whispers that might just as well have been shouts.

"What do you know about training dragons?"

"What does the Tsar know?"

"You are so rash, my old friend." It was as if Borutsch had never had a drop of the *schnapps*, for he certainly seemed cold sober now. "The Tsar has never trained a dragon, but his money has. And where will *you*, Lev Bronstein, find that kind of money?"

Bronstein laid a finger to the side of his nose and laughed. It was not a humorous sound at all. "Where Jews always find money," he said. "In other people's pockets."

Bronstein turned and looked at the morning sun. Soon it would be full day. Not that there was that much difference between day and night, this far north in the Russias in the winter. All was a kind of deep gray.

"And when I turn my dragons loose to destroy the Tsar's armies, *he* will return."

"If he returns," Borutsch shouted, throwing the flask to the ground, "it will be at the head of a German column!"

"*He* has fought thirty years for the revolution!"

"Not here, he hasn't. By now, Ulyanov knows less about this land than the Tsar's German wife does."

"He is Russian, not German. And he is even a quarter Jew." Bronstein sounded petulant. "And why do you not call him by the name he prefers?"

"Very well," Borutsch said. "Lenin will burn this land to the ground before saving it, just to show that his reading of Marx is more *oisgezeihent* than mine."

Bronstein raised his hand as if to slap Borutsch, who was proud of the fact that he didn't flinch. Then, without touching his friend at all, Bronstein walked away down the hill at a sharp clip. He did not turn to see if Borutsch followed or not, did not even acknowledge his friend was there at all.

"You don't need to destroy the army," Borutsch called after him. "They'd come over to us eventually." Bending over, he picked up the flask. Gave it a shake. Smiled at the reassuring slosh it still made. "Given the passage of time," he said more quietly. Bronstein was already out of earshot.

Borutsch wondered if he'd ever see Bronstein again. Wondered if he'd recognize him if he did. What did it matter? He was not going back to the *shtetl*; not going to cower in that burrow ever again; not going to drink any more cheap *schnapps*. "If there's going to be a war with all those dragons," he said to himself, "I will leave me out of it." He'd already started the negotiations to sell his companies. He'd take his family into Europe, maybe even into Berlin. It would certainly be safer than here when the dragon smoke began to cover all of the land. When the Tsar and his family would be as much at risk as the Jews.

I took the stairs two at a time. Coming around the corner on the floor where my apartments were situated, I told myself that it no longer mattered who was there with Ninotchka. Out they would go. I would send her to her room. Though I rarely gave orders, she knew when she had to listen to me. It's in the voice, of course. After I locked her in, I would send out invitations to those I knew were already against the monk. I counted them on my fingers as I strode down the hall. The Archbishop, of course, because Rasputin had called rather too often for the peasants to forgo the clergy and find God in their own hearts. The head of the army, because of the monk's antiwar passions. To his credit, the Tsar did not think highly of the madman's stance, and when Rasputin had expressed a desire to bless the troops at the front, Nicholas had roared out, "Put a foot on that sacred ground, and I will have you hanged at once!" I had never heard him be so decisive and magnificent before or—alas—since.

Perhaps, I thought, *I should also ask Prince Yusupov and Grand Duke*

Pavlovich, who have their own reasons for hating him. And one or two others. But another thought occurred to me. *Too many in a conspiracy will make it fail. We need not a net but a hammer, for as the old* babuschkas *like to say, "A hammer shatters glass but forges steel."*

I already knew that I would have my old friend Vladimir on my side. He had called out Rasputin in the Duma, saying in a passionate speech that the monk had taken the Tsar's ministers firmly in hand. How did he put it? Oh yes, that the ministers "have been turned into marionettes." That was a good figure of speech. I hardly knew he had it in him. A good man with a pistol, though.

But we would have to be careful. Rasputin was thought by the peasants to be unkillable. Especially after that slattern tried to gut him, calling him the Antichrist. She had missed her opportunity. Yes, her knife slid through his soft belly, and he stood before her with his entrails spilled out. But some local doctor pushed the tangled mess back in the empty cavity and sewed him up again.

Oh yes, he might be the very devil to kill.

And realizing that I'd made a joke—rare enough for me—I entered the apartments, giggling.

Ninotchka was alone, working on her sewing. She looked up, the blond hair framing that perfect heart-shaped face. "A joke, my darling?" she asked.

"A joke," I said, "but not one a man can share with his adorable wife." I cupped her chin with my right hand.

She wrinkled her nose. "You stink, my love. What *is* that smell?"

I had forgotten to wash the stench of dragon off my hands.

"It is nothing. I was talking to the horses that pull our carriage, reminding them of what sweet cargo they will have aboard tonight."

"Tonight?" The look in her eyes forgave me the stench. It was not the start of the Season, and she was growing feverish for some fun. I would take her to the Maryinski Theater and to dinner afterwards. And she would reward me later.

"I have planned a special treat out for us. It was to have been a surprise." It was amazing how easily the lie came out. "And now I have business," I added. "I beg you to go to your rooms. You and your women."

"Government business?" she asked, so sweetly that I knew that she was trying to find out some bit of gossip she could sell to the highest bidder. After all, I alone could not keep her in jewels. Later in bed, I would sleepily let out a minor secret. Not this one, of course. I am a patriot, after all. I serve the Tsar. Even though the Tsar has not lately served me at all.

I smiled back. "Very definitely government business."

After she went in, I locked the door from the outside. Then I sat at my desk and wrote my letters. Satisfied with the way I had suggested but never actually said what the reason for the meeting was, I called my man in to deliver them and to make a reservation at the Maryinski and *Chez Galouise,* the finest French restaurant in the city, for their last sitting. I knew I could trust Alexie completely. He, at least, would never shop me to my enemies. After all, I had saved his life upon three separate occasions. That kind of loyalty is what distinguishes a man from a woman.

Spring would break in Russia like the smiles of women Bronstein had known: cautious, cold, and a long time coming. But now they were in the deepest part of the winter. Snow lay indifferently on the ground, as if it knew that it still had months of discomfort to visit on the people, rich and poor alike. *But,* Bronstein told himself, *on the poor even more.* The peasants, at the bottom of the heap, might even have to tear the thatch from their roofs to feed the livestock if things got much worse.

He'd visited the eggs a dozen more times, going each visit by a different route and always brushing away his back trail carefully. He spent hours with the eggs, squatting in the cold, snowy field and talking out his plans as if the dragons could hear him. He had no one else to tell. Borutsch had fled to Berlin, and Bronstein feared that the old man had spilled his secret before leaving. But he spotted no one following him, and the eggs had never been disturbed.

But not this time.

Bronstein could see something was wrong as soon as he spotted the lightning-split pine. The ground beneath it was torn up, the leaves scattered. Running up to the tree, he gaped in horror at a hole in the ground that was completely devoid of eggs.

Mein Gott und Marx, he swore in silent German. *The Tsar's men have found them!*

There was no time to tear his hair or weep uncontrollably; he knew that he had to flee.

Perhaps I can join Borutsch in Berlin. If he'll have me.

Bronstein turned to run but was stopped cold by a rustling sound in the brush behind him.

Soldiers! he thought desperately. Reaching into his pocket and pulling out the small pistol he'd taken to carrying, he waved it at his unseen enemies before realizing how useless it would be against what sounded like an entire company of soldiers.

Swiveling his head from side to side as more rustling came from all around him, he came to a grim decision.

So this is how it ends.

The gun shook as he raised it to his temple.

"Long live the revolution!" he shouted, then winced. *Oh, to have not died with a cliché on my lips!*

His finger tightened on the trigger, then stopped just short of firing as a dragon the size of a newborn lamb—and just as unsteady on its feet—pushed through the bushes and into view.

"*Gevalt!*"

The dragon emitted a sound somewhere between a mew and a hiss and wobbled directly up to Bronstein, who took an involuntary step back. Even as a hatchling, the creature was fearsome to look at, all leathery hide and oversized bat wings, and came up to his knees. Its eyes were the gold of a full-grown beast, though still cloudy from the albumin that coated its skin and made it glisten in the thin forest light. He wondered if they would stay that color, or change, as babies' eyes do. He'd heard the Tsar's dragons had eyes like shrouds. Of course, the man who told him that could have been exaggerating for effect. And though the pronounced teeth that gave the adult dragons their truly sinister appearance had yet to grow in, the egg tooth at the tip of the little dragonling's beak looked sharp enough to kill if called upon. And the claws that scritch-scratched through the sticks and leaves looked even now as though they could easily gut a cow.

But Bronstein quickly remembered Lenin's advice.

Dragons respect only power. And fresh-hatched, you must be the only power they know.

So he pocketed the pistol that he still held stupidly to his head and stepped forward, putting both hands on the dragon's moist skin.

"Down, beast," he said firmly, pressing down. The beast collapsed on its side, mewling piteously. Grabbing a handful of dead leaves from the trees, Bronstein began scraping and scrubbing, cleaning the egg slime from the dragon's skin, talking the whole time. "Down, beast," and, "Stay still, monster!"

More dragons wandered out of the brush, attracted, no doubt, by the sound of his voice.

Perhaps, Bronstein thought, *they could hear me through their shells these last months.* Whether that was true or not, he was glad that he'd spoken to them all that while.

"Down!" he bade the new dragons, and they, too, obeyed.

As he scraped and scrubbed, Bronstein could see the dragons' color emerging. They were red, not black.

Red, like fire. Red, like blood.

Somehow that was comforting.

The mad monk had heard talk of dragons. Of course he'd often heard talk of dragons. But this time there was something different in the tenor of the conversations, and he was always alert to changes in gossip.

It had something to do with a red terror, which was odd, since the Tsar's dragons were black. But when his sources were pressed further—a kitchen maid, a bootboy, the man-boy who exercised the Tsar's dogs and slept with them as well—they couldn't say more than that.

Red terror! He tried to imagine what they meant, his hands wrangling together. It could mean nothing or everything. It could have nothing to do with dragons at all and everything to do with assassination attempts. A palace was the perfect place for such plots. Like a dish of stew left on the stove too many days, there was a stink about it.

But if there was a plot, he would know about it. He would master it. He would use it for his own good.

"Find me more about this red terror," he whispered to the kitchen maid, a skinny little thing with a crooked nose. "And we will talk of marriage." That he was already married mattered not a bit. He would find her a mate, and she knew it.

"Find me more about this red terror," he told the bootboy, "and I shall make sure you rise to footman." It was his little joke, that. The boy was not smart enough for the job he already had. But there were always ways to make the boy think he'd tried.

He said nothing more to the dog's keeper. As his old mother used to tell him: *A spoken word is not a sparrow. Once it flies out, you can't catch it.* He knew that the dog boy spoke in his sleep, his hands and feet scrabbling on the rushes the way his hounds did when they dreamed. Everybody listened in.

The truth that peasants speak is not the same as the truth that the powerful know. Having been one and become the other, the mad monk knew this better than most. He wrung his hands once more. "Find me more about this red terror," he muttered to no one in particular.

But even as he asked, he drew in upon himself, becoming moody, cautious, worried. Walking alone by the frozen River Neva, he tried to puzzle through all he'd heard. It was as if the world was sending him messages in code. He asked his secretary, Simanovich, for paper, and wrote a letter to the Tsar telling him of the signs and warning him, too. But he did not send it. It was too soon. Once he found out all about this red terror, he would personally hand the letter to the Tsar.

The red dragons were restless, snapping at their keepers and tugging at their leads. Bronstein tried to keep them in line—he was the only one they really listened to—but even he was having trouble with them tonight.

"Why do they act this way?"

"And why do you not stop them?"

The speakers were Koba and Kamo, two middlemen sent by Lenin to oversee the training of the beasts. Or the "Red Terror," as Lenin had dubbed them. That was so like Lenin, trusting no one. Not even his own handpicked men.

He'd told them nothing beside the fact that they would be underground. They'd assumed they were to be spies. And so they were, of a sort.

Bronstein couldn't tell Koba and Kamo apart. And he didn't like their manner: arrogance compounded by . . . by . . . He couldn't quite put his finger on it.

"The dragons are bred to the sky," he said archly, "and this stay underground irks them." He fixed one of them—the one with the slightly thicker moustache, *Koba, maybe*—with a glare. "And you may try to stop them if you wish."

Maybe-Koba looked at the dragons for a moment as if considering it. He didn't look hopeful. But he didn't look frightened either.

Bronstein snapped his fingers. That was it! Arrogance compounded by blind stupidity. They didn't know enough to be afraid of the dragons. Or of Lenin. *Or*—he thought carefully—*of me.*

"My apologies, Comrade Bronstein."

He didn't sound sorry. *The man is an entire library of negatives,* Bronstein thought.

Maybe-Koba went on. "We shall let you return to your work. Comrade Lenin will be here within days. Then we shall release the Red Terror to cleanse this land. Lenin has said it, and now I understand what he means. Come, Kamo."

Koba it is, then, Bronstein thought, adding aloud, "Cleanse it of what? Of Russians?"

Bronstein knew that Koba—or maybe Kamo. Did it matter?—had been a Georgian Social Democrat and nationalist, and, some whispered, a separatist before joining Lenin to free the entire working class. Some said that Koba—or maybe Kamo—still was. The fractures in the revolution made Bronstein's head hurt. Without realizing it, he rubbed his cigarette-stained fingers against his temples.

Koba stared at Bronstein with no trace of emotion on his face. "Of the Tsar. And his followers. Are you feeling ill?" As if a headache dropped Bronstein even further in his estimation.

There was something hard about Koba, Bronstein decided, like his innards were made of stone or steel rather then flesh and blood. But the men followed him. Followed him without question. Not that the men who followed Koba asked a lot of questions. They might fight for the workers, but they looked like idlers and ne'er-do-wells to Bronstein. Actually, they looked like thieves and murderers, and most likely anti-Semites, but sometimes those were the kind of men you needed.

Revolution was a dirty business.

He grunted. So was tyranny.

"I will provide the dragons, Koba, and you provide the men. And together we will *free* this land."

"Comrade Lenin will be here soon. He will say if there will be freedom or not. Make sure his dragons are ready."

With that, Koba turned and left, Kamo right behind.

Lenin's dragons? Bronstein's hand twitched. *Who stayed up nights with the beasts? Who imprinted them? Who fed them by hand?* How he would have loved to wring the necks of these interlopers. But that was not his way. Besides, one of the dragons chose that moment to bite the finger of a young man who was grooming him, and Bronstein had to run and help wrench the digit out of the dragon's mouth before it was swallowed.

Lenin will be here soon, he thought, smacking the dragon on the top of its stone-hard head until it opened its mouth. The finger was still on the creature's tongue, and Bronstein snatched it out before the jaws snapped shut. He tossed it to its bleeding and howling former owner before wiping his hands on his shirt. Perhaps the doctor could sew it back on. Perhaps not.

Fingers, dragons, revolutionaries, his thoughts cascaded. *There's no way we'll be ready in time.*

I had to admit, it was a masterful plan. Especially since my presence was necessary at its execution. I giggled at my play on words, and Ninotchka glanced at me coldly. Her face was as powdered as her hair, which made her look surprisingly old. And haggard.

"Did I say something to amuse you, my husband?"

She'd grown distant over the last weeks, probably due to my spending long hours pulling the threads of my plot together into a web that Father Grigori could not hope to escape. He could neither refuse the invitation nor survive the meal I had planned for him.

And I *would* be there. Nothing on Earth could keep me from seeing the look on his arrogant face as he realized who the architect of his destruction was. Did he think he could cuckold me without a response? I had destroyed better men than he in the service of the Tsar. Occasionally I had even killed them on the Tsar's orders. Not with my own hands, of course. But with a word in the right ear, with a bit of money passed carefully. Knowing the right men for such tasks *is* my job. And it seems that I am very good at what I do. If the monk's mad eyes seemed to look through me whenever we met in the palace halls—well, I would soon see them close forever.

"No," I said to Ninotchka. Having planned to dispose of Rasputin on her behalf, I now grew tired of her sniping. A man does what he must to protect his spouse, and if she is especially unappreciative of his efforts, he may very well find himself a new wife who is. "No, you say *nothing* that amuses me these days."

Taking pleasure in the wide-eyed look of surprise she gave me, I spun smartly on my heel and quick-marched from the sitting room, my boots tip-tapping a message to her with every step.

After all, I had a group of high-level men to shore up. Just in case . . . just in case the borscht-cum-poison didn't kill Rasputin on the first go-round.

A week later, in his apartment, Rasputin looked in the great mirror. He grimaced at his reflection, his teeth so white compared to the smiles of the peasants he had known. Brushing his fingers through his beard, he loosened a few scattered bits of bread stuck in the hairs. *Always go to a dinner full*, his mother had warned. *The hungry man looks like a greedy man.* He had no desire to look greedy to these men. Hard, yes. Powerful, definitely. But not greedy. A greedy man is considered prey.

"Prince Yusupov's house in Petrograd at 9," the invitation had read. He knew that Yusupov's palace was a magnificent building on the Nevska, though he'd never before been invited to dine there. He and the prince had parted company some time ago. He'd heard it had a great hall with six equal sides, each guarded by a large wooden door. This morning, after receiving the invitation, he'd played the cards and saw that six would be a number of change for him. He was ready. But then, he was *always* ready. Didn't he always carry a charm around his neck against death by a man's hand? He never took it off, not in the bathhouse, not in bed. A man with so many enemies had to be prepared.

And really, Yusupov is but a boy in man's clothing, Rasputin thought. *He got his place at court through marriage. He needs me more than I need him.* Still, going to the palace would give him the opportunity to meet the prince's wife, the Tsar's lovely niece, Irina of the piercing eyes. He had heard many things about her and all of them wonderful. Rasputin had not yet had the pleasure. *Well, it would be her pleasure, too.*

That dog, Vladimir Purishkevich, was picking him up in a state automobile. He supposed that he could abide the man for the time it took to drive to the prince's palace. Then he would turn his back and mesmerize the princess right there, in front of her husband and his friends. They'd make a game of it. But it would not be a game. Not entirely.

Really, he felt, *no one can stop me.* He began to laugh. It began softly but soon rose to almost maniacal heights.

A knock on the door recalled him to himself.

"Father Grigori," his man asked. "Are you choking?"

"I am laughing, imbecile," he answered, but gently, because the man had been with him since the days of the flagellants, and a man of such fervid loyalty could not be found elsewhere.

The door opened and Father Grigori's man shuffled in, hunched and slow. "My . . . apologies, Father," he stuttered. "But I have news." He hauled one of the dragon boys in with him. The boy had a nose clotted with snot, and he sniveled.

Rasputin waited, but the man said nothing more. *He really is an imbecile*, the mad monk thought. The boy said nothing, either. Waiting, Rasputin assumed, for a sign from his elders. And betters.

Raising an eyebrow, Rasputin finally cued the man. "And this news is . . ."

It was the boy who spoke, trembling, the clot loosened, snot running down towards his mouth. "Your Holiness, I . . . I have found the red terror."

Rasputin stood and waved them fully inside his chambers. "Quickly, quickly," he said. "Come in where we will not be overheard. And tell me everything."

"It is about dragons, Father, and there is a man called Lenin who will free them, but he will not be here until the month's end. Three days from now. When the moon is full. Only when he comes . . ."

"Dragons . . ." Rasputin's voice was calm, but underneath his heart seemed to skip a beat. Soon he would be able to tell the Tsar.

Shoring up my co-conspirators had been tougher work than I'd imagined it would be. *Really, they have no stomach for this stuff. Aristocrats are ever prepared to pronounce sentence but rarely willing to carry that same sentence out themselves.* Not that I liked to get my hands dirty, either—but if you really want something done, occasionally you have to be the one to do it. And these men wanted Father Grigori dead almost as much as I did. And now, a week later, they had knives in their boots and revolvers in their waistbands so they that could finish the job properly if needed. But I could not presume that they would actually use their weapons. Better to be prepared myself.

In just a few hours, the mad monk will be dead, I thought.

I practically skipped down the halls of the palace thinking about it. Though first I had a few administrative duties to deal with, afterwards I'd be there to watch Rasputin die.

Except instead of sitting down to drink a beet stew full of poison, that son of a Siberian peasant was marching quickly down the same hall as me dressed in his best embroidered blouse, black velvet trousers, and shiny new boots.

"Good evening, Father Grigori," I said as calmly as I could. *What is he doing here? He dare not insult the men I set him up with openly. Is he that arrogant? Or is he really that powerful?* My hands began to tremble, and I willed them to stop, to freeze.

Subtly, I put myself into his path, so that he would have to either pull up or plow me down. For a moment, I thought he was going to march right over me, but, at the last second, he stopped, looming above me, uncomfortably close. He smelled of cheap soap. I barely kept myself from wrinkling my nose.

"Out of my way, lackey," he said, eyes as cold as his mother's breast milk must have been. "I have important news for the Tsar."

I was close to panic. What news could he have to cause him to miss his dinner and insult me openly but that of my plans for him? I reached inside my jacket surreptitiously. Got my fingers on the hilt of a dagger I kept hidden there.

I may have to cut him down here in the hall, I thought. I wasn't sure I could. He was far bigger than I and certainly stronger, and if I missed with my first stroke, he could probably snap me in two with his huge peasant's hands.

"Why not give it to me to pass along then, Father," I said, hoping my voice didn't sound as querulous and weak to him as it did to me. "I assume by your outfit that you have somewhere else you must be?"

I was really just trying to buy some time. I needed to be just a few steps back, so that I would have room to draw steel, but not so far away as to be unable to close and strike. I had no idea what I might tell His Majesty to explain my murder of his wife's closest advisor in the halls outside his chambers. But tales could be fabricated, evidence planted. I was not terribly good with a knife, but I had skills in that other department.

But the knife will have to come out first.

With that in mind, I took a small step back and prepared to pull my blade.

But, surprisingly, the mad monk stood just a single moment in thought, then turned and spoke to me.

"You are right, my son. I have somewhere to be. Somewhere important. The Tsar, bless him, is probably already closeted with his beautiful wife. No man should be disturbed at such a time. I will speak to him in the morning after our prayers." He managed to pack information and insult in five short sentences before turning on his heel and marching away from me.

I stood and watched him disappear around a corner, sweat from my knife hand drip-dripping into my jacket.

My car followed Rasputin's, but not that closely. I did not want to frighten him off. As we were both going to Prince Yusupov's palace, and I knew where it was—well, didn't everybody?—I could take a slightly longer route.

I'd never actually been to the palace before. The prince was sole heir to the largest fortune in Russia, and I was certainly not in his set. But if I could help pull off this coup, perhaps he would reward me greatly. After all, he had tired of his old friend in carousal, Rasputin, who had gone with him to all the dubious nightclubs long before his marriage.

The prince had said quite plainly a year ago, "Will no one kill this *starets* for me?"

I hadn't known it then, but when I spoke of my own plan to Pavlovich, he brought me in on this one. Because of Pavlovich's extensive social calendar, the first time he was free was this evening, December 31. We didn't want him canceling any of his other engagements and thus arousing suspicion.

I felt marvelous to have been able to move the monk along and could not wait to hear their applause. It warmed me on such a cold night. I leaned forward and told my driver, "Faster! Faster now."

It was pitch-black outside, lit only by the car's lights illuminating the swirling snow. The driver had a heavy foot, and soon we approached the palace.

I went in the back way, as if a servant, as planned. One of the stewards took me down to the cellar room where the dinner was to be. I peeked out from behind the curtain. No one was there yet.

The cellar room was of gray stone with a granite floor. It had a low, vaulted ceiling. *Ah,* I thought, *it already feels like a mausoleum.* Only the carved wooden chairs, the small tables covered with embroidered cloths, and the cabinet of inlaid ebony indicated that it was a place of habitation by the living. A white bearskin rug and a brilliant fire in the hearth further softened the room's cemeterial aspect.

In the center of the room, a table was laid for six: the prince, the monk, Pavolovich, two other conspirators, and the prince's wife, who had been the bait to lure Rasputin to the place. Though he was not to know it, Princess Irina was off in the Crimea with her parents, not here.

I smiled. What a plot we have hatched! What a coil!

A samovar in the middle of the table was already smoking away, surrounded by plates of cakes and dainties. On the sideboard were the drinks, filled with poison, and the glasses, their rims soaked in poison as well. Dr. Lazovert had told me himself that each cake was filled with enough cyanide potassium to kill several men in an instant.

Several! We only wanted to dispatch *one.*

My smile grew larger. All was at the ready. As soon as Rasputin dropped, it would be my job to get the body out of there. But just in case he was slow to die, I had a pistol as well. And my knife.

From upstairs came the sound of music. I think it was "Yankee Doodle Dandy," that damned American song. The music was supposed to be part of a party that Princess Irina was throwing for some women friends before joining the men. I would have to hide again. They would soon be bringing Rasputin down.

I feared being found behind a curtain and situated myself on the other side of the wooden serving door. It had a small window. I could see but not be seen. Perfect.

And then the door opened, and in walked the mad monk himself, followed by a nervous-looking Prince Yusupov. I wanted to shout at him, "Stop sweating! You will give the game away." But we were already well into it. It would play as it would play. I shrank back for a moment, away from the window in the door, took a deep breath, and waited.

✡

Rasputin sauntered into the room, smiling. He could feel his body tingling, starting at his feet. That always meant something huge would happen soon. Perhaps Princess Irina would declare her love openly. Perhaps the prince would simply offer her to him.

But no—he preferred the chase, the slow seduction, the whimpering of the whipped dog that would be the prince. He must not jump the fence before it was close enough. His mother always said that. The old folk wisdom was true.

He touched the charm around his neck. The prince would hate him but could not harm him.

"Have some cakes," Prince Yusupov said, gesturing with a hand toward the table. There were beads of sweat on his forehead.

Rasputin wondered at that. It was, indeed, too warm down in the cellar, but he himself was not sweating.

"The cakes were made especially. Especially for you," Yusupov said.

And indeed, they were the very kind of he loved best. Honey cakes topped with crushed almonds, *skorospelki* covered with branches of fresh dill, caviar *blinis*, and so much more. But Rasputin did not want to appear greedy.

"Please," Yusupov said. "Irina had them made especially. We would not want her to be disappointed."

"No, we would not," Rasputin said, managing to make the four words sound both engaging and insulting at the same time. He picked up a honey cake and a *blini* and ate them, savoring the taste. Surprisingly, they were too sweet and dry. "Some Madeira, if you please," he told the prince.

Yusupov himself went to the sideboard and poured the wine with exquisite care into a glass.

The first glass went down quickly but barely moved the dry taste out of Rasputin's mouth. Forgetting that he didn't want to appear greedy, he held out the glass for refill.

Eagerly, the prince filled it for him.

"And the princess?" Rasputin said, after downing the second glass.

"Here shortly. She had to see off her own guests and change costume," Yusupov said.

"Ah, women," said the monk. "God bless them. My mother used to say, 'A wife is not a pot, she will not break so easily.' Ha-ha. But I would rather say, 'Every seed knows its time.'"

Yusupov started. "What do you mean by that? What do you mean?" He was sweating again.

Rasputin put his hand out and clapped Yusupov on the shoulder. "Just that women, God bless them, are like little seeds and know their own time, even though we poor fellows do not." He slashed a hand across his forehead. "Is it very hot in here?"

"Yes, very," said Yusupov using a handkerchief to wipe his own forehead.

"Well, sing to me then, to pass the time till your wife gets here," the monk said. He pointed to the guitar that rested against the wall. "I heard you singing often in those far-off days when we went into the dark sides of the city. I would hear you again. For old times' sake. And for your lovely wife Irina's."

Yusupov nodded, gulped, nodded again. Then he went over and picked the guitar. Strumming, he began to sing.

I could not believe my ears. Downstairs, someone was singing, slightly off-key. I moved back and peeked carefully through the window. Rasputin was still on his feet. There seemed to be cakes missing from the table. An empty glass stood on the table as well. And Yusupov, that damned upper-class clown, was strumming his guitar and singing. Had he gone faint with worry? Had he decided not to kill his old friend after all? I turned away from the sight, raced up the servants' stairs, and found Dr. L., Purishkevich, and Grand Duke Dmitri at the top of the stairs that led down to the cellar.

"For the Lord's sake, what is going on?" I asked, my voice barely more than a whisper. "To my certain knowledge, the man ate several cakes. And had a glass of wine."

"Two at least," said Dr. L. "We heard him ask for a refill. He is . . . " he whispered as well, "not a man at all, but the very devil. There was enough poison to fell an entire unit of Cossacks. I know; I put the stuff in it myself." He looked wretched and—as we watched—he sank into a stupor.

I took his hands and finally had to slap his face to revive him.

All the while we whispered together, Yusupov's thready voice, singing tune after tune, made its way up the stairs.

"Should we go down?" I asked.

"No, no, no," Purishkevich whispered vehemently, "that will give the game away."

"But surely he is already suspicious."

"He is a peasant," said the Grand Duke, which explained nothing.

I was a-tremble. After all we had planned, for it to come to this? *This, I thought, is the worst possible thing.* Oh, had I but known!

Suddenly the door to the cellar opened, and we all backed up, I the fastest. But it was just poor Yusupov, saying over his shoulder, "Have another cake, Father. I will see what is keeping my wife."

And Rasputin's voice, somewhat hoarsened, called up to him, "Love and eggs are best when they are fresh!"

"A peasant," the Grand Duke repeated, as Yusupov came up to find us.

If I was trembling, Yusupov was a leaf on a tree, all aflutter and sweating. "What should I do? What can I do?"

"He cannot be allowed to leave half-dead," Purishkevich said laconically.

The Grand Duke handed Yusupov a pistol. "Be a man." And Yusupov went back down the stairs, holding the pistol behind him.

We heard Rasputin call out, "For the Lord's sake, give me more wine." And then he added, "With God in thought, but mankind in the flesh."

A moment later we heard a shot. And a scream.

"Come," said the Grand Duke, "that will have done it."

I was not so sure, but in this company it was not my place to say. We ran down the stairs one right after another, the Grand Duke first, Dr. L. second. Purishkevich stayed behind.

The monk had fallen backward onto the white bearskin rug, his eyes closed.

Dr. L. knelt by his side, felt for his pulse. "He is dead."

But of course, that was premature, for not a moment later, Rasputin's left eye, then his right, opened, and he stared straight at Yusupov with those green eyes that reminded me of dragon eyes. They were filled suddenly with hatred. Yusupov screamed.

I could not move, nor could poor Yusupov. The Grand Duke was cursing under his breath. And I thought we were about to lose Dr. L. again.

"Long whiskers cannot take the place of brains," said Rasputin to the ceiling, and as he spoke, he began to foam at the mouth. A moment later, he leaped up, grabbed poor Yusupov by the throat, tore an epaulet from Yusupov's jacket.

Yusupov was sweating so badly that the monk's hand slipped from his throat, and Yusupov broke away from him, which threw Rasputin down on his knees.

That gave Yusupov time to escape, and he turned and raced up the stairs. He was screaming out to Purishkevich to fire his gun, shouting, "He's alive! Alive!" His voice was inhuman, a terrified scream the likes of which I'd never heard before or since.

The three of us watched as Rasputin, foaming and fulminating, and on all fours, climbed after him.

Prince Yusupov made it to his parents' apartments and locked the door after him, but the mad monk, maddened further by all that had happened to him, went straight out the front door. The rest of us followed him to see what he would do, Dr. L. muttering all the while that he was a devil and would probably sprout red wings and fly away.

But he was not flying; he was running across the snow-covered courtyard towards the iron gate that led to the street, shouting all the while, "Felix, Felix, I will tell everything to the Empress."

At last, Purishkevich raised his gun and fired.

The night seemed one long, dark echo. But he had missed.

"Fire again!" I cried. If Rasputin got away, we were all dead men.

He fired again and, unbelievably, missed once more.

"Fool!" the Grand Duke said as Purishkevich bit his own left hand to force himself to concentrate.

When he fired a third time, the bullet struck Rasputin between the shoulders, and he stopped running though he did not fall.

"A devil, I tell you!" cried the doctor.

"I am surrounded by fools," the Grand Duke said, and I was inclined to agree with him.

But Purishkevich shot one last time, and this one hit Rasputin in the head, and he fell to his knees. Purishkevich ran over to him and kicked him hard, a boot to the temple. At that, the monk finally fell down prostrate in the snow.

Suddenly Yusupov appeared with a rubber club and began hitting Rasputin hysterically over and over and over again.

The Grand Duke took hold of Yusupov's shoulders and led him away.

Only then did I take out my knife and plunge it deep into Rasputin's heart. I wanted to say something, anything, but there was nothing more to say.

A servant came out a little later with a rope, and we pulled the body to the frozen Neva and left it there.

"Should we find a hole and push him in?" I asked.

"Let the world see him," the Grand Duke said. "Dead is dead."

I looked at the mad monk splayed out on the ice and wondered at that. By my count, he should have died five times tonight before my knife decided the thing. But, "Dead is dead," I agreed with the Grand Duke, and left him lying there.

I went home but could not scrub away the feel of my hand touching his back, the knife going deep into his body.

"It is ended," I told my image in the mirror. But it had only begun.

The mad monk lay on the ice. His back hurt abominably where the knife had plunged in. He couldn't move.

"I curse you," he muttered, or tried to. His lips were frozen shut, and anyway, he wasn't sure whom he should be cursing, not knowing who had set the blade deep in his back. Instead, he cursed his old drinking companion, his betrayer.

Felix, may you lose all that is dear to you.

His shoulder and the back of his head hurt, too, though not as badly, Oddly enough his stomach and throat were burning as well. He wondered if the cakes—how many had he eaten?—had disagreed with him. *Trust the* prvidvorny, *the courtiers, to make stale and rotten cakes. His own mother could have done better.*

He was cold, but he had been colder. The Lord knew how cold a *muzhik* from Siberia could get without succumbing. He was wearing his charm, so men couldn't kill him. Nor women, it turned out. The whore who had slit him from stem to sternum had learned that. He would survive this.

But he could not move.

How long till the full moon? he thought. *How long till that fool Lenin arrives and lets the dragons out of their hole?*

Dragons, when caught in their lairs, can be drowned, starved out, slaughtered by massed rifle fire—in fact, killed in any number of ways. It was why the Tsar's dragons' stables were better guarded than his own home. In the skies, they were unstoppable: swift fire from the night skies and death to all who stood against them, like Jews and revolutionaries. But not now.

The fools haven't killed me. But if I don't recover before the moon is full, they will have killed Russia.

He tried to twitch a finger, blink an eyelid. Nothing.

I must rest. I will try again in the morning.

The moon rose over the frozen Neva, a near-perfect circle.

I have perhaps two days, he thought, his mind perfectly clear. *Maybe three.*

The red dragons were no longer restless, because, for the first time, they'd been led up into the night air. Long noses sniffed at the sky; wings unfurled and caught the slight breeze. But they were not loosed to fly. Not yet. Not till Lenin gave the word.

The man in question, who had arrived just the night before, stood watching the dragons critically. Bronstein knew that the Bolshevik leader had never seen dragons before tonight, but he was showing neither awe nor fear in their presence. On the contrary, he was eyeing them critically, one hand stroking his beard.

"You are sure they will function, Leon?"

Lenin meant him, Bronstein. He insisted on calling Bronstein by his revolutionary name. Bronstein realized just now that he didn't much care for it. It was an ugly name, *Leon. And Trotsky sounds like a town in Poland.* He wondered how soon he could go back to the name he'd been born with. And he thought at the same time that taking revolutionary names was like a boys' game. *Such silliness!*

"Leon!" Lenin snapped. "Will they function?"

"I . . . I do not know for sure," Bronstein said, too quickly, knowing that he should have lied and said that he was certain. "But they are the same stock as the Tsar's dragons," he added. "And those function well enough."

Bronstein was certain of that at least. He'd traced the rumor of a second brood bred from the Great Khan's dragons with the thoroughness of a Talmudic

scholar. Traced the rumor through ancient documents detailing complex trea-
ties and Byzantine trades to a kingdom in North Africa. Traced it by rail and
camel and foot to a city that drought had turned to desert when the pharaohs
were still young. Traced it with maps and bribes and a little bit of luck to a patch
of sand that hadn't seen a drop of rain in centuries.

Then he'd dug.

And dug.

And dug some more.

He dug till he'd worn through three shovels and done what he was sure was
irreparable damage to his arms and shoulders. Dug till the sun scorched the
Russian pall from his face and turned it to dragon-leather. Dug till the desert
night froze him colder than any Russian would ever care to admit.

Dug till he found the first new dragon eggs in over 120 years. The Tsar's
dragon queen hadn't dropped a hatch of eggs in a century, nor was she likely
to anytime soon. And even if she did, it would be years before the eggs would
hatch.

Dragon eggs weren't like other eggs. They didn't need warmth and heat to
bring forth their hatchlings. They were already creatures of fire; they needed a
cool, damp place to develop.

Nothing colder and wetter than a Russian spring, Bronstein knew. So he'd
brought them home in giant wooden boxes and planted them on the hillside
overlooking his town, doing all the work himself.

Another thing that set dragon eggs apart: they could sit for years, even
centuries, until the conditions were right to be born.

"And some would say," Bronstein said to Lenin, "they should be more
powerful, having lain in their eggs for so much longer."

Lenin stared at him blankly for a moment, then turned to Koba. "Are your
men ready?"

Koba grinned, and his straight teeth reflected orange from the fire of a
snorting dragon. The handler calmed the beast as Koba spoke.

"Ready to kill at my command, Comrade."

Lenin turned a stern gaze at the moon as if he could command it to rise
faster. Koba glanced at Bronstein and grinned wider.

A dragon coughed a gout of flame, and Koba's eyes reflected the fire. Bronstein
looked into those eyes of flame and knew that if he let Koba loose his men before
Bronstein launched his dragons, then he had lost. There would be no place for
him in the new Russia. The land would be ruled by Georgian murderers and
cutthroat thieves; new *kruks* to replace the old, and the proletariat worse off
than before. Not the Eden he'd dreamed of. And the Jews? Well, they, of course,
would be blamed.

"Lenin," Bronstein said, as firmly as he could. "The dragons are ready."

"Truly?" Lenin asked, not looking back. "Yes, Comrade."

Lenin waited just a beat, nothing more, then said, "Then let them fly."

Bronstein nodded to Lenin's back and practically leaped toward the dragons. "Fly!" he shouted. "Let them fly!"

The command was repeated down the line. Talon boys dashed bravely beneath broad, scaly chests to cut the webbings that held the dragons' claws together.

"Fly!" Bronstein shouted, and the handlers let slip the rings that held the pronged collars tight to the dragons' necks before scurrying back, as the beasts were now free to gnash and nip with teeth the size of scythe blades.

"Fly!" the lashers shouted as they cracked their long whips over the dragons' heads. But the dragons needed no encouragement. They were made for this. For the night sky, the cool air, the fire from above.

"Fly," Bronstein said softly, as giant wings enveloped the moon, and the Red Terror took to the skies.

Fifty yards away, Lenin turned to Koba. "Release your men to do their duty, as well." And Koba laughed in answer, waving his hand.

Bronstein saw Koba's men scurry away and knew for certain that Russia was lost. Releasing the dragons was a mistake; releasing Koba's men a disaster. Borutsch had been right all along.

It will be years before we struggle free from these twin terrors from land and sky. What I wanted was a clean start. But this is not it.

He shivered in the cold.

I need warmth, he thought suddenly. By that he did not mean a stove in a tunnel, a cup of tea, *schnapps. I want palm trees. Soft music. Women with smiling faces. I want to live a long and merry life, with a* zaftik *wife.* He thought of Greece, southern Italy, Mexico. The dragon wings were but a murmur by then. And the shouts of men.

In the blackness before dawn, the mad monk's left index finger moved. It scraped across the ice and the slight *scritching* sound it made echoed loud and triumphant in his ears.

He'd lain unmoving for three days.

A peasant child had thrown rocks at him on the second day, trying to ascertain whether the drunk on the ice was alive or dead. The mad monk was surprised when the child didn't come out on the ice and loot his body. But then he realized why.

The ice was melting.

The days had grown warmer, and the ice was melting. Soon, the mighty Neva would break winter's grip and flow freely to the Baltic Sea once more. Icy water was already pooling in his best boots and soaking his black velvet trousers. It splashed in his left ear, the one that lay against the ice, and he thought that he could feel it seeping through his skin to freeze his very bones.

Terror crept in with the cold as he realized that his attempted murderers would not need to kill him. The river would do their work for them. Drown him, as his sister had drowned, or cause him to waste away in fever, like his brother. He would have shivered with fear or cold, but he could not move.

Night fell, and, for the first time, Father Grigori felt the terror of the mortals he'd ministered to. Through the night, he felt like Jesus on the cross, his iron faith wavering. *Why hast thou forsaken me?*

The night brought no answer, just more cold water in his boots.

But then, before dawn, the finger moved.

If one finger can move, the rest can move as well.

And putting thought to deed, he moved the index finger on his other hand. Moved it as if he'd never been hurt, tapping it on the ice, once, twice, a third time. His spirits soared as the sun broke the horizon, and, with a great effort, he bent up at the waist, levering himself to a sitting position. He was sore. He was cold. Every bit of his body ached. But he was alive. And moving!

However, he was also very tired, and he decided not to try to stand quite yet. Facing the rising sun, he waited for the heat to reach him.

"When I am warmed straight through," he said, his voice calm despite the creaking and popping of his stiff limbs, "I shall go ashore and deal with Felix and the others."

Watching the sun rise and turn from red to gold, he saw a flock of birds pass before it. A big flock of birds, not just in size, but in number, hundreds of them, casting long shadows across the ice.

What are those? he thought. *Egrets leaving their roost?* But it was winter. There were no egrets here.

And the birds were too big. Even from far away, he could tell that they were huge. Suddenly, he knew that he was too late. He'd lain on the ice too long, and Lenin had come to loose the Red Terror on the land.

Now staring in horror, he watched the flock move closer, revealing red scales and leathery wings, smoke curling from their nostrils. He made a small cry, like a rabbit in extremis, and struggled to stand. But the movement that had come so easily just moments ago was a trial now. His limbs cried in protest and refused to budge. Despite straining and sweating, he'd only achieved an ungainly half crouch when the dragons were upon him.

The lead dragon swooped in low and swatted him aside with its forefoot. He went skittering across the ice, feeling his ribs shatter. Crawling for the shore, he dragged himself along far too slowly, and his fingernails broke on the ice. Finally—*finally*—he was able to shiver. But this was in fear. He no longer felt cold. Terror rushed hot in his blood.

A shadow enveloped him, and he looked up into the black eyes of a hovering dragon. Before he could react, the dragon's talons shot toward him, and one long claw pierced him through the chest, pinning him to the ice. It looked as if it were laughing at him, its teeth filling its horrible great mouth. He tried to scream, but suddenly he had no breath. Lungs pierced, he could only stare stupidly as the dragon's wing beats slowed and it landed on the ice beside him, as gently as any songbird.

But the dragon was no songbird, and the ice shattered under its weight. Water splashed the beast's belly, and it roared its displeasure, flapping madly, trying to get aloft. Then it belched out a lash of fire, which further melted the ice around itself and the ice below Rasputin. When the dragon managed to lift out of the water, it slowly shook itself free of water and prey at the same time. The wind from the dragon's wings was so strong that it pushed Father Grigori Rasputin over the melting edge of ice and down into the dark water.

We have put a rope through the nose of Leviathan, he thought as the leaves closed over his head. He could still see the dragons, distorted by the water, hovering over the hole in the ice like terns. *But he is king over all the sons of pride.*

And then, like his sister, Maria, so many years before, Father Grigori drowned.

I did not wake Ninotchka. All was falling apart. She would need her sleep.

Prying open the old desk where I keep my treasures—the key was long lost—I filled my pockets with gold coinage, my real certificate of birth, my other papers, several strands of rare pearls, my mother's diamonds, my father's gold watch and fob. I would leave my wife with what paltry jewels she had. She would need them. Alas, the Tsar would not look kindly on me and mine once the story of the mad monk's death came out. And come out it would. Servants can be forced to tell what their masters will not. Better that I leave Ninotchka to what fate her beauty could buy her.

As for me, I would cross the line, find the men who held the new reins of terror. Who knows if the Tsar will even last through this time? The wheel turns and turns again. Revolution is a messy business. Yet, there is always a need for a good functionary, a secretary, a man of purpose. I'd always known I was the first two, and now I know I can be hard, too. I can kill. My hand can wield a knife. Yes, I am someone who has much to offer, to *muzhik* or Tsar. And I will let it be known—I work equally well with men and with dragons.

Going East

Elana Gomel

July 17, 1941

I'm going east. I may be excused for feeling slightly nervous. A strange phrase is haunting me: "A poisonous wind from the east that blows no good." The phrase is trailing a billowing, yellow cloud.

July 20, 1941

The smell of ashes is in the air. This place is a shambles. There was a dead cat in the street, emaciated, with patchy ginger fur falling out in clumps. Laura used to work on a crappy wall hanging of two kittens playing with a ball; not in the best of tastes, but she never finished it anyway.

Cats have no loyalty and no race: they are all the same. Unlike dogs and people.

August 3, 1941.

Yesterday I went over the draft of my research paper. Not bad at all! Overly ambitious perhaps but all advances in science begin with impossible dreams. If I can prove, scientifically prove, that races are indeed different species, what a boost this will give to our enterprise! (Not to mention my own career taking off!) I know I'm right. All I need is a tangible proof.

August 5, 1941

The weather is horrible; wind and lashing rain. Kremer tells me that the best way of overcoming the nausea that seizes me when I see corpses is to keep looking. Then it becomes a habit.

August 10, 1941

I have torn up Father's letter. It's a miracle that it passed the censor. What was the old fool thinking?

"You are destroying everything I have dedicated my life to studying and understanding," he writes. "How can you do it? You grew up with medieval Hebrew manuscripts and rare Yiddish chapbooks. Have you forgotten it all? Do you remember what happened when you were six, when I received my Jewish Studies appointment at Leipzig? Your mother baked cookies with Hebrew letters on them to celebrate. You ate the letter 'Aleph' straight from the oven and burned your mouth.

. . . Now you burn books. How soon will you begin to burn people?"

Sooner than you know, Father. But this is what you have never understood, will never understand: they are not people.

Yes, I remember the cookie. And I remember how you locked yourself in your study and pored over those spidery alien letters while we survived on potato peel and ersatz coffee. Your family starved but you had money for your books!

Well, no matter. My parents have bequeathed me the only inheritance that matters: the purity of my blood. Blood is everything; letters—nothing.

October 20, 1941.

A limited action today. The Jews have to be sorted out. The chaos can no longer be endured.

The Jews were ordered to gather in the market square. Lists had been made of the skilled workers and their families. Those were separated from the rest, the unproductive population. Of course, it all degenerated into a complete mess. Cries, screaming, stench . . . Finally, Kremer had a bright idea and told everybody to lie face down on the ground.

The site was in the woods, some distance away. The people marched in surprising quiet. Their screeching stopped once they started moving. We drove past them but suddenly I told my driver to stop.

On the edge of the column walked a young woman who, all my anthropological instincts told me, was a pure Aryan. Disregarding the grumbling of the policemen, I pulled her aside and examined her. Slender, long-legged, dolichocephalic, light gray eyes, almost white hair, straight narrow nose. I did not want to remove her clothing in the presence of the jeering policemen but I had no doubt that I would find all the markers of Nordic femininity: small upright breasts, clear division between the thorax and the pelvis, long firm thighs.

"What are you doing here?" I said indignantly. "You don't belong with them!"

She replied in Viennese German.

"I do."

And she thrust her documents at me. According to them, she was Lila Sara Schwartz, originally from Vienna, relocated to the General Government of Poland in 1940. Her second name was a giveaway: according to the law of 1938 it was added to the names of all female Jews.

Documents may be forged but the body does not lie!

"Get into the car!" I commanded.

The local policemen snickered but I paid no attention. How can sub-humans like them understand a scientist's dedication?

The woman, Lila, obeyed and we drove on until we came to the place. The ground was covered with what seemed to be drifts of snow. In fact it was shredded documents and paper money; the Jews were tearing them up, God knows why. There was a smell of pine resin in the air. Everything seemed to be peaceful and orderly compared to the mess at the gathering point.

Kremer staggered away from the ditch and was sick.

Some people prayed but not many. An old man stood before me, his stomach flabby, grizzled hair covering his chest. He said: "What do you want from me? I'm only a composer."

October 21, 1941.

I did the anthropometric measurements of Lila. Beautiful, she is very beautiful.

I gave her some food, which she ate daintily despite her malnutrition. Seeing this only confirmed my belief that she is human.

I sat her in front of me and demanded to know why she pretended to be a Jew. To put her at ease, I added (perhaps incautiously):

"You can be open with me. I know how one can be beguiled by them. My own father, pure Aryan that he is, is . . . was a Hebraist."

She knew what it meant, which supported my theory that she is an educated woman, somehow ensnared by their alien wiles. But her reaction was disconcerting. She laughed.

"A Hebraist?" she repeated. "So you must be a real authority on Jews."

"I know some things," I replied huffily. "Enough to see that you're not one of them."

"So who am I? One of you?"

"Undoubtedly. Science is infallible."

"But scientists aren't. What if I am a half-breed?"

"A Mischling? Still, since your Aryan blood obviously predominates, you're entitled to life. Perhaps you can be sterilized . . . "

She laughed again, showing those perfectly even, sugar-white teeth. The only flaw in that beautiful face is its color, or rather the lack of it: her skin, her eyebrows and lashes, even her eyes, seem to be bleached. But suddenly her transparent irises sparked with icy, diamond lights and I felt a strange slow shiver go through me. I did not immediately realize what it was.

"Sterilize me?" she said mockingly. "Well, that would be quite a feat! Do you know how many children I've already borne?"

She must be mad; that explains it all. But I was not at this moment concerned with her mental state for I knew what was happening to me, my body presenting me with an irrefutable proof, no matter how horrified and disgusted my mind was.

I snatched up my gun, pushing it under her chin. But as my finger tightened on the trigger, a liquid instability washed over her face and for a moment I saw Laura's blue eyes look into mine, and her soft pink lips go white with fear. I dropped the gun.

"Go away!" I screamed.

For a moment everything went black and when I came to my senses, she was gone. I questioned my orderly: he claims he had not seen anybody.

[Later that night]

I've given most of my *schnapps* to Kremer but I have one emergency bottle left. A man is entitled to oblivion after such a dream.

There was a red steaming sea in it, languidly lapping at the pinkish shore.

There was a woman coming out of the sea, her body diamond-shiny, diamond-sharp.

She bent down, so that her white hair covered her face, and pulled a baby from between her thighs. She lifted it into the air. It didn't cry; it smiled, and she dropped it into the red sea and it floated peacefully on its viscous swell. And with every step she was bringing forth more and more babies.

My orderly came in when he heard my shriek, stupid idiot! I told him it was a nightmare. A childhood nightmare. An SS officer has to be civil, even to his underlings.

The worst thing is that if it becomes known, the comrades will think the strain of the action is to blame. They will see me as a weakling, a crybaby.

I did not lie. It is indeed a childhood dream. I first had it after Father had received his appointment in Leipzig. I was too small to realize the shame of his profession. But big enough to be frightened by those poisonous Talmudic tales he told me, the tales of Lilith, a vampire succubus, Adam's first wife, who does not share in the curse of the exile from Eden.

They say she gives birth to a hundred babies each day. Enough to fill the world with her litter, imitation people. To make them, she steals men's sperm. She is so beautiful no man can resist her.

How could he do it? Poisoning my mind with this Jewish trash . . .

March 15, 1942

Laura and I are married.

November 21, 1942

I woke up with a terrible hangover. Never again!

Yesterday I had to assist the police forces of the town named Talnoe. They wanted a racial expert to examine the children of mixed marriages.

The Russian and Ukrainian women with their offspring were locked up in three rooms of the local school when I arrived. There were about a hundred people. Even a cursory examination of the children (ages 0-15) confirmed my theory. I pointed out the specimens I wanted to add to my collection and the commandant—unfortunately, I forgot his name—immediately agreed to ship them to my headquarters after processing.

A woman was sitting quietly in the corner, holding a sleeping toddler. A typical Ukrainian peasant, large, raw-boned, with puffed-up weepy eyes. I diagnosed trachoma.

"Is this your child?" I asked through the translator.

"No," she replied unexpectedly in decent German but with a harsh, grating accent. "I'm his nurse."

The child woke up when I took him but did not cry. He was relatively plump but his coordination was deficient. Nevertheless, his expression seemed almost adult and he looked at me as if he understood who I was.

"I want him too," I said to the commandant and then told the nurse she could go home.

"You are taking them to the local slaughterhouse," the nurse said. I did not know where the designated site was but the translator nodded. She smiled. Her teeth were sugar-white, perfect, and horrible in that dusky seamed face.

"Release the mothers," she said. "I will stay with the children."

I was suddenly aware that the hubbub of shrill voices had died out. Everybody was looking at us: the mothers, clutching their spawn; the local policemen; the two SS men.

"Do as she says," I ordered.

She addressed the mothers in Ukrainian. I don't know what she said; the translator later claimed not to have heard. And the women, who had been tearing their hair and banging their heads on the wall, got up quietly, one by one, kissed their children, and went out. None of the children cried as they clustered around the nurse.

I don't know what prompted me to do it. I had my lunch with me, a hunk of rye bread and a piece of salted pork wrapped in a newspaper. I offered it to the nurse.

She looked at me but did not touch the food and I felt a strange burning in my eyes, as if her disease had communicated itself to me.

"You should know better than offer me salt, Untersturmführer," she said. "The children are quiet now. Do you want them to start crying again?"

I stared at her stupidly. I don't know how long I would have stood there, destroying my self-respect as a German officer, had not the translator tugged at my hand. It is an index of how lost I was that I was actually grateful to him.

In the morning the policemen took the children to the slaughterhouse where they were terminated. They went quietly and without fear. The nurse refused to be parted from them. She was terminated too.

Why should I be surprised that she knew the legend? This is where they all originated, those venomous, debilitating, polluting superstitions, here, in the miasma of the *shtetl*. It is not surprising at all that she knew the legend of the *astri*, a ghostly nurse who takes care of orphans. The *astri*'s true face, monstrous and ape-like, is only revealed when she is forced to taste salt.

This was the only story I had liked as a child.

February 5, 1943

Laura is pregnant! Finally! I can confess now that I had started worrying . . . An SS officer whose wife is childless can kiss his career goodbye. But everything is going to be fine now.

Her letter was less enthusiastic than I expected: vague fears, feminine shilly-shallying and damp hints of depression. I wrote back to her immediately, trying to sound reassuring but firm. I am a little disappointed in her.

I am going to call my son Günter, a good Germanic name.

March 12, 1943

Today we are cleaning up the "small ghetto." No exemptions this time, no skilled workers to preserve, no Mischlinge to beg for mercy. Everybody, everybody must go!

The sky is feverish-bright with the reflection of fires. There are no more than three thousand Jews left but somehow this action seems to be going on forever.

I have been handing out triple doses of sleeping pills. We are overtaxed and undermanned; there are too many of them.

In the morning I walked along the main street. The snow was gray with red veins. The pavement looked as if a giant garbage bin had been upended over the entire town. Rags and open purses trampled into the slush; a dirty baby shoe; a pacifier; a rat; a half-eaten apple.

Suddenly I noticed a scatter of black spiders crawling on the sidewalk. I stopped and looked down: these were twisted Hebrew letters, a large "Aleph" among them.

I fairly jumped up. Fortunately, nobody saw me tiptoeing around the Jewish gravestones that Kremer had ordered to be used for pavement. Eventually I got a grip upon myself and walked straight. The writing was obscured by the dirty slush anyway.

The burial crew sat on the sodden ground, guarded by Klemke. One of them looked at me. Arkady, a stonemason by trade.

"My wife, son, and daughter are dead," he said, painstakingly stringing German words together. It is horrible to hear them speak; as if a mouse in a mousetrap addressed you with a plea for mercy. Klemke barked something and pulled the trigger, striking the iron fence a couple of meters away.

"Stop it, you idiot!" I yelled.

The fence consists of dense ironwork perched on widely spaced stone pillars. The ironwork ends about twenty-five centimeters off the ground. I heard shuffling at the same time as I saw the heads of mounted policemen appear above the fence. I idly watched the feet passing by, trying to guess their owners' sex and age. It was not difficult. The gaping shoes of old men held together by twine; the dainty sandals of girls, the toes curling inwards from the cold; the pomponed booties of children, their bright colors dimmed by dirt. And then I saw something else.

Mixed into this procession of feet that crawled past me like a weird caterpillar were bare extremities so deformed they appeared scarcely human. They resembled a bird's scaled talons, except they were of a size no living bird could match. Grayish or sand-colored, with a rudimentary spur, they scratched the pavement as their owners passed along the fence. There was more than one pair.

"Halt!" I yelled and run to the gate.

The column dissolved into a confused melee, the people turning to watch me with wild or apathetic eyes. The policemen grumbled. But I was not to be deterred. I ordered the prisoners to stand in a row and went along, examining their feet. I did not care that I must have looked like a crazed Prince Charming looking for his Cinderella. I looked for something far more beautiful: scientific truth.

I reached a slender youth and stopped before him. Dark curly hair, thick lips, a typical Oriental physiognomy. He was barefoot and his feet, heavily splattered with mud, looked no different from everybody else's. But as I looked at him, something peculiar happened, a moment of double vision, as if a different body flickered into being, superimposed itself upon this young vermin, his real body that was in no way human.

I told him to stand aside and went on. Passing twice along the row, I discovered three more: two women and a boy. I told the policemen to proceed with their task and took the specimens to the dissecting room.

One of the females was a girl of about sixteen, the other an older woman, between thirty and thirty-five. The boy was about six. They all appeared undernourished and suffering from skin diseases. As ordinary a group of Jews as one is likely to encounter, with nothing to distinguish them from their racial brethren. But I knew what I had seen and my heart was racing wildly in presentiment of a major discovery.

I gestured the policeman out of the room and addressed the four as they stood against the wall, nude, with their crossed hands covering their genitals.

"I know who you are," I said, not bothering with the pretense that they could not understand my German. "I have penetrated your disguise. I am the first one to see what the Führer has divined in his genius: that the Jews are shape-shifters, alien parasites taking on a human form to deceive and destroy. If you tell me how you do it; how you manage to adhere to your form even after death, maddening our soldiers; how you insinuate yourself into our families, mate with our women; I will let the four of you live. In fact, I guarantee you will survive as precious proofs of the rightness of our cause. You will not be allowed to breed, of course, but you will be well taken care of. I give you my word."

They exchanged glances. And oh, how my heart drummed when the girl addressed me in my own language, a fluent, beautiful speech, and yet tinged with something indescribably alien, as if a rock or a tree cried out in human voice.

"You are destroying our people anyway," she said. "What proof do you need?"

"I want to know the truth!" I responded.

"The truth is in the eye of the beholder," said the child.

"No!" I protested. "The truth is absolute and I have dedicated my life to serving it."

"Is this why you take the lives of others?" asked the youth.

"I take no human lives!" I cried. "I'm not a murderer! Show me who you really are! Show me your true faces!"

"You've tasted the sweetness of the letter," said the woman. "You may see."

A strange shudder went through the four of them, a ripple as if the ice-cold air in the room suddenly boiled with heat haze. And then they began to change. Their flesh flowed together like mud, off-white and pink, the gleaming bones poking momentarily through the viscous flood, and then the streams separated and crawled up the bony frames like a congeries of fat snakes, interweaving and clothing the skeletons anew.

Their trunks retained a roughly human appearance, but the skin was of a dead pinkish-gray, thick and pitted like orange peel. The overall impression was of the bodies melted down and congealed in random shapes. But below the hips even this residual humanity was lost: the trunks were perched on scrawny chicken-like legs and splayed fleshless feet with curving talons, scrabbling in the dust on the floor.

Their faces . . . Scaled skin tightly stretched across deformed skulls, lash-less watery eyes with a brilliant, icy flame burning in each pupil, slit-like mouths, stretched open by pointed fangs. And yet, the most horrifying thing was precisely the degree to which they retained their deceptive individuality, so that one could still recognize in these beastly masks a young girl's sullen prettiness, a woman's tired resignation, a teenager's desperate courage, a child's pathetic bewilderment.

I surveyed this ultimate proof of the rightness of our cause, this acquittal from the charge, which I had never quite dared naming to myself. This was the moment of justification. But such is the deviousness of the enemy that precisely at that moment I was overcome by a shameful, unmanning flood of pity. I pitied them in their monstrous nakedness as I had not pitied the women, the children, the old men, the babies, the wounded soldiers, Arkady with his dead family, the bullet-riddled mother buried with her living son . . .

"You recognize us," said the woman. "You know who we are."

"Of course! You are Jews!"

"No, we are Jews' nightmares. We are the demons of the people you're destroying. We have preyed upon them for millennia. We have been nourished by their fears; we have eaten their desires. But now their fears and desires are ashes. Your madness is consuming our people like a raging fire. And we have to go down with them, to be their comfort in darkness, for they have no other."

"I don't believe in demons!" I cried. "It's another of your filthy deceits. But science will dispel your lies! Science will reveal you for what you are!"

"You don't believe in demons, Klaus?" said the boy. "How come? You believed in us well enough after you ate a cookie with an Aleph on it. Don't you remember me? I used to be your playmate, little Klaus. I used to come at night and we'd play hide-and-seek. Don't you remember how you spread flour on the bedroom's floor one night and next morning there was a giant chicken's footprint in it? But Father didn't believe you, he laughed at you, and you were so angry you tore up one of his Hebrew manuscripts. He spanked you. And afterwards you didn't want to play with me, little Klaus, you turned away and threw a pillow at me when I came in . . ."

I don't know how my gun leapt into my hand. I don't know how I pulled the trigger. I don't know which of them fell first.

But I remember as I stood in sudden silence. It's not too bad, I keep telling myself, dead they would be as much proof as living, I only need to start autopsy and preparation immediately . . .

I dropped the gun and knelt over the bodies.

Lying in the spreading pool of blood were four ordinary executed Jews, a youth with a bullet hole in his forehead, a young girl, a woman, and a child. All naked, all starved and filthy, all dead.

I think I screamed at Kremer who came in, having heard the shots. I pulled him toward the bodies; I lifted their sore-covered feet and pushed them in his blank face. And he did not even bother to shame me or bring me to my senses. He turned around and walked out.

November 15, 1943

I am on home leave. It's fortunate since Laura is about to give birth.

Our reunion was not all I had hoped it would be. Why do women have to swell like sacks of rotting grain in pregnancy? Yes, nature would have her due, but does it have to include blotched skin, dull hair, bloated ankles, bad temper, and random tears?

I didn't tell her this is a compassionate leave. After my supposed nervous breakdown, I was given a pep talk and told, in a sickeningly false paternalistic tone, "to make the SS proud with my newborn son." Unofficially they also suggested I should pop the next bun into the oven as soon as possible. Not bloody likely!

I am not mad! I saw what I saw!

[Later the same day]
Laura went into labor. I sent for Frau Richter, the neighborhood's best midwife. She is the bedroom now with Laura. I've steeled myself for a long wait. I don't expect an easy birth; she's let herself go physically and she is hysterical and frightened. I expect her to start screaming every moment now.

But I won't go outside. I'll do my duty as a German father, even if she is less than a German mother. Perhaps my fortitude will rub off on her.

Strange; the midwife has been inside for over half an hour and I hear no cries. Everything is quiet, deadly quiet. Perhaps I should go in—I'm a doctor, after all.

The door opens, Frau Richter stands on the threshold, beaming:

"Herr Schlosser," she says, "come and see your son!"

November 23, 1943

I'm to be court-martialed tomorrow. I'm lucky: normally an SS Court of Honor would sentence me to death. But I can expect clemency. They say that Reichsführer Himmler himself has been troubled by reports about the psychological deterioration of Einzatsgruppen members. He now puts his trust in gassing.

Yesterday I had a visitor, another sign of special consideration. Father.

He came in and I was struck by how old and thin he looked, yellow skin hanging loosely on his face like a rumpled suit.

"So, Klaus," he said, "it was too much for you, after all."

"No!" I spat. "I want to fight! I'm not a deserter. I hope they'll send me to the front. I don't care for my rank; I'll go as a simple soldier, as long as they give me another chance to fight the enemy!"

"The war is lost," he said softly.

"This is treason!"

"What will you do? Denounce me? Will they listen to you, a . . . "

"A madman? Don't be afraid to say it, Father. I know what they think of me. And I know I'm perfectly sane. It's just that I've seen the truth, which they still cannot accept. They mouth the Party line but they refuse to believe what they say. But they'll see it one day, and I'll be vindicated."

He looked at me, those pale washed-out eyes in the nest of wrinkles.

"I'm afraid you're right," he said. "A madman would be easier to talk to."

"Never mind! I don't want to discuss metaphysics with you. I just want to see Günter. Ask them to bring him to me."

"Günter?"

"My son!"

"Your son's name isn't Günter," said Father. "It's Adam."

"What kind of name is it? It's not a German name!"

"This is what his mother wanted to call him."

"Laura? You talked to Laura?'

"Of course. We became very close during her pregnancy. She asked me to take care of my grandson. She was afraid she'd die in childbirth. How ironic!"

I should have known. Father, dripping poison into Laura's ear, polluting her weak mind with his Jewish tales . . .

"Father," I said, "I saw them."

"Who?"

"Your Jewish demons. Creatures from the stories you told me. The *astri*, the vampire nurse; the chicken-footed ghosts; and . . . and Lilith, the succubus, who gives birth without pain . . . "

Yes, I saw her. When I walked on trembling legs into the birthing chamber where my wife lay in bed, radiant, her face unmarred by labor, her eyes clear, and the midwife swaddling the loud baby and babbling on about the miracle, the easiest birth she'd seen in her thirty years, no pain at all, just came out as sweetly as you please, like a cork from a bottle . . . And Laura, smiling at me . . . And then her puffy cheeks thinning out, adhering to the diamond-sharp bones, her blue eyes paling to the unnatural transparency of ice, her blond hair turning as white as the pillow on which it was spread . . .

I didn't shoot my wife. I shot Lila, Lilith, the eternal deceiver. That they found Laura's body riddled with bullets proves no more than the seemingly human bodies buried in the mass graves in the East.

I expected Father to react as they all did, with the mingled horror and pity, which are the emotional alms thrown by the sane to the mad. But he didn't.

"You saw them?" he asked seriously.

"Yes, I did. And I killed them I killed all of them. They are no more."

Father smiled a tired, pale smile.

"You killed the demons of the Jews," he said. "But Jews still live. And now you've become their demon. When they wake up at night, it's you they'll see in the darkness. You're a Jewish bogeyman. The last and the most horrifying of them all."

I gaped at him. He got up.

"I'll take care of Adam," he said. "I'm sorry, son."

[Undated]

Is he right? Is the war lost? Will our struggle to rid humanity of parasites come to nothing?

I have questioned myself again and again, and my conscience is clear. I am not a murderer! I am not a baby killer!

If the proof eluded me, then it is the scientist who failed, not the science. Another will come and show the world what I've seen.

And yet, as I'm lying here on the stinking bunk bed, I keep seeing my father, walking into a billowing yellow cloud. He is carrying a swaddled baby. Adam. His name begins with an "Aleph" in Hebrew: I still remember that much, a poisonous, accursed knowledge that permeates me like dirt, like sweat. I will never be rid of it, no matter how hard I try.

My father and my newborn son disappear into the cloud. And I follow.

There are still Jews there, I know. A people cannot live without its demons. And so here I am, going east.

Dark Coffee, Bright Light and the Paradoxes of Omnipotence

Ben Burgis

Avi realized with moments to spare that the coffee house was about to go up in flames.

He'd been sitting alone at a table by the window, sipping strong sweet coffee from a ceramic cup and trying to grade a pile of Intro to Philosophy papers, when the man in the trench coat came in off the street. This guy would have caught Avi's attention anyway, if only because he was the only other Jew in the trendy East Jerusalem café.

A Sephardic guy who could afford the pricey designer jeans below that trench coat was hard to tell from a Palestinian, but there was a colorful, hand-knit *yarmulke* poking out from underneath the man's baseball cap. That identified him as being not only a Jew, but an observant one, and of the "national-religious" variety at that.

Avi was close enough to him to see that the man's face was glowing with sweat, his eyes dilated with excitement. If Avi had been more paranoid by nature, those physical details, combined with the sheer improbability of that kind of Jew stopping in a place like this for a cup of coffee, would be all he needed to know.

He didn't put it together, though, not until the man opened his mouth and began to very softly recite the Shema, the last prayer a devout Jew utters before he dies.

"Shema Yisroel . . . " *Hear, O Israel.*

Avi spit out his mouthful of dark coffee and got to his feet.

"Adonai Eloheinu . . . " *The Lord is our God.*

"Get the fuck out of here!" Avi shouted as loud as he could in his Hebrew-accented Arabic. He earned stares of incomprehension from the other patrons.

"Adonai . . . " *The Lord . . .*

Avi barreled past the bomber so fast that he went right past the sidewalk and fell onto the street in a heap. Cars swerved around him. Horns honked. He threw his hands over his head.

"Ehad." . . . *is one.*

Avi didn't actually hear that last word, or see the man open up his trench coat and pull the string, but he could feel the reverberations.

From where he sat, covering his head with his hands, he could only see a momentary impression of bright light in the periphery of his vision. As he rocked back and forth on the baking pavement of that Jerusalem street, deafened by the explosion, Avi mouthed "Baruch Hashem," a quick thoughtless prayer of thanks, to a God in which he had long since ceased to believe, for the kindness of sparing his life.

Avi lost his religion fifteen years earlier, a few weeks before his thirteenth birthday.

Of course, he hadn't had all that much faith to lose. His parents had both spent their childhoods on a secular *kibbutz* before the Twelve-Day War of 1967 put an end to that experiment in collective farming. The Jordanians, and later their "independent" Palestinian client state, argued that they were simply restoring refugees to their lawful homes, but Avi knew that was bullshit. His grandparents' generation of Zionists had drained the swamp where that *kibbutz* was built. Any Arabs who'd lived there before '48 must have been very good swimmers.

The net effect was that, along with hundreds of thousands of other refugees from the countryside, Avi's parents had raised him and his brother David in the over-crowded city centre of Tel Aviv, at the heart of what the Palestinian authorities called the "the Jewish Autonomy Zone" and the embittered residents called "the *shtetl*" or sometimes "the world's biggest fucking prison camp." An awful lot of those residents, faced with a regime of identity cards and house-to-house weapons searches, deadly air strikes on "suspected Jewish Underground militants" and a thousand daily humiliations in what for nineteen glorious years had been their own country, found comfort in a return to the faith of their fathers.

Avi's mother was one of the *ba'al teshuvim*, the newly devout. His father was not. The uneasy compromise was a *kosher* kitchen with two sets of plates and dishes to become dirtied by his father's cooking on Yom Kippur, Shabbat meals in front of the television as the family cheered for their teams in Friday night soccer games, and religious training for both of the boys until they reached the age of thirteen, at which point they would be allowed to choose for themselves.

Avi and David dutifully joined a couple of dozen other neighborhood boys after school twice a week to study Torah and Talmud in pairs as an old Rabbi with a gray beard and a broad-rimmed black hat paced back and forth to yell at them in his own pidgin of Yiddish, Russian and Hebrew. Many years later, when he was in grad school at Al-Quds University, some of Avi's more liberal Palestinian friends would ask him if the intellectual rigors of that kind of study, all those commentaries and commentaries on commentaries, had been a good preparation for his later interest in analytic philosophy.

He'd always told them that they weren't, certainly not as much as a good course in calculus or physics would have been, but that his real philosophical training had begun on the day he'd been kicked out. He'd been paired with a dark-eyed Sephardic boy whose name he subsequently forgot, but whose soft olive complexion lingered in his memory. At the time, Avi was too confused to really understand much about his fascination with the boy or his own nascent bisexuality. He'd just known that he liked to spar about tricky Talmudic passages with him, teasing out subtly heretical interpretations for the joy of seeing the faint blush on the other boy's cheek.

It was in the middle of just such an exchange, about a particularly bizarre Talmudic reference to "demons" infesting abandoned buildings, that the rabbi had stopped in his usual exhortations to the room at large to stare incredulously at them. For just a moment, time stopped. Every detail of the room, the brown paint peeling from its walls and the pervasive smell of the cheap clove cigarettes the rabbi smoked every day before class, imprinted itself on Avi's mind.

In his own personal mythology, the event later came to resemble something in between Socrates being forced to drink poison by the Athenian court and Martin Luther's rebuke to the Papal authorities at the Diet of Worms. The truth was that at the time Avi's chief concern had been his irrational certainty that the rabbi had read his mind, that he knew what sort of thoughts Avi was having about the Sephardic boy. That, more than anything, fueled his attempt at coolly arrogant defiance. "I said," Avi repeated, "that it has to be metaphorical. Someone as smart as Maimonides must have known that there aren't really any demons."

The rabbi demanded in a shaky voice to know why God couldn't have created demons, Avi muttered something about science and the rabbi started shouting. "Hashem separated the light from the darkness! He can do anything!"

The room was in a hush, only David smirking as he tried to contain his hilarity at the way his big brother was taking the piss out of the old rabbi. The Sephardic boy looked like he wanted to crawl under his desk.

Avi stuck a finger at the old wooden door at the front of the room, the one that no one could ever quite close. "Could Hashem make it so that door was always closed instead of always open?"

"*Da*," the rabbi answered.

Avi took a second to remember that "*da*" was "yes" in Russian, then he plunged forward. "Could he make it so no one could open it?"

"*Da*."

"Could he make it so He Himself couldn't open it?"

The rabbi sputtered, and started quoting poetic passages from the psalms about the power and majesty of God. David started laughing. Avi smirked. "It's a simple question. Yes or no. Which is it?"

He never got his answer.

Six days before his twenty-eighth birthday, Avi found himself back in Tel Aviv, writing on the chalkboard of a junior college classroom that could have been the twin of the classroom in which his atheism had been born fifteen years before. The peeling paint was orange instead of brown, and no clove cigarettes covered the smell of the *kosher* butchery next door, but the two rooms were of a type, right down to doors that didn't quite close.

By all rights, Avi should be teaching in Palestine proper, not the backwater of the Jewish Autonomy Zone. Not only were the classes he'd TA'd while he was getting his PhD wildly popular, he'd had papers published in symbolic logic journals in both Palestine and the United States. Everyone agreed he was one of the brightest students in the department.

None of that mattered. After the wave of suicide bombings that had rocked Jerusalem on the anniversary of the 12-Day War, the Temporary Autonomy Zone Co-Authority was in no mood to renew the educational travel visa of a philosopher whose kid brother had spent time in prison as a suspected Jewish Underground agitator. The campus liberals at Al-Quds had made a fuss on Avi's behalf, but at the end of the day, here he was, trying to teach modal logic to about two dozen bored students who could barely follow lectures in Arabic.

The chalk board was full of logical formulas prefaced with diamond-shaped possibility operators and square-shaped necessity operators. An Ashkenazi boy in his twenties, a hand-knit purple *yarmulke* pinned to his thick brown hair, was standing up at his desk, trying to translate the formula Avi had circled from the symbolism into ordinary talk. His skin was a few shades too light to be exactly Avi's usual taste, but "Dr. Cohen" still had to remind himself not to stare at the boy. What you could get away with in cosmopolitan East Jerusalem was very different from the way things were back home.

"It says that it's possible that it's necessary that . . . "

"Necessary that it's possible that," Avi corrected.

"Right. Necessary that it's possible that the Morning Star and the Evening Star are not identical."

Avi nodded encouragingly, and took a sip of sludgy black coffee from his travel mug before he responded. Sarah, sitting in the front row, smirked at that. Avi ignored her. "Good. Now what does that mean?"

The student started to repeat himself, and Avi cut him off. "What I mean is what would it mean for the Morning Star to fail to be identical to the Evening

Star? Remember, we said that 'necessary' means that it's true in all possible worlds, and 'possible' means that it's true in at least one possible world."

The student tried the same line a third time, but with "necessary" replaced with "in all possible worlds." Avi cut him off, told him to sit back down and started writing the names of books and authors on the chalkboard. One was *Identity and Necessity* by Saul Kripke. Some of students in the back briefly perked up in interest when Avi mentioned that Kripke was an American Jew, but leaned back in their seats when they realized that *Identity and Necessity* had nothing to do with politics. They couldn't use it as an opportunity to bait Dr. Cohen into yet another round of the endless off-topic argument about whether violence was justified in "the struggle against the Arab aggressors."

The other book was *Counterfactuals* by an Australian philosopher named David Lewis. Avi explained that Kripke saw possible worlds as a metaphor, whereas Lewis believed that alternate worlds literally existed, one for every possible state of affairs. Since two people in different spatio-temporal worlds couldn't literally be "identical," possibility-statements really referred to the actions of your "counterpart" in that other world. "So, for example, if I say that it is possible that Rebecca"—the redhead giggled and squirmed in her seat like she always did when she was used in an example, and behind her Sarah rolled her eyes like she always did when Rebecca acted that way—"might have lived in Sefad instead of here if we'd won the 12-Day War, according to David Lewis, what I really mean is that in the closest possible world where that happened— I mean, the one that most resembles our world despite that difference—the inhabitant of that world who is most similar to Rebecca lives in Sefad."

The student in the purple *yarmulke* seized the conversational opening. "In that world, are the Arabs willing to treat us like human beings?"

Avi sighed, took a sip of his sweet coffee, and decided to stop fighting the drift of the conversation. "Maybe. Or maybe in that world they have it just as bad as we do in this one. Maybe they're even desperate enough to use dumb, counter-productive tactics like suicide bombings."

Avi leaned back on his desk and finished his coffee as his students interrupted each other in their angry responses. He was resigned to the fact that even in the most distant possible worlds, his counterparts weren't going to be able to steer the conversation back to modal logic before the end of the hour.

David, to his credit, laughed when Avi relayed that line the next night over Shabbat dinner conversation with him and his wife Sarah.

The couple's combined salary was almost nothing, since Sarah was living off of student loans and David's security level made him almost completely ineligible for legal employment in the Autonomy Zone, but they always managed to put together an amazing dinner. With the plates of steaming chicken, *challah* and baked noodle *kugel*, the intricately decorated table cloth and the faux-silver Shabbat candles, they'd created an atmosphere that made it well worth sitting through the prayers—Avi drew the line at saying them—and having to argue about politics the whole time.

"That's good," David said, "but you really do have to be more careful than that."

Sarah ladled more chicken onto Avi's plate. He smiled up at her. "Hey, if known terrorist elements like you still want me over for dinner, I figure I can't be saying anything that bad."

David smirked at the Co-Authority-speak. "Sure, but even if I really was involved in the JU's military wing, which I never have been"—he made a comical show of looking around for Co-Authority spy cameras—"I'd still agree with your point. The JU hasn't engaged in martyrdom operations for ten years, and we've called on the other factions to stop too. 'Suicide bombings' are stupid."

Avi put down his fork and stared his brother in the eye. "And there's such a big difference between that and roadside bombs, right? Enough of those and we'll get our independence back for sure."

The smirk didn't leave David's face, but his eyes went cold. "There's a huge difference. You can leave a roadside bomb and live to build another one the next day."

" . . . and since doing it for forty years has been so wildly successful in breaking the will of the occupiers, maybe we should just try the same fucking thing for forty more."

Sarah slammed her wine glass on the table. If it had been made of real glass instead of reinforced plastic, it probably would have shattered. Her usual cheerful expression was replaced with a deep flush that reduced both her husband and her Intro to Philosophy professor to silence.

"Avi," she finally said. "Why don't you tell David about modal logic?"

Avi began to re-gain his religion five days later, on his twenty-eighth birthday.

He taught at the junior college that night, and left the class proud that he'd been able to spend nearly the whole hour on-topic. He was going to go to Sarah and David's for a bottle of black market single malt scotch that David had been bragging about. It belatedly occurred to him to wonder why Sarah had skipped class that night.

When he stepped out into the dry heat of the September night, everything had changed.

By the time Avi had unlocked his bicycle from the lamppost, he'd realized that the streets were deserted. He could hear the moan of sirens in the distance, but he biked for five minutes without seeing a single car. When he did see one, it was a lime green, open-back truck bearing the symbol of the Palestine Defense Forces.

It screeched to a halt when he biked by. Two soldiers, identical looking except for a few inches difference in height and the thick glasses one of them wore perched on his nose, jumped out and started screaming in Arabic with thick Galilean accents. They pointed their sleek black assault rifles at Avi, and for a horrible second he thought he was going to piss his pants.

Following their instructions, he abandoned his bike and sank to his knees, his hands cupped behind his head. He asked—first, unthinkingly, in Hebrew, and then in Arabic—what had happened. The taller of the two soldiers, the one with the glasses, swung the rifle to smash Avi's jaw.

Avi's field of vision filled with red spots.

As soon as his identity card had pinned him as a blood relation of one of the "known terrorist leaders," another rifle swing knocked Avi unconscious.

Moments before, he finally made out the two words the soldier was repeating over and over again, "Arafat" and "dead."

The Jewish Underground had assassinated the Prime Minister.

He woke up in a four-by-four foot detention cell, which he shared with two other detainees. They smoked and speculated about the news and once or twice a day each of them was pulled out for interrogation.

At first, Avi thought that they were interrogating him because they thought he might know something. He was well aware of the Palestinian Supreme Court's ruling that "coercive interrogation" was justified in suspected terrorism cases, and he'd heard the horror stories, but he honestly thought that anything they did to him would be about extracting information.

It wasn't. It was about the commander—Mahmud something-or-other—working out his anger issues about terrorism, about the way Jews smelled, and just how shitty he found service in godforsaken places like Tel Aviv. His favored methods of therapy were a lit cigarillo, a pair of pliers, and a bucket of stagnant water.

During his third session in the back room, Avi came up from the bucket angry enough to respond out of turn. "You said that if 'the Jews' stopped blowing themselves up, you wouldn't have to be stationed here. There are two problems there. I'd think that in the closest possible worlds . . . "

Responding to a nod from the commander, the two PDF soldiers holding his head dunked it back in the water.

It took Avi almost thirty seconds to get his voice back. " . . . in which you never occupied us in the first place, there wouldn't be any suicide bombings."

Mahmud nodded again, and Avi was back in the water. When he got back out, he had to take several ragged breaths before continuing. "The second problem is the scope of that phrase, 'the Jews.' If all Jews blew themselves up, there would be no one to occupy. Maybe if you took a Deductive Logic class . . . "

That was the day Mahmud introduced the pliers.

Back in the cell, Avi got to know his two fellow inmates in the way that is unique to people who spend all day and all night in each other's company. Ehud was an agnostic, and Gershom was extremely religious, so there was some conversation there in between the endless guesswork about current events. By the second day, Gershom and Ehud both knew all the standard philosophical arguments for and against the existence of God backwards and forwards. Gershom surprised and delighted Avi by being a good student and coming up with all sorts of clever objections and counter-arguments.

Gershom started demanding a Siddur for his daily prayers in his interrogation sessions, and the guards eventually gave him one. They put it in the shared toilet in the back of the cell.

Gershom grimly fished the prayer book out of the toilet bowl, left it out to dry on the floor for a day, separated the pages and began to use it. They couldn't say the prayers that required a *minyan*, but Ehud and Avi immediately and unquestioningly joined in the chanting every morning as a matter of solidarity. As soon as that was over, they would re-start the argument about the existence of God.

Once Avi was missing two of the fingernails on his right hand and one of the ones on the left, he pretty much figured the worst of the "interrogation" was over. He was wrong.

His little outburst about logic had resulted in a new line of verbal abuse, this one revolving around Mahmud's contention that Avi "talked like a fucking queer." The day before he was released, Mahmud told his two confederates to leave the room and announced with great pride that he'd talked to some people who'd met Avi at Al Quds. "Turns out you don't just talk like one."

If Avi had been less addled by the days of "interrogation" and sleep in the constant bright light of the detention cell, he might have had some idea of where Mahmud was going with this before the commander unzipped his pants.

"I guess that means you won't even mind this, will you?"

When Avi was dumped back onto the streets at the end of the week, his first visit was to Sarah and David's apartment. He had to fight down vomit when he saw the bruises covering Sarah's face and neck, but he forced himself to be relieved that she was in one piece and not in a detention cell herself.

Sarah hugged him, hard, until he winced and she pulled back. She invited him in and held it together long enough to get him a cup of coffee. She didn't even start crying until he asked whether David was still in detention.

Avi was a coffin bearer at his brother's funeral, and from then on he attended the *minyan* at Gershom's *shul* three times a day, praying with an intensity and devotion that rivaled the rabbi's. He went through the motions of teaching his class for the remainder of the semester—his new rabbi had reminded him, after all, of the importance of honoring contracts—and went to services on the last Friday of the school year with his new intention fully formed.

He had discussed it with the rabbi, who was a member of the "Real JU" splinter faction, and he was far from surprised when the topic of that night's sermon was the biblical story of Samson.

"Samson said, 'Let me die with the Philistines!' and pulled the temple down around those wicked men. This was a great *mitzvah*, and Samson was a hero of the Jewish people." The Rabbi stared straight into Avi's eyes as he said that part. For a moment, there seemed to be a flame dancing in the Rabbi's glasses as pure and bright as the verses of the law, inscribed according to tradition in black fire on white fire in the mind of God.

Avi nodded, and his heart lifted in joy. He wept as he sang the prayer about the resurrection of the dead. When the Torah was passed around the congregation, Avi was the first to kiss it.

As he climbed the hill to the PDF checkpoint on the border of the neighborhood the next morning and waited for the civilians to pass through, Avi reflected that he still didn't know whether an all-powerful being could create a door that He Himself could not open. He was, however, no longer bothered by the question.

He got to the checkpoint and began to whisper, suffused with the happy knowledge that in a few minutes all of the cards would be turned over, all of his questions answered, as his body was transfigured into a pillar of light.

"Shema, Yisroel . . . "

Biographical Notes to "A Discourse on the Nature of Causality, with Air-planes" by Benjamin Rosenbaum

Benjamin Rosenbaum

On my return from PlausFab-Wisconsin (a delightful festival of art and inquiry, which styles itself "the World's Only Gynarchist Plausible-Fable Assembly") aboard the *P.R.G.B. Śri George Bernard Shaw*, I happened to share a compartment with Prem Ramasson, Raja of Outermost Thule, and his consort, a dour but beautiful woman whose name I did not know.

Two great blond barbarians bearing the livery of Outermost Thule (an elephant astride an iceberg and a volcano) stood in the hallway outside, armed with sabres and needlethrowers. Politely they asked if they might frisk me, then allowed me in. They ignored the short dagger at my belt—presumably accounting their liege's skill at arms more than sufficient to equal mine.

I took my place on the embroidered divan. "Good evening," I said.

The Raja flashed me a white-toothed smile and inclined his head. His consort pulled a wisp of blue veil across her lips, and looked out the porthole.

I took my notebook, pen, and inkwell from my valise, set the inkwell into the port provided in the white pine table set in the wall, and slid aside the strings that bound the notebook. The inkwell lit with a faint blue glow.

The Raja was shuffling through a Wisdom Deck, pausing to look at the incandescent faces of the cards, then up at me. "You are the plausible-fabulist, Benjamin Rosenbaum," he said at length.

I bowed stiffly. "A pen name, of course," I said.

"Taken from *The Scarlet Pimpernel*?" he asked, cocking one eyebrow curiously.

"My lord is very quick," I said mildly.

The Raja laughed, indicating the Wisdom Deck with a wave. "He isn't the most heroic or sympathetic character in that book, however."

"Indeed not, my lord," I said with polite restraint. "The name is chosen ironically. As a sort of challenge to myself, if you will. Bearing the name of a notorious anti-Hebraic caricature, I must needs be all the prouder and more subtle in my own literary endeavors."

"You are a Karaite, then?" he asked.

"I am an Israelite, at any rate," I said. "If not an orthodox follower of my people's traditional religion of despair."

The prince's eyes glittered with interest, so—despite my reservations—I explained my researches into the Rabbinical Heresy which had briefly flourished in Palestine and Babylon at the time of Ashoka, and its lost Talmud.

"Fascinating," said the Raja. "Do you return now to your family?"

"I am altogether without attachments, my liege," I said, my face darkening with shame.

Excusing myself, I delved once again into my writing, pausing now and then to let my Wisdom Ants scurry from the inkwell to taste the ink with their antennae, committing it to memory for later editing. At PlausFab-Wisconsin, I had received an assignment—to construct a plausible-fable of a world without zeppelins—and I was trying to imagine some alternative air conveyance for my characters when the Prince spoke again.

"I am an enthusiast for plausible-fables myself," he said. "I enjoyed your 'Droplet' greatly."

"Thank you, Your Highness."

"Are you writing such a grand extrapolation now?"

"I am trying my hand at a shadow history," I said.

The prince laughed gleefully. His consort had nestled herself against the bulkhead and fallen asleep, the blue gauze of her veil obscuring her features. "I adore shadow history," he said.

"Most shadow history proceeds with the logic of dream, full of odd echoes and distorted resonances of our world," I said. "I am experimenting with a new form, in which a single point of divergence in history leads to a new causal chain of events, and thus a different present."

"But the world *is* a dream," he said excitedly. "Your idea smacks of Democritan materialism—as if the events of the world were produced purely by linear cause and effect, the simplest of the Five Forms of causality."

"Indeed," I said.

"How fanciful!" he cried.

I was about to turn again to my work, but the prince clapped his hands thrice. From his baggage, a birdlike Wisdom Servant unfolded itself and stepped agilely onto the floor. Fully unfolded, it was three cubits tall, with a trapezoidal head and incandescent blue eyes. It took a silver tea service from an alcove in the wall, set the tray on the table between us, and began to pour.

"Wake up, Sarasvati Sitasdottir," the prince said to his consort, stroking her shoulder. "We are celebrating."

The servitor placed a steaming teacup before me. I capped my pen and shooed my Ants back into their inkwell, though one crawled stubbornly towards the tea. "What are we celebrating?" I asked.

"You shall come with me to Outermost Thule," he said. "It is a magical place—all fire and ice, except where it is greensward and sheep. Home once of epic heroes, Rama's cousins." His consort took a sleepy sip of her tea. "I have need of a plausible-fabulist. You can write the history of the Thule that might have been, to inspire and quell my restive subjects."

"Why me, Your Highness? I am hardly a fabulist of great renown. Perhaps I could help you contact someone more suitable—Karen Despair Robinson, say, or Howi Qomr Faukota."

"Nonsense," laughed the Raja, "for I have met none of them by chance in an airship compartment."

"But yet . . . ," I said, discomfited.

"You speak again like a materialist! This is why the East, once it was awakened, was able to conquer the West—we understand how to read the dream that the world is. Come, no more fuss."

I lifted my teacup. The stray Wisdom Ant was crawling along its rim; I positioned my forefinger before her, that she might climb onto it.

Just then there was a scuffle at the door, and Prem Ramasson set his teacup down and rose. He said something admonitory in the harsh Nordic tongue of his adopted country, something I imagined to mean "come now, boys, let the conductor through." The scuffle ceased, and the Raja slid the door of the compartment open, one hand on the hilt of his sword. There was the sharp hiss of a needlethrower, and he staggered backward, collapsing into the arms of his consort, who cried out.

The thin and angular Wisdom Servant plucked the dart from its master's neck. "Poison," it said, its voice a tangle of flutelike harmonics. "The assassin will possess its antidote."

Sarasvati Sitasdottir began to scream.

It is true that I had not accepted Prem Ramasson's offer of employment—indeed, that he had not seemed to find it necessary to actually ask. It is true also that I am a man of letters, neither spy nor bodyguard. It is furthermore true that I was unarmed, save for the ceremonial dagger at my belt, which had thus far seen employment only in the slicing of bread, cheese, and tomatoes.

Thus, the fact that I leapt through the doorway, over the fallen bodies of the prince's bodyguard, and pursued the fleeting form of the assassin down the long and curving corridor, cannot be reckoned as a habitual or forthright action. Nor, in truth, was it a considered one. In Śri Grigory Guptanovich Karthaganov's typology of action and motive, it must be accounted an impulsive-transformative action: the unreflective moment which changes forever the path of events.

Causes buzz around any such moment like bees around a hive, returning with pollen and information, exiting with hunger and ambition. The assassin's strike was the proximate cause. The prince's kind manner, his enthusiasm for plausible-fables (and my work in particular), his apparent sympathy for my people, the dark eyes of his consort—all these were inciting causes.

The psychological cause, surely, can be found in this name that I have chosen—"Benjamin Rosenbaum"—the fat and cowardly merchant of *The Scarlet Pimpernel* who is beaten and raises no hand to defend himself; just as we, deprived of our Temple, found refuge in endless, beautiful elegies of despair, turning our backs on the Rabbis and their dreams of a new beginning. I have always seethed against this passivity. Perhaps, then, I was waiting—my whole life—for such a chance at rash and violent action.

The figure—clothed head to toe in a dull gray that matched the airship's hull—raced ahead of me down the deserted corridor, and descended through a maintenance hatch set in the floor. I reached it, and paused for breath, thankful my enthusiasm for the favorite sport of my continent—the exalted Lacrosse—had prepared me somewhat for the chase. I did not imagine, though, that I could overpower an armed and trained assassin. Yet, the weave of the world had brought me here—surely to some purpose. How could I do aught but follow?

Beyond the proximate, inciting, and psychological causes, there are the more fundamental causes of an action. These address how the action embeds itself into the weave of the world, like a nettle in cloth. They rely on cosmology and epistemology. If the world is a dream, what caused the dreamer to dream that I chased the assassin? If the world is a lesson, what should this action teach? If the world is a gift, a wild and mindless rush of beauty, riven of logic or purpose—as it sometimes seems—still, seen from above, it must possess its own aesthetic harmony. The spectacle, then, of a ludicrously named practitioner of a half-despised art (bastard child of literature and philosophy), clumsily attempting the role of hero on the middledeck of the *P.R.G.B. Śri George Bernard Shaw*, must surely have some part in the pattern—chord or discord, tragic or comic.

Hesitantly, I poked my head down through the hatch. Beneath, a spiral staircase descended through a workroom cluttered with tools. I could hear the faint hum of engines nearby. There, in the canvas of the outer hull, between the *Shaw*'s great aluminum ribs, a door to the sky was open.

From a workbench, I took and donned an airman's vest, supple leather gloves, and a visored mask, to shield me somewhat from the assassin's needle. I leaned my head out the door.

A brisk wind whipped across the skin of the ship. I took a tether from a nearby anchor and hooked it to my vest. The assassin was untethered. He crawled along a line of handholds and footholds set in the airship's gently curving surface. Many cubits beyond him, a small and brightly colored glider clung to the *Shaw*—like a dragonfly splayed upon a watermelon.

It was the first time I had seen a glider put to any utilitarian purpose—espionage rather than sport—and immediately I was seized by the longing to return to my notebook. Gliders! In a world without dirigibles, my heroes could travel in some kind of immense, powered gliders! Of course, they would be forced to land whenever winds were unfavorable.

Or would they? I recalled that my purpose was not to repaint our world anew, but to speculate rigorously according to Democritan logic. Each new cause could lead to some wholly new effect, causing in turn some unimagined consequence. Given different economic incentives, then, and with no overriding, higher pattern to dictate the results, who knew what advances a glider-based science of aeronautics might achieve? Exhilarating speculation!

I glanced down, and the sight below wrenched me from my reverie:

The immense panoply of the Great Lakes—

—their dark green wave-wrinkled water—

—the paler green and tawny yellow fingers of land reaching in among them—

—puffs of cloud gamboling in the bulk of air between—

—and beyond, the vault of sky presiding over the Frankish and Athapascan Moeity.

It was a long way down.

"Malkat Ha-Shamayim," I murmured aloud. "What am I doing?"

"I was wondering that myself," said a high and glittering timbrel of chords and discords by my ear. It was the recalcitrant, tea-seeking Wisdom Ant, now perched on my shoulder.

"Well," I said crossly, "do you have any suggestions?"

"My sisters have tasted the neurotoxin coursing the through the prince's blood," the Ant said. "We do not recognize it. His servant has kept him alive so far, but an antidote is beyond us." She gestured towards the fleeing villain with one delicate antenna. "The assassin will likely carry an antidote to his venom. If you can place me on his body, I can find it. I will then transmit the recipe to my sisters through the Brahmanic field. Perhaps they can formulate a close analogue in our inkwell."

"It is a chance," I agreed. "But the assassin is half-way to his craft."

"True," said the Ant pensively.

"I have an idea for getting there," I said. "But you will have to do the math."

The tether which bound me to the *Shaw* was fastened high above us. I crawled upwards and away from the glider, to a point the Ant calculated. The handholds ceased, but I improvised with the letters of the airship's name, raised in decoration from its side.

From the top of an *R*, I leapt into the air—struck with my heels against the resilient canvas—and rebounded, sailing outwards, snapping the tether taut.

The Ant took shelter in my collar as the air roared around us. We described a long arc, swinging past the surprised assassin to the brightly colored glider; I was able to seize its aluminum frame.

I hooked my feet onto its seat, and hung there, my heart racing. The glider creaked, but held.

"Disembark," I panted to the Ant. "When the assassin gains the craft, you can search him."

"Her," said the Ant, crawling down my shoulder. "She has removed her mask, and in our passing I was able to observe her striking resemblance to Sarasvati Sitasdottir, the prince's consort. She is clearly her sister."

I glanced at the assassin. Her long black hair now whipped in the wind. She was braced against the airship's hull with one hand and one foot; with the other hand she had drawn her needlethrower.

"That is interesting information," I said as the Ant crawled off my hand and onto the glider. "Good luck."

"Good-bye," said the Ant.

A needle whizzed by my cheek. I released the glider and swung once more into the cerulean sphere.

Once again I passed the killer, covering my face with my leather gloves—a dart glanced off my visor. Once again I swung beyond the door to the maintenance room and towards the hull.

Predictably, however, my momentum was insufficient to attain it. I described a few more dizzying swings of decreasing arc-length until I hung, nauseous, terrified, and gently swaying, at the end of the tether, amidst the sky.

To discourage further needles, I protected the back of my head with my arms, and faced downwards. That is when I noticed the pirate ship.

It was sleek and narrow and black, designed for maneuverability. Like the *Shaw*, it had a battery of sails for fair winds, and propellers in an aft assemblage. But the *Shaw* traveled in a predictable course and carried a fixed set of coiled tensors, whose millions of microsprings gradually relaxed to produce its motive force. The new craft spouted clouds of white steam; carrying its own generatory, it could rewind its tensor batteries while underway. And, unlike the *Shaw*, it was armed—a cruel array of arbalest-harpoons was mounted at either side. It carried its sails below, sporting at its top two razor-sharp saw-ridges with which it could gut recalcitrant prey.

All this would have been enough to recognize the craft as a pirate—but it displayed the universal device of pirates as well, that parody of the Yin-Yang: all Yang, declaring allegiance to imbalance. In a yellow circle, two round black dots stared like unblinking demonic eyes; beneath, a black semicircle leered with empty, ravenous bonhomie.

I dared a glance upward in time to see the glider launch from the *Shaw*'s side. Whoever the mysterious assassin-sister was, whatever her purpose (political symbolism? personal revenge? dynastic ambition? anarchic mania?), she was a fantastic glider pilot. She gained the air with a single, supple back-flip, twirled the glider once, then hung deftly in the sky, considering.

Most people, surely, would have wondered at the *meaning* of a pirate and an assassin showing up together—what resonance, what symbolism, what hortatory or aesthetic purpose did the world intend thereby? But my mind was still with my thought-experiment.

Imagine there are no causes but mechanical ones—that the world is nothing but a chain of dominoes! Every plausible-fabulist spends long hours teasing apart fictional plots, imagining consequences, conjuring and discarding the antecedents of desired events. We dirty our hands daily with the simplest and grubbiest of the Five Forms. Now I tried to reason thus about life.

Were the pirate and the assassin in league? It seemed unlikely. If the assassin intended to trigger political upheaval and turmoil, pirates surely spoiled the attempt. A death at the hands of pirates while traveling in a foreign land is not the stuff of which revolutions are made. If the intent was merely to kill Ramasson, surely one or the other would suffice.

Yet was I to credit chance, then, with the intrusion of two violent enemies, in the same hour, into my hitherto tranquil existence?

Absurd! Yet the idea had an odd attractiveness. If the world was a blind machine, surely such clumsy coincidences would be common!

The assassin saw the pirate ship; yet, with an admirable consistency, she seemed resolved to finish what she had started. She came for me.

I drew my dagger from its sheath. Perhaps, at first, I had some wild idea of throwing it, or parrying her needles, though I had the skill for neither.

She advanced to a point some fifteen cubits away; from there, her spring-fired darts had more than enough power to pierce my clothing. I could see her face now, a choleric, wild-eyed homunculus of her phlegmatic sister's.

The smooth black canvas of the pirate ship was now thirty cubits below me.

The assassin banked her glider's wings against the wind, hanging like a kite. She let go its aluminum frame with her right hand, and drew her needlethrower.

Summoning all my strength, I struck the tether that held me with my dagger's blade.

My strength, as it happened, was extremely insufficient. The tether twanged like a harp-string, but was otherwise unharmed, and the dagger was knocked from my grasp by the recoil.

The assassin burst out laughing, and covered her eyes. Feeling foolish, I seized the tether in one hand and unhooked it from my vest with the other.

Then I let go.

Since that time, I have on various occasions enumerated to myself, with a mixture of wonder and chagrin, the various ways I might have died. I might have snapped my neck, or, landing on my stomach, folded in a *V* and broken my spine like a twig. If I had struck one of the craft's aluminum ribs, I should certainly have shattered bones.

What is chance? Is it best to liken it to the whim of some being of another scale or scope, the dreamer of our dream? Or to regard the world as having an inherent pattern, mirroring itself at every stage and scale?

Or could our world arise, as Democritus held, willy-nilly, of the couplings and patternings of endless dumb particulates?

While hanging from the *Shaw*, I had decided that the protagonist of my Democritan shadow-history (should I live to write it) would be a man of letters, a dabbler in philosophy like myself, who lived in an advanced society committed to philosophical materialism. I relished the apparent paradox—an intelligent man, in a sophisticated nation, forced to account for all events purely within the rubric of overt mechanical causation!

Yet those who today, complacently, regard the materialist hypothesis as dead—pointing to the Brahmanic field and its Wisdom Creatures, to the predictive successes, from weather to history, of the Theory of Five Causal Forms—forget that the question is, at bottom, axiomatic. The materialist hypothesis—the primacy of Matter over Mind—is undisprovable. What successes might some other science, in another history, have built, upon its bulwark?

So I cannot say—I cannot say!—if it is meaningful or meaningless, the fact that I struck the pirate vessel's resilient canvas with my legs and buttocks, was flung upwards again, to bounce and roll until I fetched up against the wall of the airship's dorsal razor-weapon. I cannot say if some Preserver spared my life through will, if some Pattern needed me for the skein it wove—or if a patternless and unforetellable Chance spared me all unknowing.

There was a small closed hatchway in the razor-spine nearby, whose overhanging ridge provided some protection against my adversary. Bruised and weary, groping inchoately among theories of chance and purpose, I scrambled for it as the boarding gongs and klaxons began.

The *Shaw* knew it could neither outrun nor outfight the swift and dangerous corsair—it idled above me, awaiting rapine. The brigand's longboats launched—lean and maneuverable black dirigibles the size of killer whales, with parties of armed sky-bandits clinging to their sides.

The glider turned and dove, a blur of gold and crimson and verdant blue disappearing over the pirate zeppelin's side—abandoning our duel, I imagined, for some redoubt many leagues below us.

Oddly, I was sad to see her go. True, I had known from her only wanton violence; she had almost killed me; I crouched battered, terrified, and nauseous on the summit of a pirate corsair on her account; and the kind Raja, my almost-employer, might be dead. Yet I felt our relations had reached as yet no satisfactory conclusion.

It is said that we fabulists live two lives at once. First we live as others do: seeking to feed and clothe ourselves, earn the respect and affection of our fellows, fly from danger, entertain and satiate ourselves on the things of this world. But then, too, we live a second life, pawing through the moments of the first, even as they happen, like a market-woman of the bazaar sifting trash for treasures. Every agony we endure, we also hold up to the light with great excitement, expecting it will be of use; every simple joy, we regard with a critical eye, wondering how it could be changed, honed, tightened, to fit inside a fable's walls.

The hatch was locked. I removed my mask and visor and lay on the canvas, basking in the afternoon sun, hoping my Ants had met success in their apothecary and saved the Prince; watching the pirate longboats sack the unresisting *P.R.G.B. Śri George Bernard Shaw* and return laden with valuables and—perhaps—hostages.

I was beginning to wonder if they would ever notice me—if, perhaps, I should signal them—when the cacophony of gongs and klaxons resumed—louder, insistent, angry—and the longboats raced back down to anchor beneath the pirate ship.

Curious, I found a ladder set in the razor-ridge's metal wall that led to a lookout platform.

A war-city was emerging from a cloudbank some leagues away.

I had never seen any work of man so vast. Fully twelve great dirigible hulls, each dwarfing the *Shaw*, were bound together in a constellation of outbuildings and propeller assemblies. Near the center, a great plume of white steam rose from a pillar; a Heart-of-the-Sun reactor, where the dull yellow ore called Yama's-flesh is driven to realize enlightenment through the ministrations of Wisdom-Sadhus.

There was a spyglass set in the railing by my side; I peered through, scanning the features of this new apparition.

None of the squabbling statelets of my continent could muster such a vessel, certainly; and only the Powers—Cathay, Gabon, the Aryan Raj—could afford to fly one so far afield, though the Khmer and Malay might have the capacity to build them.

There is little enough to choose between the meddling Powers, though Gabon makes the most pretense of investing in its colonies and believing in its supposed civilizing mission. This craft, though, was clearly Hindu. Every cubit of its surface was bedecked with a façade of cytoceramic statuary—couples coupling in five thousand erotic poses; theromorphic gods gesturing to soothe or menace; Rama in his chariot; heroes riddled with arrows and fighting on; saints undergoing martyrdom. In one corner, I spotted the Israelite avatar of Vishnu, hanging on his cross between Shiva and Ganesh.

Then I felt rough hands on my shoulders.

Five pirates had emerged from the hatch, cutlasses drawn. Their dress was motley and ragged, their features varied—Sikh, Xhosan, Baltic, Frankish, and Aztec, I surmised. None of us spoke as they led me through the rat's maze of catwalks and ladders set between the ship's inner and outer hulls.

I was queasy and light-headed with bruises, hunger, and the aftermath of rash and strenuous action; it seemed odd indeed that the day before, I had been celebrating and debating with the plausible-fabulists gathered at Wisconsin. I recalled that there had been a fancy-dress ball there, with a pirate theme; and the images of yesterday's festive, well-groomed pirates of fancy interleaved with those of today's grim and unwashed captors on the long climb down to the bridge.

The bridge was in the gondola that hung beneath the pirate airship's bulk, forwards of the rigging. It was crowded with lean and dangerous men in pantaloons, sarongs and leather trousers. They consulted paper charts and the liquid, glowing forms swimming in Wisdom Tanks, spoke through bronze tubes set in the walls, barked orders to cabin boys who raced away across the airship's webwork of spars.

At the great window that occupied the whole of the forward wall, watching the clouds part as we plunged into them, stood the captain.

I had suspected whose ship this might be upon seeing it; now I was sure. A giant of a man, dressed in buckskin and adorned with feathers, his braided red hair and bristling beard proclaimed him the scion of those who had fled the destruction of Viking Eire to settle on the banks of the Father-of-Waters.

This ship, then, was the *Hiawatha MacCool*, and this the man who terrorized commerce from the shores of Lake Erie to the border of Texas.

"Chippewa Melko," I said.

He turned, raising an eyebrow.

"Found him sightseeing on the starboard spine," one of my captors said.

"Indeed?" said Melko. "Did you fall off the *Shaw*?"

"I jumped, after a fashion," I said. "The reason thereof is a tale that strains my own credibility, although I lived it."

Sadly, this quip was lost on Melko, as he was distracted by some pressing bit of martial business.

We were descending at a precipitous rate; the water of Lake Erie loomed before us, filling the window. Individual whitecaps were discernible upon its surface.

When I glanced away from the window, the bridge had darkened—every Wisdom Tank was gray and lifeless.

"You there! Spy!" Melko barked. I noted with discomfiture that he addressed me. "Why would they disrupt our communications?"

"What?" I said.

The pirate captain gestured at the muddy tanks. "The Aryan war-city— they've disrupted the Brahmanic field with some damned device. They mean to cripple us, I suppose—ships like theirs are dependent on it. Won't work. But how do they expect to get their hostages back alive if they refuse to parley?"

"Perhaps they mean to board and take them," I offered.

"We'll see about that," he said grimly. "Listen up, boys—we hauled ass to avoid a trap, but the trap found us anyway. But we can outrun this bastard in the high airstreams if we lose all extra weight. Dinky—run and tell Max to drop the steamer. Red, Ali—mark the aft, fore, and starboard harpoons with buoys and let 'em go. Grig, Ngube—same with the spent tensors. Fast!"

He turned to me as his minions scurried to their tasks. "We're throwing all dead weight over the side. That includes you, unless I'm swiftly convinced otherwise. Who are you?"

"Gabriel Goodman," I said truthfully, "but better known by my quill-name—'Benjamin Rosenbaum'."

"Benjamin Rosenbaum?" the pirate cried. "The great Iowa poet, author of 'Green Nakedness' and 'Broken Lines'? You are a hero of our land, sir! Fear not, I shall—"

"No," I interrupted crossly. "Not that Benjamin Rosenbaum."

The pirate reddened, and tapped his teeth, frowning. "Aha, hold then, I have heard of you—the children's tale-scribe, I take it? 'Legs the Caterpillar'? I'll spare you, then, for the sake of my son Timmy, who—"

"No," I said again, through gritted teeth. "I am an author of plausible-fables, sir, not picture-books."

"Never read the stuff," said Melko. There was a great shudder, and the steel bulk of the steam generatory, billowing white clouds, fell past us. It struck the lake, raising a plume of spray that spotted the window with droplets. The forward harpoon assembly followed, trailing a red buoy on a line.

"Right then," said Melko. "Over you go."

"You spoke of Aryan hostages," I said hastily, thinking it wise now to mention the position I seemed to have accepted *de facto*, if not yet *de jure*. "Do you by any chance refer to my employer, Prem Ramasson, and his consort?"

Melko spat on the floor, causing a cabin boy to rush forward with a mop. "So you're one of those quislings who serves Hindoo royalty even as they divide up the land of your fathers, are you?" He advanced towards me menacingly.

"Outer Thule is a minor province of the Raj, sir," I said. "It is absurd to blame Ramasson for the war in Texas."

"Ready to rise, sir," came the cry.

"Rise then!" Melko ordered. "And throw this dog in the brig with its master. If we can't ransom them, we'll throw them off at the top." He glowered at me. "That will give you a nice long while to salve your conscience with making fine distinctions among Hindoos. What do you think he's doing here in our lands, if not plotting with his brothers to steal more of our gold and helium?"

I was unable to further pursue my political debate with Chippewa Melko, as his henchmen dragged me at once to cramped quarters between the inner and outer hulls. The prince lay on the single bunk, ashen and unmoving. His consort knelt at his side, weeping silently. The Wisdom Servant, deprived of its animating field, had collapsed into a tangle of reedlike protuberances.

My valise was there; I opened it and took out my inkwell. The Wisdom Ants lay within, tiny crumpled blobs of brassy metal. I put the inkwell in my pocket.

"Thank you for trying," Sarasvati Sitasdottir said hoarsely. "Alas, luck has turned against us."

"All may not be lost," I said. "An Aryan war-city pursues the pirates, and may yet buy our ransom; although, strangely, they have damped the Brahmanic field and so cannot hear the pirates' offer of parley."

"If they were going to parley, they would have done so by now," she said dully. "They will burn the pirate from the sky. They do not know we are aboard."

"Then our bad luck comes in threes." It is an old rule of thumb, derided as superstition by professional causalists. But they, like all professionals, like to obfuscate their science, rendering it inaccessible to the layman; in truth, the old rule holds a glimmer of the workings of the third form of causality.

"A swift death is no bad luck for me," Sarasvati Sitasdottir said. "Not when he is gone." She choked a sob, and turned away.

I felt for the Raja's pulse; his blood was still beneath his amber skin. His face was turned towards the metal bulkhead; droplets of moisture there told of his last breath, not long ago. I wiped them away, and closed his eyes.

We waited, for one doom or another. I could feel the zeppelin rising swiftly; the *Hiawatha* was unheated, and the air turned cold. The princess did not speak.

✡

My mind turned again to the fable I had been commissioned to write, the materialist shadow-history of a world without zeppelins. If by some unlikely chance I should live to finish it, I resolved to make do without the extravagant perils, ironic coincidences, sudden bursts of insight, death-defying escapades and beautiful villainesses that litter our genre and cheapen its high philosophical concerns. Why must every protagonist be doomed, daring, lonely, and overly proud? No, my philosopher-hero would enjoy precisely those goods of which I was deprived—a happy family, a secure situation, a prosperous and powerful nation, a conciliatory nature; above all, an absence of immediate physical peril. Of course, there must be conflict, worry, sorrow—but, I vowed, of a rich and subtle kind!

I wondered how my hero would view the chain of events in which I was embroiled. With derision? With compassion? I loved him, after a fashion, for he was my creation. How would he regard me?

If only the first and simplest form of causality had earned his allegiance, he would not be placated by such easy saws as "bad things come in threes." An assassin, and a pirate, and an uncommunicative war-city, he would ask? All within the space of an hour?

Would he simply accept the absurd and improbable results of living within a blind and random machine? Yet his society could not have advanced far, mired in such fatalism!

Would he not doggedly seek meaning, despite the limitations of his framework?

What if our bad luck were no coincidence at all, he would ask. What if all three misfortunes had a single, linear, proximate cause, intelligible to reason?

"My lady," I said, "I do not wish to cause you further pain. Yet I find I must speak. I saw the face of the prince's killer—it was a young woman's face, in lineament much like your own."

"Shakuntala!" the princess cried. "My sister! No! It cannot be! She would never do this—" she curled her hands into fists. "No!"

"And yet," I said gently, "it seems you regard the assertion as not utterly implausible."

"She is banished," Sarasvati Sitasdottir said. "She has gone over to the Thanes—the Nordic Liberation Army—the anarcho-gynarchist insurgents in our land. It is like her to seek danger and glory. But she would not kill Prem! She loved him before I!"

To that, I could find no response. The *Hiawatha* shuddered around us—some battle had been joined. We heard shouts and running footsteps.

Sarasvati, the prince, the pirates—any of them would have had a thousand gods to pray to, convenient gods for any occasion. Such solace I could sorely have used. But I was raised a Karaite. We acknowledge only one God, austere and magnificent; the One God of All Things, attended by His angels and His consort, the Queen of Heaven. The only way to speak to Him, we are taught, is in His Holy Temple; and it lies in ruins these two thousand years. In times like these, we are told to meditate on the contrast between His imperturbable magnificence and our own abandoned and abject vulnerability, and to be certain that He watches us with immeasurable compassion, though He will not act. I have never found this much comfort.

Instead, I turned to the prince, curious what in his visage might have inspired the passions of the two sisters.

On the bulkhead just before his lips—where, before, I had wiped away the sign of his last breath—a tracery of condensation stood.

Was this some effluvium issued by the organs of a decaying corpse? I bent, and delicately sniffed—detecting no corruption.

"My lady," I said, indicating the droplets on the cool metal, "he lives."

"What?" the princess cried. "But how?"

"A diguanidinium compound produced by certain marine dinoflagellates," I said, "can induce a deathlike coma, in which the subject breathes but thrice an hour; the heartbeat is similarly undetectable."

Delicately, she felt his face. "Can he hear us?"

"Perhaps."

"Why would she do this?"

"The body would be rushed back to Thule, would it not? Perhaps the revolutionaries meant to steal it and revive him as a hostage?"

A tremendous thunderclap shook the *Hiawatha MacCool*, and I noticed we were listing to one side. There was a commotion in the gangway; then Chippewa Melko entered. Several guards stood behind him.

"Damned tenacious," he spat. "If they want you so badly, why won't they parley? We're still out of range of the war-city itself and its big guns, thank Buddha, Thor, and Darwin. We burned one of their launches, at the cost of many of my men. But the other launch is gaining."

"Perhaps they don't know the hostages are aboard?" I asked.

"Then why pursue me this distance? I'm no fool—I know what it costs them to detour that monster. They don't do it for sport, and I don't flatter myself I'm worth that much to them. No, it's you they want. So they can have you—I've no more stomach for this chase." He gestured at the prince with his chin. "Is he dead?"

"No," I said.

"Doesn't look well. No matter—come along. I'm putting you all in a launch with a flag of parley on it. Their war-boat will have to stop for you, and that will give us the time we need."

So it was that we found ourselves in the freezing, cramped bay of a pirate longboat. Three of Melko's crewmen accompanied us—one at the controls, the other two clinging to the longboat's sides. Sarasvati and I huddled on the aluminum deck beside the pilot, the prince's body held between us. All three of Melko's men had parachutes—they planned to escape as soon as we docked. Our longboat flew the white flag of parley, and—taken from the prince's luggage—the royal standard of Outermost Thule.

All the others were gazing tensely at our target—the war-city's fighter launch, which climbed toward us from below. It was almost as big as Melko's flagship. I, alone, glanced back out the open doorway as we swung away from the *Hiawatha*.

So only I saw a brightly colored glider detach itself from the *Hiawatha*'s side and swoop to follow us.

Why would Shakuntala have lingered with the pirates thus far? Once the rebels' plan to abduct the prince was foiled by Melko's arrival, why not simply abandon it and await a fairer chance?

Unless the intent was not to abduct—but to protect.

"My lady," I said in my halting middle-school Sanskrit, "your sister is here."

Sarasvati gasped, following my gaze.

"Madam—your husband was aiding the rebels."

"How dare you?" she hissed in the same tongue, much more fluently.

"It is the only—" I struggled for the Sanskrit word for 'hypothesis', then abandoned the attempt, leaning over to whisper in English. "Why else did the pirates and the war-city arrive together? Consider: the prince's collusion with the Thanes was discovered by the Aryan Raj. But to try him for treason would provoke great scandal and stir sympathy for the insurgents. Instead, they made sure rumor of a valuable hostage reached Melko. With the prince in the hands of the pirates, his death would simply be a regrettable calamity."

Her eyes widened. "Those monsters!" she hissed.

"Your sister aimed to save him, but Melko arrived too soon—before news of the prince's death could discourage his brigandy. My lady, I fear that if we reach that launch, they will discover that the Prince lives. Then some accident will befall us all."

There were shouts from outside. Melko's crewmen drew their needlethrowers and fired at the advancing glider.

With a shriek, Sarasvati flung herself upon the pilot, knocking the controls from his hands.

The longboat lurched sickeningly.

I gained my feet, then fell against the prince. I saw a flash of orange and gold—the glider, swooping by us.

I struggled to stand. The pilot drew his cutlass. He seized Sarasvati by the hair and spun her away from the controls.

Just then, one of the men clinging to the outside, pricked by Shakuntala's needle, fell. His tether caught him, and the floor jerked beneath us.

The pilot staggered back. Sarasvati Sitasdottir punched him in the throat. They stumbled towards the door.

I started forward. The other pirate on the outside fell, untethered, and the longboat lurched again. Unbalanced, our craft drove in a tight circle, listing dangerously.

Sarasvati fought with uncommon ferocity, forcing the pirate towards the open hatch. Fearing they would both tumble through, I seized the controls.

Regrettably, I knew nothing of flying airship-longboats, whose controls, it happens, are of a remarkably poor design.

One would imagine that the principal steering element could be moved in the direction that one wishes the craft to go; instead, just the opposite is the case. Then, too, one would expect these brawny and unrefined air-men to use controls lending themselves to rough usage; instead, it seems an exceedingly fine hand is required.

Thus, rather than steadying the craft, I achieved the opposite.

Not only were Sarasvati and the pilot flung out the cabin door, but I myself was thrown through it, just managing to catch with both hands a metal protuberance in the hatchway's base. My feet swung freely over the void.

I looked up in time to see the Raja's limp body come sliding towards me like a missile.

I fear that I hesitated too long in deciding whether to dodge or catch my almost-employer. At the last minute courage won out, and I flung one arm around his chest as he struck me.

This dislodged my grip, and the two of us fell from the airship.

In an extremity of terror, I let go the prince, and clawed wildly at nothing.

I slammed into the body of the pirate who hung, poisoned by Shakuntala's needle, from the airship's tether. I slid along him, and finally caught myself at his feet.

As I clung there, shaking miserably, I watched Prem Ramasson tumble through the air, and I cursed myself for having caused the very tragedies I had endeavored to avoid, like a figure in an Athenian tragedy. But such tragedies proceed from some essential flaw in their heroes—some illustrative hubris, some damning vice. Searching my own character and actions, I could find only that I had endeavored to make do, as well as I could, in situations for which I was ill-prepared. Is that not the fate of any of us, confronting life and its vagaries?

Was my tale, then, an absurd and tragic farce? Was its lesson one merely of ignominy and despair?

Or perhaps—as my shadow-protagonist might imagine—there was no tale, no teller—perhaps the dramatic and sensational events I had endured were part of no story at all, but brute and silent facts of Matter.

From above, Shakuntala Sitasdottir dove in her glider. It was folded like a spear, and she swept past the prince in seconds. Nimbly, she flung open the glider's wings, sweeping up to the falling Raja, and rolling the glider, took him into her embrace.

Thus encumbered—she must have secured him somehow—she dove again (chasing her sister, I imagine) and disappeared in a bank of cloud.

A flock of brass-colored Wisdom Gulls, arriving from the Aryan war-city, flew around the pirates' launch. They entered its empty cabin, glanced at me and the poisoned pirate to whom I clung, and departed.

I climbed up the body to sit upon its shoulders, a much more comfortable position. There, clinging to the tether and shivering, I rested.

The *Hiawatha MacCool,* black smoke guttering from one side of her, climbed higher and higher into the sky, pursued by the Aryan war-boat. The sun was setting, limning the clouds with gold and pink and violet. The war-city, terrible and glorious, sailed slowly by, under my feet, its shadow an island of darkness in the sunset's gold-glitter, on the waters of the lake beneath.

Some distance to the east, where the sky was already darkening to a rich cobalt, the Aryan war-boat which Melko had successfully struck was bathed in white fire. After a while, the inner hull must have been breached, for the fire went out, extinguished by escaping helium, and the zeppelin plummeted.

Above me, the propeller hummed, driving my launch in the same small circle again and again.

I hoped that I had saved the prince after all. I hoped Shakuntala had saved her sister, and that the three of them would find refuge with the Thanes.

My shadow-protagonist had given me a gift; it was the logic of his world that had led me to discover the war-city's threat. Did this mean his philosophy was the correct one?

Yet the events that followed were so dramatic and contrived—precisely as if I inhabited a pulp romance. Perhaps he was writing my story, as I wrote his; perhaps, with the comfortable life I had given him, he longed to lose himself in uncomfortable escapades of this sort. In that case, we both of us lived in a world designed, a world of story, full of meaning.

But perhaps I had framed the question wrong. Perhaps the division between Mind and Matter is itself illusory; perhaps Randomness, Pattern, and Plan are all but stories we tell about the inchoate and unknowable world which fills the darkness beyond the thin circle illumed by reason's light. Perhaps it is foolish to ask if I or the protagonist of my world-without-zeppelins story is the more real. Each of us is flesh, a buzzing swarm of atoms; yet each of us also a tale contained in the pages of the other's notebook. We are bodies. But we are also the stories we tell about each other. Perhaps not knowing is enough.

Maybe it is not a matter of discovering the correct philosophy. Maybe the desire that burns behind this question is the desire to be real. And which is more real—a clod of dirt unnoticed at your feet, or a hero in a legend?

And maybe behind the desire to be real is simply wanting to be known.

To be held.

The first stars glittered against the fading blue. I was in the bosom of the Queen of Heaven. My fingers and toes were getting numb—soon frostbite would set in. I recited the prayer the ancient heretical Rabbis would say before death, which begins, "Hear, O Israel, the Lord is Our God, the Lord is One."

Then I began to climb the tether.

Alienation and Love in the Hebrew Alphabet

Lavie Tidhar

Aleph

An apple tree. A little girl standing beside it.

The apples are small and bitter, like old men; they are wizened and sour.

Somewhere, a chime sounds, a wind blows leaves on the ground.

Somewhere, the hiss of escaping air.

Bet

"Where have you been?" Mother says. Anger makes her brow damp and she fights the dark hair that sticks to her skin. "I told you not to go off on your own. You could have met anyone. Anyone! Sometimes I don't know what to do with you."

The little girl smiles, but it is a private smile, an inward smile, one that Mother cannot, will not, see.

"Well?"

The little girl mumbles something. Mother snorts and moves her hair to behind her ears.

"Spacemen and spaceships! Honest, I don't know what to do with you. Go and watch television. I have to go."

The girl goes upstairs. A few minutes later she hears the front door bang. Mother going out. She will be back late.

There is a window in her room. Beyond the window lie fields, hills, forests; in the horizon lights begin to appear from distant towns.

In the darkening skies more lights begin to appear.

Gimel

There are less apples on the tree. Around the trunk the cores of eaten apples lie like unmoving ants.

There are footsteps in the wet earth, large and asymmetrical. They lead away, down to the valley, to the brook, and disappear beyond it.

The girl examines the marks in the ground. she is becoming used to marks in the ground—the *W*-shape of birds' feet, the branded footsteps of children, the wide, linear marks of vehicles—and these are new.

Experimentally, she picks an apple from the tree and bites it, but it tastes disgusting, unripe and bitter, and she lets it drop to the ground uneaten.

Then Mother, calling for her from the house, and she has to go back.

Daled

She watches the lights play in the sky.

In her new language, the word for star is *kochav*, the middle sound throaty like a smoker's cough. At least, that's what Mother says, and she cries when she says it, and says they should never have come here, to this place called a *kibbutz* and to a man called Nathan, who works in the factory now. When Mother met him in Canada Nathan was on holiday, away from the *kibbutz* for a year, and he had painted such a lovely picture of the place that when he asked Mother to come there with him she agreed almost at once.

"Look at this place!" she says to her daughter. "What was I thinking?" she had cut her hair short—'because of the heat,' she said—and her ears stick out, making the girl smile. "Do you know what they want me to do now? Work in the dining room! Wash dishes!" her voice turns ugly as she mimics the voice of the man responsible for allocating jobs on the *kibbutz*, a short, dark man with too-tight shorts and a belly that hangs over them, covered in a checkered shirt like many of the men on the *kibbutz*. "There are no bad jobs. All jobs are equal. All jobs are important. And after all, what skills do you have? Singing won't feed the sheep. Singing won't make the wheat grow. I'm sorry, but if you want to stay here you must work."

The girl nods, but she isn't listening. She is thinking about the apple tree, and the marks in the ground.

Later, Nathan arrives, a quiet man carrying himself well, carrying also a bunch of flowers for Mother.

"From my garden," he said.

"They're lovely," she says.

They go out arm in arm, leaving the girl alone to her thoughts.

Heh

The brook is shallow and smells of soap; she has been warned not to drink the water, that the *kibbutz*'s shampoo factory needs to dump waste into it, otherwise where will it go?

The footsteps lead to the water's edge and disappear.

Crossing the brook isn't easy. There are stones left in equal lengths, stepping stones, but her legs are too short and she slips and falls into the water, briefly, and then gives up and just strides across, shoes filling up with water.

On the other side the footsteps disappear. She sees a long, curving mark in the ground, and thinks it must have been made by a snake. Somewhere in the bushes, a frogs harrumphs.

She doesn't like frogs.

She walks farther, past the squat building that holds the water drill; the walls are graffitied with army marks.

She picks blackberries from the thick bushes growing by the brook, picking the red ones, the ones that haven't ripened yet. Those are sour, not sweet, and taste delicious.

She knows she shouldn't be walking here by herself, but she has no one to go with. Mother is away, gone to the nearest city with Nathan, and the other children avoid her. She can't speak the language yet and when she does try they laugh.

She rounds a bend and reaches the beginning of a forest. The pine trees are all equally spaced, and there is a sharp scent in the air, of the amber liquid that comes out when a tree is cut.

She wades into the trees and starts climbing the hill.

Vav

"I. Don't. Believe. It!" Mother pronounces each word like a slap to the face, and the girl starts to cry, helpless in the face of such injustice. She is cold, and wet, and covered in mud and bruises, and all she wants right now is a bath and a soup and her bed.

"Don't cry. Don't." Mother holds her tight, squatting down so their faces are close. "Don't. I'm sorry."

They hold each other for a long moment in silence.

"I'm sorry."

Zain

She saw nothing that first time.

But now, when she goes to the apple tree, she feels invisible eyes on her, as if someone, something in the wilds about her had noted her presence and was showing discreet interest.

And the next day, there are new marks around the tree, and less apples.

And this time, the footsteps extend beyond the brook, like signposts, just for her.

But she doesn't follow them. Not yet.

Chet

Nathan is downstairs, helping Mother with dinner. He's a nice man, really, and he wants them to be there, with him.

Both of them. But he doesn't understand.

"What have you been up to then?" he says in that way adults have, who are not used to talking to children. "Were you playing a nice game?"

She tries to tell him about the apple tree, about the footmarks, about the lights in the skies, and Nathan nods, and smiles, and winks at her. "She has such a fertile imagination!" he says to Mother as they sit down to eat, *kibbutz*-dinner, fried eggs and salad cut into tiny pieces and bread, "such wonderful imagination!"

Mother serves him a fried egg, sunny side up, and scrambled eggs with cheese for her daughter.

"Sometimes I worry about her," she says quietly to Nathan, later, when they are both curled up together in front of the television, alone. "She doesn't have friends here. I think it was a mistake to come here."

Nathan holds her to him. "Give her time," he says. "Give yourself time."

"Yes."

They watch an American movie in silence.

Tet

"Hey, stupid!" the big kid, Oran, holds her down in the mud and slaps her. 'You can't even talk, can you! Stuuuu-pid!"

her knee rises, a reflex, connects with something soft.

Oran lets go of her and falls in the mud himself, crying. His hands try desperately to hold something between his legs.

The girl stands and looks at him until he stops twitching and rolling in the mud and then she walks off, towards the apple tree.

Yud

Down to the stream. Cross, shoes again filling up with water. Pass the water tower, pass the blackberry bushes.

The forest, the damp, the scent of pine.

She follows the marks in the ground, the way the other children play Arrow, when one group runs ahead, chalking the way on the pavements.

Someone, something, is chalking the marks.

And she follows.

Kaf

The silver disc lay half-buried in the ground.

She walks around the circumference, looking at it.

It's large, she can't tell how large because of the parts hidden in the earth, but it is big; darkened windows are carved into it, evenly spaced.

The forest is silent.

Somewhere nearby there is the hiss of escaping air.

Lamed

She sits on the ground, cross-legged under shifting pine-needles and damp earth.

She sits opposite the green man.

His skin is the color of the trees, dark green changing to brown towards the head, in which two large, narrow eyes are cut into the face. A small nose, a smooth skin, a small mouth. large head. Small ears.

No hair.

He is dressed in a silver suit that looks strange but feels (when she reaches a hand and touches it) like cloth, silky and fine and warm.

They don't talk.

Just sit there, for a long time, until it begins to get dark.

Then she gets up, turns and makes her way back through the foliage, back home.

When she turns her head to look again, he has disappeared.

But from her window, overlooking the hills, she can catch the sudden flash of silver, moonlight on metal, and she knows they are still there.

Mem

Mother is crying in the kitchen. "Look at my hands," she says, "look at my fingers!"

Her hands are red, splotchy, the nails worn, the skin coarsened. "I can't do this anymore!"

The girl comes up to her and puts her arms around her. She tries to tell Mother about the man in the forest, about the silver disc and the quiet that surrounds it.

"Will you never stop? You and your dreaming . . . " Mother sighs, wipes her hands on a kitchen cloth. "I know it's hard for you, honey," she says. She puts the girl on her lap, curls her hair with a finger. "We'll manage. Nathan is a good man. Everyone says it's a good place to raise children."

The girl doesn't say anything.

"I wish we could go," her mother whispers, close to the girl's ear. "I wish there was a spaceman in the woods, and he could take us away in his silver ship, away into the stars . . . "

"He can't," the girl says. "His spaceship is broken."

Mother smiles. "Go and watch television," she says.

The girl goes up to her room. She knows Mother is waiting for Nathan.

She waits to here his steps coming up to the front of the house.

She waits to hear his knock on the door, Mother's voice, the rustle of flowers, the door banging as they go out.

But there is no noise, no sound, only the cries of the hyenas in the hills, and she falls asleep, still waiting for a sound that doesn't come.

Nun

The spaceman is waiting for her by the apple tree.

Here, in broad daylight, she can see his feet, the curious imprint they make in the ground.

He is eating the apples, quickly, biting all around until only the core remains. Then he drops the core on the ground and starts on the next.

"Why can't you leave?" she asks.

The smooth, alien face doesn't move. The narrow eyes blink, once.

Something unexplainable passes from him, to her. Not words, exactly, not thoughts, exactly; a mixture of emotions, a whole palate of them. The girl has never realized how many there were, before, how many shades of each.

The spaceman uses them like speech.

"You need . . . " she searches for the words.

He nods.

His eyes blink.

She senses desperation, sadness, loneliness.

He drops the last apple core on the ground and walks away, towards the brook.

Samech

Mother has a new job: taking care of the children in the *peuton*, the pre-kindergarten class.

She finishes early, then comes home and sits outside, looking at the hills and the forest with a king of longing in her eyes, almost like a farmer looks, hoping for rain.

Praying for change.

She drinks in moderation, she says.

The sun sets beyond the hills. In its place comes darkness, one more profound, deeper than the ones they have ever experienced in the city. Stars unveil in the sky, more and more of them, until they cover the darkness like pearls viewed through water.

The girl watches the skies with her mother; sitting out on the veranda, they search the stars together.

Nathan doesn't come anymore. Mother says he "needed to find himself. Thought that maybe the *kibbutz* wasn't for him, that he needed his freedom. He was still searching for his real self." She said it like it was a fact, just a fact and nothing more.

But the girl knew that it wasn't. And she thought of what the spaceman in the forest had passed to her, the things he needed for his spacecraft to fly.

But she wasn't sure it would be enough.

Ain

There is a circle of children around her, chanting. Pointing fingers. Laughing.

They push her in the puddle and kick water and mud on her clothes and face.

They have bright, colorful boots, with trousers tucked inside into thick socks. She can see them from where she lies, and her feelings are a complex, angry maze through which she runs.

Peh

Down to the stream. Cross, shoes again filling up with water. Pass the water tower, pass the blackberry bushes.

The forest, the damp, the scent of pine.

The ship.

"How come no one sees it?" she says. "Sees you?"

Something like fear from the green man. Something like care. And something like pride.

"You make them not see it?"

An emotion signifying assent.

"What do you do all the time?" she kicks the ground, a little too hard. "How do you cope with it?"

Sadness again. A shade of anger. The scent of hope.

"Will you meet me by the apple tree?" she says. "Tomorrow?"

Again, assent.

She turns away and runs through the forest, her heart beating hard with a mixture of emotions.

Tzadik

Night. They sit on the veranda.

The stars above are like a fractured mirror, slivers of shining glass scattered across the heavens.

Beyond the hills the hyenas laugh.

Kuf

"Can you see him?" the girl demands.

Mother makes a show of looking around. "It's time you made some real friends."

"He's here!" the girl protests, pointing at the green man. He stands by the tree, blinking his eyes rapidly.

"Stop!"

He does.

He envelopes them in a rainbow of emotions. Above them all hope, like a wide ray of light obscuring all others.

"Please," he says. His voice is uncertain and reedy, like a feather on the wind.

And, "yes," they say, in unison, mother and daughter, linking hands.

Resh

Alienation and love. Like a mother and daughter, like two refugees in a crowd.

The spaceman walked away from the tree, towards the brook. Cross. Pass the water tower, pass the blackberry bushes.

The forest, the damp, the scent of pine.

The great silver disc, motionless in the ground.

Mother and daughter wait, holding hands.

Shin

There was a deep thrum, a vibration that shook the pine-needles A flash of silver in the sunlight.

A swathe of emotions seen through a prism, where two burn brightest of all, and conquer the spectrum. The quiet hurts, the silent tenderness, the invisible loves and the visible pains.

They channel their being into the silver disc in the woods and the skies dim and night steals on the *kibbutz* and the stars come out, one by one, until they fill the sky like a map.

Alienation and love; the things that move worlds.

Tav

An apple tree. A little girl standing besides it, holding her mother's hand.

Somewhere, a chime sounds, a wind blows leaves on the ground.

Somewhere, the hiss of escaping air.

Then silence.

The Problem of Susan

Neil Gaiman

She has the dream again that night.

In the dream, she is standing, with her brothers and her sister, on the edge of the battlefield. It is summer, and the grass is a peculiarly vivid shade of green: a wholesome green, like a cricket pitch or the welcoming slope of the South Downs as you make your way north from the coast. There are bodies on the grass. None of the bodies are human; she can see a centaur, its throat slit, on the grass near her. The horse half of it is a vivid chestnut. Its human skin is nut-brown from the sun. She finds herself staring at the horse's penis, wondering about centaurs mating, imagines being kissed by that bearded face. Her eyes flick to the cut throat, and the sticky red-black pool that surrounds it, and she shivers.

Flies buzz about the corpses.

The wildflowers tangle in the grass. They bloomed yesterday for the first time in . . . how long? A hundred years? A thousand? A hundred thousand? She does not know.

All this was snow, she thinks, as she looks at the battlefield.

Yesterday, all this was snow. Always winter, and never Christmas.

Her sister tugs her hand, and points. On the brow of the green hill they stand, deep in conversation. The lion is golden, his arms folded behind his back. The witch is dressed all in white. Right now she is shouting at the lion, who is simply listening. The children cannot make out any of their words, not her cold anger, nor the lion's thrum-deep replies. The witch's hair is black and shiny, her lips are red.

In her dream she notices these things.

They will finish their conversation soon, the lion and the witch . . .

There are things about herself that the professor despises. Her smell, for example. She smells like her grandmother smelled, like old women smell, and for this she cannot forgive herself, so on waking she bathes in scented water and, naked and towel-dried, dabs several drops of Chanel toilet water beneath her arms and on her neck. It is, she believes, her sole extravagance.

Today she dresses in her dark brown dress suit. She thinks of these as her interview clothes, as opposed to her lecture clothes or her knocking-about-the-house clothes. Now she is in retirement, she wears her knocking-about-the-house clothes more and more. She puts on lipstick.

After breakfast, she washes a milk bottle, places it at her back door. She discovers that the next-door's cat has deposited a mouse head and a paw, on the doormat. It looks as though the mouse is swimming through the coconut matting, as though most of it is submerged. She purses her lips, then she folds her copy of yesterday's *Daily Telegraph*, and she folds and flips the mouse head and the paw into the newspaper, never touching them with her hands.

Today's *Daily Telegraph* is waiting for her in the hall, along with several letters, which she inspects, without opening any of them, then places on the desk in her tiny study. Since her retirement she visits her study only to write. Now she walks into the kitchen and seats herself at the old oak table. Her reading glasses hang about her neck on a silver chain, and she perches them on her nose and begins with the obituaries.

She does not actually expect to encounter anyone she knows there, but the world is small, and she observes that, perhaps with cruel humor, the obituarists have run a photograph of Peter Burrell-Gunn as he was in the early 1950s, and not at all as he was the last time the professor had seen him, at a Literary Monthly Christmas party several years before, all gouty and beaky and trembling, and reminding her of nothing so much as a caricature of an owl. In the photograph, he is very beautiful. He looks wild, and noble.

She had spent an evening once kissing him in a summer house: she remembers that very clearly, although she cannot remember for the life of her in which garden the summer house had belonged.

It was, she decides, Charles and Nadia Reid's house in the country. Which meant that it was before Nadia ran away with that Scottish artist, and Charles took the professor with him to Spain, although she was certainly not a professor then. This was many years before people commonly went to Spain for their holidays; it was an exotic and dangerous place in those days. He asked her to marry him, too, and she is no longer certain why she said no, or even if she had entirely said no. He was a pleasant-enough young man, and he took what was left of her virginity on a blanket on a Spanish beach, on a warm spring night. She was twenty years old, and had thought herself so old . . .

The doorbell chimes, and she puts down the paper, and makes her way to the front door, and opens it.

Her first thought is how young the girl looks.

Her first thought is how old the woman looks. "Professor Hastings?" she says. "I'm Greta Campion. I'm doing the profile on you. For the *Literary Chronicle*."

The older woman stares at her for a moment, vulnerable and ancient, then

she smiles. It's a friendly smile, and Greta warms to her. "Come in, dear," says
the professor. "We'll be in the sitting room."

"I brought you this," says Greta. "I baked it myself." She takes the cake tin
from her bag, hoping its contents hadn't disintegrated *en route*. "It's a chocolate
cake. I read on-line that you liked them."

The old woman nods and blinks. "I do," she says. "How kind. This way."

Greta follows her into a comfortable room, is shown to her armchair, and
told, firmly, not to move. The professor bustles off and returns with a tray, on
which are teacups and saucers, a teapot, a plate of chocolate biscuits, and Greta's
chocolate cake.

Tea is poured, and Greta exclaims over the professor's brooch, and then
she pulls out her notebook and pen, and a copy of the professor's last book, *A
Quest for Meanings in Children's Fiction*, the copy bristling with Post-it notes
and scraps of paper. They talk about the early chapters, in which the hypothesis
is set forth that there was originally no distinct branch of fiction that was only
intended for children, until the Victorian notions of the purity and sanctity of
childhood demanded that fiction for children be made . . .

"Well, pure," says the professor.

"And sanctified?" asks Greta, with a smile.

"And sanctimonious," corrects the old woman. "It is difficult to read *The
Water Babies* without wincing."

And then she talks about ways that artists used to draw children—as adults,
only smaller, without considering the child's proportions—and how the Grimms'
stories were collected for adults and, when the Grimms realized the books were
being read in the nursery, were bowdlerized to make them more appropriate.
She talks of Perrault's "Sleeping Beauty in the Wood," and of its original coda in
which the Prince's cannibal ogre mother attempts to frame the Sleeping Beauty
for having eaten her own children, and all the while Greta nods and takes notes,
and nervously tries to contribute enough to the conversation that the professor
will feel that it is a conversation or at least an interview, not a lecture.

"Where," asks Greta, "do you feel your interest in children's fiction came from?"

The professor shakes her head. "Where do any of our interests come from?
Where does your interest in children's books come from?"

Greta says, "They always seemed the books that were most important to me.
The ones that mattered. When I was a kid, and when I grew. I was like Dahl's
Matilda. . . . Were your family great readers?"

"Not really . . . . I say that, it was a long time ago that they died. Were killed.
I should say."

"All your family died at the same time? Was this in the war?"

"No, dear. We were evacuees, in the war. This was in a train crash, several
years after. I was not there."

"Just like in Lewis's Narnia books," says Greta, and immediately feels like a fool, and an insensitive fool. "I'm sorry. That was a terrible thing to say, wasn't it?"

"Was it, dear?"

Greta can feel herself blushing, and she says, "It's just I remember that sequence so vividly. In *The Last Battle*. Where you learn there was a train crash on the way back to school, and everyone was killed. Except for Susan, of course."

The professor says, "More tea, dear?" and Greta knows that she should leave the subject, but she says, "You know, that used to make me so angry."

"What did, dear?"

"Susan. All the other kids go off to Paradise, and Susan can't go. She's no longer a friend of Narnia because she's too fond of lipsticks and nylons and invitations to parties. I even talked to my English teacher about it, about the problem of Susan, when I was twelve."

She'll leave the subject now, talk about the role of children's fiction in creating the belief systems we adopt as adults, but the professor says, "And tell me, dear, what did your teacher say?"

"She said that even though Susan had refused Paradise then, she still had time while she lived to repent."

"Repent what?"

"Not believing, I suppose. And the sin of Eve."

The professor cuts herself a slice of chocolate cake. She seems to be remembering. And then she says, "I doubt there was much opportunity for nylons and lipsticks after her family was killed. There certainly wasn't for me. A little money—less than one might imagine—from her parents' estate, to lodge and feed her. No luxuries . . . "

"There must have been something else wrong with Susan," says the young journalist, "something they didn't tell us. Otherwise she wouldn't have been damned like that—denied the Heaven of further up and further in. I mean, all the people she had ever cared for had gone on to their reward, in a world of magic and waterfalls and joy. And she was left behind."

"I don't know about the girl in the books," says the professor, "but remaining behind would also have meant that she was available to identify her brothers' and her little sister's bodies. There were a lot of people dead in that crash. I was taken to a nearby school—it was the first day of term, and they had taken the bodies there. My older brother looked okay. Like he was asleep. The other two were a bit messier."

"I suppose Susan would have seen their bodies, and thought, they're on holidays now. The perfect school holidays. Romping in meadows with talking animals, world without end."

"She might have done. I only remember thinking what a great deal of damage a train can do, when it hits another train, to the people who were traveling inside. I suppose you've never had to identify a body, dear?"

"No."

"That's a blessing. I remember looking at them and thinking, What if I'm wrong, what if it's not him after all? My younger brother was decapitated, you know. A god who would punish me for liking nylons and parties by making me walk through that school dining room, with the flies, to identify Ed, well . . . he's enjoying himself a bit too much, isn't he? Like a cat, getting the last ounce of enjoyment out of a mouse. Or a gram of enjoyment, I suppose it must be these days. I don't know, really."

She trails off. And then, after some time, she says, "I'm sorry dear. I don't think I can do any more of this today. Perhaps if your editor gives me a ring, we can set a time to finish our conversation."

Greta nods and says of course, and knows in her heart, with a peculiar finality, that they will talk no more.

That night, the professor climbs the stairs of her house, slowly, painstakingly, floor by floor. She takes sheets and blankets from the airing cupboard, and makes up a bed in the spare bedroom, at the back. It is empty but for a wartime austerity dressing table, with a mirror and drawers, an oak bed, and a dusty applewood wardrobe, which contains only coathangers and a cardboard box. She places a vase on the dressing table, containing purple rhododendron flowers, sticky and vulgar.

She takes from the box in the wardrobe a plastic shopping bag containing four old photographic albums. Then she climbs into the bed that was hers as a child, and lies there between the sheets, looking at the black-and-white photographs, and the sepia photographs, and the handful of unconvincing color photographs. She looks at her brothers, and her sister, and her parents, and she wonders how they could have been that young, how anybody could have been that young.

After a while she notices that there are several children's books beside the bed, which puzzles her slightly, because she does not believe she keeps books on the bedside table in that room. Nor, she decides, does she usually have a bedside table there. On the top of the pile is an old paperback book—it must be more than forty years old: the price on the cover is in shillings. It shows a lion, and two girls twining a daisy chain into its mane.

The professor's lips prickle with shock. And only then does she understand that she is dreaming, for she does not keep those books in the house. Beneath the paperback is a hardback, in its jacket, of a book that, in her dream, she has always wanted to read: *Mary Poppins Brings in the Dawn,* which P. L. Travers had never written while alive.

She picks it up and opens it to the middle, and reads the story waiting for her: Jane and Michael follow Mary Poppins on her day off, to Heaven, and they meet the boy Jesus, who is still slightly scared of Mary Poppins because she was once his nanny, and the Holy Ghost, who complains that he has not been able to get his sheet properly white since Mary Poppins left, and God the Father, who says, "There's no making her do anything. Not her. She's Mary Poppins."

"But you're God," said Jane. "You created everybody and everything. They have to do what you say."

"Not her," said God the Father once again, and he scratched his golden beard flecked with white. "I didn't create her. She's Mary Poppins."

And the professor stirs in her sleep, and afterward dreams that she is reading her own obituary. It has been a good life, she thinks, as she reads it, discovering her history laid out in black and white. Everyone is there. Even the people she had forgotten.

Greta sleeps beside her boyfriend, in a small flat in Camden, and she, too, is dreaming.

In the dream, the lion and the witch come down the hill together.

She is standing on the battlefield, holding her sister's hand. She looks up at the golden lion, and the burning amber of his eyes. "He's not a tame lion, is he?" she whispers to her sister, and they shiver.

The witch looks at them all, then she turns to the lion, and says, coldly, "I am satisfied with the terms of our agreement. You take the girls: for myself, I shall have the boys."

She understands what must have happened, and she runs, but the beast is upon her before she has covered a dozen paces.

The lion eats all of her except her head, in her dream. He leaves the head, and one of her hands, just as a housecat leaves the parts of a mouse it has no desire for, for later, or as a gift.

She wishes that he had eaten her head, then she would not have had to look. Dead eyelids cannot be closed, and she stares, unflinching, at the twisted thing her brothers have become. The great beast eats her little sister more slowly, and, it seems to her, with more relish and pleasure than it had eaten her; but then, her little sister had always been its favorite.

The witch removes her white robes, revealing a body no less white, with high, small breasts, and nipples so dark they are almost black. The witch lies back upon the grass, spreads her legs. Beneath her body, the grass becomes rimed with frost. "Now," she says.

The lion licks her white cleft with its pink tongue, until she can take no more of it, and she pulls its huge mouth to hers, and wraps her icy legs into its golden fur . . . .

Being dead, the eyes in the head on the grass cannot look away. Being dead, they miss nothing.

And when the two of them are done, sweaty and sticky and sated, only then does the lion amble over to the head on the grass and devour it in its huge mouth, crunching her skull in its powerful jaws, and it is then, only then, that she wakes.

Her heart is pounding. She tries to wake her boyfriend, but he snores and grunts and will not be roused.

It's true, Greta thinks, irrationally, in the darkness. She grew up. She carried on. She didn't die.

She imagines the professor, waking in the night and listening to the noises coming from the old applewood wardrobe in the corner: to the rustlings of all these gliding ghosts, which might be mistaken for the scurries of mice or rats, to the padding of enormous velvet paws, and the distant, dangerous music of a hunting horn.

She knows she is being ridiculous, although she will not be surprised when she reads of the professor's demise. *Death comes in the night,* she thinks, *before she returns to sleep. Like a lion.*

The white witch rides naked on the lion's golden back. Its muzzle is spotted with fresh, scarlet blood. Then the vast pinkness of its tongue wipes around its face, and once more it is perfectly clean.

Uncle Chaim and Aunt Rifke and the Angel

Peter S. Beagle

My Uncle Chaim, who was a painter, was working in his studio—as he did on every day except Shabbos—when the blue angel showed up. I was there.

I was usually there most afternoons, dropping in on my way home from Fiorello LaGuardia Elementary School. I was what they call a "latchkey kid," these days. My parents both worked and traveled full-time, and Uncle Chaim's studio had been my home base and my real playground since I was small. I was shy and uncomfortable with other children. Uncle Chaim didn't have any kids, and didn't know much about them, so he talked to me like an adult when he talked at all, which suited me perfectly. I looked through his paintings and drawings, tried some of my own, and ate Chinese food with him in silent companionship, when he remembered that we should probably eat. Sometimes I fell asleep on the cot. And when his friends—who were mostly painters like himself—dropped in to visit, I withdrew into my favorite corner and listened to their talk, and understood what I understood. Until the blue angel came.

It was very sudden: one moment I was looking through a couple of the comic books Uncle Chaim kept around for me, while he was trying to catch the highlight on the tendons under his model's chin, and the next moment there was this angel standing before him, actually posing, with her arms spread out and her great wings taking up almost half the studio. She was not blue herself—a light beige would be closer—but she wore a blue robe that managed to look at once graceful and grand, with a white undergarment glimmering beneath. Her face, half-shadowed by a loose hood, looked disapproving.

I dropped the comic book and stared. No, I *gaped*, there's a difference. Uncle Chaim said to her, "I can't see my model. If you wouldn't mind moving just a bit?" He was grumpy when he was working, but never rude.

"*I* am your model," the angel said. "From this day forth, you will paint no one but me."

"I don't work on commission," Uncle Chaim answered. "I used to, but you have to put up with too many aggravating rich people. Now I just paint what I paint, take it to the gallery. Easier on my stomach, you know?"

His model, the wife of a fellow painter, said, "Chaim, who are you talking to?"

"Nobody, nobody, Ruthie. Just myself, same way your Jules does when he's working. Old guys get like that." To the angel, in a lower voice, he said, "Also, whatever you're doing to the light, could you not? I got some great shadows going right now." For a celestial brightness was swelling in the grubby little warehouse district studio, illuminating the warped floor boards, the wrinkled tubes of colors scattered everywhere, the canvases stacked and propped in the corners, along with several ancient rickety easels. It scared me, but not Uncle Chaim. He said. "So you're an angel, fine, that's terrific. Now give me back my shadows."

The room darkened obediently. "*Thank* you. Now about *moving . . .* " He made a brushing-away gesture with the hand holding the little glass of Scotch.

The model said, "Chaim, you're worrying me."

"What, I'm seventy-six years old, I'm not entitled to a hallucination now and then? I'm seeing an angel, you're not—this is no big deal. I just want it should move out of the way, let me work." The angel, in response, spread her wings even wider, and Uncle Chaim snapped, "Oh, for God's sake, shoo!"

"It is for God's sake that I am here," the angel announced majestically. "The Lord—Yahweh—I Am That I Am—has sent me down to be your muse." She inclined her head a trifle, by way of accepting the worship and wonder she expected.

From Uncle Chaim, she didn't get it, unless very nearly dropping his glass of Scotch counts as a compliment. "A muse?" he snorted. "I don't need a muse—I got models!"

"That's it," Ruthie said. "I'm calling Jules, I'll make him come over and sit with you." She put on her coat, picked up her purse, and headed for the door, saying over her shoulder, "Same time Thursday? If you're still here?"

"I got more models than I know what to do with," Uncle Chaim told the blue angel. "Men, women, old, young—even a cat, there's one lady always brings her cat, what am I going to do?" He heard the door slam, realized that Ruthie was gone, and sighed irritably, taking a larger swallow of whiskey than he usually allowed himself. "Now she's upset, she thinks she's my mother anyway, she'll send Jules with chicken soup and an enema." He narrowed his eyes at the angel. "And what's this, how I'm only going to be painting you from now on? Like Velázquez stuck painting royal Hapsburg imbeciles over and over? Some hope you've got! Listen, you go back and tell,"—he hesitated just a trifle—"tell whoever sent you that Chaim Malakoff is too old not to paint what he likes, when he likes, and for who he likes. You got all that? We're clear?"

It was surely no way to speak to an angel; but as Uncle Chaim used to warn me about everyone from neighborhood bullies to my fourth-grade teacher, who hit people, "You give the bastards an inch, they'll walk all over you. From me they get *bupkes, nichevo,* nothing. Not an inch." I got beaten up more than once in those days, saying that to the wrong people.

And the blue angel was definitely one of them. The entire room suddenly filled with her: with the wings spreading higher than the ceiling, wider than the walls, yet somehow not touching so much as a stick of charcoal; with the aroma almost too impossibly haunting to be borne; with the vast, unutterable beauty that a thousand medieval and Renaissance artists had somehow not gone mad (for the most part) trying to ambush on canvas or trap in stone. In that moment, Uncle Chaim confided later, he didn't know whether to pity or envy Muslims their ancient ban on depictions of the human body.

"I thought maybe I should kneel, what would it hurt? But then I thought, *what would it hurt?* It'd hurt my left knee, the one had the arthritis twenty years, that's what it would hurt." So he only shrugged a little and told her, "I could manage a sitting on Monday. Somebody cancelled, I got the whole morning free."

"Now," the angel said. Her air of distinct disapproval had become one of authority. The difference was slight but notable.

"Now," Uncle Chaim mimicked her. "All right, already—Ruthie left early, so why not?" He moved the unfinished portrait over to another easel, and carefully selected a blank canvas from several propped against a wall. "I got to clean off a couple of brushes here, we'll start. You want to take off that thing, whatever, on your head?" Even I knew perfectly well that it was a halo, but Uncle Chaim always told me that you had to start with people as you meant to go on.

"You will require a larger surface," the angel instructed him. "I am not to be represented in miniature."

Uncle Chaim raised one eyebrow (an ability I envied him to the point of practicing—futilely—in the bathroom mirror for hours, until my parents banged on the door, certain I was up to the worst kind of no good). "No, huh? Good enough for the Persians, good enough for Holbein and Hilliard and Sam Cooper, but not for you? So okay, so we'll try this one . . . " Rummaging in a corner, he fetched out his biggest canvas, dusted it off, eyed it critically—"Don't even remember what I'm doing with anything this size, must have been saving it for you"—and finally set it up on the empty easel, turning it away from the angel. "Okay, Malakoff's rules. Nobody—*nobody*—looks at my painting till I'm done. Not angels, not Adonai, not my nephew over there in the corner, that's David, Duvidl—not even my wife. Nobody. Understood?"

The angel nodded, almost imperceptibly. With surprising meekness, she asked, "Where shall I sit?"

"Not a lot of choices," Uncle Chaim grunted, lifting a brush from a jar of turpentine. "Over there's okay, where Ruthie was sitting—or maybe by the big window. The window would be good, we've lost the shadows already. Take the red chair, I'll fix the color later."

But sitting down is not a natural act for an angel: they stand or they fly; check any Renaissance painting. The great wings inevitably get crumpled, the halo always winds up distinctly askew; and there is simply no way, even for Uncle Chaim, to ask an angel to cross her legs or to hook one over the arm of the chair. In the end they compromised, and the blue angel rose up to pose in the window, holding herself there effortlessly, with her wings not stirring at all. Uncle Chaim, settling in to work—brushes cleaned and Scotch replenished— could not refrain from remarking, "I always imagined you guys sort of hovered. Like hummingbirds."

"We fly only by the Will of God," the angel replied. "If Yahweh, praised be His name,"—I could actually *hear* the capital letters—"withdrew that mighty Will from us, we would fall from the sky on the instant, every single one."

"Doesn't bear thinking about," Uncle Chaim muttered. "Raining angels all over everywhere—falling on people's heads, tying up traffic—"

The angel looked first startled and then notably shocked. "I was speaking of *our* sky," she explained haughtily, "the sky of Paradise, which compares to yours as gold to lead, tapestry to tissue, heavenly choirs to the bellowing of feeding hogs—"

"All *right* already, I get the picture." Uncle Chaim cocked an eye at her, poised up there in the window with no visible means of support, and then back at his canvas. "I was going to ask you about being an angel, what it's like, but if you're going to talk about us like that—badmouthing the *sky*, for God's sake, the whole *planet*."

The angel did not answer him immediately, and when she did, she appeared considerably abashed and spoke very quietly, almost like a scolded schoolgirl. "You are right. It is His sky, His world, and I shame my Lord, my fellows and my breeding by speaking slightingly of any part of it." In a lower voice, she added, as though speaking only to herself, "Perhaps that is why I am here."

Uncle Chaim was covering the canvas with a thin layer of very light blue, to give the painting an undertone. Without looking up, he said, "What, you got sent down here like a punishment? You talked back, you didn't take out the garbage? I could believe it. Your boy Yahweh, he always did have a short fuse."

"I was told only that I was to come to you and be your model and your muse," the angel answered. She pushed her hood back from her face, revealing hair that was not bright gold, as so often painted, but of a color resembling the night sky when it pales into dawn. "Angels do not ask questions."

"Mmm." Uncle Chaim sipped thoughtfully at his Scotch. "Well, one did, anyway, you believe the story."

The angel did not reply, but she looked at him as though he had uttered some unimaginable obscenity. Uncle Chaim shrugged and continued preparing the ground for the portrait. Neither one said anything for some time, and it was the angel who spoke first. She said, a trifle hesitantly, "I have never been a muse before."

"Never had one," Uncle Chaim replied sourly. "Did just fine."

"I do not know what the duties of a muse would be," the angel confessed. "You will need to advise me."

"What?" Uncle Chaim put down his brush. "Okay now, wait a minute. I got to tell you how to get into my hair, order me around, probably tell me how I'm not painting you right? Forget it, lady—you figure it out for yourself, I'm working here."

But the blue angel looked confused and unhappy, which is no more natural for an angel than sitting down. Uncle Chaim scratched his head and said, more gently, "What do I know? I guess you're supposed to stimulate my creativity, something like that. Give me ideas, visions, make me see things, think about things I've never thought about." After a pause, he added, "Frankly, Goya pretty much has that effect on me already. Goya and Matisse. So that's covered, the stimulation—maybe you could just tell them, *him*, about that . . ."

Seeing the expression on the angel's marble-smooth face, he let the sentence trail away. Rabbi Shulevitz, who cut his blond hair close and wore shorts when he watered his lawn, once told me that angels are supposed to express God's emotions and desires, without being troubled by any of their own. "Like a number of other heavenly dictates," he murmured when my mother was out of the room, "that one has never quite functioned as I'm sure it was intended."

They were still working in the studio when my mother called and ordered me home. The angel had required no rest or food at all, while Uncle Chaim had actually been drinking his Scotch instead of sipping it (I never once saw him drunk, but I'm not sure that I ever saw him entirely sober), and needed more bathroom breaks than usual. Daylight gone, and his precarious array of 60-watt bulbs proving increasingly unsatisfactory, he looked briefly at the portrait, covered it, and said to the angel, "Well, *that* stinks, but we'll do better tomorrow. What time you want to start?"

The angel floated down from the window to stand before him. Uncle Chaim was a small man, dark and balding, but he already knew that the angel altered her height when they faced each other, so as not to overwhelm him completely. She said, "I will be here when you are."

Uncle Chaim misunderstood. He assured her that if she had no other place to sleep but the studio, it wouldn't be the first time a model or a friend had spent the night on that trundle bed in the far corner. "Only no peeking at the picture, okay? On your honor as a muse."

The blue angel looked for a moment as though she were going to smile, but she didn't. "I will not sleep here, or anywhere on this Earth," she said. "But you will find me waiting when you come."

"Oh," Uncle Chaim said. "Right. Of course. Fine. But don't change your clothes, okay? Absolutely no changing." The angel nodded.

When Uncle Chaim got home that night, my Aunt Rifke told my mother on the phone at some length, he was in a state that simply did not register on her long-practiced seismograph of her husband's moods. "He comes in, he's telling jokes, he eats up everything on the table, we snuggle up, watch a little TV, I can figure the work went well today. He doesn't talk, he's not hungry, he goes to bed early, tosses and tumbles around all night . . . okay, not so good. Thirty-seven years with a person, wait, you'll find out." Aunt Rifke had been Uncle Chaim's model until they married, and his agent, accountant and road manager ever since.

But the night he returned from beginning his portrait of the angel brought Aunt Rifke a husband she barely recognized. "Not up, not down, not happy, not *not* happy, just . . . *dazed*, I guess that's the best word. He'd start to eat something, then he'd forget about it, wander around the apartment—couldn't sit still, couldn't keep his mind on anything, had trouble even finishing a sentence. One sentence. I tell you, it scared me. I couldn't keep from wondering, is *this how it begins*? A man starts acting strange, one day to the next, you think about things like that, you know?" Talking about it, even long past the moment's terror, tears still started in her eyes.

Uncle Chaim did tell her that he had been visited by an angel who demanded that he paint her portrait. *That* Aunt Rifke had no trouble believing, thirty-seven years of marriage to an artist having inured her to certain revelations. Her main concern was how painting an angel might affect Uncle Chaim's working hours, and his daily conduct. "Like actors, you know, Duvidl? They become the people they're doing, I've seen it over and over." Also, blasphemous as it might sound, she wondered how much the angel would be paying, and in what currency. "And saying we'll get a big credit in the next world is not funny, Chaim. Not funny."

Uncle Chaim urged Rifke to come to the studio the very next day to meet his new model for herself. Strangely, that lady, whom I'd known all my life as a legendary repository of other people's lives, stories and secrets, flatly refused to take him up on the offer. "I got nothing to wear, not for meeting an angel in. Besides, what would we talk about? No, you just give her my best, I'll make some *rugelach*." And she never wavered from that position, except once.

The blue angel was indeed waiting when Uncle Chaim arrived in the studio early the next morning. She had even made coffee in his ancient glass percolator, and was offended when he informed her that it was as thin as rain and tasted like used dishwater. "Where I come from, no one ever *makes* coffee," she returned fire. "We command it."

"That's what's wrong with this crap," Uncle Chaim answered her. "Coffee's like art, you don't order coffee around." He waved the angel aside and set about a second pot, which came out strong enough to widen the angel's eyes when she sipped it. Uncle Chaim teased her—"Don't get stuff like *that* in the Green Pastures, huh?"—and confided that he made much better coffee than Aunt Rifke. "Not her fault. Woman was raised on decaf, what can you expect? Cooks like an angel, though."

The angel either missed the joke or ignored it. She began to resume her pose in the window, but Uncle Chaim stopped her. "Later, later, the sun's not right. Just stand where you are, I want to do some work on the head." As I remember, he never used the personal possessive in referring to his models' bodies: it was invariably "turn the face a little," "relax the shoulder," "move the foot to the left." Amateurs often resented it; professionals tended to find it liberating. Uncle Chaim didn't much care either way.

For himself, he was grateful that the angel proved capable of holding a pose indefinitely, without complaining, asking for a break, or needing the toilet. What he found distracting was her steadily emerging interest in talking and asking questions. As requested, her expression never changed and her lips hardly moved; indeed, there were times when he would have sworn he was hearing her only in his mind. Enough of her queries had to do with his work, with how he did what he was doing, that he finally demanded point-blank, "All those angels, seraphs, cherubim, centuries of them—all those Virgins and Assumptions and whatnot—and you've never once been painted? Not one time?"

"I have never set foot on Earth before," the angel confessed. "Not until I was sent to you."

"Sent to me. Directly. Special Delivery, Chaim Shlomovitch Malakoff—one angel, totally inexperienced at modeling. Or anything else, got anything to do with human life." The angel nodded, somewhat shyly. Uncle Chaim spoke only one word. "*Why?*"

"I am only eleven thousand, seven hundred and twenty-two years old," the angel said, with a slight but distinct suggestion of resentment in her voice. "No one tells me a *thing.*"

Uncle Chaim was silent for some time, squinting at her face from different angles and distances, even closing one eye from time to time. Finally he grumbled, more than half to himself, "I got a very bad feeling that we're both supposed to learn something from this. Bad, bad feeling." He filled the little glass for the first time that day, and went back to work.

But if there was to be any learning involved in their near-daily meetings in the studio, it appeared to be entirely on her part. She was ravenously curious about human life on the blue-green ball of damp dirt that she had observed so distantly for so long, and her constant questioning reminded a weary Uncle

Chaim—as he informed me more than once—of me at the age of four. Except that an angel cannot be bought off, even temporarily, with strawberry ice cream, or threatened with loss of a bedtime story if she can't learn to take "I don't *know!*" for an answer. At times he pretended not to hear her; on other occasions, he would make up some patently ridiculous explanation that a grandchild would have laughed to scorn, but that the angel took so seriously that he was guiltily certain he was bound to be struck by lightning. Only the lightning never came, and the tactic usually did buy him a few moments' peace—until the next question.

Once he said to her, in some desperation, "You're an angel, you're supposed to know everything about human beings. Listen, I'll take you out to Bleecker, MacDougal, Washington Square, you can look at the books, magazines, TV, the classes, the beads and crystals . . . it's all about how to get in touch with angels. Real ones, real angels, never mind that stuff about the angel inside you. Everybody wants some of that angel wisdom, and they want it bad, and they want it right now. We'll take an afternoon off, I'll show you."

The blue angel said simply, "The streets and the shops have nothing to show me, nothing to teach. You do."

"No," Uncle Chaim said. "No, no, no, no no. I'm a painter—that's all, that's it, that's what I know. Painting. But you, you sit at the right hand of God—"

"He doesn't have hands," the angel interrupted. "And nobody exactly *sits*—"

"The point I'm making, you're the one who ought to be answering questions. About the universe, and about Darwin, and how everything really happened, and what is it with God and shellfish, and the whole business with the milk and the meat—*those* kinds of questions. I mean, I should be asking them, I know that, only I'm working right now."

It was almost impossible to judge the angel's emotions from the expressions of her chillingly beautiful porcelain face; but as far as Uncle Chaim could tell, she looked sad. She said, "I also am what I am. We angels—as you call us—we are messengers, minions, lackeys, knowing only what we are told, what we are ordered to do. A few of the Oldest, the ones who were there at the Beginning— Michael, Gabriel, Raphael—*they* have names, thoughts, histories, choices, powers. The rest of us, we tremble, we *hide* when we see them passing by. We think, *if those are angels, we must be something else altogether,* but we can never find a better word for ourselves."

She looked straight at Uncle Chaim—he noticed in some surprise that in a certain light her eyes were not nearly as blue as he had been painting them, but closer to a dark sea-green—and he looked away from an anguish that he had never seen before, and did not know how to paint. He said, "So okay, you're a low-class angel, a heavenly grunt, like they say now. So how come they picked you to be my muse? Got to mean *something*, no? Right?"

The angel did not answer his question, nor did she speak much for the rest of the day. Uncle Chaim posed her in several positions, but the unwonted sadness in her eyes depressed him past even Laphroaig's ability to ameliorate. He quit work early, allowing the angel—as he would never have permitted Aunt Rifke or me—to potter around the studio, putting it to rights according to her inexpert notions, organizing brushes, oils, watercolors, pastels and pencils, fixatives, rolls of canvas, bottles of tempera and turpentine, even dusty chunks of rabbit skin glue, according to size. As he told his friend Jules Sidelsky, meeting for their traditional weekly lunch at a Ukrainian restaurant on Second Avenue, where the two of them spoke only Russian, "Maybe God could figure where things are anymore. Me, I just shut my eyes and pray."

Jules was large and fat, like Diego Rivera, and I thought of him as a sort of uncle too, because he and Ruthie always remembered my birthday, just like Uncle Chaim and Aunt Rifke. Jules did not believe in angels, but he knew that Uncle Chaim didn't necessarily believe in them either, just because he had one in his studio every day. He asked seriously, "That helps? The praying?" Uncle Chaim gave him a look, and Jules dropped the subject. "So what's she like? I mean, as a model? You like painting her?"

Uncle Chaim held his hand out, palm down, and wobbled it gently from side to side. "What's not to like? She'll hold any pose absolutely forever—you could leave her all night, morning I guarantee she wouldn't have moved a muscle. No whining, no bellyaching—listen, she'd make Cinderella look like the witch in that movie, the green one. In my life I never worked with anybody gave me less *tsuris*."

"So what's with—?" and Jules mimicked his fluttering hand. "I'm waiting for the *but*, Chaim."

Uncle Chaim was still for a while, neither answering nor appearing to notice the steaming *varyniki* that the waitress had just set down before him. Finally he grumbled, "She's an angel, what can I tell you? Go reason with an angel." He found himself vaguely angry with Jules, for no reason that made any sense. He went on, "She's got it in her head she's supposed to be my muse. It's not the most comfortable thing sometimes, all right?"

Perhaps due to their shared childhood on Tenth Avenue, Jules did not laugh, but it was plainly a near thing. He said, mildly enough, "Matisse had muses. Rodin, up to here with muses. Picasso about had to give them serial numbers— I think he married them just to keep them straight in his head. You, me . . . I don't see it, Chaim. We're not muse types, you know? Never were, not in all our lives. Also, Rifke would kill you dead. Deader."

"What, I don't know that? Anyway, it's not what you're thinking." He grinned suddenly, in spite of himself. "She's not that kind of girl, you ought to be ashamed. It's just she wants to help, to inspire, that's what muses do. I don't mind her messing around with my mess in the studio—I mean, yeah, I mind it, but I can live with it. But the other day,"—he paused briefly, taking a long breath—"the other day she wanted to give me a haircut. A haircut. It's all right, go ahead."

For Jules was definitely laughing this time, spluttering tea through his nose, so that he turned a bright cerise as other diners stared at them. "A haircut," he managed to get out, when he could speak at all clearly. "An angel gave you a haircut."

"No, she didn't *give* me a haircut," Uncle Chaim snapped back crossly. "She wanted to, she offered—and then, when I said *no, thanks*, after awhile she said she could play music for me while I worked. I usually have the news on, and she doesn't like it, I can tell. Well, it wouldn't make much sense to her, would it? Hardly does to me anymore."

"So she's going to be posing *and* playing music? What, on her harp? That's true, the harp business?"

"No, she just said she could command the music. The way they do with coffee." Jules stared at him. "Well, *I* don't know—I guess it's like some heavenly Muzak or something. Anyway, I told her no, and I'm sorry I told you anything. Eat, forget it, okay?"

But Jules was not to be put off so easily. He dug down into his *galushki poltavski* for a little time, and then looked up and said with his mouth full, "Tell me one thing, then I'll drop it. Would you say she was beautiful?"

"She's an angel," Uncle Chaim said.

"That's not what I asked. Angels are all supposed to be beautiful, right? Beyond words, beyond description, the works. So?" He smiled serenely at Uncle Chaim over his folded hands.

Uncle Chaim took so long to answer him that Jules actually waved a hand directly in front of his eyes. "Hello? Earth to Malakoff—this is your wake-up call. You in there, Chaim?"

"I'm there, I'm there, stop with the kid stuff." Uncle Chaim flicked his own fingers dismissively at his friend's hand. "Jules, all I can tell you, I never saw anyone looked like her before. Maybe that's beauty all by itself, maybe it's just novelty. Some days she looks eleven thousand years old, like she says—some days . . . some days she could be younger than Duvidl, she could be the first child in the world, first one ever." He shook his head helplessly. "I don't *know*, Jules. I wish I could ask Rembrandt or somebody. Vermeer. Vermeer would know."

Strangely, of the small corps of visitors to the studio—old painters like himself and Jules, gallery owners, art brokers, friends from the neighborhood—I seemed to be the only one who ever saw the blue angel as anything other than one of his unsought acolytes, perfectly happy to stretch canvases, make sandwiches and occasionally pose, all for the gift of a growled thanks and the privilege of covertly studying him at work. My memory is that I regarded her as a nice-looking older lady with wings, but not my type at all, I having just discovered Alice Faye. Lauren Bacall, Lizabeth Scott, and Lena Horne came a bit later in my development.

I knew she was an angel. I also knew better than to tell any of my own friends about her: we were a cynical lot, who regularly got thrown out of movie theatres for cheering on the Wolf Man and booing Shirley Temple and Bobby Breen. But I was shy with the angel, and—I guess—she with me, so I can't honestly say I remember much either in the way of conversation or revelation. Though I am still haunted by one particular moment when I asked her, straight out, "Up there, in heaven—do you ever see Jesus? Jesus Christ, I mean." We were hardly an observant family, any of us, but it still felt strange and a bit dangerous to say the name.

The blue angel turned from cleaning off a palette knife and looked directly at me, really for the first time since we had been introduced. I noticed that the color of her wings seemed to change from moment to moment, rippling constantly through a supple spectrum different from any I knew; and that I had no words either for her hair color, or for her smell. She said, "No, I have never seen him."

"Oh," I said, vaguely disappointed, Jewish or not. "Well—uh—what about his mother? The—the Virgin?" Funny, I remember that *that* seemed more daringly wicked than saying the other name out loud. I wonder why that should have been.

"No," the angel answered. "Nor,"—heading me off—"have I ever seen God. You are closer to God now, as you stand there, than I have ever been."

"That doesn't make any sense," I said. She kept looking at me, but did not reply. I said, "I mean, you're an angel. Angels live with God, don't they?"

She shook her head. In that moment—and just for that moment—her richly empty face showed me a sadness that I don't think a human face could ever have contained. "Angels live alone. If we were with God, we would not be angels." She turned away, and I thought she had finished speaking. But then she looked back quite suddenly to say, in a voice that did not sound like her voice at all, being lower than the sound I knew, and almost masculine in texture, *"Dark and dark and dark . . . so empty . . . so dark . . . "*

It frightened me deeply, that one broken sentence, though I couldn't have said why: it was just so dislocating, so completely out of place—even the rhythm of those few words sounded more like the hesitant English of our old Latvian rabbi than that of Uncle Chaim's muse. He didn't hear it, and I didn't tell him about it, because I thought it must be me, that I was making it up, or I'd heard it wrong. I was accustomed to thinking like that when I was a boy.

"She's got like a dimmer switch," Uncle Chaim explained to Aunt Rifke; they were putting freshly washed sheets on the guest bed at the time, because I was staying the night to interview them for my Immigrant Experience class project. "Dial it one way, you wouldn't notice her if she were running naked down Madison Avenue at high noon, flapping her wings and waving a gun. Two guns. Turn that dial back the other way, all the way . . . well, thank God she wouldn't ever do that, because she'd likely set the studio on fire. You think I'm joking. I'm not joking."

"No, Chaim, I know you're not joking." Rifke silently undid and remade both of his attempts at hospital corners, as she always did. She said, "What I want to know is, just where's that dial set when you're painting her? And I'd think a bit about that answer, if I were you." Rifke's favorite cousin Harvey, a career social worker, had recently abandoned wife and children to run off with a beautiful young dope dealer, and Rifke was feeling more than slightly edgy.

Uncle Chaim did think about it, and replied, "About a third, I'd say. Maybe half, once or twice, no more. I remember, I had to ask her a couple times, turn it down, please—go work when somebody's *glowing* six feet away from you. I mean, the moon takes up a lot of space, a little studio like mine. Bad enough with the wings."

Rifke tucked in the last corner, smoothed the sheet tight, faced him across the bed and said, "You're never going to finish this one, are you? Thirty-seven years, I know all the signs. You'll do it over and over, you'll frame it, you'll hang it, you'll say, *okay, that's it, I'm done*—but you won't be done, you'll just start the whole thing again, only maybe a different style, a brighter palette, a bigger canvas, a smaller canvas. But you'll never get it the way it's in your head, not for you." She smacked the pillows fluffy and tossed them back on the bed. "Don't even bother arguing with me, Malakoff. Not when I'm right."

"So am I arguing? Does it look like I'm arguing?" Uncle Chaim rarely drank at home, but on this occasion he walked into the kitchen, filled a glass from the dusty bottle of *grappa*, and turned back to his wife. He said very quietly, "Crazy to think I could get an angel right. Who could paint an angel?"

Aunt Rifke came to him then and put her hands on his shoulders. "My crazy old man, that's who," she answered him. "Nobody else. God would know."

And my Uncle Chaim blushed for the first time in many years. I didn't see this, but Aunt Rifke told me.

Of course, she was quite right about that painting, or any of the many, many others he made of the blue angel. He was never satisfied with any of them, not a one. There was always *something* wrong, something missing, something there but not there, glimpsed but gone. "Like that Chinese monkey trying to grab the moon in the water," Uncle Chaim said to me once. "That's me, a Chinese monkey."

Not that you could say he suffered financially from working with only one model, as the angel had commanded. The failed portraits that he lugged down to the gallery handling his paintings sold almost instantly to museums, private collectors and corporations decorating their lobbies and meeting rooms, under such generic titles as *Angel in the Window, Blue Wings, Angel with Wineglass*, and *Midnight Angel*. Aunt Rifke banked the money, and Uncle Chaim endured the unveilings and the receptions as best he could—without ever looking at the paintings themselves—and then shuffled back to his studio to start over. The angel was always waiting.

I was doing my homework in the studio when Jules Sidelsky visited at last, lured there by other reasons than art, beauty, or deity. The blue angel hadn't given up the notion of acting as Uncle Chaim's muse, but never seemed able to take it much beyond making a tuna salad sandwich, or a pot of coffee (at which, to be fair, she had become quite skilled), summoning music, or reciting the lost works of legendary or forgotten poets while he worked. He tried to discourage this habit; but he did learn a number of Shakespeare's unpublished sonnets, and was able to write down for Jules three poems that drowned with Shelley off the Livorno coast. "Also, your boy Pushkin, his wife destroyed a mess of his stuff right after his death. My girl's got it all by heart, you believe that?"

Pushkin did it. If the great Russian had been declared a saint, Jules would have reported for instruction to the Patriarch of Moscow on the following day. As it was, he came down to Uncle Chaim's studio instead, and was at last introduced to the blue angel, who was as gracious as Jules did his bewildered best to be. She spent the afternoon declaiming Pushkin's vanished verse to him in the original, while hovering tirelessly upside down, just above the crossbar of a second easel. Uncle Chaim thought he might be entering a surrealist phase.

Leaving, Jules caught Uncle Chaim's arm and dragged him out his door into the hot, bustling Village streets, once his dearest subject before the coming of the blue angel. Uncle Chaim, knowing his purpose, said, "So now you see? Now you see?"

"I see." Jules's voice was dark and flat, and almost without expression. "I see you got an angel there, all right. No question in the world about that." The grip on Uncle Chaim's arm tightened. Jules said, "You have to get rid of her."

"*What?* What are you *talking* about? Just finally doing the most important work of my life, and you want me . . . ?" Uncle Chaim's eyes narrowed, and he pulled forcefully away from his friend. "What is it with you and my models? You got like this once before, when I was painting that Puerto Rican guy, the teacher, with the big nose, and you just couldn't stand it, you remember? Said I'd stolen him, wouldn't speak to me for weeks, *weeks*, you remember?"

"Chaim, that's not true—"

"And so now I've got this angel, it's the same thing—worse, with the Pushkin and all—"

"Chaim, damn it, I wouldn't care if she were Pushkin's sister, they played Monopoly together—"

Uncle Chaim's voice abruptly grew calmer; the top of his head stopped sweating and lost its crimson tinge. "I'm sorry, I'm sorry, Jules. It's not I don't understand, I've been the same way about other people's models." He patted the other's shoulder awkwardly. "Look, I tell you what, anytime you want, you come on over, we'll work together. How about that?"

Poor Jules must have been completely staggered by all this. On the one hand he knew—I mean, even I knew—that Uncle Chaim never invited other artists to share space with him, let alone a model; on the other, the sudden change can only have sharpened his anxiety about his old friend's state of mind. He said, "Chaim, I'm just trying to tell you, whatever's going on, it isn't good for you. Not her fault, not your fault. People and angels aren't supposed to hang out together—we aren't built for it, and neither are they. She really needs to go back where she belongs."

"She can't. Absolutely not." Uncle Chaim was shaking his head, and kept on shaking it. "She got *sent* here, Jules, she got sent to *me*—"

"By whom? You ever ask yourself that?" They stared at each other. Jules said, very carefully, "No, not by the Devil. I don't believe in the Devil any more than I believe in God, although he always gets the good lines. But it's a free country, and I *can* believe in angels without swallowing all the rest of it, if I want to." He paused, and took a gentler hold on Uncle Chaim's arm. "And I can also imagine that angels might not be exactly what we think they are. That an angel might lie, and still be an angel. That an angel might be selfish—jealous, even. That an angel might just be a little bit out of her head."

In a very pale and quiet voice, Uncle Chaim said, "You're talking about a fallen angel, aren't you?"

"I don't know what I'm talking about," Jules answered. "That's the God's truth." Both of them smiled wearily, but neither one laughed. Jules said, "I'm dead serious, Chaim. For your sake, your sanity, she needs to go."

"And for my sake, she can't." Uncle Chaim was plainly too exhausted for either pretense or bluster, but there was no give in him. He said, "*Landsmann*, it doesn't matter. You could be right, you could be wrong, I'm telling you, it doesn't matter. There's no one else I want to paint anymore—there's no one else I *can* paint, Jules, that's just how it is. Go home now." He refused to say another word.

In the months that followed, Uncle Chaim became steadily more silent, more reclusive, more closed-off from everything that did not directly involve the current portrait of the blue angel. By autumn, he was no longer meeting

Jules for lunch at the Ukrainian restaurant; he could rarely be induced to appear at his own openings, or anyone else's; he frequently spent the night at his studio, sleeping briefly in his chair, when he slept at all. It had been understood between Uncle Chaim and me since I was three that I had the run of the place at any time; and while it was still true, I felt far less comfortable there than I was accustomed, and left it more and more to him and the strange lady with the wings.

When an exasperated—and increasingly frightened—Aunt Rifke would challenge him, "You've turned into Red Skelton, painting nothing but clowns on velvet—Margaret Keane, all those big-eyed war orphans," he only shrugged and replied, when he even bothered to respond, "You were the one who told me I could paint an angel. Change your mind?"

Whatever she truly thought, it was not in Aunt Rifke to say such a thing to him directly. Her only recourse was to mumble something like, "Even Leonardo gave up on drawing cats," or "You've done the best anybody could ever do—let it go now, let *her* go." Her own theory, differing somewhat from Jules's, was that it was as much Uncle Chaim's obsession as his model's possible madness that was holding the angel to Earth. "Like Ella and Sam," she said to me, referring to the perpetually quarrelling parents of my favorite cousin Arthur. "Locked together, like some kind of punishment machine. Thirty years they hate each other, cats and dogs, but they're so scared of being alone, if one of them died,"— she snapped her fingers—"the other one would be gone in a week. Like that. Okay, so not exactly like that, but like that." Aunt Rifke wasn't getting a lot of sleep either just then.

She confessed to me—it astonishes me to this day—that she prayed more than once herself, during the worst times. Even in my family, which still runs to atheists, agnostics, and cranky anarchists, Aunt Rifke's unbelief was regarded as the standard by which all other blasphemy had to be judged, and set against which it invariably paled. The idea of a prayer from her lips was, on the one hand, fascinating—how would Aunt Rifke conceivably address a Supreme Being?—and more than a little alarming as well. Supplication was not in her vocabulary, let alone her repertoire. Command was.

I didn't ask her what she had prayed for. I did ask, trying to make her laugh, if she had commenced by saying, "To whom it may concern . . . " She slapped my hand lightly. "Don't talk fresh, just because you're in fifth grade, sixth grade, whatever. Of course I didn't say that, an old Socialist Worker like me. I started off like you'd talk to some kid's mother on the phone, I said, 'It's time for your little girl to go home, we're going to be having dinner. You better call her in now, it's getting dark.' Like that, polite. But not fancy."

"And you got an answer?" Her face clouded, but she made no reply. "You didn't get an answer? Bad connection?" I honestly wasn't being fresh: this was my story too, somehow, all the way back, from the beginning, and I had to know where we were in it. "Come *on*, Aunt Rifke."

"I got an answer." The words came slowly, and cut off abruptly, though she seemed to want to say something more. Instead, she got up and went to the stove, all my aunts' traditional *querencia* in times of emotional stress. Without turning her head, she said in a curiously dull tone, "*You* go home now. Your mother'll yell at me."

My mother worried about my grades and my taste in friends, not about me; but I had never seen Aunt Rifke quite like this, and I knew better than to push her any further. So I went on home.

From that day, however, I made a new point of stopping by the studio literally every day—except Shabbos, naturally—even if only for a few minutes, just to let Uncle Chaim know that someone besides Aunt Rifke was concerned about him. Of course, obviously, a whole lot of other people would have been, from family to gallery owners to friends like Jules and Ruthie; but I was ten years old, and feeling like my uncle's only guardian, and a private detective to boot. A guardian against what? An angel? Detecting what? A portrait? I couldn't have said for a minute, but a ten-year-old boy with a sense of mission definitely qualifies as a dangerous flying object.

Uncle Chaim didn't talk to me anymore while he was working, and I really missed that. To this day, almost everything I know about painting—about *being* a painter, every day, all day—I learned from him, grumbled out of the side of his mouth as he sized a canvas, touched up a troublesome corner, or stood back, scratching his head, to reconsider a composition or a subject's expression, or simply to study the stoop of a shadow. Now he worked in bleak near-total silence; and since the blue angel never spoke unless addressed directly, the studio had become a far less inviting place than my three-year-old self had found it. Yet I felt that Uncle Chaim still liked having me there, even if he didn't say anything, so I kept going, but it was an effort some days, mission or no mission.

His only conversation was with the angel—Uncle Chaim always chatted with his models; paradoxically, he felt that it helped them to concentrate—and while I honestly wasn't trying to eavesdrop (except sometimes), I couldn't help overhearing their talk. Uncle Chaim would ask the angel to lift a wing slightly, or to alter her stance somewhat: as I've said, sitting remained uncomfortable and unnatural for her, but she had finally been able to manage a sort of semi-recumbent posture, which made her look curiously vulnerable, almost like a tired child after an adult party, playing at being her mother, with the grown-ups all asleep upstairs. I can close my eyes today and see her so.

One winter afternoon, having come tired, and stayed late, I was half-asleep on a padded rocker in a far corner when I heard Uncle Chaim saying, "You ever think that maybe we might both be dead, you and me?"

"We angels do not die," the blue angel responded. "It is not in us to die."

"I told you, lift the chin," Uncle Chaim grunted. "Well, it's built into *us*, believe me, it's mostly what we do from day one." He looked up at her from the easel. "But I'm trying to get you into a painting, and I'll never be able to do it, but it doesn't matter, got to keep trying. The head a *little* bit to the left—no, that's too much, I said a *little*." He put down his brush and walked over to the angel, taking her chin in his hand. He said, "And you . . . whatever you're after, you're not going to get that right, either, are you? So it's like we're stuck here together—and if we *were* dead, maybe this is hell. Would we know? You ever think about things like that?"

"No." The angel said nothing further for a long time, and I was dozing off again when I heard her speak. "You would not speak so lightly of hell if you had seen it. I have seen it. It is not what you think."

"*Nu?*" Uncle Chaim's voice could raise an eyebrow itself. "So what's it like?"

"*Cold.*" The words were almost inaudible. "So cold . . . so lonely . . . so *empty*. God is not there . . . no one is there. No one, no one, no one . . . no one . . . "

It was that voice, that other voice that I had heard once before, and I have never again been as frightened as I was by the murmuring terror in her words. I actually grabbed my books and got up to leave, already framing some sort of gotta-go to Uncle Chaim, but just then Aunt Rifke walked into the studio for the first time, with Rabbi Shulevitz trailing behind her, so I stayed where I was. I don't know a thing about ten-year-olds today; but in those times one of the major functions of adults was to supply drama and mystery to our lives, and we took such things where we found them.

Rabbi Stuart Shulevitz was the nearest thing my family had to an actual regular rabbi. He was Reform, of course, which meant that he had no beard, played the guitar, performed Bat Mitzvahs and interfaith marriages, invited local priests and imams to lead the Passover ritual, and put up perpetually with all the jokes told, even by his own congregation, about young, beardless, terminally tolerant Reform rabbis. Uncle Chaim, who allowed Aunt Rifke to drag him to *shul* twice a year, on the High Holidays, regarded him as being somewhere between a mild head cold and mouse droppings in the pantry. But Aunt Rifke always defended Rabbi Shulevitz, saying, "He's smarter than he looks, and anyway he can't help being blond. Also, he smells good."

Uncle Chaim and I had to concede the point. Rabbi Shulevitz's immediate predecessor, a huge, hairy, bespectacled man from Riga, had smelled mainly of rancid hair oil and cheap peach *schnapps*. And he couldn't sing "Red River Valley," either.

Aunt Rifke was generally a placid-appearing, *hamishe* sort of woman, but now her plump face was set in lines that would have told even an angel that she meant business. The blue angel froze in position in a different way than she usually held still as required by the pose. Her strange eyes seemed almost to change their shape, widening in the center and somehow *lifting* at the corners, as though to echo her wings. She stood at near-attention, silently regarding Aunt Rifke and the rabbi.

Uncle Chaim never stopped painting. Over his shoulder he said, "Rifke, what do you want? I'll be home when I'm home."

"So who's rushing you?" Aunt Rifke snapped back. "We didn't come about you. We came the rabbi should take a look at your *model* here." The word burst from her mouth trailing blue smoke.

"What look? I'm working, I'm going to lose the light in ten, fifteen minutes. Sorry, Rabbi, I got no time. Come back next week, you could say a *barucha* for the whole studio. Goodbye, Rifke."

But my eyes were on the rabbi, and on the angel, as he slowly approached her, paying no heed to the quarreling voices of Uncle Chaim and Aunt Rifke. Blond or not, "Red River Valley" or not, he was still magic in my sight, the official representative of a power as real as my disbelief. On the other hand, the angel could fly. The Chasidic wonder-*rebbes* of my parents' Eastern Europe could fly up to heaven and share the Shabbos meal with God, when they chose. Reform rabbis couldn't fly.

As Rabbi Shulevitz neared her, the blue angel became larger and more stately, and there was now a certain menacing aspect to her divine radiance, which set me shrinking into a corner, half-concealed by a dusty drape. But the rabbi came on.

"Come no closer," the angel warned him. Her voice sounded deeper, and slightly distorted, like a phonograph record when the Victrola hasn't been wound tight enough. "It is not for mortals to lay hands on the Lord's servant and messenger."

"I'm not touching you," Rabbi Shulevitz answered mildly. "I just want to look in your eyes. An angel can't object to that, surely."

"The full blaze of an angel's eyes would leave you ashes, impudent man." Even I could hear the undertone of anxiety in her voice.

"That is foolishness." The rabbi's tone continued gentle, almost playful. "My friend Chaim paints your eyes full of compassion, of sorrow for the world and all its creatures, every one. Only turn those eyes to me for a minute, for a very little minute, where's the harm?"

Obediently he stayed where he was, taking off his hat to reveal the black *yarmulke* underneath. Behind him, Aunt Rifke made as though to take Uncle Chaim's arm, but he shrugged her away, never taking his own eyes from Rabbi Shulevitz and the blue angel. His face was very pale. The glass of Scotch in his left hand, plainly as forgotten as the brush in his right, was beginning to slosh over the rim with his trembling, and I was distracted with fascination, waiting for him to drop it. So I wasn't quite present, you might say, when the rabbi's eyes looked into the eyes of the blue angel.

But I heard the rabbi gasp, and I saw him stagger backwards a couple of steps, with his arm up in front of his eyes. And I saw the angel turning away, instantly; the whole encounter couldn't have lasted more than five seconds, if that much. And if Rabbi Shulevitz looked stunned and frightened—which he did—there is no word that I know to describe the expression on the angel's face. No words.

Rabbi Shulevitz spoke to Aunt Rifke in Hebrew, which I didn't know, and she answered him in swift, fierce Yiddish, which I did, but only insofar as it pertained to things my parents felt were best kept hidden from me, such as money problems, family gossip, and sex. So I missed most of her words, but I caught anyway three of them. One was *shofar*, which is the ram's horn blown at sundown on the High Holidays, and about which I already knew two good dirty jokes. The second was *minyan*, the number of adult Jews needed to form a prayer circle on special occasions. Reform *minyanim* include women, which Aunt Rifke always told me I'd come to appreciate in a couple of years. She was right.

The third word was *dybbuk*.

I knew the word, and I didn't know it. If you'd asked me its meaning, I would have answered that it meant some kind of bogey, like the Invisible Man, or just maybe the Mummy. But I learned the real meaning fast, because Rabbi Shulevitz had taken off his glasses and was wiping his forehead, and whispering, "No. No. *Ich vershtaye nicht . . .* "

Uncle Chaim was complaining, "What the hell is this? See now, we've lost the light already, I *told* you." No one—me included—was paying any attention.

Aunt Rifke—who was never entirely sure that Rabbi Shulevitz *really* understood Yiddish—burst into English. "It's a *dybbuk*, what's not to understand? There's a *golem* in that woman, you've got to get rid of it! You get a *minyan* together, right now, you get rid of it! Exorcise!"

Why on Earth did she want the rabbi to start doing push-ups or jumping-jacks in this moment? I was still puzzling over that when he said, "That woman, as you call her, is an angel. You cannot . . . Rifke, you do not exorcise an angel." He was trembling—I could see that—but his voice was steady and firm.

"You do when it's possessed!" Aunt Rifke looked utterly exasperated with everybody. "I don't know how it could happen, but Chaim's angel's got a *dybbuk* in her,"—she whirled on her husband—"which is why she makes you just keep painting her and painting her, day and night. You finish—really finish, it's done, over—she might have to go back out where it's not so nice for a *dybbuk*, you know about that? Look at her!" and she pointed an orange-nailed finger straight in the blue angel's face. "She hears me, she knows what I'm talking about. You

know what I'm talking, don't you, Miss Angel? Or I should say, Mister Dybbuk?
You tell me, okay?"

I had never seen Aunt Rifke like this; she might have been possessed herself.
Rabbi Shulevitz was trying to calm her, while Uncle Chaim fumed at the intruders
disturbing his model. To my eyes, the angel looked more than disturbed—she
looked as terrified as a cat I'd seen backed against a railing by a couple of dogs,
strays, with no one to call them away from tearing her to pieces. I was anxious
for her, but much more so for my aunt and uncle, truly expecting them to be
struck by lightning, or turned to salt, or something on that order. I was scared
for the rabbi as well, but I figured he could take care of himself. Maybe even
with Aunt Rifke.

"A *dybbuk* cannot possibly possess an angel," the rabbi was saying. "Believe
me, I majored in Ashkenazic folklore—wrote my thesis on Lilith, as a matter
of fact—and there are no accounts, no legends, not so much as a single *bubbe-
meise* of such a thing. *Dybbuks* are wandering spirits, some of them good, some
malicious, but all houseless in the universe. They cannot enter heaven, and
Gehenna won't have them, so they take refuge within the first human being
they can reach, like any parasite. But an angel? Inconceivable, take my word.
Inconceivable."

"In the mind of God," the blue angel said, "nothing is inconceivable."

Strangely, we hardly heard her; she had almost been forgotten in the dispute
over her possession. But her voice was that other voice—I could see Uncle
Chaim's eyes widen as he caught the difference. That voice said now, "She is
right. I am a *dybbuk*."

In the sudden absolute silence, Aunt Rifke, serenely complacent, said, "Told
you."

I heard myself say, "Is she bad? I thought she was an angel."

Uncle Chaim said impatiently, "What? She's a model."

Rabbi Shulevitz put his glasses back on, his eyes soft with pity behind the
heavy lenses. I expected him to point at the angel, like Aunt Rifke, and thunder
out stern and stately Hebrew maledictions, but he only said, "Poor thing, poor
thing. Poor creature."

Through the angel's mouth, the *dybbuk* said, "Rabbi, go away. Let me alone,
let me be. I am warning you."

I could not take my eyes off her. I don't know whether I was more fascinated
by what she was saying, and the adults having to deal with its mystery, or by
the fact that all the time I had known her as Uncle Chaim's winged and haloed
model, someone else was using her the way I played with my little puppet theatre
at home—moving her, making up things for her to say, perhaps even putting
her away at night when the studio was empty. Already it was as though I had
never heard her strange, shy voice asking a child's endless questions about the

world, but only this grown-up voice, speaking to Rabbi Shulevitz. "You cannot force me to leave her."

"I don't want to force you to do anything," the rabbi said gently. "I want to help you."

I wish I had never heard the laughter that answered him. I was too young to hear something like that, if anyone could ever be old enough. I cried out and doubled up around myself, hugging my stomach, although what I felt was worse than the worst bellyache I had ever wakened with in the night. Aunt Rifke came and put her arms around me, trying to soothe me, murmuring, half in English, half in Yiddish, "Shh, shh, it's all right, *der rebbe* will make it all right. He's helping the angel, he's getting rid of that thing inside her, like a doctor. Wait, wait, you'll see, it'll be all right." But I went on crying, because I had been visited by a monstrous grief not my own, and I was only ten.

The *dybbuk* said, "If you wish to help me, rabbi, leave me alone. I will not go into the dark again."

Rabbi Shulevitz wiped his forehead. He asked, his tone still gentle and wondering, "What did you do to become . . . what you are? Do you remember?"

The *dybbuk* did not answer him for a long time. Nobody spoke, except for Uncle Chaim muttering unhappily to himself, "Who needs this? Try to get your work done, it turns into a *ferkockte* party. Who needs it?" Aunt Rifke shushed him, but she reached for his arm, and this time he let her take it.

The rabbi said, "You are a Jew."

"I was. Now I am nothing."

"No, you are still a Jew. You must know that we do not practice exorcism, not as others do. We heal, we try to heal both the person possessed and the one possessing. But you must tell me what you have done. Why you cannot find peace."

The change in Rabbi Shulevitz astonished me as much as the difference between Uncle Chaim's blue angel and the spirit that inhabited her and spoke through her. He didn't even look like the crew-cut, blue-eyed, guitar-playing, basketball-playing (well, he tried). college-student-dressing young man whose idea of a good time was getting people to sit in a circle and sing "So Long, It's Been Good to Know You" or "Dreidel, Dreidel, Dreidel" together. There was a power of his own inhabiting him, and clearly the *dybbuk* recognized it. It said slowly, "You cannot help me. You cannot heal."

"Well, we don't know that, do we?" Rabbi Shulevitz said brightly. "So, a bargain. You tell me what holds you here, and I will tell you, honestly, what I can do for you. *Honestly.*"

Again the *dybbuk* was slow to reply. Aunt Rifke said hotly, "What is this? What *help*? We're here to expel, to get rid of a demon that's taken over one of God's angels, if that's what she really is, and enchanted my husband so it's all he can paint, all he can think about painting. Who's talking about *helping* a demon?"

"The rabbi is," I said, and they all turned as though they'd forgotten I was there. I gulped and stumbled along, feeling like I might throw up. I said, "I don't think it's a demon, but even if it is, it's given Uncle Chaim a chance to paint a real angel, and everybody loves the paintings, and they buy them, which we wouldn't have had them to sell if the—the *thing*—hadn't made her stay in Uncle Chaim's studio." I ran out of breath, gas and show-business ambitions all at pretty much the same time, and sat down, grateful that I had neither puked nor started to cry. I was still grandly capable of both back then.

Aunt Rifke looked at me in a way I didn't recall her ever doing before. She didn't say anything, but her arm tightened around me. Rabbi Shulevitz said quietly, "Thank you, David." He turned back to face the angel. In the same voice, he said, "Please. Tell me."

When the *dybbuk* spoke again, the words came one by one—two by two, at most. "A girl . . . .There was a girl . . . a young woman . . . "

"*Ai*, how not?" Aunt Rifke's sigh was resigned, but not angry or mocking, just as Uncle Chaim's "*Shah*, Rifkela" was neither a dismissal nor an order. The rabbi, in turn, gestured them to silence.

"She wanted us to marry," the *dybbuk* said. "I did too. But there was time. There was a world . . . there was my work . . . there were things to see . . . to taste and smell and do and be . . . .It could wait a little. She could wait . . . "

"Uh-huh. Of course. You could die waiting around for some damn man!"

"*Shah*, Rifkela!"

"But this one did not wait around," Rabbi Shulevitz said to the *dybbuk*. "She did not wait for you, am I right?"

"She married another man," came the reply, and it seemed to my ten-year-old imagination that every tortured syllable came away tinged with blood. "They had been married for two years when he beat her to death."

It was my Uncle Chaim who gasped in shock. I don't think anyone else made a sound.

The *dybbuk* said, "She sent me a message. I came as fast as I could. I *did* come," though no one had challenged his statement. "But it was too late."

This time we were the ones who did not speak for a long time. Rabbi Shulevitz finally asked, "What did you do?"

"I looked for him. I meant to kill him, but he killed himself before I found him. So I was too late again."

"What happened then?" That was me, once more to my own surprise. "When you didn't get to kill him?"

"I lived. I wanted to die, but I lived."

From Aunt Rifke—how not? "You ever got married?"

"No. I lived alone, and I grew old and died. That is all."

"Excuse me, but that is *not* all." The rabbi's voice had suddenly, startlingly, turned probing, almost harsh. "That is only the beginning." Everyone looked at him. The rabbi said, "So, after you died, what did happen? Where did you go?"

There was no answer. Rabbi Shulevitz repeated the question. The *dybbuk* responded finally, "You have said it yourself. Houseless in the universe I am, and how should it be otherwise? The woman I loved died because I did not love her enough—what greater sin is there than that? Even her murderer had the courage to atone, but I dared not offer my own life in payment for hers. I chose to live, and living on has been my punishment, in death as well as in life. To wander back and forth in a cold you cannot know, shunned by heaven, scorned by purgatory . . . do you wonder that I sought shelter where I could, even in an angel? God himself would have to come and cast me out again, Rabbi—you never can."

I became aware that my aunt and uncle had drawn close around me, as though expecting something dangerous and possibly explosive to happen. Rabbi Shulevitz took off his glasses again, ran his hand through his crew cut, stared at the glasses as though he had never seen them before, and put them back on.

"You are right," he said to the *dybbuk*. "I'm a rabbi, not a *rebbe*—no Solomonic wisdom, no magical powers, just a degree from a second-class seminary in Metuchen, New Jersey. You wouldn't know it." He drew a deep breath and moved a few steps closer to the blue angel. He said, "But this *gornisht* rabbi knows anyway that you would never have been allowed this refuge if God had not taken pity on you. You must know this, surely?" The *dybbuk* did not answer. Rabbi Shulevitz said, "And if God pities you, might you not have a little pity on yourself? A little forgiveness?"

"Forgiveness . . . " Now it was the *dybbuk* who whispered. "Forgiveness may be God's business. It is not mine."

"Forgiveness is everyone's business. Even the dead. On this Earth or under it, there is no peace without forgiveness." The rabbi reached out then, to touch the blue angel comfortingly. She did not react, but he winced and drew his hand back instantly, blowing hard on his fingers, hitting them against his leg. Even I could see that they had turned white with cold.

"You need not fear for her," the *dybbuk* said. "Angels feel neither cold nor heat. You have touched where I have been."

Rabbi Shulevitz shook his head. He said, "I touched you. I touched your shame and your grief—as raw today, I know, as on the day your love died. But the cold . . . the cold is yours. The loneliness, the endless guilt over what you should have done, the endless turning to and fro in empty darkness . . . none of that comes from God. You must believe me, my friend." He paused, still flexing his frozen fingers. "And you must come forth from God's angel now. For her sake and your own."

The *dybbuk* did not respond. Aunt Rifke said, far more sympathetically than she had before, "You need a *minyan*, I could make some calls. We'd be careful, we wouldn't hurt it."

Uncle Chaim looked from her to the rabbi, then back to the blue angel. He opened his mouth to say something, but didn't.

The rabbi said, "You have suffered enough at your own hands. It is time for you to surrender your pain." When there was still no reply, he asked, "Are you afraid to be without it? Is that your real fear?"

"It has been my only friend!" the *dybbuk* answered at last. "Even God cannot understand what I have done so well as my pain does. Without the pain, there is only me."

"There is heaven," Rabbi Shulevitz said. "Heaven is waiting for you. Heaven has been waiting a long, long time."

"*I am waiting for me!*" It burst out of the *dybbuk* in a long wail of purest terror, the kind you only hear from small children trapped in a nightmare. "You want me to abandon the one sanctuary I have ever found, where I can huddle warm in the consciousness of an angel and sometimes—for a little— even forget the thing I am. You want me to be naked to myself again, and I am telling you *no, not ever, not ever, not ever*. Do what you must, Rabbi, and I will do the only thing I can." It paused, and then added, somewhat stiffly, "Thank you for your efforts. You are a good man."

Rabbi Shulevitz looked genuinely embarrassed. He also looked weary, frustrated and older than he had been when he first recognized the possession of Uncle Chaim's angel. Looking vaguely around at us, he said, "I don't know— maybe it *will* take a *minyan*. I don't want to, but we can't just . . . " His voice trailed away sadly, too defeated even to finish the sentence.

Or maybe he didn't finish because that was when I stepped forward, pulling away from my aunt and uncle, and said, "He can come with me, if he wants. He can come and live in me. Like with the angel."

Uncle Chaim said, "*What?*" and Aunt Rifke said, "*No!*" and Rabbi Shulevitz said, "*David!*" He turned and grabbed me by the shoulders, and I could feel him wanting to shake me, but he didn't. He seemed to be having trouble breathing. He said, "David, you don't know what you're saying."

"Yes, I do," I said. "He's scared, he's so scared. I know about scared."

Aunt Rifke crouched down beside me, peering hard into my face. "David, you're ten years old, you're a little boy. This one, he could be a thousand years, he's been hiding from God in an angel's body. How could you know what he's feeling?"

I said, "Aunt Rifke, I go to school. I wake up every morning, and right away I think about the boys waiting to beat me up because I'm small, or because I'm Jewish, or because they just don't like my face, the way I look at them. Every day I want to stay home and read, and listen to the radio, and play my All-Star Baseball game, but I get dressed and I eat breakfast, and I walk to school. And every day I have to think how I'm going to get through recess, get through gym class, get home without running into Jay Taffer, George DiLucca. Billy Kronish. I know all about not wanting to go outside."

Nobody said anything. The rabbi tried several times, but it was Uncle Chaim who finally said loudly, "I got to teach you to box. A little Archie Moore, a little Willie Pep, we'll take care of those *mamzers*." He looked ready to give me my first lesson right there.

When the *dybbuk* spoke again, its voice was somehow different: quiet, slow, wondering. It said, "Boy, you would do that?" I didn't speak, but I nodded.

Aunt Rifke said, "Your mother would *kill* me! She's hated me since I married Chaim."

The *dybbuk* said, "Boy, if I come . . . outside, I cannot go back. Do you understand that?"

"Yes," I said. "I understand."

But I was shaking. I tried to imagine what it would be like to have someone living inside me, like a baby, or a tapeworm. I was fascinated by tapeworms that year. Only this would be a spirit, not an actual physical thing—that wouldn't be so bad, would it? It might even be company, in a way, almost like being a comic-book superhero and having a secret identity. I wondered whether the angel had even known the *dybbuk* was in her, as quiet as he had been until he spoke to Rabbi Shulevitz. Who, at the moment, was repeating over and over, "No, I can't permit this. This is wrong, this can't be allowed. No." He began to mutter prayers in Hebrew.

Aunt Rifke was saying, "I don't care, I'm calling some people from the *shul*, I'm getting some people down here right away!" Uncle Chaim was gripping my shoulder so hard it hurt, but he didn't say anything. But there was really no one in the room except the *dybbuk* and me. When I think about it, when I remember, that's all I see.

I remember being thirsty, terribly thirsty, because my throat and my mouth were so dry. I pulled away from Uncle Chaim and Aunt Rifke, and I moved past Rabbi Shulevitz, and I croaked out to the *dybbuk*, "Come on, then. You can come out of the angel, it's safe, it's okay." I remember thinking that it was like trying to talk a cat down out of a tree, and I almost giggled.

I never saw him actually leave the blue angel. I don't think anyone did. He was simply standing right in front of me, tall enough that I had to look up to meet his eyes. Maybe he wasn't a thousand years old, but Aunt Rifke hadn't missed by much. It wasn't his clothes that told me—he wore a white turban that looked almost square, a dark red vest sort of thing and white trousers, under a gray robe that came all the way to the ground—it was the eyes. If blackness is the absence of light, then those were the blackest eyes I'll ever see, because there was no light in those eyes, and no smallest possibility of light ever. You couldn't call them sad: *sad* at least knows what joy is, and grieves at being exiled from *joy*. However old he really was, those eyes were a thousand years past sad.

"Sephardi," Rabbi Shulevitz murmured. "Of course he'd be Sephardi."

Aunt Rifke said, "You can see through him. Right through."

In fact he seemed to come and go: near-solid one moment, cobweb and smoke the next. His face was lean and dark, and must have been a proud face once. Now it was just weary, unspeakably weary—even a ten-year-old could see that. The lines down his cheeks and around the eyes and mouth made me think of desert pictures I'd seen, where the earth gets so dry that it pulls apart, cracks and pulls away from itself. He looked like that.

But he smiled at me. No, he smiled *into* me, and just as I've never seen eyes like his again, I've never seen a smile as beautiful. Maybe it couldn't reach his eyes, but it must have reached mine, because I can still see it. He said softly, "Thank you. You are a kind boy. I promise you, I will not take up much room."

I braced myself. The only invasive procedures I'd had any experience with then were my twice-monthly allergy shots and the time our doctor had to lance an infected finger that had swollen to twice its size. Would possession be anything like that? Would it make a difference if you were sort of inviting the possession, not being ambushed and taken over, like in *Invasion of the Body Snatchers*? I didn't mean to close my eyes, but I did.

Then I heard the voice of the blue angel.

"There is no need." It sounded like the voice I knew, but the *breath* in it was different—I don't know how else to put it. I could say it sounded stronger, or clearer, or maybe more musical; but it was the breath, the free breath. Or maybe that isn't right either, I can't tell you—I'm not even certain whether angels breathe, and I knew an angel once. There it is.

"Manassa, there is no need," she said again. I turned to look at her then, when she called the *dybbuk* by his name, and she was smiling herself, for the first time. It wasn't like his; it was a faraway smile at something I couldn't see, but it was real, and I heard Uncle Chaim catch his breath. To no one in particular, he said, "*Now* she smiles. Never once, I could never once get her to smile."

"Listen," the blue angel said. I didn't hear anything but my uncle grumbling, and Rabbi Shulevitz's continued Hebrew prayers. But the *dybbuk*—Manassa—lifted his head, and the endlessly black eyes widened, just a little.

The angel said again, "Listen," and this time I did hear something, and so did everyone else. It was music, definitely music, but too faint with distance for me to make anything out of it. But Aunt Rifke, who loved more kinds of music than you'd think, put her hand to her mouth and whispered, "*Oh*."

"Manassa, listen," the angel said for the third time, and the two of them looked at each other as the music grew stronger and clearer. I can't describe it properly: it wasn't harps and psalteries—whatever a psaltery is, maybe you use it singing psalms—and it wasn't a choir of soaring heavenly voices, either. It was almost a little scary, the way you feel when you hear the wild geese passing over in the autumn night. It made me think of that poem of Tennyson's, with that line about *the horns of Elfland faintly blowing.* We'd been studying it in school.

"It is your welcome, Manassa," the blue angel said. "The gates are open for you. They were always open."

But the *dybbuk* backed away, suddenly whimpering. "I cannot! I am afraid! They will see!"

The angel took his hand. "They see now, as they saw you then. Come with me, I will take you there."

The *dybbuk* looked around, just this side of panicking. He even tugged a bit at the blue angel's hand, but she would not let him go. Finally he sighed very deeply—lord, you could feel the dust of the tombs in that sigh, and the wind between the stars—and nodded to her. He said, "I will go with you."

The blue angel turned to look at all of us, but mostly at Uncle Chaim. She said to him, "You are a better painter than I was a muse. And you taught me a great deal about other things than painting. I will tell Rembrandt."

Aunt Rifke said, a little hesitantly, "I was maybe rude. I'm sorry." The angel smiled at her.

Rabbi Shulevitz said, "Only when I saw you did I realize that I had never believed in angels."

"Continue not to," the angel replied. "We rather prefer it, to tell you the truth. We work better that way."

Then she and the *dybbuk* both looked at me, and I didn't feel even ten years old; more like four or so. I threw my arms around Aunt Rifke and buried my face in her skirt. She patted my head—at least I guess it was her, I didn't actually see her. I heard the blue angel say in Yiddish, "*Sei gesund,* Chaim's Duvidl. You were always courteous to me. Be well."

I looked up in time to meet the old, old eyes of the *dybbuk.* He said, "In a thousand years, no one has ever offered me freely what you did." He said something else, too, but it wasn't in either Hebrew or Yiddish, and I didn't understand.

The blue angel spread her splendid, shimmering wings one last time, filling the studio—as, for a moment, the mean winter sky outside seemed to flare with a sunset hope that could not have been. Then she and Manassa, the *dybbuk,* were gone, vanished instantly, which makes me think that the wings aren't really for flying. I don't know what other purpose they could serve, except they did seem somehow to enfold us all and hold us close. But maybe they're just really decorative. I'll never know now.

Uncle Chaim blew out his breath in one long, exasperated sigh. He said to Aunt Rifke, "I never did get her right. You know that."

I was trying to hear the music, but Aunt Rifke was busy hugging me, and kissing me all over my face, and telling me not ever, ever to do such a thing again, what was I thinking? But she smiled up at Uncle Chaim and answered him, "Well, she got *you* right, that's what matters." Uncle Chaim blinked at her. Aunt Rifke said, "She's probably telling Rembrandt about you right now. Maybe Vermeer, too."

"You think so?" Uncle Chaim looked doubtful at first, but then he shrugged and began to smile himself. "Could be."

I asked Rabbi Shulevitz, "He said something to me, the *dybbuk*, just at the end. I didn't understand."

The rabbi put his arm around me. "He was speaking in old Ladino, the language of the Sephardim. He said, *'I will not forget you.'*" His smile was a little shaky, and I could feel him trembling himself, with everything over. "I think you have a friend in heaven, David. Extraordinary Duvidl."

The music was gone. We stood together in the studio, and although there were four of us, it felt as empty as the winter street beyond the window where the blue angel had posed so often. A taxi took the corner too fast, and almost hit a truck; a cloud bank was pearly with the moon's muffled light. A group of young women crossed the street, singing. I could feel everyone wanting to move away, but nobody did, and nobody spoke, until Uncle Chaim finally said, "Rabbi, you got time for a sitting tomorrow? Don't wear that suit."

Eliyahu ha-Navi

Max Sparber

Although he was not recognizably human, in 1908 the old man was nevertheless recognizably Jewish. He looked as I imagine he must have looked for a thousand years. He was dwarfish and twisted, with long, gnarled limbs that grasped whatever they could clutch with a fierce clawing motion. His gray, matted beard and sidelocks met on the ground, where they tangled with each other and with the filthy fringes from his prayer shawl. He was small enough that my great-grandparents could fit him into an accordion case, and this is what they did, so that his moans and wheezing might be mistaken for the sound of wind running through an instrument's reeds. They carried him aboard the *Lusitania*, and my great-grandfather never let go of the accordion case, holding it to his side and whispering to it as they sat in steerage. When they eventually saw the Statue of Liberty, my great-grandfather kissed the accordion case and whispered to it, "Nyu York, Eliyahu, Nyu York!" The accordion case coughed and rattled back, unconcerned.

This is how the Jews brought the prophet Elijah to the New World.

My great-grandparents kept him under the sink of their tiny Brownsville apartment, feeding him dates and fortunes cookies, which he devoured—fortunes and all—by pulverizing the food against his gums with short, spastic jabs of his crooked hands. Elijah terrified the children, as a series of strokes had left him foul tempered, and he frequently flew into rages. His fits could last for hours, during which he would fling plates and silverware at my great-grandmother, who would do her best to subdue him by beating the prophet with a carpet whisk.

When my grandfather Jack was a boy, Elijah terrified him; every Passover, Jack was required to bring the old man a glass of wine, as tradition dictated. Jack knew through bitter experience that it was a bad idea to get too near the prophet. He recounted that one year he attempted to push the glass of wine across the floor to Elijah with a mop handle. The old man watched Jack warily, peering at him sideways through half-closed, yellow eyes, and when the mop handle got close enough Elijah lunged.

As they did every year, the neighbors stood outside in the hallway, ears pressed to my great-grandparents' door. When they heard Jack's screams, they gossiped, as they always did. "Ach, it is the Sparbers," they muttered to each other. "Every Passover it is the same. They beat their children! Ten times, once for each plague!"

While Elijah's temper seemed boundless, as years passed and the prophet grew older he quieted almost to the point of docility. My father does not like to discuss it, as he feels responsible, but the prophet's change in temperament came swiftly, with a tragic incident that occurred in my childhood home in Minneapolis.

My father owned a large German shepherd. Once when we were out, the dog got into the old man's crawlspace in the basement. We returned home to a house littered with clumps of hair and shreds of the old man's leather phylacteries. We found the dog and the prophet in the living room. Elijah lay face down on the floor with his arms splayed, looking very much like a rag doll that somebody had casually tossed aside. The German shepherd, growling and wagging his tail, pounced repeatedly at the prone figure and chewed at its leg. Madness still glowed in the eye of the prophet after that incident, but it was the madness of fear rather than the madness of rage.

Elijah grew very quiet, huddling against walls when we came near and fleeing into closets or hiding under beds when he was able. At night, we could hear his terrified voice whispering in Yiddish, the sound creeping up from his basement crawlspace through vents and emerging into our bedrooms as hoarse mumbling. These sounds unnerved me, and were the cause of uncountable nightmares. I would wake, screaming, and my father would come into my room and sit on the side of my bed, wiping the sweat from my brow with the back of his hand and telling me stories about the Messiah. When the Messiah came, he explained, there would be peace throughout the world. All the Jews would converge in Jerusalem, and God would slay Leviathan in the deep. God would spread the skin of Leviathan over Jerusalem, where it would hang like a great, glowing canopy. We would gather at tables to hear the words of the Messiah, we would eat the sweet flesh of Leviathan, and both would be more delightful than anything we knew.

"This is why the prophet Elijah is so important, Max," he would tell me. "It is Elijah that will tell the world of the Messiah's coming! He will go from door to door, knocking and saying, 'Gather your prayer shawl, gather your phylacteries! He is here! The Messiah is here!' "

However, by the time I entered college, I no longer ate meat, and I no longer hoped for a Messiah. I did not wish to go to Jerusalem and devour the flesh of Leviathan. It was at this time that I received the prophet, along with a pen set, as a gift to celebrate the onset of my adult life. I despised my responsibility for Elijah. I had no love for this man, who had been a burden on my family for too long. He was little more than rags and bones now, and he gave off a powerful odor that I could not inhale without gagging. I did not want to tend to Elijah.

I hid the prophet in the closet of my dormitory room, opening the door only long enough to fling scraps from my dinner plate onto him. I felt a mixture of guilt and resentment toward the old man. At night, when I would hear the voice of the prophet mumbling in Yiddish from inside the closet, I would close my eyes and secretly hope that God rejected those incomprehensible prayers. I imagined the words of Elijah rising to Heaven as wisps of smoke, and entering through the nostrils of God. I imagined God spitting the prophet's prayers out of His mouth as though they were filthy rags. Then I would sleep, and in my dreams, I would be terrified.

Elijah disgusted my girlfriend, who shared her dorm room with an easily shocked girl from Iran. This rendered neither of our rooms suitable for intimacy. We struggled to find locations to satisfy our desires, but every abandoned classroom or empty soccer field failed us. In the first instance, just as we were flinging our discarded clothes onto the chalkboard and front row of desks, a dozen first-year calculus students filed in and burst into embarrassed giggling. In the second instance, as we lay on the grass, furiously pawing at each other and gasping for air, a squad of cheerleaders stormed the field and stood above us, arms akimbo, demanding that we leave.

Unfortunately, my girlfriend's Iranian roommate never seemed to leave their dorm room, where she spent hours on the telephone speaking in rapid-fire Farsi. If we intruded during her conversations, she would stare at us from underneath her veil and her eyes would widen, followed by an inevitable high-pitched gasp. My girlfriend did not want to imagine how her roommate would respond if she witnessed us doing so much as holding hands.

My room was no better an option. No amount of discussion concerning Elijah made the prophet any less offensive to my girlfriend. She was not Jewish, and did not care one way or the other if he was a figure from the Old Testament. "Whoever he is," she would complain, "he needs to be in an nursing home. At least there they would clean him!"

Finally, in order to act on my lust, I decided to pay fifty dollars to the two wrestlers who lived in the dorm room next to mine. I asked them to look after the prophet for several hours. When I left the old man with the wrestlers, he turned away from me and pressed his head and hands to the wall, shoulders rising and falling gently as he wept. The wrestlers seemed unconcerned. "He'll be all right," they promised me. "Go and take care of your lady."

While my girlfriend and I indulged our desires, the wrestlers fed Elijah beer and pizza. They turned their music up and danced around the old man, clubbing each other with their massive arms and howling. They went through their drawers and found their cheapest cologne, which they dumped on Elijah to cover his smell. They watched a pornographic movie with the prophet, smoking marihuana out of a six-foot plastic bong and blowing the smoke in Elijah's face. They used cigarette lighters to singe his beard and sidelocks, and they brought trinkets from their Hawaiian vacation out of their closet and decorated the old man with them. When I came for Elijah, two hours after I had left him, he was slumped on one of their beds with a plastic tropical-flower lei around his neck, a grass skirt around his waist, and a coconut-half bikini top slung over his shoulders. He lay there, staring up at the ceiling, not blinking. One of the wrestlers lifted a tiki mug to me, toasting me with a tropical cocktail. "Hey," he said blearily. "Your grandfather is pretty cool."

The prophet was not breathing.

It took twnty minutes of CPR before paramedics produced a heartbeat. I visited Elijah every afternoon for a month, drowning in shame. I sat by his hospital bed and stared at the old man. I spoke quietly to him and grasped his hand, rubbing his dry, paper-like skin and praying he would come out of the coma. At the end of the afternoon, my father would join me, and we would go down to the hospital's cafeteria and eat dinner in silence. At first, I tried to apologize to my father, but he raised his hand to silence me. "It was too big a responsibility," he said, his voice breaking. "This is my fault. I should never have asked you to care for Elijah."

I would walk with my father to the hospital room, and he would take a seat alongside the prophet's bed. He would lean down towards the old man, whispering. "What now, Eliyahu?" my father would ask. "What now?"

My grades plummeted and my relationship with my girlfriend ended. I did not attend class, but instead wandered around the campus, filled with black thoughts. At night, I would watch the news, and I would hear of wars and murders, and wonder if it was not somehow my fault. What if the Messiah was ready to come, I wondered, but could not? What if the Messiah waited in Heaven, astride his white stallion, waiting for Elijah to announce him—and because of my stupidity, that announcement would never come?

Unable to bear these thoughts, I drank, and the more I drank the angrier I grew. What sort of God, I asked myself, would keep the prophet alive in such a debilitated state? What sort of God would allow Elijah to grow mad and frail, so that a little bit of excitement might kill him? Was this my fault, I asked, or God's?

Drunk, I stumbled to the hospital. It was late at night, and the building seemed abandoned. I passed through the hallways unnoticed, as though I were in a dream, until I reached Elijah's room. I stood above the prophet and wept, wanting to press a pillow into the old man's face until he stopped breathing again. If the Messiah cannot come without this ruin of a man, I told myself, then the Messiah does not deserve to come.

I leaned over and pressed my lips to the old man's ear and, for the first time in my life, I whispered to him. "Gather your prayer shawl, gather your phylacteries," I whispered. "He is here!" Then I returned to my dorm room and slept without nightmares.

When I came to the hospital the next day, Elijah was gone. An orderly went through the old man's room, changing the sheets on his empty bed and spraying air freshener. On the floor, swept into a little pile, were half-eaten dates and fragments of a fortune cookie. From outside the room, from some distant hallway, I heard the moans and wheezes of an accordion.

Reuben

Tamar Yellin

When I was nine years old, my Uncle Esdras came to visit.

He was a traveller, and a handsome man. Though short, he had the body of an acrobat, and with his shock of fair hair looked much like my father had in earlier life. Both wore glasses, and both possessed the family characteristics: sobriety, generosity, intellect, bad temper, the wealth of too many talents, and an obsessive nature.

There are birds, the albatross for example, which spend their entire lives in the air. My uncle was like that. He set down only occasionally, and when he did so it was never for long. His visits were rare and always unexpected, for he was always *en route*, and the fact that we lay on his route was just a happy accident. He was a bird of passage, and we were his way station.

My father did not share his wanderlust. He was a man of books, an earnest autodidact, whom travelling invariably made ill. He preferred to cover distances on paper, and to read about those faraway places he did not have the stamina to reach. To him there was something faintly reprehensible in Esdras, clicking his heels across the continents.

I still remember the day of his arrival. He wore a pale suit, and carried a small brown valise. This, from the state of its broken corners and the numerous labels pasted onto it, must have travelled with him for many years. He smelt strongly of nicotine, and when he bent down to greet me I was struck by a strange sense of recognition. It would be unfair to say that he was my father made handsome, for my father too had once been a handsome man. Truer to say he was my father turned hero: a swashbuckler version bronzed by the desert sun.

My mother must have recognized it also, for her embrace of welcome was a little longer and tighter than was strictly necessary. She had squeezed into her black dress, puffed up her hair, and sprayed herself with the perfume she saved for special occasions. The house was a glade of sunshine and fluttering chintz, and she had set the table with angel cake and flowers.

Into this haven of suburban peace Uncle Esdras entered like a light aircraft, battered and bleached, footsore and world-weary, wanting only an oil-change and a wash. But he was not a man to insult hospitality; he had, after all, accepted it the world over. And really it only took a few moments for him to adjust himself. He sat down to tea and promptly turned the table into a map as he proceeded to describe, with cartographic exactness, the route he had lately followed to bring him to us. It was a typical act of conquest. He would never, in all the time he spent there, seem natural in our house, but would become a kind of resident anomaly, like the bizarre carving he had brought us from Africa, which sat on the mantelpiece next to the eight-day clock.

Later I found he had taken over my room, and turned it, in a few moves, into his own, a sort of explorer's base hut. Strange objects were scattered among my childish possessions, dark, worn, heavy things, whose presence made every-thing else unfamiliar: a pair of thick boots, a leather-covered camera, a canvas knapsack fastened with giant buckles. I did not see how they could all have emerged from that one modest suitcase, but my uncle, along with his many other talents, was an expert and indefatigable packer.

On the bedside table a black sticky volume was lying, bound round with an ancient elastic band and decorated with stains and squashed mosquitoes: my uncle's travel journal. I opened it. It was written in purple ink, in a strange spidery code. Here and there it was splashed with a crude drawing: a temple, a tree, a tremulous smoking mountain.

I do not know, to this day, what precisely it was my uncle did. I thought of him then as a kind of scholar-adventurer, performing in actuality what my father only read about in books: leaping crevasses, discovering hidden cities, recording the dialects of distant clans. I imagined him living a life more dangerous and romantic than that of anyone else I had ever met.

He did not take much notice of me at first. Apparently he valued his privacy, for as soon as he entered the room I was dismissed with a clap of the hands. Later I peeped in to find him lying back on the bed with his boots on, blowing smoke meditatively at the ceiling. This struck me as entirely an adventurer's thing to do.

Afterwards I found that by standing on a flowerpot beneath the window I could satisfactorily spy on him, although there wasn't much to see. However rest-less his lifestyle, he had the capacity to lie still for long periods. His expression was neither troubled nor entirely peaceful: from the depth of the grooves on his forehead he seemed to be calculating the solution to a particularly difficult sum.

I managed to sit quietly through dinner while my parents and uncle talked, but found it impossible to follow the conversation studded with foreign and exotic words. During dessert I nodded off to sleep, and was ignominiously sent to bed. Three hours later I was up again: creeping down in my pajamas I found them, like mountaineers in a tent, playing kitchen-roulette on the tablecloth. My uncle had set up a circle of condiments, my father with skill and dexterity spun the knife; my mother had got out an heirloom bottle of brandy. The stakes, it seemed, were more spiritual than monetary. They all smoked cigarettes, and

I felt I had stumbled on something adult, sinister, and exclusive, an intimate threesome where I was an unwanted fourth.

This was my first introduction to Uncle Esdras. Next morning I discovered him, a dawn riser, sitting in the lounge with his inevitable cigarette and a line of curious objects ranged on the coffee table in front of him. He did not glance at me, but raised a finger. I stopped at a deferential distance of about three feet and looked at the objects. There was a ball of patterned metal, a fragment of red coral, and a string of beads. A tooth, a gourd, a coin, and what I knew later to be a lemur's foot.

Uncle Esdras contemplated this booty, and while wielding his cigarette in one hand, adjusted their positions relative to one another as though playing an odd kind of solitaire. There seemed to be great deliberation in the way he did this, and if I had known better I would have said he was trying to pique my interest.

After a while, having arranged them to his satisfaction, he sat back with a sigh, and finally deigned to turn his eyes on me. I suppose you would like to take a closer look, he said, and patting the cushion invited me to sit down next to him. I hesitated at first. There was something of the predator in Esdras which I instinctively recognized, but I let my curiosity get the better of me and slid in beside him onto the green sofa.

Then he proceeded to explain the origins of his seven objects. He asked me if I knew the meaning of the word *talisman*. Each of these was a kind of talisman and very necessary to the traveller. The coin, for instance, which was decorated with a curly script, if kept in a pocket guaranteed you would always have two coins to rub together. He had found it by chance in an Arabian market. The coral he had won from an old sailor in Calcutta, who in turn had obtained it from a great fakir. It had the power of calming bad weather when thrown into the sea.

As he described their powers and provenance he threw me quick glances every so often, as if to check whether I believed his tales. My expression must have looked suitably wonderstruck, for he continued to tell even more fantastic stories. The gourd, for example, was a magical source of water which had saved his life once when crossing the Sahara. The tooth had mystical healing properties.

I picked up the coffee-colored beads which hung limply on a dirty piece of string. Uncle Esdras frowned.

Oh, they are just worry beads, he said.

I would have liked to have them for my father, who worried a great deal; but all my acquisitiveness, which Uncle Esdras had so successfully stimulated, seemed hopeless in the face of such valuable items. I laid the beads down, and pushed out my lower lip.

You may handle them if you wish, Uncle Esdras said with formality, and feeling obliged, I rolled the ball of metal embossed with symbols which, apparently, brought its possessor genuine good luck. Of course, he continued, they are only useful to the person who rightfully owns them. If you were to steal that, for instance, it wouldn't work for you.

Indignantly I denied any such intention. I put down the charm, and one by one he plopped the items into a canvas bag, including, last of all, the lemur's foot, which I had longed but didn't dare to touch, and for which he had still provided no explanation.

And what about that? I asked, pointing.

That, he answered, is a lemur's foot. If you throw it down on the ground when you are lost, its toes will point you in the right direction.

Of course, a compass might have done the same; but this tool dealt in destiny rather than magnetism, and I watched him place it in the bag with envy.

After that, Uncle Esdras ignored me again. At breakfast he spoke to my mother and forgot my presence. When we went for a walk he strolled arm-in-arm with her and indulged in a tensely murmured conversation. Skipping close, I caught a few mysterious fragments.

But why not? my mother purred into his ear. You should settle down. Waiting for you somewhere is a nice woman—

Later I went up to him where he sat reading the newspaper on the patio.

Those talismans, I said. Do you often use them?

Now and then, he answered.

I thought for a moment. I asked: And a traveller—someone who wanted to be a traveller. Would they need to have talismans like those?

Esdras replied that they were more or less essential. Seeing my crestfallen look, he modified this by saying that they were certainly a great help.

I wandered off, and resorting to my room (which at the moment hardly seemed to be mine) spent the afternoon going through a certain drawer, which my mother habitually referred to as my "mess drawer" but which to me was full of irreplaceable treasures. There was my school badge for good conduct, the peacock feather my father had given me, and a war-scarred, tournament-winning bouncy ball. A plastic ruby which had fallen out of a piece of cheap costume jewelry and a glass drop from a vanished chandelier. Every one of these objects carried for me a kind of magical and irrational power, quite out of proportion to their actual value; the ball for example I regarded as almost human. They had been endowed with the significance which belongs only to children's playthings and ritual artifacts.

As I sorted through them I wondered if I could convince Uncle Esdras of their special qualities. But I doubted that I would succeed in persuading him to exchange even one of them for a genuine talisman.

✡

Of the three main family traits—short sight, a bad stomach, and an anxious temperament—my father had more than his fair measure. It was not surprising that he should take refuge in an increasing bibliomania.

For as long as I could remember he had enclosed himself, evening after evening, in his small windowless study lined with tottering books: rabbinic treatises, Kabbalistic novels, anthropological surveys of the Jewish nose; histories of seventy generations, lists of innumerable dead. Here, surrounded by wreaths of his own breath (he believed in cold) he would study the art of biblical numerology, trace his ancestry to the house of Solomon or follow the spurious trail of the ten lost tribes. Or, turning the pages of an enormous picture book, he would sate himself with images: with one hundred-and-one representations of Jerusalem. Jerusalem in woodcuts, Jerusalem in gilt with glittering minarets, Jerusalem as a chessboard with the temple in the middle; mosaic maps, archaeological plans, medieval diagrams with Jerusalem the navel of the world, the world peeled and quartered like an orange with Jerusalem at its center.

In his youth he had dreamed of becoming an engineer. His first ambition had been to design bridges. He filled his sketchbooks with flying arcs of steel, all of them unviable and unstable, hanging perilously in empty air. He had a supernatural affinity with numbers, and no idea what he might do with it.

Instead he went into business, worked himself to exhaustion and left his other ambitions to lie and rust. Time slipped through his fingers. He knew he should have done something exceptional in the world, and at his worst moments, could at least comfort himself with that knowledge.

Sometimes on an evening I would sit with him and, perched on his skinny knee, turn the pages of some enigmatic text: a poem in Gothic script, a plan of the universe embellished with dragons. He would tell me stories of the ten lost tribes, who were carried away and shut up beyond the Sambatyon, a river of rocks and stones which poured six days and was peaceful on the Sabbath; of the Black Jews of Malabar and their red Pentateuch; of the Jews of Yemen, who refused to return until the Messiah came. For this they were cursed, and their messiah, when he did come, was a disappointment. He challenged the king to chop off his head and watch him rise again; and the king did, and he didn't.

As I grew older I would read aloud while my father sat, his eyes closed, smoking an endless chain of Consulates; and while my father played a game of chess with himself in which neither side ever seemed to win, I would browse through fantastic chronicles of how the Children of Israel were led by Moses through the wilderness of Russia, across the Red Sea at the Bering Strait, and down to the promised land of America.

I asked my father once why he never spoke about my Uncle Esdras. There was nothing to be said, my father replied, placing a hand to his forehead, as though the very mention of it gave him a headache. The brothers had not been close for many years. Esdras never wrote or telephoned. Long ago they had quarreled, but that was unimportant: the crust had long since cooled on that altercation. Most of all, my father was disappointed. Esdras could have done anything: whatever he turned his hand to he would have excelled. Yet he became nothing; became this wanderer, this will-o'-the-wisp, this drifter. A man of wasted talents and broken dreams.

Now I had seen my uncle, I could not prevent myself from making comparisons: my father the businessman, Esdras the adventurer; Esdras tanned and dynamic, my father sedentary and pale. I could not understand my father's hostility, and thought his reserve must stem from some deep-seated jealousy of his more youthful and enterprising brother.

I thought I detected, too, a certain disdain in my uncle's attitude. He spoke to my father with one corner of his mouth always cynically turned up, and never, I noticed, looked him in the eye. While my father was out at work he went into his room and sat on the corner of his desk, finished his chess game, and flicked through his precious books with the half-smile of one who had no need of them. Yet communication between the two cannot have been entirely frozen, for once, when I came home from school, I caught sight of them closeted together in the study, and my father, with an air of profound gloom, handing a significant envelope to his brother.

For my part, I was dazzled by the romance of my Uncle Esdras, which was made all the more tantalizing by his habit of ignoring me for long periods, and only speaking to me when he chose. He took up his place in our house with the suave negligence of a visiting dignitary, and was waited on hand and foot by my mother, with whom he held urgent, whispered conversations behind the kitchen door.

It took me a little while therefore to pluck up sufficient courage and present him with my first proposal: the exchange of his worry beads for my champion ball, plus the accumulated savings in my piggy bank. I had chosen the worry beads for our first transaction, not because they were what I most wanted, but because I thought that of all the talismans in the bag they were probably of the least value. In any event, I didn't think Uncle Esdras was likely to need them much. He was cutting his toenails in the bedroom at the time; at first I thought he was going to say nothing, but then to my surprise he laid the scissors down and handed me the cuttings on a small piece of paper. Throw these in the stove for me, will you, he said. And don't drop any. You'd be surprised what a witch can get up to with your toenails. I did as he asked, and returned. Well then, he said, let me have a look at this ball. I brought it out, and we proceeded to go into detail about its tournament record.

To this day I cannot fathom the motivations of my Uncle Esdras: whether he was moved by spite or mischievousness or pure casual greed, or, as seems likely, by a combination of all three, he took up my offer and pocketed both ball and cash. There is, of course, another possibility: that he really believed in the value of his talismans, and only took what he considered fair payment.

As a result of this successful first deal I was both heartened and dismayed. Heartened because the other items now looked attainable; dismayed because I had already parted with all my money. I had a lot to learn, I realized, on the subject of bargaining.

I went off to regroup my strategies, and this required some considerable thought, because I saw that if I was to make the most of my remaining assets I would need to invest them with greater properties than they really had. I did not feel this would be lying exactly. It was more a kind of psychic discovery. By concentrating hard enough I would discover the true powers of these seemingly worthless objects.

So it was that I found myself presenting the plastic jewel for inspection as the seed of a great treasure, which, if planted in a certain spot in China, would produce in due time an actual treasure tree. The jewels, I explained, grew as stones inside the fruit. Uncle Esdras examined it carefully, and threw me a curious look, half-skeptical and half-impressed, raising one eyebrow and turning up the corner of his mouth. He wondered what he would do with a treasure tree, and speculated that it might be more of a liability than a benefit. And then, perhaps he didn't have any plans to go to China. He was a difficult customer, but I was ready to fight back. I said it would be a terrible waste not to go to China, and think of all the good he could do with the money; and if the tree were a nuisance he could always chop it down. We argued like this for a while, but the final result was that he took the jewel and I got the lucky charm in exchange for it.

I could see that this game of swaps was going to be hard work, not least because Uncle Esdras was such a moody chap. There were times when he refused to acknowledge my existence, and others when he positively snarled at me. I learned to recognize the signs, however. We were entangled now in a peculiar conspiracy, and when the moment was right he was as eager as I to negotiate.

It wasn't all business though. My uncle had other things to teach me, too. Lying on his back under the moon (since for nine weeks he had not slept in a bed, his body gave him no choice at first but to sleep in the garden) he taught me the names of the stars and the constellations, and described, in his detailed, *National Geographic* manner, the nights he had passed under a desert sky. He recalled nights in the mountains with stars as big as snowflakes, and low tropical moons the color of brass. He invoked the cry of the jackal and the song of the bulbul, the call of the cicada, and the howl of the wolf.

Why did he travel so much? He started out as a species of shady salesman;

invested his money, spent nothing, had no home of his own: not one chair leg, he liked to say with a smile. This was how he afforded his airline tickets, and an endless succession of rooms in cheap hotels. More and more he had gone for the gypsy life, joining a series of ill-planned expeditions: crossing the desert with a flotsam of outcasts, climbing mountains on the bootstraps of lunatics, and dragging through jungles in the wake of gangsters. For years now he had preferred to travel alone, and showed no mercy to tagalongs and companions.

It was easy for him to undergo privations. Nothing clung to him: even his clothes were borrowed. He described his sufferings with obvious pleasure, and showed off his forearm, ripped by an angry scar. Every few minutes his face contracted with pain. Sciatica, he told me, adding, with a wry smile, that pain too was a kind of companionship.

I begged him to tell me more stories, and he obliged with tall ones: how he had sailed by raft down the Orinoco River and visited the Bermuda Triangle. How he had survived snakebite and caught malaria, and escaped an erupting volcano by the skin of his teeth. He told his tales always with a twinkle in his eye, as though silently acknowledging their spuriousness. But I longed to believe him; and while I did so, I think he even believed himself.

I asked him once if he had ever encountered any of the ten lost tribes. He paused and drew breath, as though about to spin another yarn. Then he frowned, and seemed to change his mind.

There was an old junkseller he had met, once, in the backstreets of Shanghai, who claimed to belong to the missing tribe of Reuben, and who had tried to sell him some ancient biblical parchments. But he hadn't been taken in: the man was a charlatan.

The story was obviously true; and this seemed an appropriate moment for us to engage in a little business transaction of our own. I reached into a pocket for my latest offering: one of the onyx eggs from the mantelpiece. It wasn't, strictly speaking, mine to exchange, but I was beyond caring about such minor details. I told him it was the egg of a phoenix. I wanted the lemur's foot desperately, and so far nothing I could offer would persuade my uncle to part with it.

Night after night, my father and mother and uncle played the knife game in a welter of cigarette smoke and brandy and an increasingly portentous atmosphere. I would come down to find them gathered round the table, watching the knife spin with the faces of hardened gamblers.

My mother would be gazing at my Uncle Esdras. My father would be gazing at my mother. Esdras, calm and detached, spun the knife with the deftness of long practice. As the blade turned the mood intensified, so that when it finally slowed and came to rest, it seemed to point with prophetic significance.

And then, one night: You spin it, said Esdras, pulling me onto his knee ; and as he did so my father's head jerked up, like that of a horse does when it senses danger. For the stakes were now immeasurably higher. His eyes met those of his brother, my mother observed them both; all three watched my small hand spin the knife. Quickly at first, then slower, the blade flashed round. It was as though my whole future depended on it.

My father said to him: It's not your place.

My uncle replied: It isn't your place either.

You've no business to interfere, my father said.

None of us can prevent it, my uncle answered.

Then the knife slowed down, and came to a halt, and pointed at neither my uncle nor my father. It pointed away, through a gap in the condiments: out of the circle, into the distance; nowhere.

What did my uncle do on his long wanderings? He looked at the landscape. He gazed at and examined the faces of people. He listened to language, traffic, music, banter. He smelled rot and incense; he tried all sorts of food. He slept under rocks and on benches, in trains and in boats, his cheek against granite, metal, sawdust, velvet.

It was, all in all, an intensely physical life. A life in which thought was consumed by practical matters, and long hours of travel by uninterrupted thought. A life of consulting maps and haggling for tickets, of planning the next destination and bartering clothes; of riding the dragon of the imagination all across Asia.

At least, said my uncle Esdras, his eyes on the stars, that was the way it appeared to him just now. Just now, with his eyes on the stars and his body in stasis, the friendly pain of sciatica streaking his leg, he really believed his travels to be romantic. It was an illusion, of course: and one he fell victim to every time he resolved to end his journey.

I'll let you into a secret, my uncle said. This time I'd really decided to call it a day. But I knew as soon as I got here that that was impossible. Why? I asked him. Well, he said vaguely, I'd already bought my ticket. And he held up an airline ticket against the moon.

Then Esdras told me the truth about his existence. How life was reduced to the merely physical. How slow and tedious were the long void hours of travel. How cold the nights spent sleeping under the heavens. How sordid the far-flung places of the world.

The truth of it is, I am shattered, said Uncle Esdras, and turned on me a pair of exhausted eyes. At that moment I felt a strange presentiment. He turned his face away and looked at the sky.

That was the price of freedom, said my uncle: always to be counting the miles from nowhere; always to travel hopefully, never to arrive. Never to go home, never to be at peace.

But he was depressed just now, he immediately added. Whenever he stopped he got into this mood. As soon as he moved on he would feel better. That was why he never lingered long.

You see, he explained, fixing his gaze on the stars (and I wondered how he could see them without his glasses): my mother and father thought he was always unhappy. But when he visited them, he always was.

Night after night my uncle spun the knife; and as went round it wound a spring tighter and tighter inside my father, tighter and tighter inside my uncle too, so that one night as I lay in bed I heard a glass break and my father shouting. Then my mother's voice, querulous and distressed. The deep, impassive tones of my Uncle Esdras.

This time I didn't dare to venture downstairs.

Next morning I found him seated as usual, his bag packed and waiting in the hall; phlegmatic as ever, he turned the pages of the newspaper with a leisurely air. My mother was red-eyed in the kitchen. My father, of course, was nowhere to be seen.

Uncle Esdras was leaving as suddenly as he had come, and I still had not bargained successfully for the lemur's foot.

Nor had I begun to broach the possibility of my coming with him, if not this time, then when I was old enough. We simply hadn't had the opportunity to discuss it. But he was sour and distant this morning, and shook out the paper violently when I approached; so I went off in desperation to hunt through the contents of my mother's dressing-table.

His taxi was coming at twelve, and while my mother packed sandwiches and my father sat dourly among his books, Uncle Esdras paced the garden and I made my last reckless offer. Fortunately he was in a mood to negotiate. He wore a sardonic smile; I wondered whether to trust him. But it was his ability to play seriously which was at once so disconcerting and so irresistible.

Transaction completed, he smiled and ruffled my hair. Poor kid, he said. Looks like you're going to take after your worthless uncle.

It was the best compliment I had ever had. We walked down the driveway together, hand in hand. And there was an aura then about Uncle Esdras: a radiance of utter happiness. He had the ecstatic air of a man beginning, all over again, the great undiscovered adventure of his life.

As my mother and I saw him off at the gate (I with a handshake, she with an epic embrace) I felt a sudden pang, not only of disappointment at being left behind, but of guilt at sending him into the world so bare, so unprotected and without talismans: with only a false jewel, a badge for good conduct, a peacock's feather and a bouncy ball.

Returning indoors, I took out my frustrations on my father, who listened incredulously while I told him it was all his fault, that I was going to the Sahara with Uncle Esdras, that I loved Uncle Esdras more than I did him. Slowly, with a pained face, he rose to his feet.

He's a bum! he shouted, and the word sounded all the uglier flying from his unaccustomed mouth. He's never even been to the Sahara. Don't you know he only came here to borrow money?

It was a lie and I said so, running off then to shut myself in my room. My room was tidy, and bore no trace of Uncle Esdras, whose sheets, even, my mother had hastened to remove. It was as though he had never visited. And yet it was not. The dawn of some unpleasant change was breaking in me. For the rest of that day I valiantly held it off, while my mother hunted and inquired after her diamond ring. But after all, I told myself, she didn't realize that it could summon a genie. A fair exchange is no robbery, I told myself over and over, as I rearranged my seven talismans, and ran my acquisitive fingers along the knuckles of the lemur's foot.

The Muldoon

Glen Hirshberg

"He found that he could not even concentrate for more than an instant on Skeffington's death, for Skeffington, alive, in multiple guises, kept getting in the way."

— John O'Hara

That night, like every night we spent in our grandfather's house, my older brother Martin and I stayed up late to listen. Sometimes, we heard murmuring in the white, circular vent high up the cracking plaster wall over our heads. The voices were our parents', we assumed, their conversation captured but also muffled by the pipes in the downstairs guest room ceiling. In summer, when the wind went still between thunderstorms, we could almost make out words. Sometimes, especially in August, when the Baltimore heat strangled even the thunderclouds, we heard cicadas bowing wildly in the grass out our window and twenty feet down.

On the dead-still September night after my grandfather's *shiva*, though, when all of the more than two thousand well-wishers we'd hosted that week had finally filed through the house and told their stories and left, all Martin and I heard was the clock. *Tuk, tuk, tuk,* like a prison guard's footsteps. I could almost see it out there, hulking over the foyer below, nine feet of carved oak and that bizarre, glassed-in face, brass hands on black velvet with brass fittings. Even though the carvings all the way up the casing were just wiggles and flourishes, and even though the velvet never resembled anything but a blank, square space, the whole thing had always reminded me more of a totem pole than a clock, and it scared me, some.

"Miriam," my brother whispered. "Awake?"

I hesitated until after the next *tuk*. It had always seemed bad luck to start a sentence in rhythm with that clock. "Think they're asleep?"

He sat up. Instinctively, my glance slipped out our open door to the far hallway wall. My grandfather had died right out there, felled at last by the heart attack his physician had warned him for decades was coming if he refused to drop fifty pounds. It seemed impossible that his enormous body had left not the slightest trace in the threadbare hallway carpet, but there was none. What had he even been doing up here? In the past four years or so, I'd never once seen him more than two steps off the ground floor.

The only thing I could see in the hallway now was the mirror. Like every other mirror in the house, it had been soaped for the *shiva*, and so, instead of the half-reassuring, half-terrifying blur of movement I usually glimpsed there, I saw only darkness, barely penetrated by the single butterfly nightlight plugged in beneath it.

Reaching over the edge of the bed, I found my sweatpants and pulled them on under my nightgown. Then I sat up, too.

"Why do they soap the mirrors?"

"Because the Angel of Death might still be lurking. You don't want him catching sight of you." Martin turned his head my way, and a tiny ray of light glinted off his thick owl-glasses.

"That isn't why," I whispered.

"You make the ball?"

"Duh."

With a quick smile that trapped moonlight in his braces, my brother slid out of bed. I flipped my own covers back but waited until he reached the door, poked his head out, and peered downstairs. Overhead, the vent pushed a useless puff of cold air into the heat that had pooled around us. In the foyer, the clock *tuk*-ed.

"Voices," I hissed, and Martin scampered fast back to bed. His glasses tilted toward the vent. I grinned. "Ha. We're even."

Now I could see his eyes, dark brown and huge in their irises, as though bulging with all the amazing things he knew. One day, I thought, if Martin kept reading like he did, badgered my parents into taking him to enough museums, just stood there and *watched* the way he could sometimes, he'd literally pop himself like an over-inflated balloon.

"For what?" he snapped.

"Angel of Death."

"That's what Roz told me."

"She would."

He grinned back. "You're right."

From under my pillow, I drew out the sock-ball I'd made and flipped it to him. He turned it in his hands as though completing an inspection. Part of the ritual. Once or twice, he'd even torn balls apart and made me redo them. The DayGlo-yellow stripes my mother hoped looked just a little athletic on his spindle-legs had to curve just so, like stitching on a baseball. And the weight had to be right. Three, maybe four socks, depending on how worn they were and what brand mom had bought. Five, and the thing just wouldn't arc properly.

"You really think we should play tonight?"

Martin glanced up, as though he hadn't even considered that. Then he shrugged. "Grandpa would've."

I knew that he'd considered it plenty. And that gave me my first conscious inkling of just how much our grandfather had meant to my brother.

This time, I followed right behind Martin to the door, and we edged together onto the balcony. Below us, the grandfather clock and the double-doored glass case where our Roz, the tall, orange-skinned, sour-faced woman grandpa had married right after I was born, kept her prized porcelain poodle collection and her milky blue oriental vases with the swans gliding around the sides lay hooded in shadow. Beyond the foyer, I could just see the straightened rows of chairs we'd set up for the week's last mourner's Kaddish, the final chanting of words that seemed to have channeled a permanent groove on my tongue. The older you get, my mother had told me, the more familiar they become. *Yit-barah, v'yish-tabah, v'yit-pa-ar, v'yit-roman, v'yit-na-sey . . .*

"You can throw first," my brother said, as though granting me a favor.

"Don't you want to?" I teased. "To honor him?" Very quietly, I began to make chicken clucks.

"Cut it out," Martin mumbled, but made no move toward the stairs. I clucked some more, and he shot out his hand so fast I thought he was trying to hit me. But he was only flapping in that nervous, spastic wave my parents had been waiting for him to outgrow since he was three. "Shush. Look."

"I am look . . ." I started, then realized he wasn't peering over the balcony at the downstairs hall from which Roz would emerge to scream at us if she heard movement. He was looking over his shoulder toward the mirror. "Not funny," I said.

"Weird," said Martin. Not until he took a step across the landing did I realize what he meant.

The doors to the hags' rooms were open. Not much. I couldn't see anything of either room. But both had been pushed just slightly back from their usual positions. Clamminess flowed from my fingertips up the peach fuzz on my arms.

Naturally, halfway across the landing, Martin stopped. If I didn't take the lead, he'd never move another step. The clammy sensation spread to my shoulders, down my back. I went to my brother anyway. We stood, right in the spot where the mirror should have reflected us. Right where Grandpa died. In the butterfly-light, Martin's face looked wet and waxy, the way it did when he had a fever.

"You really want to go through those doors?" I whispered.

"Just trying to remember."

I nodded first toward Mrs. Gold's room, then Sophie's. "Pink. Blue." The shiver I'd been fighting for the past half-minute snaked across my ribs.

Martin shook his head. "I mean the last time we saw them open. Either one."

But he already knew that. So did I. We'd last glimpsed those rooms the week before the hags had died. Four years—almost half my life—ago.

"Let's not," I said, and Martin shuffled to the right, toward Mrs. Gold's. "Martin, come on, let's play. I'm going downstairs."

But I stayed put, amazed, as he scuttled forward with his eyes darting everywhere, like a little ghost-shrimp racing across an exposed patch of sea bottom. *He'll never do it,* I thought, *not without me.* I tried chicken-clucking again, but my tongue had dried out. Martin stretched out his hand and shoved.

The door made no sound as it glided back, revealing more shadows, the dark humps of four-poster bed and dresser, a square of moonlight through almost-drawn curtains. A split second before, if someone had asked me to draw Mrs. Gold's room, I would have made a big, pink smear with a crayon. But now, even from across the hall, I recognized that everything was just the way I'd last seen it.

"Coming?" Martin asked.

More than anything else, it was the plea in his voice that pulled me forward. I didn't bother stopping, because I knew I'd be the one going in first anyway. But I did glance at my brother's face as I passed. His skin looked even waxier than before, as though it might melt right off.

Stopping on the threshold, I reached into Mrs. Gold's room with my arm, then jerked it back.

"*What?*" my brother snapped.

I stared at the goose bumps dimpling the skin above my wrist like bubbles in boiling water. But the air in Mrs. Gold's room wasn't boiling. It was freezing cold. "I think we found this house's only unclogged vent," I said.

"Just flick on the lights."

I reached in again. It really was freezing. My hand danced along the wall. I was imagining fat, pink spiders lurking right above my fingers, waiting while I stretched just that last bit closer . . .

"Oh, *fudder,*" I mumbled, stepped straight into the room, and switched on the dresser lamp. The furniture leapt from its shadows into familiar formation, *surprise*! But there was nothing surprising. How was it that I remembered this so perfectly, having spent a maximum of twenty hours in here in my entire life, none of them after the age of six?

There it all was, where it had always been: The bed with its crinoline curtain and beige sheets that always looked too heavy and scratchy to me, something to make drapes out of, not sleep in; the pink wallpaper; the row of perfect pink powder puffs laid atop closed pink clam-lids full of powder or God-knows-what, next to dark pink bottles of lotion; the silver picture frame with the side-by-side posed portraits of two men in old army uniforms. Brothers? Husbands? Sons? I'd been too young to ask. Mrs. Gold was Roz's mother, but neither of them had ever explained about the photographs, at least not in my hearing. I'm not sure even my mother knew.

As Martin came in behind me, the circular vent over the bed gushed frigid air. I clutched my arms tight against myself and closed my eyes and was surprised to find tears between my lashes. Just a few. Every visit to Baltimore for the first six years of my life, for one hour per day, my parents would drag chairs in here and plop us down by this bed to *"chat"* with Mrs. Gold. That was my mother's word for it. Mostly, what we did was sit in the chairs or—when I was a baby—crawl over the carpet—and make silent faces at each other while Mrs. Gold prattled endlessly, senselessly, about horses or people we didn't know with names like Ruby and Selma, gobbling the Berger cookies we brought her and scattering crumbs all over those scratchy sheets. My mother would nod and smile and wipe the crumbs away. Mrs. Gold would nod and smile, and strands of her poofy white hair would blow in the wind from the vent. As far as I could tell, Mrs. Gold had no idea who any of us were. All those hours in here, and really, we'd never even met her.

Martin had slipped past me, and now he touched the fold of the sheet at the head of the bed. I was amazed again. He'd done the same thing at the funeral home, stunning my mother by sticking his hand into the coffin during the visitation and gently, with one extended finger, touching my grandfather's lapel. Not typical timid Martin behavior.

"Remember her hands?" he said.

Like shed snakeskin. So dry no lotion on Earth, no matter how pink, would soften them

"She seemed nice," I said, feeling sad again. For Grandpa, mostly, not Mrs. Gold. After all, we'd never known her when she was . . . whoever she was. "I bet she was nice."

Martin took his finger off the bed and glanced at me. "Unlike the one we were actually related to." And he walked straight past me into the hall.

"Martin, no." I paused only to switch out the dresser lamp. As I did, the clock in the foyer *tuk*-ed, and the dark seemed to pounce on the bed, the powder puffs, and the pathetic picture frame. I hurried into the hall, conscious of my clumping steps. Was I *trying* to wake Roz?

Martin stood before Sophie's door, hand out, but he hadn't touched it. When he turned to me, he had a grin on his face I'd never seen before. *"Mamzer,"* he drawled.

My mouth dropped open. He sounded exactly like her. "Stop it."

"Come to Gehenna. Suffer with me."

"Martin, *shut up!"*

He flinched, bumped Sophie's door with his shoulder and then stumbled back in my direction. The door swung open, and we both held still and stared.

Balding carpet, yellow-white where the butterfly light barely touched it. Everything else stayed shadowed. The curtains in there had been drawn completely. When was the last time light had touched this room?

"Why did you say that?" I asked

"It's what she said. To Grandpa, every time he dragged himself up here. Remember?"

"What's *mamzer*?"

Martin shook his head. "Aunt Paulina slapped me once for saying it."

"What's *henna*?"

"*Gehenna*. One sixtieth of Eden."

Prying my eyes from Sophie's doorway, I glared at my brother. "What does that mean?"

"It's like hell. Jew hell."

"Jews don't believe in hell. Do we?"

"Somewhere wicked people go. They can get out, though. After they suffer enough."

"Can we play our game now?" I made a flipping motion with my hand, cupping it as though around a sock-ball.

"Let's . . . take one look. Pay our respects."

"Why?"

Martin looked at the floor, and his arms gave one of their half-flaps. "Grandpa did. Every day, no matter what she called him. If we don't, no one ever will again."

He strode forward, pushed the door all the way back, and actually stepped partway over the threshold. The shadows leaned toward him, and I made myself move, half-thinking I might snatch him back. With a flick of his wrist, Martin switched on the lights.

For a second, I thought the bulbs had blown, because the shadows glowed rather than dissipated, and the plain, boxy bed in there seemed to take slow shape, as though reassembling itself. Then I remembered. Sophie's room wasn't blue because of wallpaper or bed coverings or curtain fabric. She'd liked dark blue light, barely enough to see by, just enough to read if you were right under the lamp. She'd lain in that light all day, curled beneath her covers with just her thin, knife-shaped head sticking out like a moray eel's.

Martin's hand had found mine, and after a few seconds, his touch distracted me enough to glance away, momentarily, from the bed, the bare dresser, the otherwise utterly empty room. I stared down at our palms. *"Your brother's only going to love a few people,"* my mother had told me once, after he'd slammed the door to his room in my face for the thousandth time so he could work on his chemistry set or read Ovid aloud to himself without me bothering him. *"You'll be one of them."*

"How'd they die?" I asked.

Martin seemed transfixed by the room, or his memories of it, which had to be more defined than mine. Our parents had never made us come in here. But Martin had accompanied grandpa, at least some of the time. When Sophie wasn't screaming, or calling everyone names. He took a long time answering. "They were old."

"Yeah. But didn't they like die on the same day or something?"

"Same week, I think. Dad says that happens a lot to old people. They're barely still in their bodies, you know? Then someone they love goes, and it's like unbuckling the last straps holding them in. They just slip out."

"But Sophie and Mrs. Gold hated each other."

Martin shook his head. "Mrs. Gold didn't even know who Sophie was, I bet. And Sophie hated everything. You know, Mom says she was a really good grandma, until she got sick. Super smart, too. She used to give lectures at the synagogue."

"Lectures about what?"

"Hey," said Martin, let go of my hand, and took two shuffling steps into Sophie's room. Blue light washed across his shoulders, darkening him. On the far wall, something twitched. Then it rose off the plaster. I gasped, lunged forward to grab Martin, and a second something joined the first, and I understood.

"No one's been in here," I whispered. The air was not cold, although the circular vent I could just make out over the bed coughed right as I said that. Another thought wriggled behind my eyes, but I shook it away. "Martin, the mirror."

Glancing up, he saw what I meant. The glass on Sophie's wall—aimed toward the hall, not the bed, she'd never wanted to see herself—stood unsoaped, pulling the dimness in rather than reflecting it, like a black hole. In that light, we were just shapes, our faces featureless. Even for grandpa's *shiva*, no one had bothered to prepare this room.

Martin turned from our reflections to me, his pointy nose and glasses familiar and reassuring, but only until he spoke.

"Miriam, look at this."

Along the left-hand wall ran a long closet with sliding wooden doors. The farthest door had been pulled almost all the way open and tipped off its runners, so that it hung half-sideways like a dangling tooth.

"Remember the dresses?"

I had no idea what he was talking about now. I also couldn't resist another glance in the mirror, but then quickly pulled my eyes away. There were no pictures on Sophie's bureau, just a heavy, wooden gavel. My grandfather's, of course. He must have given it to her when he retired.

"This whole closet used to be stuffed with them. Fifty, sixty, maybe more, in plastic cleaners bags. I don't think she ever wore them after she moved here. I can't even remember her getting dressed."

"She never left the room," I muttered.

"Except to sneak into Mrs. Gold's."

I closed my eyes as the clock *tuk*-ed and the vent rasped.

It had only happened once while we were in the house. But Grandpa said she did it all the time. Whenever Sophie got bored of accusing her son of kidnapping her from her own house and penning her up here, or whenever her ravaged, rotting lungs allowed her enough breath, she'd rouse herself from this bed, inch out the door in her bare feet with the blue veins popping out of the tops like rooster crests, and sneak into Mrs. Gold's room. There she'd sit, murmuring God knew what, until Mrs. Gold started screaming.

"It always creeped me out," Martin said. "I never liked looking over at this closet. But the dresses blocked *that*."

"Blocked wh—" I started, and my breath caught in my teeth. Waist-high on the back inside closet wall, all but covered by a rough square of wood that had been leaned against it rather than fitted over it, there was an opening. A door. "Martin, if Roz catches us in here—"

Hostility flared in his voice like a lick of flame. "Roz hardly ever catches us playing the balcony ball game right outside her room. Anyway, in case you haven't noticed, she *never* comes in here."

"What's with you?" I snapped. Nothing about my brother made sense tonight.

"What? Nothing. It's just . . . Grandpa brings Roz's mother here, even though she needs constant care, can't even feed herself unless she's eating Berger cookies, probably has no idea where she is. Grandpa takes care of her, like he took care of everyone. But when it comes to *his* mother, Roz won't even bring food in here. She makes him do everything. And after they die, Roz leaves her own mother's room exactly like it was, but she cleans out every trace of Sophie, right down to the closet."

"Sophie was mean."

"She was sick. And ninety-two."

"And mean."

"I'm going in there," Martin said, gesturing or flapping, I couldn't tell which. "I want to see Grandpa's stuff. Don't you? I bet it's all stored in there."

"I'm going to bed. Goodnight, Martin."

In an instant, the hostility left him, and his expression turned small, almost panicked.

"I'm going to bed," I said again.

"You don't want to see Grandpa?"

This time, the violence in my own voice surprised me. "Not in there." I was thinking of the way he'd looked in his coffin. His dead face had barely even resembled his real one. His living one. His whole head had been transformed into a waxy, vaguely grandpa-shaped *bulge* balanced atop his bulgy, overweight body, like the top of a snowman.

"Please," Martin said, and something moved downstairs.

"Shit," I mouthed, going completely still.

Clock tick. Clock tick. Footsteps. *Had I left the lights on in Mrs. Gold's room?* I couldn't remember. If Roz wasn't looking, she might not see Sophie's blue light from downstairs. Somehow, I knew she didn't want us in here.

I couldn't help glancing behind me, and then my shoulders clenched. The door had swung almost all the way shut.

Which wasn't so strange, was it? How far had we even opened it?

Footsteps. Clock tick. Clock tick. Clock tick. Clock tick. When I turned back to Martin, he was on his hands and knees, scuttling for the closet.

"Martin, *no*," I hissed. Then I was on my knees too, hurrying after him. When I drew up alongside him, our heads just inside the closet, he looked my way and grinned, tentatively.

"Sssh," he whispered.

"What do you think you'll find in there?"

The grin slid from his face. "Him." With a nod, he pulled the square of wood off the opening. Then he swore and dropped it. His right hand rose to his mouth, and I saw the sliver sticking out of the bottom of his thumb like a porcupine quill.

Taking his wrist, I leaned over, trying to see. In that murky, useless light, the wood seemed to have stabbed straight through the webbing into his palm. It almost looked like a new ridge forming along his lifeline. "Hold still," I murmured, grabbed the splinter as low down as I could, and yanked.

Martin sucked in breath, staring at his hand. "Did you get it all?"

"Come where it's light and I'll see."

"No." He pulled his hand from me, and without another word crawled through the opening. For one moment, as his butt hovered in front of me and his torso disappeared, I had to stifle another urge to drag him out, splinters be damned. Then he was through. For a few seconds, I heard only his breathing, saw only his bare feet through the hole. The rest of him was in shadow.

"Miriam, get in here," he said.

In I went. I had to shove Martin forward to get through, and I did so harder than I had to. He made no protest. I tried lifting my knees instead of sliding them to keep the splinters off. When I straightened, I was surprised to find most of the space in front of us bathed in moonlight.

"What window is that?" I whispered.

"Must be on the side."

"I've never seen it."

"How much time have you spent on the side?"

None, in truth. No one did. The space between my grandfather's house and the ancient gray wooden fence that bordered his property had been overrun by spiders even when our mom was young. I'd glimpsed an old bike back there once, completely draped in webs like furniture in a dead man's room.

"Probably a billion spiders in here, too, you know," I said.

But Martin wasn't paying attention, and neither was I, really. We were too busy staring. All around us, stacked from floor to four-foot ceiling all the way down the length of the half-finished space, cardboard boxes had been stacked, sometimes atop each other, sometimes atop old white suitcases or trunks with their key-coverings dangling like the tongues on strangled things. With his shoulder, Martin nudged one of the nearest stacks, which tipped dangerously but slid back a bit. Reaching underneath a lid flap, Martin stuck his hand in the bottom-most box. I bit my cheek and held still and marveled, for the hundredth time in the last fifteen minutes, at my brother's behavior. When he pulled out a *Playboy*, I started to laugh, and stopped because of the look on Martin's face.

He held the magazine open and flat across both hands, looking terrified to drop it, almost in awe of it, as though it were a Torah scroll. It would be a long time, I thought, before Martin started dating.

"You said you wanted to see grandpa's stuff," I couldn't resist teasing.

"This wasn't his."

Now I did laugh. "Maybe it was Mrs. Gold's."

I slid the magazine off his hands, and that seemed to relieve him, some. The page to which it had fallen open showed a long, brown-haired woman with strangely pointed feet poised naked atop a stone backyard well, as though she'd just climbed out of it. The woman wasn't smiling, and I didn't like the picture at all. I closed the magazine and laid it face down on the floor.

Edging forward, Martin began to reach randomly into other boxes. I did the same. Mostly, though, I watched my brother. The moonlight seemed to pour over him in layers, coating him, so that with each passing moment he grew paler. Other than Martin's scuttling as he moved down the row on his knees, I heard nothing, not even the clock. That should have been a comfort. But the silence in that not-quite-room was worse.

To distract myself, I began to run my fingers over the boxes on my right. Their cardboard skin had sticky damp patches, bulged outward in places but sank into itself in others. From one box, I drew an unpleasantly damp, battered, black rectangular case I thought might be for pens, but when I opened it, I found four pearls strung on a broken chain, pressed deep into their own impressions in the velvet lining like little eyes in sockets. My real grandmother's, I realized. Roz liked showier jewelry. I'd never met my mother's mother. She'd died three months before Martin was born. Dad had liked her a lot. I was still gazing at the pearls when air gushed across me, pouring over my skin like ice.

Martin grunted, and I caught his wrist. We crouched and waited for the torrent to sigh itself out. Eventually, it did. Martin started to speak, and I tightened my grasp and shut him up.

Just at the end, as the gush had died . . .

"Martin," I whispered.

"It's the air-conditioning, Miriam. See?"

"Martin, did you hear it?"

"Duh. Look at—"

"Martin. The vents."

He wasn't listening, didn't understand. Dazed, I let him disengage, watched him crab-walk to the next stack of boxes and begin digging. I almost started screaming at him. If I did, I now knew, the sound would pour out of the walls above our bed, and from the circular space above Mrs. Gold's window, and from Sophie's closet. Because these vents didn't connect to the guest room where our parents were, like we'd always thought. They connected the upstairs rooms and this room. And so the murmuring we'd always heard—that we'd heard as recently as twenty minutes ago—hadn't come from our parents at all. It had come from right—

"Jackpot," Martin muttered.

Ahead, wedged between the last boxes and the wall, something stirred. Flapped. Plastic. Maybe.

"Martin . . . "

"Hi, Grandpa."

I spun so fast I almost knocked him over, banging my arms instead on the plaque he was wiping free of mold and dust with the sleeve of his pajamas. Frozen air roared over us again, as though I'd rattled a cage and woken the house itself. Up ahead, whatever it was flapped some more.

"Watch *out*," Martin snapped. He wasn't worried about me, of course. He didn't want anything happening to the plaque.

"We have to get out of here," I said.

Wordlessly, he held up his treasure. Black granite, with words engraved in it, clearly legible despite the fuzzy smear of grime across the surface. *To the Big Judge, who takes care of his own. A muldoon, and no mistake. From his friends, the Knights of Labor.*

"The Knights of Labor?"

"He knew everyone," Martin said. "They all loved him. The whole city."

This was who my grandfather was to my brother, I realized. Someone as smart and weird and defiant and solitary as he was, except that our grand-father had somehow figured out people enough to wind up a judge, a civil rights activist, a bloated and beloved public figure. Slowly, like a snake stirring, another shudder slipped down my back.

"What's a *muldoon*?"

"Says right here, stupid." Martin nodded at the plaque. "He took care of his own."

"We should go, Martin. Now."

"What are you talking about?"

As the house unleashed another frigid breath, he tucked the plaque lovingly against his chest and moved deeper into the attic. The plastic at the end of the row was rippling now, flattening itself. It reminded me of an octopus I'd seen in the Baltimore Aquarium once, completely changing shape to slip between two rocks.

"There," I barked suddenly, as the air expired. "Hear it?"

But Martin was busy wedging open box lids, prying out cufflinks in little boxes, a ceremonial silver shovel marking some sort of groundbreaking, a photograph of grandpa with Earl Weaver and two grinning grounds crew guys in the Orioles dugout. The last thing he pulled out before I moved was a book. Old, blue binding, stiff and jacketless. Martin flipped through it once, mumbled, "Hebrew," and dumped it behind him. Embossed on the cover, staring straight up at the ceiling over my brother's head, I saw a single, lidless eye.

Martin kept going, almost to the end now. The plastic had gone still, the air-conditioning and the murmurs that rode it temporarily silent. I almost left him there. If I'd been sure he'd follow—as, on almost any other occasion, he would have—that's exactly what I'd have done. Instead, I edged forward myself, my hand stretching for the book. As much to get that eye hidden again as from any curiosity, I picked the thing up and opened it. Something in the binding snapped, and a single page slipped free and fluttered away like a dried butterfly I'd let loose.

"*Ayin Harah*," I read slowly, sounding out the Hebrew letters on the title page. But it wasn't the words that set me shuddering again, if only because I wasn't positive what they implied; I knew they meant "Evil Eye." But our Aunt Pauline had told us that was a protective thing, mostly. Instead, my gaze locked on my great-grandmother's signature, lurking like a blue spider in the top left-hand corner of the inside cover. Then my head lifted, and I was staring at the box from which the book had come.

Not my grandfather's stuff in there. Not my grandmother's, or Roz's, either. That box—and maybe that one alone—was hers.

I have no explanation for what happened next. I knew better. That is, I knew, already. Thought I did. I didn't want to be in the attic even one second longer, and I was scared, not curious. I crept forward and stuck my hand between the flaps anyway.

For a moment, I thought the box was empty. My hand kept sliding deeper, all the way to my elbow before I touched fabric and closed my fist over it. Beneath whatever I'd grabbed was plastic, wrapped around some kind of heavy fabric. The plastic rustled and stuck slightly to my hand like an anemone's tentacles, though everything in that box was completely dry. I pulled, and the boxes balanced atop the one I'd reached into tipped back and bumped against the wall of the attic, and my hands came out, holding the thing I'd grasped, which fell open as it touched the air.

"Grandpa with two presidents, look," Martin said from down the row, waving a picture frame without lifting his head from whatever box he was looting.

Cradled in my palms lay what could have been a *matzoh* covering, maybe for holding the *afikomen* at a *seder*. When I spread out the folds, though, I found dark, rust-colored circular stains in the white fabric. Again I thought of the seder, the ritual of dipping a finger in wine and then touching it to a plate or napkin as everyone chanted plagues God had inflicted upon the Egyptians. In modern Hagadahs, the ritual is explained as a symbol of Jewish regret that the Egyptian people had to bear the brunt of their ruler's refusal to free the slaves. But none of the actual ceremonial instructions say that. They just order us to chant the words. *Dam. Tzfar de'ah. Kinim. Arbeh.*

Inside the fold where matzoh might have been tucked, I found only a gritty, black residue. It could have been dust from the attic, or split spider sacs, or tiny dead things. But it smelled, faintly, on my fingers. An old and rotten smell, with just a hint of something else. Something worse.

Not worse. *Familiar.* I had no idea what it was. But Sophie had smelled like this.

"Martin, please," I heard myself say. But he wasn't listening. Instead, he was leaning almost *into* the last box in the row. The plastic jammed against the wall had gone utterly still. At any moment, I expected it to hump up like a wave and crash down on my brother's back. I didn't even realize my hands had slipped back inside Sophie's box until I touched wrapping again.

Gasping, I dragged my hands away, but my fingers had curled, and the plastic and the heavy fabric it swaddled came up clutched between them.

A *dress*, I thought, panicking, shoving backward. *From her closet.* I stared at the lump of fabric, draped now half out of the box, the plastic covering rising slightly in the stirring air.

Except it wasn't a dress. It was two dresses, plainly visible now through the plastic. One was gauzy and pink, barely there, with wispy flowers stitched up the sleeves. The other, white and heavy, had folded itself inside the pink one, the long sleeves encircling the waist. Long, black smears spread across the back of the white dress, like finger-marks, from fingers dipped in Sophie's residue . . .

I don't think I had any idea, at first, that I'd started shouting. I was too busy scuttling backwards on my hands, banging against boxes on either side as I scrambled for the opening behind us. The air-conditioning triggered, blasting me with its breath, which didn't stink, just froze the hairs to the skin of my arms and legs. Martin had leapt to his feet, banging his head against the attic ceiling, and now he was waving his hands, trying to quiet me. But the sight of him panicked me more. The dresses on the ground between us shivered, almost rolled over, and the plastic behind him rippled madly, popping and straining against the weight that held it, all but free. My hand touched down on the *Playboy*, and I imagined the well-woman climbing out of the magazine on her pointy feet and finally fell hard half out of the attic opening, screaming now, banging my spine on the wood and bruising it badly.

Then there were hands on my shoulder, hard and horny and orange-ish, yanking me out of the hole and dragging me across the floor. Yellow eyes flashing fury, Roz leaned past me and ducked her head through the hole, screeching at Martin to get out. Then she stalked away, snarling *"Out"* and *"Come on."*

Never had I known her to be this angry. I'd also never been happier to see her pinched, glaring, unhappy face, the color of an overripe orange thanks to the liquid tan she poured all over herself before her daily mah-jongg games at the club where she sometimes took us swimming. Flipping over and standing, I hurried after her, the rattle of the ridiculous twin rows of bracelets that ran halfway up her arms sweet and welcome in my ears as the tolling of a dinner bell. I waited at the lip of the closet until Martin's head appeared, then fled Sophie's room.

A few seconds later, my brother emerged, the *Knights of Labor* plaque clutched against his chest, glaring bloody murder at me. But Roz took him by the shoulders, guided him back to his bed in my mother's old room, and sat him down. I followed, and fell onto my own bed. For a minute, maybe more, she stood above us and glowed even more than usual, as though she might burst into flame. Then, for the first time in all my experience of her, she crossed her legs and sat down between our beds on the filthy floor.

"Oh, kids," she sighed. "What were you doing in there?"

"Where are Mom and Dad?" Martin demanded. The shrillness in his tone made me cringe even farther back against the white wall behind me. Pushing with me feet, I dug myself under the covers and lay my head on my pillow.

"Out," Roz said, in the same weary voice. "They're on a walk. They've been cooped up here, same as the rest of us, for an entire week."

"Cooped up?" Martin's voice rose still more, and even Roz's leathery face registered surprise. "As in, sitting *shiva*? Paying tribute to Grandpa?"

After a long pause, she nodded. "Exactly that, Martin."

From the other room, I swore I could hear the sound of plastic sliding over threadbare carpet. My eyes darted to the doorway, the lit landing, the streaks of soap in the mirror, the floor.

"How'd they die?" I blurted.

Roz's lizard eyes darted back and forth between Martin and me. "What's with you two tonight?"

"Mrs. Gold and Sophie. Please, please, please. Grandma." I didn't often call her that. She scowled even harder.

"What are you babbling about?" Martin said to me. "Roz, Miriam's been really—"

"Badly, Miriam" Roz said, and Martin went quiet. "They died badly."

Despite what she'd said, her words had a surprising, almost comforting effect on me. "Please tell me."

"Your parents wouldn't want me to."

"Please."

Settling back, Roz eyed me, then the vent overhead. I kept glancing into the hall. But I didn't hear anything now. And after a while, I only watched her. She crossed her arms over her knees, and her bracelets clanked.

"It was an accident. A horrible accident. It really was. You have to understand . . . you have no idea how awful those days were. May you never have such days."

"What was so awful?" Martin asked. There was still a trace of petulance in his tone. But Roz's attitude appeared to be having the same weirdly soothing effect on him as on me.

She shrugged. "In the pink room, you've got my mother. Only she's not my mother anymore. She's this sweet, stupid, chattering houseplant."

I gaped. Martin did, too, and Roz laughed, kind of, without humor or joy.

"Every single day, usually more than once, she shit all over the bed. The rest of the time, she sat there and babbled mostly nice things about cookies or owls or whatever. Places she'd never been. People she may have known, but I didn't. She never mentioned me, or my father, or my brother, or anything about our lives. It was like she'd led some completely different life, without me in it."

Roz held her knees a while. Finally, she went on. "And in the blue room, there was Sophie, who remembered everything. How it had felt to walk to the market, or lecture a roomful of professors about the Kabbalah or whatever other weird stuff she knew. How it had been to live completely by herself, with her books, in her own world, the way she had for twenty-two years after your great-grandfather died. Best years of her life, I think. And then, just like that, her bones gave out on her. She couldn't move well. Couldn't drive. She couldn't really see. She broke her hip twice. When your grandpa brought her here, she was so angry, kids. So angry. She didn't want to die. She didn't want to be dependent. It made her mean. That's pretty much your choices, I think. Getting old—getting *that* old, anyway—makes you mean, or sick, or stupid, or lonely. Take your pick. Only you don't get to pick. And sometimes, you get all four."

Rustling, from the vent. The faintest hint. Or had it come from the hallway?

"Grandma, what happened?"

"An accident, Miriam. Like I said. Your goddamn grandfather . . . "

"You can't—" Martin started, and Roz rode him down.

"Your goddamn grandfather wouldn't put them in homes. Either one. *'Your mother's your mother.'* " When she said that, she rumbled, and sounded just like grandpa. " *'She's no trouble. And as for my mother . . . it'd kill her.'*

"But having them here, kids . . . it was killing us. Poisoning every single day. Wrecking every relationship we had, even with each other."

Grandma looked up from her knees and straight at us. "Anyway," she said. "We had a home care service. A private nurse. Mrs. Gertzen. She came one night a week, and a couple weekends a year when we just couldn't take it and had to get away. When we wanted to go, we called Mrs. Gertzen, left the dates, and she came and took care of both our mothers while we were gone. Well, the last time . . . when they died . . . your grandfather called her, same as always. Sophie liked Mrs. Gertzen, was probably nicer to her than anyone else, most of the time. Grandpa left instructions, and we headed off to the Delaware shore for five days. But Mrs. Gertzen had a heart attack that first afternoon, and never even made it to the house. And no one else on Earth had any idea that my mother and Sophie were up here."

"Oh my God," I heard myself whisper, as the vent above me rasped pathetically. For the first time in what seemed hours, I became aware of the clock, *tuk*-ing away. I was imagining being trapped in this bed, hearing that sound. The metered pulse of the living world, just downstairs, plainly audible. And—for my great-grandmother and Mrs. Gold—utterly out of reach.

When I looked at my grandmother again, I was amazed to find tears leaking out of her eyes. She made no move to wipe them. "It must have been worse for Sophie," she half-whispered.

My mouth fell open. Martin had gone completely still as well as silent.

"I mean, I doubt my mother even knew what was happening. She probably prattled all the way to the end. If there is an Angel of Death, I bet she offered him a Berger cookie."

"You're . . . " *nicer than I thought,* I was going to say, but that wasn't quite right. *Different than I thought.*

"But Sophie. Can you imagine how horrible? How infuriating? To realize— she must have known by dinner time—that no one was coming? She couldn't make it downstairs. We'd had to carry her to the bathroom, the last few weeks. All she'd done that past month was light candles and read her Zohar and mutter to herself. I'm sure she knew she'd never make it to the kitchen. I'm sure that's why she didn't try. But I think she came back to herself at the end, you know? Turned back into the person she must have been. The woman who raised your grandfather, made him who he was or at least let him be. Because somehow she dragged herself into my mother's room one last time. They died with their arms around each other."

The dresses, I thought. *Had they been arranged like that on purpose? Tucked together, as a memory or a monument?* Then I was shivering, sobbing, and my brother was, too. Roz sat silently between us, staring at the floor.

"I shouldn't have told you," she mumbled. "Your parents will be furious."

Seconds later, the front door opened, and our mom and dad came hurtling up the stairs, filling our doorway with their flushed, exhausted, everyday faces.

"What are you doing up?" my mother asked, moving forward fast and stretching one arm toward each of us, though we were too far apart to be gathered that way.

"I'm afraid I—" Roz started.

"Grandpa," I said, and felt Roz look at me. "We were feeling bad about Grandpa."

My mother's mouth twisted, and her eyes closed. "I know," she said. "Me, too."

I crawled over to Martin's bed. My mother held us a long time, while my father stood above her, his hands sliding from her back to our shoulders to our heads. At some point, Roz slipped silently from the room. I didn't see her go.

For half an hour, maybe more, our parents stayed. Martin showed them the plaque he'd found, and my mother seemed startled mostly by the realization of where we'd been.

"You know I forgot that room was there?" she said. "Your cousins and I used to hide in it all the time. Before the hags came."

"You shouldn't call them that," Martin said, and my mother straightened, eyes narrowed. Eventually, she nodded, and her shoulders sagged.

"You're right. And I don't think of them that way, it's just, at the end . . . Goodnight, kids."

After they'd gone, switching out all the lights except the butterfly in the hall, I thought I might sleep. But every time I closed my eyes, I swore I felt something pawing at the covers, as though trying to draw them back, so that whatever it was could crawl in with me. Opening my eyes, I found the dark room, the moon outside, the spider shadows in the corners. Several times, I glanced toward my brother's bed. He was lying on his back with the plaque he'd rescued on his chest and his head turned toward the wall, so that I couldn't see whether his eyes were open. I listened to the clock ticking and the vents rasping and muttering. *A muldoon, and no mistake*, I found myself mouthing. *Who takes care of his own.* When I tried again to close my eyes, it seemed the vent was chanting with me. *No mistake. No mistake.* My heart seemed to twist in its socket, and its beating bounced on the rhythm of the clock's tick like a skipped stone. I think I moaned, and Martin rolled over.

"Now let's play," he said.

Immediately, I was up, grabbing the sock-ball off the table where I'd left it. I wasn't anywhere near sleep, and I wasn't scared of Roz anymore. I wanted to be moving, doing anything. And my brother still wanted me with him.

I didn't wait for Martin this time, just marched straight out to the landing, casting a single, held-breath glance at Sophie's door. Someone had pulled it almost closed again, and I wondered if the wooden covering over the opening to the attic had also been replaced. Mrs. Gold's door, I noticed, had been left open. *Pushed open?*

Squelching that thought with a shake of my head, I started down the stairs. But Martin galloped up beside me, pushed me against the wall, took the sock-ball out of my hands, and hurried ahead.

"My ups," he said.

"Your funeral," I answered, and he stopped three steps down and turned and grinned. A flicker of butterfly light danced in his glasses, which made it look as though something reflective and transparent had moved behind me, but I didn't turn around, didn't turn around, turned and found the landing empty.

"She's asleep," Martin said, and for one awful moment, I didn't know whom he meant.

Then I did, and grinned weakly back. "If you say so." Retreating upstairs, I circled around the balcony into position.

The rules of Martin-Miriam Balcony Ball were simple. The person in the foyer below tried to lob the sock-ball over the railing and have it hit the carpet anywhere on the *L*-shaped landing. The person on the landing tried to catch the sock and slam it to the tile down in the foyer, triggering an innings change in which both players tried to bump each other off balance as they passed on the steps, thereby gaining an advantage for the first throw of the next round. Play ended when someone had landed ten throws on the balcony, or when Roz came and roared us back to bed, or when any small porcelain animal or *tuk*-ing grandfather clock or crystal chandelier got smashed. In the five year history of the game, that latter ending had only occurred once. The casualty had been a poodle left out atop the cabinet. This night's game lasted exactly one throw.

In retrospect, I think the hour or so between the moment our parents left and his invitation to play were no more restful for Martin than they had been for me. He'd lain more still, but that had just compressed the energy the evening had given him, and now he was fizzing like a shaken pop bottle. I watched him glance toward Roz's hallway, crouch into himself as though expecting a hail of gunfire, and scurry into the center of the foyer. He looked skeletal and small, like some kind of armored beetle, and the ache that prickled up under my skin was at least partially defensive of him. He would never fill space the way our grandfather had. No one would. That ability—*was that the right word?*—to love people in general more than the people closest to you, was a rare and only partly desirable thing. Martin, I already knew, didn't have it.

He must have been kneading the sock-ball all the way down the stairs, because as soon as he reared back and threw, one of the socks slipped free of the knot I'd made and dangled like the tail of a comet. Worse, Martin had somehow aimed straight up, so that instead of arching over the balcony, the sock-comet shot between the arms of the chandelier, knocked crystals together as it reached its apex, and then draped itself, almost casually, over the arm nearest the steps. After that, it just hung.

The chandelier leaned gently left, then right. The clock *tuk*-ed like a clucking tongue.

"Shit," Martin said, and something rustled.

"*Sssh.*" I resisted yet another urge to jerk my head around. I turned slowly instead, saw Sophie's almost closed door, Mrs. Gold's wide-open one. Butterfly light. Our room. Nothing else. If the sound I'd just heard had come from downstairs, then Roz was awake. "Get up here," I said, and Martin came, fast.

By the time he reached me, all that fizzing energy seemed to have evaporated. His shoulders had rounded, and his glasses had clouded over with his exertion. He looked at me through his own fog.

"Mir, what are we going to do?"

"What do you think we're going to do, we're going to go get it. *You're* going to go get it."

Martin wiped his glasses on his shirt, eyeing the distance between the landing where we stood and the gently swinging chandelier. "We need a broom." His eyes flicked hopefully to mine. He was Martin again, alright.

I glanced downstairs to the hallway I'd have to cross to get to the broom closet. "Feel free," I said.

"Come on, Miriam."

"You threw it."

"You're braver."

Abruptly, the naked woman from the well in the magazine flashed in front of my eyes. I could almost see—almost *hear*—her stepping out of the photograph, balancing on those pointed feet. Tiptoeing over the splinter-riddled floor toward those wrapped-together dresses, slipping them over her shoulders.

"What?" Martin said.

"I can't."

For the second time that night, Martin took my hand. Before the last couple hours, Martin had last held my hand when I was six years old, and my mother had made him do it whenever we crossed a street, for his protection more than mine, since he was usually thinking about something random instead of paying attention.

"I have a better idea," he whispered, and pulled me toward the top of the staircase.

As soon as he laid himself flat on the top step, I knew what he was going to do. "You can't," I whispered, but what I really meant was that I didn't believe he'd dare. There he was, though, tilting onto his side, wriggling his head through the railings. His shoulders followed. Within seconds he was resting one elbow in the dust atop the grandfather clock.

Kneeling, I watched his shirt pulse with each *tuk*, as though a second, stronger heart had taken root inside him. *Too* strong, I thought, *it could pop him to pieces.*

"Grab me," he said. "Don't let go."

Even at age ten, my fingers could touch when wrapped around the tops of his ankles. He slid out farther, and the clock came off its back legs and leaned with him. *"Fuck!"* he blurted, wiggling back as I gripped tight. The clock tipped back the other way and banged its top against the railings and rang them.

Letting go of Martin, I scrambled to my feet, ready to sprint for our beds as I awaited the tell-tale bloom of lights in Roz's hallway. Martin lay flat, breath heaving, either resigned to his fate or too freaked out to care. It seemed impossible that Roz hadn't heard what we'd just done, and anyway, she had a sort of lateral line for this kind of thing, sensing movement in her foyer the way Martin said sharks discerned twitching fish.

But somehow, miraculously, no one came. Nothing moved. And after a minute or so, without even waiting for me to hold his legs, Martin slithered forward once more. I dropped down next to him, held tighter. This time, he kept his spine straight, dropping as little of his weight as possible atop the clock. I watched his waist wedge briefly in the railings, then slip through as his arms stretched out. It was like feeding him to something. Worse than the clock's *tuk* was the groan from its base as it started to lean again. My hands went sweaty, and my teeth clamped down on my tongue, almost startling me into letting go. I had no idea whether the tears in my ears were fear or exhaustion or sadness for my grandfather or the first acknowledgement that I'd just heard rustling, right behind me.

"Ow," Martin said as my nails dug into his skin. But he kept sliding forward. My eyes had jammed themselves shut, so I felt rather than saw him grab the chandelier, felt it swing slightly away from, felt his ribs hit the top of the clock and the clock start to tip.

I opened my eyes, not looking back, not behind, it was only the vents, had to be, and then Roz stepped out of her hallway.

Incredibly, insanely, she didn't see us at first. She had her head down, bracelets jangling, hands jammed in the pockets of her shiny silver robe, and she didn't even look up until she was dead center under the chandelier, under my brother stretched full-length in mid-air twenty feet over her head with a sock in his hands. Then the clock's legs groaned under Martin's suspended weight, and the chandelier swung out, and Roz froze. For that one split second, none of us so much as breathed. And that's how I knew, even before she finally did lift her eyes. This time, I really had heard it.

"Get back," my grandmother said, and burst into tears.

It made no sense. I started babbling, overwhelmed by guilt I wasn't even sure was mine. "Grandma, I'm sorry. Sorry, sorry—"

"*BACK!*" Roz screamed. "*Get away! Get away from them.*" With startling speed, she spun and darted up the steps, still shouting.

Them. Meaning *us.* Which meant she wasn't talking to us.

The rest happened all in one motion. As I turned, my hands came off Martin's legs. Instantly, he was gone, tipping, the clock rocking forward and over. He didn't scream, maybe didn't have time, but his body flew face-first and smacked into the floor below just as Roz hurtled past and my parents emerged shouting from the guest bedroom and saw their son and the clock smashing and splintering around and atop him and I got my single glimpse of the thing on the landing.

Its feet weren't pointed, but bare and pale and swollen with veins. It wore some kind of pink, ruffled something, and its hair was white and flying. I couldn't see its face. But its movements . . . The arms all out of rhythm with the feet, out of order, as if they were being jerked from somewhere else on invisible strings. And the legs, the way they moved . . . not Mrs. Gold's mindless, surprisingly energetic glide . . . more of a tilting, trembling lurch. Like Sophie's.

Rooted in place, mouth open, I watched it stagger past the blacked-out mirror, headed from the pink room to the blue one.

"*Takes care of his own,*" I found myself chanting, helpless to stop. "*Takes care of his own. And no mistake. No mistake.*" There had been no mistake.

My grandmother was waving her hands in front of her, snarling, stomping her feet as though scolding a dog. *Had she already known it was here? Or just understood, immediately?* In seconds, she and the lurching thing were in the blue room, and Sophie's door slammed shut.

"*No mistake,*" I murmured, tears pouring down my face.

The door flew open again, and out Roz came. My voice wavered, sank into silence as my eyes met hers and locked. Downstairs, my father was shouting frantically into the phone for an ambulance. Roz walked, jangling, to the step above me, sat down hard, put her head on her knees and one of her hands in my hair. Then she started to weep.

Martin had fractured his spine, broken one cheekbone, his collarbone, and both legs, and he has never completely forgiven me. Sometimes I think my parents haven't, either. Certainly, they drew away from me for a long time after that, forming themselves into a sort of protective cocoon around my brother. My family traded phone calls with Roz for years. But we never went back to Baltimore, and she never came to see us.

So many times, I've lunged awake, still seeing the Sophie-Mrs. Gold creature lurching at random into my dreams. If I'd ever had the chance, I would have asked Roz only one thing: how much danger had Martin and I really been in? Would it really have hurt us? Was it inherently malevolent, a monster devouring everything it could reach? Or was it just a peculiarly Jewish sort of ghost, clinging to every last vestige of life, no matter how painful or beset by betrayal, because only in life—*this* life—is there any possibility of pleasure or fulfillment or even release?

I can't ask anyone else, because Roz is the only one other than me who knows. I have never talked about it, certainly not to Martin, who keeps the plaque he lifted from the attic that night nailed to his bedroom wall.

But I know. And sometimes, I just want to scream at all of them, make them see what's staring them right in the face, has been obvious from the moment it happened. My grandfather, the *muldoon* who took care of his own, during the whole weekend he was away with Roz, never once called his mother? Never called home? Never checked in with Mrs. Gertzen, just to see how everyone was? And Mrs. Gertzen had no family, had left no indication to the service that employed her of what jobs she might have been engaged in?

My grandfather had called Mrs. Gertzen's house before leaving for Delaware, alright. He'd learned about Mrs. Gertzen's heart attack. Then he'd weighed his shattering second marriage, his straining relationships with his children, his scant remaining healthy days, maybe even his own mother's misery.

And then he'd made his decision. Taken care of his own, and no mistake. And in the end—the way they always do, whether you take care of them or no—his own had come back for him.

Semaphore

Alex Irvine

I am thinking of my Uncle Mike because he died recently, at the ripe old age of 97, and because after his death I had the belated realization that I had at some point come to believe him immortal because of all the people I ever knew, Uncle Mike was the most able to joke about death. I wonder if he lost his sense of humor and died of the loss.

Every boy at some point worships his father. I had twin idols: my brother Daniel and my uncle Mike. Because I worshipped the ground Uncle Mike walked on, I tried to joke about death, too; but because I acquired the habit during World War II, while the world stood around watching the extinction of our extended family and the rest of European Jewry, I found that my early efforts at emulating Uncle Mike were a little tone-deaf. Like many eleven- or twelve-year-olds, I figured out how to be callous before I learned anything about reflection. This tendency, like a number of others more or less salutary, I absorbed from Daniel . . . but he has been gone long enough that I can no longer mourn him, and Uncle Mike's passing is fresh in my mind.

I'm an old man now, or at least the approach of my seventieth birthday makes me feel old, and like many old men I am trying to figure out why I was the kind of young man that I was. Trying to put in order my understanding of my previous self, the way you put your worldly affairs in order when you realize that you're closer to death than birth. The answer has to do with Uncle Mike, but more importantly with my brother Daniel, who in February of 1942 shocked the entire family by not only entering the PS 319 spelling bee but winning it—and this as a fifteen-year-old eighth grader of no academic distinction whatsoever. Because he hadn't turned sixteen or started high school, he was going to be eligible for the national tournament if he got through the regional that spring. The mystification of the Rosenthal family of 327 South Fifth, Williamsburg, was complete. None of us even knew Daniel could spell. His grades had sure never given any sign, and I don't think I'd ever seen him read a book in his life. God is mysterious that way.

Daniel, I think, was just as surprised and discombobulated as the rest of us, and as it turned out, he had his own plan for avoiding the frightening possibility that he might be exposed as something other than a garden-variety

South Williamsburg truant. He got someone to sign his papers, none of us ever figured out who, and he enlisted in the Army three days before regionals. His best friend Howard Klinkowitz, who was a year older, joined with him. The Klinkowitzes had gotten out of Leipzig in 1936; Howard, who was born there, got the nickname Klinkojoke after telling Daniel that *Witz* meant joke in German, but the one time I called him that he hit me on the arm so hard I had a knot for a week. After basic, Daniel was assigned to the Signal Corps. Five months later, and a month after the remaining Rosenthal clan turned out to watch the battleship *Iowa* launch from the Navy Yard, he drowned when a U-boat sunk his troop transport at the approach to the Straits of Gibraltar.

The word that won the spelling bee that summer was *sacrilegious*.

God is mysterious that way.

I was four years younger than Daniel, and two years behind him in school. He was my only brother. The only way I can describe the effect of his death on my four sisters is by comparing it to what happens when you take a crayon and color something as rich and as deep as the paper will hold; then you take your fingernail and scratch away the thickness of the color. My sisters were thinned out somehow. They seemed less real. Same with my father, and all I can say about my mother is that she was always strong enough to keep herself together no matter what life threw at her. The Germans got him, she muttered under her breath. The Germans got him.

Me, I had never felt more real in my life. It sounds ghoulish now, but it didn't feel that way then. Something inside me was born, or came into itself, when Daniel died. And something else fell away, which in retrospect I can identify as belief. If before I had been religious in a diffuse, osmotic kind of way, after Daniel's death I balanced my psychological scales by telling God that if he was going to take my brother away from me, I was going to take myself away from him. Not that I could have articulated any of it at the time, and in the course of events I would partially reverse this decision, reopening a space in my mind for the idea of God without giving myself any responsibility for worship or real belief. Belief—real belief—came later, with the ability to reflect. *Reflection*: from the Latin for "bending back." I indulge in puns once in a while, now that I'm too old for anyone to complain about it, and I can say without the least irony that I bent over backwards to avoid reflection through the awful years of the war.

I told my sister Miriam once—she was closest to me in age, so became my sibling confidante after Daniel died—about how strangely alive I felt even though I spent most of my days with my mind split on parallel tracks of grief and anger. This would have been just before Halloween in 1942, while we were all still stumbling around in shock. Miriam looked at me and said, "It's a *dybbuk*. It's Daniel's *dybbuk*."

Which it wasn't, but that was the kind of superficial explanation we were all grasping for. Miriam perhaps more than most; a dreamy girl, she reeled away from the news of Daniel's death, beginning a long descent into loony mysticism which culminated in her turning into a kind of den mother for a group of beatnik poets and jazz musicians holed up on Minetta Lane in the Village, and then dying of drugs and cancer and heartbreak in 1960. The world was full of *dybbuks* to her, with all of these boys leaving New York, and so many of them returning as names spoken in regretful voices, wails that riffled the laundry strung out the back windows of Williamsburg.

The conversation spooked me, even though I didn't believe in *dybbuks*. Or God, really. Especially once I started to dream about Daniel. There's no such thing as *dybbuks*, you dumb shit, he said.

Well, I thought to myself in the dream, you would know.

Yeah, he said. I would. Then he said, Yoo-Hoo will help.

What?

I woke up. The hordes in the basement were already crashing around. Children hollered, adults hollered back. I think they were speaking Polish, but I heard words I recognized as Yiddish too. It was barely dawn. I cursed all immigrants, especially those that crammed into the basement below our garden-level apartment. It was a cave down there, and now it was a cave bursting with haunted-looking people who didn't speak English and served for my parents as object lessons in why my sisters and I should feel fortunate. Occasionally this worked for a minute, but not when it was the crack of dawn and I'd just been rousted from uneasy sleep. Bad enough that my brother was dead and Hitler was taking over the world; why should I have to be woken up by screaming foreigners?

Simplicity, like I said. In retrospect it seems glib to the point of sacrilege, but in the midst of heavy emotional aftershocks, you (by which I mean me) boil things down into primary colors and the most selfish emotions. So I got out of bed, even before my father and mother had stirred in the big front bedroom and long before any of my sisters had cracked an eye in the little back room next to the kitchen, where they were compensated for the cramped arrangement by at least leaving a view of the garden. I slept in the room between, on the couch. It had been Daniel's bed; before he left, I was relegated to a pile of blankets on the floor. I thought of him every morning when I woke up, because the broken-down couch cushions seemed molded to his long, rawboned frame; I began every day conscious of the ways in which he was larger than I was, and of the way in which I had begun to struggle with the size and shape of his absence.

Grasping at the fading memory of the dream, I thought: Yoo-Hoo?

That afternoon—it was a Wednesday, I remember, I think sometime in November—I scraped up a nickel and bought myself a Yoo-Hoo. Daniel was right. It did help. I was cutting school that day, rationalizing the act as a small homage to my brother, and with my bottle of Yoo-Hoo I walked brazenly up Keap within a block of PS 319 and jumped the turnstile onto the Fourteenth Street-Canarsie Line, headed for Manhattan. In the tunnel under the river, I became suddenly conscious of the water over my head, and I started to think of Daniel. *Full fathom five my brother lies, those are pearls that were his eyes . . .* I started to cry, and just like that the Yoo-Hoo wasn't helping anymore. I got up and shoved my way out of the car to stand on the coupling until the train clacked into Union Square and I'd gotten myself under control again.

Had Daniel died quickly? My imagination boomed with the impact of the torpedo, the rolling wall of fire engulfing the passages belowdecks. I saw pieces of steel curling and tumbling through the gradations of light below the surface, finally lost in the pelagic darkness—and wondered if pieces of my brother Daniel might have danced among those fragments of his ship, until they came to rest together on the sea floor. *Epipelagic, mesopelagic, bathypelagic, abyssopelagic, hadopelagic.* Already I was absorbing words, letting them pour into me as if Daniel's death had ruptured me and a sea of language was drawing me into its depths. Walking through the pitiful last farmer's market of the year, I knew what I would do.

Or had he survived the initial impact, and felt the ship tilt, spilling him out of his bunk onto the angled steel floor? When the lights went out, had he known how to get out? After fire, water—had Daniel spent his last moments clawing at the ceiling of the ship's hold, looking for the hatch he knew must be there while around him the transport groaned and boomed its way down? I closed my eyes, to feel the darkness of drowning. I imagined that Daniel had somehow survived until the ship had come to rest on the ocean floor, and that he had had time to write a letter in the blackness, with the water slowly leaking past the stressed rivets to rise icily over his feet. At last the room, filled with water, would have been completely silent, with the letter he had written drifting loosely away from his lifeless fingers, the slow action of the water loosing graphite from paper until his last thoughts were diffused into the cold and dark.

Dear Josh, Daniel is reading in my dream. The paper crinkles in his hands, and I don't look at his face. Stop being such a shithead. I am dead. It doesn't matter how.

Drip, drip, drip, of seawater from the paper. It crinkles anyway. I smell mud.

Danny, I start to say.

Cut it out, he says. Listen. You want to do something? Fine. Quit with the torpedo and the ship and fire and smoke. How many times are you gonna play that little movie in your head? Enough already. So you got an imagination, that's great, but use it. Or don't, but anyway quit.

What do you want me to do?

You're already doing it, he says. I mean, *abyssopelagic*?

And I woke to the uproar of the refugees in the basement. *Refugee*: from the French *refugier*, to take shelter or protect, first used in reference to the Huguenots; all the way back to the Latin *refugium*, and all the way back before that to that long-lost moment when all of the little phonemes and graphemes came gasping and creeping up onto the beach of language, leaving behind them the undifferentiated ocean of sound. This is what you did to me, Danny, I thought.

At breakfast I started spelling words out loud. My sisters got into it. They collected newspapers and hit me with whatever they could find, and then it turned into a game they played among themselves. Each of them focused on words that began with the same letter as their first names: Miriam, Eva, Ruth, Deborah. After a month of this I was convinced that I knew every word in the language that began with those four letters. *Mnemonic, elegiac, rotisserie, diverticulitis. Malevolent, esoterica, rubicon, demesne.* And I think I knew every word in the language that began with a combination of those letters. *Dermatology*? Forget it. I give you *dermanyssidae*, which is a family of mites that infest birds and lizards and whatever else. I think my favorite of all of them was *merdivorous*, which means exactly what you think it might. Synonym *coprophagous*. A merdivorous grin.

My sisters knew what I was doing. So did my parents. None of them stopped me. I think they figured this was my way of working out Danny's death, and they liked the way I was serious about something. Before this I'd been flighty, accidentally good at school but never dedicated to it—or to anything else, for that matter. Like a lot of children of immigrants, I reacted to their resolve and perseverance by becoming indifferent to everything except the Dodgers . . . and, in my case, spelling.

So they quietly encouraged my newfound interest in spelling, recognizing it for the homage it was. Mom did have a tendency to stiffen and get quiet when I started spouting off Anglo-Saxon roots during one of my etymology binges. They sounded too much like German to her. She saw the effect the whole game had on my sisters, though, who started to seem more substantial again, their colors more vibrant, as they came home from the library with new words to challenge me. They asked doctors and lawyers, people whose lives revolved around jargon, for new ones. I soaked them all up, a glutton for words to fill the space left by Danny's loss.

At the same time, I was spooked by my own obsession. Miriam's *dybbuk* comment rang around in my head. If the *dybbuk* took over someone close to it to complete an unfinished task, didn't it make a certain kind of sense that Danny would come for me? Was that why I was dreaming of him?

I told you there's no such thing as *dybbuks*, he's saying to me in a dream. We're sitting next to each other, about to parachute out of a C-47 that's bucking and shuddering from flak. I think my dreaming mind has borrowed the scene from a movie, but the thought is stripped away like the streaming silk canopies opening below the plane and then ripped away out of sight.

Maybe you're just telling me that so I don't know you're one, I say.

It's his turn to jump. He cracks a smile at me over his shoulder. You have weird hang-ups, he says. Then he's gone.

Waking up, my first thought was that I'd never heard anyone say *hang-up* like that before.

It didn't stop there. Didn't stop anywhere, really, even though as the war dragged on and the news out of Europe mounted to a pitch of awful horror that penetrated even my self-obsession, I learned to stop talking about it all the time. The lesson came at the breakfast table late in 1943. The Fifth Army was in Italy, the U-boats that had murdered my brother were vanishing from the Atlantic, and Hitler was beginning to pay the price for his dream of conquering Russia. Guadalcanal and Midway had cut the Japanese down to size. The war was turning.

My father built pianos. Well, he did until Pearl Harbor. Then Steinway and Sons, like every other manufacturer in the country, tried to figure some way to make itself useful to the war effort. After backing-and-forthing with the War Production Board, Steinway settled on parts for the CG-4A glider, which was basically a vehicle for controlled crash landings. It didn't have to fly; it just had to fall from a C-47 tow plane to Earth without killing the pilot and wrecking whatever it was carrying.

It wasn't easy, that's for sure. There's a famous story about how Henry Ford tried to get into armaments production during the First World War, and found out that although he knew just about everything there was to know about making cars, that didn't mean he had the first clue about how to make boats. By World War Two, Ford had the war-materiel game figured out—they turned out a pile of CG-4A's—but Steinway sure didn't. They cut and recut, jiggered processes around, held the Army's blueprints at various angles . . . and still the glider wings came out wrong.

Until one day my dad lost his temper on the factory floor. I imagine him there, surrounded by jigsaws and racks of tools, ankle-deep in sawdust and hemmed in by the suits demanding to know why the company who made the greatest pianos in the world couldn't make something as simple as a wing for a glider that was only designed to crash.

"You leave me alone for a day," my dad said—he said a lot of other things, but I'm giving you the story as I got it in its bowdlerized (from Thomas Bowdler, eighteenth-century English physician who published a kids' version of Shakespeare without all of the dirty jokes and gore) version—"you leave me alone for a day, and I'll figure it out."

They did, and he did, and Steinway made glider wings. The company also turned a nice dime by painting a bunch of unsold uprights olive-drab and selling those to the Army as "Victory Verticals," but my dad didn't have anything to do with that, except indirectly, and that part of the story comes later.

The reason I bring up his job is that he used to come home from work and, with help from my Uncle Mike, read the letters we got from relatives in Europe. By 1943 we all knew what was going on. There had even been demonstrations in New York; that spring our whole family went and stood outside Madison Square Garden while inside various luminaries demanded that the government do something about what the newspapers were delicately calling the "plight of the European Jew." Not that any of us thought the demonstration would do any good. The way my mordant Uncle Mike put it, "We demonstrated in 1933, when the Nazis were just burning books, and look where that got us. Now they're burning us."

In 1933 I was two years old. For some reason Uncle Mike's comment got to me. I felt for weeks afterward that I was a creature of futility, doomed to witness but never act because it was impossible to act.

Anyway, in 1943 some letters were still getting out. For some reason the Nazis were more likely to let letters through if they were written in German— for that matter, Jews who spoke German were marginally more likely to get on protection lists and survive in the camps—so our cousins in Poland and Czechoslovakia wrote us in German. They got letters—don't ask me how—to another cousin in Russia, or sometimes a former business associate who fled to Sweden, and the letters got passed on, eventually, to us. My parents got some of it because they spoke Yiddish, but my Yiddish vocabulary was restricted to insults and endearments, so I waited for Uncle Mike to pause and catch me up via *extempore*—and, I'm sure, idiosyncratic—translations. (*Idiosyncratic*, from the Greek *idios + synkrasis*, "one's own mixture." *Extempore* is even better: from the Latin that means "out of time." What did you do to me, Danny?)

What I tried to do was pick out words that were interesting, or that I didn't know, or that I knew something about but not enough. Reflexively I would try to spell them, or test them against my embryonic knowledge of etymology. This time what happened was a little different. The letter mentioned Auschwitz, and I thought Klinkojoke. My mouth opened and, louder than I meant to, I said to Uncle Mike, "In German *Witz* means joke."

Of course I shouldn't have said it. Not then and there. But it was one of those moments when you suddenly discover that you're attuned to something that you find irresistibly adult—the small, gruesome ironies of language—and Uncle Mike had the blackest sense of humor of anyone I've ever known. And that little coincidence in the Germanization of Oswiecim (not so unlike the

Germanization of Kalienkowicze to Klinkowitz) was the kind of cruel witti-
cism the Nazis would have appreciated, or for all I knew did appreciate. In the
same vein as Arbeit Macht Frei. Or the "model ghetto" at Terezin. I meant it to
be a sort of letter of introduction into the mysterious and seductive adult sphere
of world-weariness and caustic humor.

Silence fell at the table. Uncle Mike put down his fork and, in a gesture for
which I have always been grateful, tried to save me from my own idiot flippancy.

"That's America," he said with a chuckle. "Education, education, education."

"You ought to be ashamed of yourself," my mother said, with a coldness in
her voice that I'd never heard before. "The Germans killed your brother. They're
killing every Jew in Europe. And you joke about it. You *spell*." She twisted the
last word, making it sound filthy somehow, as if *spelling* was something you did
to little kids when nobody was looking.

"*Zol zein*," Uncle Mike said quietly. "He's just a boy, Sarah." He folded the
letter up and handed it back to my father. I learned to stop talking about spelling
after that.

My sisters left me alone, too, so my spelling mania became a solitary pre-
occupation. I struck a balance in my head, learning to live with the sense of
triviality that came from obsessing over words while my people were being
erased from the Earth.

Danny got it, at least.

You're on a roll, kiddo, he says to me that night. We're walking along a beach. This
was fall of 1943, so I'm guessing the beach was somewhere in Italy, although it
could have been Wake or Bougainville. I followed the war in Europe more closely,
though, for obvious reasons, so I'm guessing it was Italy. Salerno, probably.

Sesquipedalian, he says to me. I spell it.

See? He says.

Screw, I say. We walk along the beach a little farther. Artillery rumbles
over the horizon. Soldiers climb out of the ground and run backwards into the
ocean. A B-24 rises up in flaming pieces from the ocean and eats its own trail
of smoke on its way back up into the sky.

Seriously, Danny says. You're a hell of a lot better at this than I was.

Sesquipedalian's easy, I say. Spelled just like it sounds. Nothing tricky about it.

Danny's laughing. I smell saltwater, and I notice his uniform is wet.

It was true, though. Compare *sesquipedalian* with the winning word in 1942,
sacrilegious. I knew that one, too, but it has that tricky transposition of the *I* and
the *E*. Like *sacristy*, not like *sacred*, which is what you would expect.

Winter came. The refugees in the basement stole our coal and erupted in
furious arguments before sunrise. I learned words. My bar mitzvah came in

January, and suddenly because I went to synagogue and read a blessing, I was supposed to follow the Commandments. I couldn't make anything make any sense because I was an obsessive with no possibility of putting my obsession to use. I was running out of eligibility, too. Age wasn't going to be a problem, at least not unless the war lasted a lot longer that people were saying it would; but I was due to finish eighth grade in June of 1944, and unless there was a regional that year, I would never get a chance to compete. This possibility ate at me, kept me up at night, had me devouring newspapers and radio broadcasts and movie newsreels for hints that the end was coming.

Do we need to apologize for the fact that as children we fail at things that no child should be expected to do? Perhaps in extraordinary times we do. Looking back—now that I've had fifty years to learn reflection—I can tell you that what I really wanted was my family safe. I wanted no more Judenfrei, no more letters that had to travel ten thousand miles to get from Poland to Brooklyn, if they got there at all. No more lists of the dead, and rumors of the missing. No more pale sisters silent in their room. No more mother bursting out in rage-fueled accusations that I wasn't good enough, wasn't serious enough, wasn't Jewish enough.

And the spelling bee started to stand in for all of that for me. Maybe it's superficial, or cowardly, but I couldn't handle it. I think I came to feel that the only way for me to survive it was to strip myself of whatever parts of my identity left me vulnerable to the horror of it all, and substitute in the endless gluttony for syllables that got me up in the morning and lulled me to sleep at night while the adults conferred in the kitchen over school, work, the war, the Shoah.

Which nobody was yet calling the Holocaust, at least not with a capital H. (*Holocaust*: from the Greek *holokaustos*, "burnt whole." Word used by Greek translators of the Torah for burnt offerings to God; there's irony for you.)

"He turns to words," I heard Uncle Mike say to my mother one night in the kitchen, when they thought I was asleep. "What could be more Jewish than that?"

God is mysterious that way.

I decided to fail the eighth grade. By the spring of 1944 it was clear that there would be no spelling bee that year, and although I was failing at so much else I would not fail the memory of my brother—even if not failing meant I had to fail.

So I quit doing homework, and started cutting school almost every day. It was late enough in the school year that I had to work pretty hard at being held back, since my grades from earlier in the year were pretty good, but I was counting on the establishment of a downward trend to make up for that.

The truant officer came to our house three times. My mother slapped my face. My father, skinny with sorrow and overtime, shook his head in weary disgust. On Passover, my sisters, taking a break from helping my mother cook for the *seder*, huddled like a flock of birds and sent Miriam over to make overtures. "We know what you're doing," she said. "Daniel wouldn't have wanted you to."

"Maybe I'll ask him," I said, cruelly, and she went back to her flock of four.

I do ask him, while we're walking through the pulverized rubble of some European city that night. Fires smolder in the ruins. Danny, me, and a couple of stray dogs. Aircraft engines thrum overhead, but the sky is a featureless black.

So am I wrong, Danny?

What do I know, he says. I'm just a *dybbuk*.

What you are is fish food, I say. In waking life, he is the only thing I can't be flip about. Here it's different.

Not even that anymore, he says.

What were you doing when it happened? I ask him.

He looks me in the eye. It?

When you got killed, I say. When the torpedo hit.

Signaling, he says, and pantomimes a semaphore. I don't catch the letters. Telling the ship behind us that one of our engines was acting up and we could only make eight knots.

He sees the question in my eyes and goes on. Yeah, he says. I was on deck, astern over the engine room. The fish hit us square under my feet, bounced me into the drink. Then the water coming in through the hole sucked me right along with it.

His retelling is pitiless, and makes me ashamed of the movies I played in my head. Still I want him to answer my first question, but I can't ask it again.

Never was a very good swimmer, Danny says. But it doesn't matter.

I can feel onrushing wakefulness, like the Dopplering sound of a train whistle. Then he's crying, my dead not-*dybbuk* fish-food maybe-ghost of a brother. Yesterday Howard went home, he says.

Morning brought news that it was true. Klinkojoke had died when the B-24 on which he was a nose gunner got shot up over Bad Voslau, Austria, and crashed in the English Channel on the way back. Deborah, Ruth, and Eva cried for a week (Eva from the great distance of Morningside Heights because she'd gotten a scholarship to go to Barnard and was living in a dormitory there). They'd loved Klinkojoke, and Miriam cried because they did. I was so scared because of what Danny had told me that I had to scare somebody else, so I told Miriam.

"Danny told me about it last night," I said. We were out in the backyard garden, which was the one of the few good things about having a ground-floor apartment. The air was cool, and beyond the concrete patio the whole yard was turned up and cordoned off into a victory garden. "He also told me how he died."

She'd been suffering a recurrent sniffle over Klinkojoke, but it stopped and she got absolutely still. "That's not funny, Josh."

"Remember what I told you right after he died? It's been happening ever since."

Miriam got up from the bench where were sitting and went back inside. We never talked about Danny again. I always felt that what happened to her after the war was my fault, and that if it hadn't started when Danny died, it started that April Sunday morning, just after Passover, on the patio next to the stakes and strings and shoots of the victory garden. But—and here's the reflection again—I don't know how I could have done it any different.

In June—the day after the Allies landed at Normandy—my parents were notified that I would be required to repeat the eighth grade unless I completed summer school. My father took me aside, and we both understood that he was doing me a favor by relieving my mother of the duty. "You're thirteen years old, Joshua," he said, "and for twelve of those years you've been the smart one of my boys. Now I want you to tell me, man to man. Are you doing this because you got the idea that you need to be more like your brother now that he's dead?"

This was the longest speech I'd ever heard my father give, and it took me a minute to recover my surly equanimity. "What if I am?" I asked him.

"Then I'll get you on at Steinway," he said without missing a beat. "If you're just going to clown around at school, you might as well get the hell out of it and make some use of yourself."

For as long as I've been alive since then, I've been trying to figure out if there was something I expected less than that. I thought about it.

"Can I work for the summer and then go back?"

My father laughed. "That's exactly what Mike said you would say. Okay. That's what we'll do."

And we did. I got on the train with my father every morning that summer, while the Allied pincer tightened on Germany and the Marines ground their way toward Japan. My job was to tape the keyboards and pedals of old unsalable Steinway uprights so they could be spray-painted Army green. Victory Verticals. I taped them, they went in for spraying, the paint dried, I peeled the tape. Then came the best part of my job, which was stenciling PROPERTY OF THE U.S. ARMY on the back of every one. At the end of every day I rode the subway home with my dad; he complained about the lousy quality of the wood they were getting for the glider wings, and I picked white paint out from under my fingernails. I never did ask him how he got me the job. The wartime economy had the country as close to full employment as it ever got, but it's my guess that plenty of grown men—or women—would have taken the job I had as a thirteen-year-old kid. I imagine a conversation in which my father, covered with grease and sawdust from the factory floor, goes to Mr. Steinway and explains the situation, whereupon Mr. Steinway does a favor for the guy who finally got the wing design right. It's the only time in my life I indulged in a little nepotism (from the Latin *nepos*, "nephew"; originally the favors bestowed by a pope on his illegitimate children). Something about the daily physical work, the routine of getting up early and working had an effect on my dreams. I didn't talk to Danny all summer, even in July when Majdanek became the first concentration camp to be liberated and all of our worst intuitions began to be confirmed.

Maybe that was coincidence, but I don't think so, since Danny was there again as soon as I decided to go back to school in the fall.

It's raining like hell, and we're dangling our legs off one of the tracks of a burned-out Panzer tank. You think it's going to be over this year? I ask him.

How should I know? Danny says. You going to pass your classes this year?

The truth is, I don't know. I've got one extra year to play with age-wise, and by the time another year has gone by, I'm going to know every word in the English language. I'll be invincible. Is that worth deliberately failing another year of school? I'm inclined to think it might be.

I don't know, Danny says. How much longer do you think you can ride this grieving-for-your-brother horse?

Shithead, I say. I'm not grieving for you anymore. You won't leave me alone long enough.

What are you talking about? I left you alone all summer.

And now you're back.

You're not answering my question.

I still don't answer him. After a while he shakes his head. Your heart won't heal, he says.

Which was such a strange thing for my wiseass brother to say that I walked around for days thinking about it. Then the days stretched into weeks, and I was treading water in school, unable to concentrate on anything—even learning new words—because something about Danny's words was like a fishhook in my brain. Ambivalence was everywhere: I was passing school but barely, the Reds turned Majdanek into a brand-new concentration camp for Polish resistance fighters, Miriam had come to life but only because she was dating a boy my parents didn't like. Her dreaminess had somehow hardened into rebellion while none of us were looking.

I went to school long enough to finish an algebra test and keep my head above water, then lit out and just walked around the neighborhood. I walked down across Broadway, underneath the elevated tracks. Briefly I thought about stealing a car even though I had no idea how—or I could just get on the train, switch to another train, get on a bus at Penn Station and disappear. Except I didn't have any money. It was January. I was about to turn fourteen. Winter rain was dripping through the elevated tracks.

Something about the train made me turn and walk east on Broadway. A train thundered by overhead, and as I looked up through the slatted trackbed to follow its passage, I saw a sign. FUGACCI AND SONS, TAILORS. Each of the initial letters, even the *A*, was bigger than the others, and red while the others were black. An acrostic: FAST.

Then came one of those moments where everything that has been a mystery makes sense, and as it does you condemn yourself for an idiot because you didn't figure it out before. For so long I should have known, but at last I put it all together.

Yoo-Hoo will help. You have weird hang-ups. Yesterday Howard went home. Your heart won't heal.

YHWH.

All along, he'd been saying God. God. God. God.

Some kind of animal sound came out of me, drowned out by the train passing overhead. "Ah, Danny," I sobbed. "Why didn't you just tell me?"

I felt something break, physically break, inside me, and I leaned against one of the I-beams holding up the elevated tracks and wept for my brother. That was why I had dreamed, why he had spoken to me, why—God's will being God's will—he had died in the vortex of ocean water near the Straits of Gibraltar. There is no greater pain than complete acceptance of a fact you wish was not factual. I fought it, but that's not a fight you can win.

New Yorkers being New Yorkers, people left me alone, and I felt it all leaking away, the resentment and obsession and the paralyzing sense of impotent witness drowned beneath the iron and the rivets and the indifference of the BMT. It ended right there in the rain, this grief-stricken rebellion against my patrimony. Because that's what it was, what I can call it after fifty years of bending back.

I went back to school, but not that day. Instead I went home, and found my mother listening to Walter Winchell on the radio. Winchell was talking about the liberation of Auschwitz.

Seven months later, it was all over. My eligibility for the spelling bee ran out in June, with an invasion of Japan looming. Then came Hiroshima and Nagasaki, and ticker-tape parades, and the counting of the dead. My older sisters Ruth and Deborah went to college like they were supposed to, Ruth to Michigan and Deborah following Eva to Barnard. I never talked to Danny again. But when a kid named John McKinney from Des Moines, Iowa, won the spelling bee the next summer, that jubilant postwar summer of 1946, I felt like the winning word was a last word from my brother, and I made a little room for belief.

Semaphore.

God is mysterious that way.

Golems I Have Known, or, Why My Elder Son's Middle Name Is Napoleon: A Trickster's Memoir

Michael Chabon

I saw my first *golem* in 1968, in Flushing, New York, shortly before my fifth birthday. It lay on a workbench in the basement of my uncle Jack's house, a few blocks away from the duplex—we called it a "two-family house"—that my parents and I shared with a Greek couple, who lived upstairs. My uncle Jack owned a candy store in Harlem, in a neighborhood where there had once been only Jews but now there were only black people, though my uncle Jack did not call them that. He called them "the coloreds." Nevertheless he always hired local Harlem people to work in his store, and he extended credit to many families in the neighborhood. I suppose he had complicated feelings about his customers, and they about him, both as a creditor and as a cranky and ill-humored man. Owning a candy store was not my uncle Jack's choice of employment; he had failed at several other trades before finally arriving, with the last of his and my aunt's savings, at the threshold of Mount Morris Candy and News. Though I was not told and did not understand any of this until much later, Uncle Jack was also a devoted Jewish scholar who nightly studied Torah and Talmud, and who had in the past year or so embarked upon the study of Kabbalah, that body of Jewish mystical teachings that have produced the Zohar, the false messiah Sabbatai Zevi, and a sense of deep understanding and inner peace, or so one presumes, for Madonna and Roseanne Barr. My parents and my uncle and aunt were not especially close, but we lived so near to them that inevitably we ended up spending time at their house, and I soon learned to fear and to long to see whatever was going on down there in Uncle Jack's basement, to which he invariably repaired as soon as decency and the serving of the *babka* allowed.

This all happened so long ago, and I was, it will be recalled, so young at the time that it's hard for me to remember just how I contrived to convey myself down there under the house, into the basement, which I had been told in no uncertain terms was filled with all kinds of deliciously dangerous power tools and chemicals, and hence strictly off-limits, to have a look. If I were writing a short story, I would figure out how to get the parents out of the way, start them arguing bitterly about Vietnam or civil rights at the dinner table, and then have my fictionalized self slip away unnoticed, perhaps with a vague murmur about going to look at the money plants in the backyard, to head down the long dark stairway into the basement, with its smell of iron filings and cold linoleum. Since this is a memoir, though, I will be truthful and say I don't know how I managed the trick. But I remember the dark stairs, and the cold iron smell.

I'm sure you will doubt what I tell you next, putting it down to the flawed memory of a small boy with a big imagination, or perhaps even, considering what I am about to say, thinking it all nothing but a pack of lies. That's precisely why I've never said anything about the real *golems* in my life before now. There was a *golem*—the most famous *golem* of all, the Golem of Prague—in my novel *The Amazing Adventures of Kavalier & Clay*, and since it was published a lot of people have asked me about my interest in that *golem* and in *golems* in general. And, because I was afraid to tell the truth and more interested in sounding smart than in sounding crazy, I usually said something about having seen, as a child, a still image from Paul Wegener's 1915 film *Der Golem* in a book about fantastic cinema, as if that explained anything, and then after that I would often say something sort of profound and sententious about how the relationship between a *golem* and its creator is usually viewed as a metaphor for that between the work of art—in my case, a novel—and its creator, and how my ideas about *golems* had been shaped by reading Gershom Scholem's famous essay "On the Idea of the *Golem*," and blah, blah, blah. When the truth is that *golems* are real, they are out there now, and they are everywhere. Well, not everywhere, perhaps, but I've seen a bunch of them in my own lifetime, and that's without even trying—believe you me—to find them. As for the Golem of Prague, and the thinly fictionalized role it plays both in *Kavalier & Clay* and in my life, I'm going to come to that in time.

I'm aware, in making this confession, that I'm revealing something that some of you already know perfectly well, something that is generally agreed to be better left undiscussed. I don't think it's exactly taboo for me to reveal the truth about *golems*—God, I hope not—but what do I know? I've never studied Kabbalah. If you see shadowy people follow me out of the hall tonight, or if a blow dart suddenly appears in my larynx and I keel over mid-sentence, you will know that I must have transgressed. I don't know what exactly is prompting me to come forward now and come out with the truth. I think it has something to do with turning forty, with the growing desire I feel to look backward over my life and to try to shore together, if I can, some kind of retrospective understanding, some sense of meaning and perhaps even wisdom to impart to my children as they grow into full consciousness of the pain and mystery of life. Maybe it has something to do with having won the Pulitzer Prize, which gives a guy a sense, however mistaken, of authority, and which, as far as I know, they will not take away from you even if it is determined that you have lost your mind.

In any event, what I saw when I reached the inner sanctum of Uncle Jack's workshop, with its tools hanging neatly from their hooks, its table saw and drill press, its swept pile of sawdust in the corner, tidily awaiting the dustpan, was a *golem*. For those of you who may not, still, be aware of or understand just what exactly a *golem* is, let me briefly state that a *golem* is an artificial being, usually but not necessarily human in shape, made from a lump of clay or earth—the word "*golem*" comes from an ancient Hebrew word meaning "lump"—and brought to life, or to a semblance of life, by mystical means. Some *golem*s are animated by the placing under their tongues of a tablet with one of the names of God written on it, others by having the Hebrew word *emet*, "truth," graved onto their broad foreheads, still others by some combination of the two. But in common all *golem*s require above all that a complicated series of alphabetical spells be chanted over them, in the proper order and combination, for hours and hours and hours. Now, according to the great Herr Scholem, the point of *golem*-making has been greatly exaggerated over the years, embroidered by liars and legend-tellers and romancers. Originally one—and when I say "one" I mean "a trained adept acting in concert with at least one other trained adept"—originally one made a *golem* not in the hope of bringing it to life but in the hope of bringing oneself to life. It was a kind of meditative exercise designed, like other kinds of chanting rituals, to free the consciousness. One imitated God's creation of Adam in the hope of approaching knowledge of the ecstasy and power of that creation.

At any rate, looking back on it, I don't seriously think my uncle Jack could have had any sincere expectation of bringing his own *golem*, the Golem of Flushing, to life. I am certain that it was intended only as a vehicle for expanding his consciousness of the Ineffable Name. It lay, as I have said, on his workbench, a big pine slab which he had nailed together himself years before. Honestly I don't remember all that much about how his *golem* looked; it had big feet, each with five clay toes; its head was squarish, its nose flat, its hair scratched in with some pointed tool in wiggly swirls. I remember the color of its skin, or rather of the clay from which it had been formed, hardened curds or handfuls of clay that were a rich dark brown like coffee grounds. A colored, I thought. The thing that impressed me the most about the thing was the air of utter inertness that it gave off, something more than lifelessness, heavier and more oppressive. In later years I would think of this *golem* when I saw cigar-store Indians, and again when I saw the giant lumpy head of John F. Kennedy in the lobby of the Kennedy Center in Washington, D.C. Its eyes were a pair of horizontal slits, slightly bulging, meant to suggest, I suppose, that it was sleeping.

What did I make of it, at the time? I knew, of course, that it was not a real person—Uncle Jack was clearly not the most talented sculptor in the world—

but there was something about it that troubled me; it had presence. I wasn't quite afraid of it, or rather I feared it obscurely, and with a stab of bright curiosity, as I feared and wondered about all kinds of other elements of the world of adults—my mother's pressing ham, filled with mysterious sand; the heavy wooden trays in which my father kept his microscope slides, smeared with the lung tissue of monkeys. There seemed inherent in that dark clay doll on the table a purpose and a power beyond my imagining.

What can I say? I reached out to touch it, grabbing clumsily at the thing's left big toe, and the toe came off with a dry tinkling of dust. That was the kind of kid I was. I had poked a hole in my mother's pressing ham so that forever after it leaked sand; I had broken five or six of my father's *pneumococcus* slides. And in my horror at this act of accidental mutilation—and I'm perfectly willing to admit that it was only this, the action of horror and dismay on a childish imagination—I saw the Golem of Flushing open its eyes. I will never forget the sight of the dull, wet gaze, blank, ignorant, afraid, that lighted on my face at that instant. I have no idea how I managed to get out of the basement again. The next thing I remember is sitting in my aunt's living room, on the slick crinkling plastic of her slipcovered sofa, and hearing my uncle Jack cry out, his voice ragged and cracked, "They killed King!"

"Oh, no," I heard my mother say. "Oh, that's just awful."

"King who?" I asked, thinking that they were lamenting the death of some monarch.

The night I broke a toe off the Golem of Flushing was the night, as it turned out—April 4, 1968—on which James Earl Ray shot Martin Luther King Jr. There was some rioting over in Harlem, in the course of which somebody set fire to the block that comprised Mount Morris Candy and News, and Uncle Jack's last-chance enterprise was burned out. In the jumble of misunderstood and half-interpreted news reports, anxious talk, and curt whispering that surrounded this calamity and that seemed to make up the bulk of adult conversation in the week that followed, I heard repeated references to "the black man." Inevitably, I guess, I was forced to the conclusion that it had been the dark man of clay in Uncle Jack's basement, angered perhaps by the loss of his toe, who had gone out to Harlem and burnt down the candy store. And it was all my fault.

I was beginning to learn the bitter truth about *golems*. A *golem*, like a lie, is the expression of a wish: a wish for peace and security; a wish for strength and control; a wish to know, in a tiny, human way, a thousandth of a millionth of the joy and power of the Greater Creation. And nothing I have learned since has ever been able to dissuade me that on that April night a *golem*, charged with all the wishes, dark and light, of a suffering people, was created and set loose in the world.

Soon after his world was set on fire, my uncle Jack fell while chasing after a young black neighborhood kid who had, or so he imagined, called him "Hymie." He broke his hip. He went into a rapid decline after that, and was dead before the following autumn. It was around that time that I managed to get down into the basement again. This part may be the embroidery of a guilty recollection, but I remember it as being on the actual day of Jack's funeral, when we all went back to the house to start the weeklong period of *shiva*. As I had suspected it would be, the giant doll with the dead, fearful eyes was gone. I got down on my hands and knees and looked around, and there, under the now barren workbench, lay the toe.

After a while my father came downstairs looking for me. Since he didn't seem to be angry at finding me in such close proximity to dangerous tools and chemicals, not to mention trespassing into forbidden zones of mystic knowledge, I told him the whole story. He laughed, and reassured me that I was not in any way responsible for my uncle's death, explaining that Uncle Jack had had his little eccentricities when it came to religion. But I could see that my father was not taking me seriously. So I showed him the toe.

"Well," he said, studying it, taking me a little more seriously now, it seemed to me. "If you had brought it to life, that wouldn't be too surprising, I guess. You know, Michael, we're descended on my father's side from Rabbi Judah ben Loew."

It was then and there, and not from any book on fantastic cinema, that I first learned about *golems* and in particular the Golem of Prague. My father explained to me that it was the great Rabbi Judah of Prague who, sometime in the sixteenth century, created the best-known of all *golems* to do his bidding around the synagogue, sweeping up the dooryard and readying the sanctuary for the Sabbath, and to help protect the Jews of Prague's ghetto against those who sought to harm them. This *golem*, like a lie, grew to a tremendous size, and in its vengeful might came in time to threaten the security of those it had been made to keep safe. Rabbi Judah lost control of it, and eventually he was obliged to destroy the life he had talked into being, in order to keep it from destroying everything else. And it was from this great wonder-working rabbi, through a grandson who left Prague and traveled across the Austrian Empire to settle in Lodz, that we were descended. Or so my father said. He had told me such things before, about other famous Jews from history, and he would continue, as I grew older, to periodically reveal new and ever more startling connections.

A writer of science fiction named Philip José Farmer once devised the amusing or tedious conceit of tracing the lineage of Lord Greystoke, better known as Tarzan of the Apes. Mr. Farmer postulated that an ancestor of the future lord of the jungle was among the passengers of two coaches that were passing Wold Newton, England, in 1795, just as a radioactive meteor fell from outer space into a meadow on the outskirts of the village. The radiation from the space rock, and the genetic mutation it caused, Mr. Farmer posited, affected all the descendents of those passengers, among them the eventual John Clayton, Lord Greystoke—Tarzan. Mr. Farmer then extended his conceit by claiming that not only Tarzan but all the great heroes and villains of popular nineteenth- and twentieth-century literature—the Scarlet Pimpernel, Sherlock Holmes and Professor Moriarty, Doc Savage, Phileas Fogg, Fu Manchu, Sam Spade, James Bond—were descended from the people riding in that pair of coaches, a super-human lineage of siblings and cousins descended from that common ancestor and that catastrophic event.

When, as a boy of nine or ten, I encountered Mr. Farmer's hypothesis in his amusing mock biography of Tarzan, it came as no surprise to me at all. My father had already articulated, in considerable detail, a similar startling theory of our own lineage.

Over the years my father has informed me—generally with no warning and without offering any explanation for the information's having gone unmentioned until that moment—that we Chabons are connected, distantly perhaps but with a kind of telling intimacy, to the following people: the great tragedienne Rachel, the humorist Art Buchwald, the vicious murderer Lepke Buchalter, Rabbi Eliyahu, known as the Gaon or Genius of Vilna, the aforementioned Rabbi Judah ben Bezalel ben Loew, Harry Houdini, the first-class spy and third-rate baseball player Moe Berg, and, most gloriously of all, Napoleon Bonaparte, through his nephew Napoleon III, who—or so my father claims—fathered an illegitimate child, my ancestor, of the above-mentioned French actress, Rachel.

I won't bother with the question of whether my father is telling the truth, or believes he is telling the truth, when he says such things. Nor is it germane to my point to ask if I believe him. After all, what he says could be true; if plausibility is good enough for me as a reader, and good enough for you as listeners, it's good enough for me as a son. The importance to me, now and as a child, of my father's stories is and was 1) their peculiar, detailed beauty, from the quirkiness of the famous personalities they involved to the complicated ways in which my father attempted to map out our relation to these people, and 2) the sense of incredible connectedness I derived, as a kid, from his stories. Listening to my father describe the deeds, crimes, and achievements of our famous cousins, scattered as they were across continents and eras, gave me an almost vertiginous sense of simultaneity, of our family's and my own small self's existing in all times, at all places.

When I was ten years old—shortly after reading Philip José Farmer's biography of Tarzan, with its genealogy of heroes and criminals almost as fantastic as my own—I produced my first sustained work of fiction. This was a short story, about twelve pages in length, entitled "The Revenge of Captain Nemo." It recounted a meeting between Verne's Captain Nemo and Doyle's Sherlock

Holmes (first cousins, according to Farmer). I won't make any claims as to its merits, but two great things happened to me in the course of writing it. One was that I consciously adopted, for the first time, a literary style: Sir Arthur Conan Doyle's, or rather that of the good Dr. John Watson. I think I had always been sensitive, before this, to variations in writers' diction and to the mood and tone of a paragraph. I was alert to the difference in vocabulary and idiom one found in British storybooks, could tell when language was trying to sound antiquated, jocular, or hard-boiled. I could hear the difference between words of Latin origin and those that came from Anglo-Saxon. I knew how Doyle's writing sounded. I could hear the tune of it in my head. Now I just had to sit down and play.

Getting the style down—that was more than half the fun for me. I used words like "postulated" and "retribution." I wrote "had the odor of" instead of "smelled." I went on about railway schedules, the harbor at Portsmouth, the fog. I referred to the infamous Moriarty as "the Napoleon of Crime," thus linking him, in my imagination, to my own family tree. When I finished it, "The Revenge of Captain Nemo" went over pretty well. I had the satisfaction of being praised by my parents and other adults and of having actually completed something that struck me as admirably substantial, even huge. The work of typing it alone had nearly killed me. But more precious to me than praise or completion was the intense pleasure I had derived from attempting to impersonate Sir Arthur Conan Doyle, from putting on his accent, following his verbal trail. It was the pleasure that a liar takes in his lie as it enters the world wearing the accent and raiment of the truth, sounding so right and plausible that—if he is any kind of liar at all—he begins, himself, to believe it. It was the pleasure that a maker of *golems* takes as the force of his words, the rhythm and accuracy of his alphabetical spells, blow life into the cold clay nostrils, and the great stony hand unclenches and reaches for his own. At some point in the exercise the power of Doyle's diction resounding in my ear carried me away. I felt intimately connected to him, as though it was not I inhabiting his literary skin but, somehow, the other way around. It was like something out of a ghost story—a child sitting down at a haunted piano and feeling a spectral hand guide his own over the keys.

That was the second important thing that happened to me when I wrote that story. It was as if I had opened a door and stepped into the room in which all my favorite writers were sitting around waiting for me to show up. They were a disparate bunch, from Judy Blume to Edgar Allan Poe, spread over different eras, continents, and genres. Some were close kin to each other—Lord Dunsany, H.P. Lovecraft—while others seemed to have nothing in common beyond their connection to me. And somehow, I sensed, their intersection defined me. They were, in other words, my family. I derived from them, they explained me. And more than anything else I wanted—I knew it now—to be accounted one of them. This was the wish—to be a credit to that far-flung family of literary heroes—that I have sought to embody, to express in the infinitely malleable clay of language, ever since.

It was around this time, as I was making up my mind to be a writer, that I encountered my second *golem*. By this time we were living in the then-new town of Columbia, a planned community in the Maryland suburbs, between Baltimore and Washington, D.C. In the waning years of my parents' marriage— it ended, draw your own conclusions, the year that I began to formulate my wish—one of the only reliable sources of pleasure for my father and me was the weekly trip we took, alone, to the Howard County Public Library's main branch, then located on Frederick Road, outside of the city limits of Columbia itself. One evening as I was rather sullenly spinning the wire rack of paperbacks intended for a group of readers who were then just becoming known, in the librarian trade, as YAs, I came across a book called *Strangely Enough!*, written by one C.B. Colby and published by Scholastic Book Services. It was one of those mysterious books that you have loved as a child but which as you go out into the world no one else ever seems to have read or even heard of, although the library's copy was tattered and well worn and had been checked out, to judge from the number of fading purplish dates stamped onto its tan pocket, by dozens of YAs before me. It was made up of a series of about a hundred short pieces, little essays, each about five hundred words long and devoted to exposing or musing over all kinds of inexplicable and supposedly factual inci- dents and phenomena: poltergeists, haunted paintings, UFO sightings, rains of frogs and stones, witch scares, phantom hitchhikers, encounters with the devil in which he left his cloven footprint clearly visible in a neighborhood rock. I read a few of the entries— enough to persuade me that it was going to turn out to be one of the best books I had ever read—and then carried it with a few other titles to wait for my father at the circulation desk.

"*Strangely Enough!*" the librarian intoned, putting a little Twilight Zone wobble into her voice. I nodded. "You know he lives here. C.B. Colby."

It turned out that C.B. Colby lived not merely in Columbia but right down the street from my family, in the small cubistic house stained dark blue, with the goldfish pond, that you had to pass whenever you went to our street's communal mailbox. His real name was Joseph Adler, and in time I discovered that in addition to Strangely Enough! he was the author of some 250 other works, fiction and nonfiction, for children and YAs, under a bewildering variety of pseudonyms. All I had known of him before now was that he was a baby chick of a man, with a soft, wavering plume of white hair and a gentle if somewhat stiff manner toward children. A reticent, courtly ghost of him, the first real writer I ever knew, can be glimpsed in the figment of a writer called

August Van Zorn, in my novel *Wonder Boys*. Mrs. Adler had died not long after we moved into the neighborhood, and my mother had made him a roast and carried it down to him. The widower, she told me when she returned from this charitable visit, was a "survivor." I hadn't heard the term before, though I had an aunt by marriage who had been interned at Auschwitz as a child, and I knew enough, the next time I saw Mr. Adler, to look for and discover the greenish-black numbers on the inside of his forearm.

I was not a bold child. It took me most of the four-week circulation period to get up the nerve to go to his front door, clutching the library's copy of his book, which by now I had read at least half-a-dozen times, terrifying myself, ruining my sleep, making the flat, sunny, avocado-and-goldenrod-colored 1973 world of Columbia, Maryland into a strange and marvelous world that contained treasures and ghosts and mysterious bright objects in the sky. Before approaching his house directly, however, I had spent several days furtively lurking nearby, concealing myself behind a bush or the neighbor's parked car, studying the bare windows behind which nothing ever seemed to move. I saw a piano. I saw a work of iron sculpture that looked something like a mace and something like a gate and something like a twist of barbed wire. I saw thousand and thousands of books. And once I caught a glimpse of Mr. Adler, drinking orange juice straight from the carton.

"Ah," he said, when he opened the door to me. "My little shadow."

It would be nice to tell you a story now about how Mr. Adler, the taciturn, intellectual, widowed author of two hundred popular pseudonymous novels, and Michael Chabon, the awkward, unhappy, budding boy-writer skulking around the margins of his neighborhood, his future, and his parents' divorce, forged an unlikely friendship while teaching each other valuable lessons about literature and life. But it didn't work out that way; I guess that's why stories are so much better than life, or rather why stories make life so much better. Mr. Adler invited me in, dismissed *Strangely Enough!* with a contemptuous wave of his hand, poured me a glass of orange juice that I felt a little bit nervous about drinking, and told me that my eyeglasses were much too big for my face. The house was filled with all kinds of spiky and unnerving sculptures, some all welded steel, like the one I'd seen from the window, others done in wood, plaster, and glass. They were the work, he explained to me, of his wife. Just before I departed his house for the first and last time, he took me into his office and pointed to the neatly stacked pages of a manuscript sitting beside his great steely battleship of an IBM Selectric. "That is the first book I will ever put my own name upon," he said. There was a faint trace of an accent; it made me think of my aunt Renée, who had been in the camps too. "What kind of book is it?" I asked him. He looked annoyed. "It's a memoir, of course," he said. "The story of my life."

It was as he was walking me, almost herding me, really, toward the door, that I noticed, lying on the glass shelf of a chrome-plated *étagère*, what I took to be another example of his late wife's work. It was a clay doll, about the size of the old G.I. Joes they used to have—big enough to whip Ken's vinyl ass. This clay figure was lumpy and crooked and almost looked as if it had been made by a kid, and I remember considering whether I ought and then deciding not to ask Mr. Adler if he had any children. You could tell, somehow, that he did not. It was a just a glimpse that I got, that day, of the little clay man. Then I was out the door.

I imagine there may be some of you who remember the name "Joseph Adler." You may have read his memoir, *The Book of Hell*, which I still see from time to time in used bookstores, its black jacket tattered or missing. My father-in-law owns a copy, though he has an extensive library of books on Jewish subjects and owns copies of a lot of books that nobody reads anymore.

I have a copy of my own, one which my father bought right after it came out. It's a well-written, fairly brutal account of the two years the author, a Prague-born Jewish journalist, spent in Theresienstadt. All the usual horrors are present, and although there is an interesting chapter on the secret camp newspaper, *Vadem*, in the end there is nothing really to distinguish the book from any of the many literary memoirs that have been written about those times. The only passage of interest to us here is a brief paragraph that concerns, very much in passing, the Golem of Prague:

> One morning I found myself in possession of five potatoes that were free of rot and not overly endowed with eyes. A man approached me offering to trade for them. In return for my potatoes he said that he would give me the magic tablet, inscribed with secret writing, that had once lain under the tongue of the famous Golem of Prague and was responsible for bringing to life that legendary Jewish automaton. He said that it was a lucky charm and would protect me from evil. We settled on two of my potatoes and went our separate ways. Shortly thereafter, I heard the man had been killed. As for the tablet, incised with Hebrew characters which I was days in trying to make out, it was lost in the disorder that followed my liberation.

Interestingly, one also encounters the Golem of Prague in the pages of *Strangely Enough!*, in a piece entitled "The Phantom of the Synagogue." In it "C.B. Colby" recounts the basic legend of Rabbi Judah's *golem*—the blood libels, the shaping of the clay of the Moldau River, the need to put an end to the Golem's career, and the persistent rumor that the lifeless form of the Golem still slumbers in the attic of the Alt-Neu Synagogue in Prague's ancient ghetto. Nothing is said, however, about the placing of any magic tablet inscribed with Hebrew letters under the Golem's tongue.

Those of you who lived in and around Washington, D.C. during that time may dimly recall the scandal that followed the book's publication, and a few particulars of the strange case of the writer the *Washington Post* called "The Liar Who Got Lost in His Lie." About six months after the book came out, you may remember, a woman came forward to denounce Joseph Adler, or C.B. Colby. This woman had stumbled upon *The Book of Hell* in her local library and, seeing the author photo, had recognized in the delicate, birdlike features of old Mr. Adler the unmistakable lineaments of a Czech Nazi journalist named Victor Fischer, an admirer and eventual successor of the notorious propagandist Julius Streicher and one of those chiefly responsible for spreading the lie about the ideal conditions to be found in Theresienstadt, where Fischer's accuser had herself been interned.

The Wiesenthal Center took an interest; the *Washington Post* investigated. Mr. Adler denied the woman's claims, hired a lawyer, and promised to fight the charges. Soon afterward, however, he collapsed, and had to be hospitalized. He had suffered a stroke. From his hospital bed, he composed a remarkable statement to the *Post*. I remember reading it to myself one morning over my bowl of Quisp cereal. In his statement, Mr. Adler acknowledged being Victor Fischer and described the destitution and despair into which he had fallen after the war, roaming penniless and starving through the Czech countryside. He described being set upon by a roving gang of Jews bent on murderous revenge, and told how his life had been spared through the kind intercession of a Jewish girl, herself a survivor, whom he eventually married—the late Mrs. Adler. In 1946 he and his new bride had emigrated to the United States, Fischer carrying the passport of a dead Jew, Joseph Adler, whose identity, on his arrival in New York, he eagerly and persuasively assumed. He resumed his journalistic career, writing for a number of newspapers and magazines, and in time came, or so he claimed, to be Joseph Adler. The whole lifelong charade had been pulled off with the knowing connivance of his wife, whose numerical tattoo had served as the model for the one which she herself pricked into his arm with a sewing needle.

Looking back I find that my recollections of the *Book of Hell* business are mingled with and effaced by concurrent memories of the Watergate scandal and with overarching outrage at my parents' divorce. I remember seeing Mr. Adler's statement in the paper, as I've said. I can remember my mother's shock and sense of betrayal by the man she had fed from her own kitchen. But the thing I remember the clearest is the day they came to take Mr. Adler's things away.

Once he entered the hospital, Mr. Adler never returned to the modest blue house on our street. One by one the goldfish in the pond fell prey to the neighborhood cats; then a kind of green pudding appeared on the surface of the water. After a few more months there was nothing in the fishpond but a slick black mat of rotten leaves. And then one day a large Mayflower van pulled up.

I happened to be passing by on my bicycle and stopped to watch the burly men carrying out the furniture, the giant twist of barbed wire, the endless boxes of books. There were a lot of crazy sculptures, and the moving men cracked jokes about them and how ugly they were and the things that some people called art. Their harshest humor they reserved, however, for an immense clay statue of a man, taller than any of them and weighing so much that it took three movers to carry it out of the house. It was a crude figure, lumpy and misshapen, with blocky feet and stubby fingers and a wide, impassive face. I recognized it at once: it was the tiny doll that I had glimpsed lying on a glass-and-metal *étagère*. It had grown, just as *golems* grew in the legends; as the Golem grew in *Strangely Enough!*, shaped by my great ancestor Rabbi Judah; as a lie grows, ugly and massive as Mr. Adler's lifelong deception, and as heavy as the burden of the guilt and horror that must have driven him so to inhabit and claim as his own the story of a dead Prague Jew.

To this day, I'm not sure what became of Mr. Adler. When I asked my mother recently, she said she thought he had eventually died in a convalescent home. She also remembered having heard sometime afterward that Mr. Adler's original accuser had later recanted, saying she was mistaken in her identification. "I think the woman was actually mentally ill," my mother said. My father, on the other hand, claims that while Mr. Adler may well have been Victor Fischer, he was certainly not C.B. Colby—that C.B. Colby was a well-known journalist and author whose works, many of them on military subjects, were only some of the books that Mr. Adler falsely claimed to have written. All those pseudonyms, according to my father, were actually the real names of writers whom Mr. Adler had chosen to claim to be. As for the *golem* that I saw them carrying out of his house that day, the three strapping men staggering under its weight as if it were a granite boulder, a chunk of iron fallen from outer space? Well, even if it did exactly resemble the little manikin I'd caught a glimpse of that day as I was leaving his house, then surely the first was a model of the second, a small preliminary work undertaken by the late Mrs. Adler before she began work on the large finished piece.

Now we come, finally, to the Golem of Prague itself. This is the part where things get weird, and I confess to being a little hesitant, having come this far, to press on. The first two *golems* I've told you about I encountered as a child, and you can blame the things I saw or thought I saw on my youth, and pardon them on the same account, and go along your way secure in the knowledge that stories of *golems* are myth, folklore, and the hokum of romancers like me. Up to this point, I am not a lunatic or even, necessarily, a liar—except of course to the degree that, professionally, I am both. From here on, however . . .

It will be recalled that on the day of my uncle Jack's funeral, my father consoled me with one of his standard accounts of our fabulous ancestry, in this case our connection to the great rabbi known as the Maharal, Rabbi Judah ben Loew of Prague. Later, my father would extend this branch laterally, to entangle the popular composer Frederick Loewe, and Marcus Loew, the man who cofounded MGM. For the twenty years that followed, I never had any more evidence to believe or disbelieve his claim of there being some kind of personal connection between me and Rabbi Judah than I did for any of the other claims he made. I grew up, and kept writing. In time, to our mutual regret, I found myself estranged from my father and from the unbelievable things I had once believed about him.

In the meantime, I had begun to publish stories of my own, stories, in some cases, about fathers who disappointed their sons. The fathers in these stories were *golem*-fathers. I wove alphabetical spells around them, and breathed life into them, and they got up and walked out into the world and caused trouble and embarrassment for the small man of flesh and blood in whose image they had been cast. Or maybe it was I who was the *golem*, my father's *golem*, animated by the enchantment of his narratives and lies, then rising up until I posed a danger to him and all the unlikely things that he, strangely enough, believed in.

Along the way I met a woman, and we decided to get married. She was not a Jew. To us—to the woman in question and me, I mean—this fact did not pose a problem. Of all the relatives of mine then living to whom it might have posed a problem, only the opinion of my grandfather mattered to me. But if he had any reservations about the match on religious grounds, he kept them to himself. Resistance, or at any rate a hint of misgiving, arose from an unexpected quarter: my father, perhaps the least observant self-identified Jew I've ever known, and believe me, that's saying a lot.

He waited to voice his doubts, as has always been his wont in such matters, until the last possible moment, when it was for all practical purposes too late to do anything about them. On the night before the wedding, at the rehearsal dinner, which was held at a French restaurant on Lake Union (I was marrying a Seattleite), he took me aside. His approach was oblique. "You know, you're a *kohen*," he said, meaning a member, by tradition, of the hereditary caste of Jewish high priests, a distinction that supposedly dates back to our forty years spent refusing to stop for directions in the Sinai desert. By now, you can't be too surprised to find my father including us among them.

"Right," I said. "Rabbi Judah."

"Oh, it goes back much farther than that," he said, and I thought, We're related to Moses himself. But instead of making the expected flight into the genealogical empyrean, my father's face softened, and his eyes grew wistful, and he looked unaccountably sad. "All those generations of Jews marrying Jews," he said. "Thousands and thousands of years of people like your mother and me."

"Yeah, well, you and Mom divorced," I said. Oh, I was feeling very cocky.

Then it was time for the toasts, and my father turned away from me. Three years from that day the Seattle girl and I would be divorced too.

After we had been married for about a month, and were living in Laguna Beach, a package arrived. In *The Amazing Adventures of Kavalier & Clay* I would employ the powers bestowed on me by Napoleon or my father and transform it into a crate, a massive wooden crate big enough to hold the huge clay man that I had seen them carrying out of Mr. Adler's house that afternoon. In reality it was just a small parcel, about the size of a paperback book—about the size, come to think of it, of *Strangely Enough!* It was wrapped in brown paper, with a pasted-on label that seemed to have been typed on an old manual typewriter. There was no return address. When I opened it I found, wrapped in a wad of cotton batting—can you guess?

It was a small, rough tablet of clay, half as big as a credit card and three times as thick. The clay was dark and worn smooth at the corners. On one side you could make out the traces of some characters—Hebrew letters, I supposed—that had been cut into the surface with a stylus or pin.

At this point, after everything I've told you so far, I expect that you realize at once what the thing was, or what it purported to be. But at the time, years removed from Uncle Jack and Mr. Adler, from *golems* and my heritage real and imagined, I had no idea what it was supposed to be, only that holding it gave me a strange sense of uneasiness. My then wife and I were graduate students, and some of our friends were artists, and I figured that somebody was having a joke at my expense. My then wife walked in on me as I was staring at it, and before I could think about what I was doing, I threw the tablet into the trash, along with the junk mail and circulars from Thrifty Drug. For some reason I didn't want her to see it.

About two years later, we had moved, trying to outrun the doom that was on us. We were living up in Puget Sound, on an island. It was a beautiful place, but I think I may have been, at the time, the only Jew living there; that, at any rate, was how I felt. One day when I drove into town to check our mailbox at the P.O., I found another small parcel awaiting me. It contained another small tablet. Actually, though I knew it was impossible, it seemed to be the same tablet, only this time the letters were so effaced as to be no more than scratches, nicks in the thing's dusty surface. I had given no thought to that other mysterious gift since throwing it away in Laguna Beach, but I had been giving increasing thought—furtively, secretly, lying awake in the middle of the night with my *goyish* wife sleeping beside me—to my father's words at the rehearsal dinner. The subject of children was beginning to come up, more and more insistently as my wife got older, and somehow, magically, every time it did we ended up having a painful, sticky, difficult argument—about religion! A subject I had never argued about with anybody in my life before! How can you tell me it's important for our children to be Jewish, she would say with perfect justification, when it doesn't seem to be at all important to you?

This time I recognized the tablet for what it was: a magic tablet for animating a *golem*, to be placed under its tongue by the hand of an adept. A reminder of Mr. Adler and his wishful lies, of the place where he claimed to have suffered. A reminder of all those who truly had died there, or at the next evil stop down the line. A reminder of all those generations of Jews, circling one another under the marriage canopy, intoning their spells, in order to bring into existence a *golem*, me, the embodiment of an ancient and simple wish: let there be more of us. Let us not disappear. I wondered who could have sent it—if perhaps old

Mr. Adler was out there somewhere, busily forging magic tablets and keeping track of my whereabouts. Or perhaps the culprit was my father. In any case, this time—my heart, my conscience, my thoughts weighed down by the *golem*-heavy burden of memory—I put the thing in my pocket. I carried it there as the marriage dissolved. I was carrying it when I met my present wife, Ayelet, herself the product of generations of Jews marrying Jews and no doubt, though my father has never said anything about it, a third cousin three times removed.

Brother, you're thinking. All this nattering on about *golems* and wishes and lies, and in the end the point comes down to one of your own kind, stick to your own kind. But that isn't the point. I don't know what the point is. All I know is that one sunny afternoon, not long after we met, I found myself in Jerusalem with Ayelet, at Yad Vashem, the Israeli national museum of the Shoah, or Holocaust, and my heart was broken. I came out into the sunshine and burst into tears and just stood there, crying, and the weight of the thing I carried, that tablet compounded of wishes and lies, that five-thousand-year burden of mothers and fathers and the wondrous, bitter story of their lives, almost knocked me down.

Our next stop before coming home was, of all places, Prague. Duly we made our way down to the ghetto, or what's left of it, and trooped around the old Jewish cemetery, with it snaggled headstones lying like teeth in a jawbone. That's where they buried old Rabbi Judah, and his grave is now a kind of pilgrimage site, strewn with memorial stones and penciled notes and withered flowers.

I knelt down beside the grave there, and in a patch of dirt I formed the hasty outline of a man. Where his mouth would be I opened a hole, and worked the clay tablet down into it. Then I took Ayelet's hand in mine and walked away.

I haven't received another one since, though I'm still looking out for it in the mail. I'm still listening to my father, too, and wishing as he wished—as we all wish, Jews and non-Jews alike— to be part of something ancient and honorable and greater than myself. And, naturally, I'm still telling lies.

The History Within Us

Matthew Kressel

On a wrist-mounted computer, Betsy Haadama watched a six thousand-year-old silent film. It was grayscale, overexposed, two-dimensional, and chronologically jumbled. On the film: a mustachioed man doting over his young son at a crowded zoo. A woman vigorously combing the boy's white hair beside a large piano. A family eating a large meal, candles burning on a table, men wearing *yarmulkes*, bodies shivering in prayer. A river, people swimming, women in white bathing caps and full-body suits. Men on rocks by the shore, pipes in mouths, smoke drifting lazily upward. A park, the boy looking down at a dead pigeon. Staring. Staring. Father picking him up, kissing him. In the sky, a bright sun.

A young sun.

"Pardon my intrusion in this time of ends," a Twirlover said, startling her. The Twirlover's six separate, hovering pink objects—like human knuckles—danced a looping, synchronized pattern in the air. "If it pleases you, will you share with me why you watch that flickering device so incessantly?"

In some parts of the galaxy one could be killed for being human. Betsy wasn't sure if this Eluder Ship was such a place. But death was coming for all soon enough. So why fear it now?

"This is an ancient film of my paternal ancestor," she said defiantly.

Puffs of air beat against her face as the Twirlover spun. "An ancient film? Indeed, such a rare treasure, an artifact of the past! If it pleases you, may we watch a portion together?"

She was about to tell it no, that she'd rather die alone, contemplating what might have been, when the alarm trilled down the cavernous halls of the Eluder Ship. A cold shiver ran down her spine as a cacophony of voices warned in ninety languages simultaneously, "Gravitational collapse imminent, my beloveds! Please take your positions inside your transitional shells!"

Angry rainbows flared across the floor and ozone and ammonia soured the air, warning those who communicated by color or smell. Betsy's mind skipped and stuttered like the ancient film playing on her wrist as a warning to the telepaths skirted the fringes of her consciousness. Still more warnings she could not perceive with her natural senses no doubt flooded the chamber now.

Hundreds of creatures ran or flew or poured inside their transitional shells, strange cocoons fitted to their variform bodies. The Twirlover tumbled away as Betsy closed the cover of her shell. She hugged her knees and shivered as the glass cover sealed her inside with a hiss and a confirmation beep. A lifeboat or a coffin? She'd find out soon enough.

Transitional shells filled the gargantuan chamber of the Eluder Ship like arrays of soldiers preparing for battle, their noses pointed toward the red-giant star looming outside. Maera—"The Daughter Star"—one of the few still-burning stars in the galaxy. It seethed before all, a conflagration as large as a solar system, turning everything the color of blood.

Forty seconds.

This was a pitiful end, but it was this or slow starvation, privation, death. The galaxy had been laid sere. No planets to grow food. No stars to keep warm. It wasn't fair. None of them deserved this. But then she remembered Julio, and what she had done to him at Afsasat.

I left you to die, Julio. And for that I deserve this.

Thirty seconds.

Soon now, Maera's heart would cool by a fraction of a degree, and billions of tons of matter, no longer kept aloft by nuclear winds, would plunge towards its gravitational center at the speed of light. The star would collapse, go nova, and in its tortured heart the universe would tear. A singularity would form, a black hole, and Betsy Haadama and the thousands of others on this Eluder Ship would ride that collapsing wave into another universe. Their matter and energy, transmuted into pure information, would seed a new creation, the World to Come. Their consciousness, over long eons, would push matter into form, coerce dust to life. In some strange new way they would live on, gods reborn further down the corridor of infinity. And they had been doing this forever, would be doing this again and again until the end of time.

Or so the litany went.

The story soothed troubled minds. But the science behind the technology was just a theory. It could be proven only by first-person observation. Any object which crossed a black hole's event horizon could never communicate with the universe again. Just as easily, she might be annihilated forever. To those witnessing from the outside, there would be no difference.

Twenty seconds.

She tried not to peer up at The Daughter, though its ember light corrupted everything with its hellish glow. Instead she watched the film on her wrist: men in fedoras, women in ostentatious hats at an airport, people descending a stairwell from plane to tarmac. A baby hoisted in the air. Smiles. Laughing. Cut to a park. The boy looking down at the dead pigeon, staring. Staring. Father picking him up, patting him on the shoulder. The boy, crying.

Why do you stare at the bird? Betsy thought. What are you thinking?

She looked up at the seething star. So beautiful, terrible, immense. A wonder that such a thing existed. A horn bellowed and Betsy screamed.

"False Alarm! Beloveds, the imminent collapse was a false alarm! Spurious readings caused us to make an erroneous conclusion. We estimate at least six hours before stellar collapse, based on present readings."

The voice announced the message in multiple languages, simulcast with aggressive rainbows, smells, alien sensations.

I'm alive! she thought. I'm still here! It felt exhilarating, for a moment. Then she remembered she'd have to do this again.

Slowly, shells opened and creatures emerged. Betsy scanned the motley lot of them as her cover retracted. A zoo of sentient species escaping from their cages, creatures made of every color, texture, and temperament.

So much life, she thought. Snuffed out by the Horde. Crimes beyond forgiveness. And made all the more vile because the Horde had been the progeny of the human race.

Betsy activated inositol in her bloodstream via thought command in order to suppress her panic/flight response. It soothed her, but only just enough to notice the hairs on the back of her neck rising from an electrostatic charge as the Twirlover returned.

"That was exciting!" it said.

"I wouldn't call it that," Betsy said.

"To be so close to annihilation and then to come back again. It renews the sense of life!"

"Or the dread of living."

"But the dread, if you explore it," the Twirlover said, "reveals the miracle of existence out of nothingness. From out of horror comes life."

The litany again. "Or out of life, horror," she said.

It tumbled quietly for a moment. "Sometimes." It moved closer to inspect her film. "That's a child of your species, is it not?"

She glanced down at her screen. "No, that's a rhinoceros."

"Ree-Nos-Ur-Us. What a marvel of composition, all those rolling mountains of flesh. Does it still exist?"

"Extinct."

The Twirlover whistled a mournful, descending arpeggio. "Like so much life in the galaxy. Like the once-glorious stars."

The Horde had obliterated stars by the billions. They had wrapped the Milky Way inside a bleak cocoon of transmatter so that nothing, no ship, no signal—not even light—could pass. And then they vanished, leaving the galaxy to rot. Such was the legacy of humanity.

She wondered if the Twirlover would kill her outright if it knew what she was. Death by physical means might be preferable, she thought, to being flash-baked into quantum-entangled gamma rays. Six in one, really.

The film cut to a boy in a crib, bouncing. His mother lifting him, smiling for the camera. The boy laughing.

"That's one of us," she said. "My paternal ancestor." Surprising herself, she felt pride.

"Ah, such wonderful protuberances!"

A wisp of dust coalesced above Betsy's head. Winking diamonds swirled in yellow clouds. An aeroform creature. For a moment she glimpsed her own face of colored sparkles reflected back at her. But the aeroform being soon spiraled away, only to pause a few seconds later before a group of fronded Whidus who turned their mushroom-like eyes in her direction. Maybe they recognized her, knew what she was. Maybe they were plotting her demise.

A second, identical Twirlover approached Betsy and said to the first, "You know, my bonded-one, that we are about to die, do you not?"

"I was about to come back to you, my flesh-bond," the first said. "And tell you about my sharing with this creature."

"Indeed you were. I saw you tumbling towards me with great haste."

"My flesh-bond, just take a good look at her smooth, auburn skin, the fine black threads that emerge from her head, the little valve at her peak where she modulates her words with a bacteria-laden pink muscle! And on her upper-left protuberance, that metal device which flicker-flashes with strange images. She watches it incessantly. She is curious, is she not?"

"There is something curious here, certainly."

"My love, let us join so I can share my thoughts with you."

"Indeed, I look forward to it!"

The two tumbled together into a single dancing, twelve-piece ring. Knuckles hopped, bounced, tumbled over each other. Music piped and whistled in Byzantine harmonies. There arose a great shriek about them, and soon after they separated again into six-pieced individuals. Betsy thought they might have interchanged pieces in the process.

"Not fair!" said the second. Or was it the first? Betsy couldn't tell them apart anymore. "You playful trickster! You gave me your segment, so now I know your thoughts. But then, you sense my emotions too."

"What joy it is to share mind with you, beloved! Yes, I feel your misplaced jealousy. And so much of it! What a waste of energy. Don't you see? This creature is alone and needs to share with someone!"

"Perhaps, but does it have to be you?"

"Not me alone, but us together!"

"In this last hour, you would defile us?"

"Please!" Betsy interjected. "I'd prefer to be alone anyway—"

"One must never be alone!" the first said. "Share with us! Let us merge gloriously with your words."

"Indeed, tell us," the second said, "Did you have a bonded-one who abandoned you, who wandered off to have intercourse with strangers when you need him?"

'Intercourse?' she thought. Perhaps there was more to the Twirlover concept of sharing than she realized. "Actually, I left him."

"Of course you did," the second said. "Like attracts like."

"Where did you abandon him?" the first said.

Interesting, the way it had interpreted her words. "I left him at the first nova," she said. "The Mother Star. Afsasat."

"You were at Afsasat and you didn't go through the event-horizon?" the second said. "I don't believe your story! Beloved, look how she defiles this union!"

"Surely," the first said, "you are joking, trying to please us with paradox? Why would you do something so idiotic? Why not escape through Afsasat when you had the chance?"

She sighed and turned her attention to the film on her wrist. Mustachioed father and blond-haired son walking down a path. Father, smiling. Boy running, falling. Crying. Father picking him up, kissing him. All better. All better.

"Did you hear our questions?" the first asked.

"Yes," she said. "It's just that it's a very long story."

"Our lives are stories. We are empty without them. Fill us so we may fill you."

Strangely, she had stopped shivering. She even felt a little warm. If this was intercourse, then she was determined to be a good lover. "This film is part of 'The Biography,' " she said. "A record of my ancestors' lives that was encoded within my genes."

"Such joy! I have heard of this technology, the sharing of such immensity," the first said. "How far back do your records go?"

"About six thousand years."

The second squealed.

"I told you, beloved," the first said. "She is share-worthy."

Her mother had told her the story in the quiet hours while drifting under the ash streams of the decimated Magellanic Clouds, or over stale, thrice-brewed tea, while the ice-blue rings of Cegmar rose above the horizon, or while her mother gently brushed her hair and chills trickled down her spine. When he turned seventy, the boy in the film digitized his aging childhood reels and then gave them to his son. His son added films, photos, and memorabilia and passed the collection to his offspring. His children added more history and passed this collection on again. This continued for generations. Eventually his descendants decided to encode this amalgamated history within their DNA, so it would never be lost or forgotten. Every child was thereafter born with the memories of their parents, and theirs before them, and theirs before them. And also in their bodily archives were the early records—the films, photos and keepsakes that started the tradition. The Biography was an ancient and unbroken chain that began with this black-and-white film playing on her wrist. The first.

And now the last.

"It's so large!" the second said.

"Excuse me?" she said.

"Your story," the first said, "To carry all that history within you!"

"It's not in me anymore. Julio and I stripped all of it, every last base-pair, from our genes. I recall only my personal experiences now. This computer . . . it holds the last copy. This is the Biography, now."

This fragile, solitary thing on her wrist.

"But why?" Moans and tweets. "That must have been an immense loss!"

The answer was complex, full of shame and guilt. Instead she offered the highly edited version. "Because we wanted to enter the World to Come without a past."

The Twirlovers tumbled noisily, screeching.

"I put the Biography on this ancient computer," she said, pointing to her wrist. "It belonged to my grandmother, five hundred and eighty years ago. Julio and I parked our starsloop in orbit around Afsasat and we stowed this wrist-player in our shrine-room. We said goodbye to our past and then we flew over to the Eluder Ship. Our starsloop and the Biography within would be destroyed when Afsasat went nova."

Chirps. Squeals.

"But Afsasat took its time. So I explored every corner of the Eluder Ship. I discovered that none of my species were there. That meant Julio and I might be the last of my kind in existence. And that meant the Biography was the last of its kind too."

A duet of whistles in a major key.

"I used to recall the smell of my great-grandmother's hair of twenty-three generations ago as her lover leaned in to kiss her pink lips. I knew every defect in the bathroom tiles of the beach house where my ancestor Rhindi lived four thousand years ago. I could hear the gulls cry as they flew in the colored dawn as the four suns rose, one green, one orange, one yellow, and one blue before Eleanor left her family for war, to die in deep space, but not before she had a son to pass on the memory. I once remembered the joy Yalta felt toward his seventeen lanky daughters, all born in zero-g, all tall, graceful, beautiful, with eyes like blue giants. These weren't others' lives. They were mine. I had lived these lives too."

Seven long, high notes.

"So many people had once lived inside of me. Even these memories that

I'm telling you about now—they come from this device! Not from me! I'm silent inside. And I realized that if I let the Biography die I would be murdering billions. Just like the Horde."

A very human gasp, then a precipitous pause.

"So I changed my mind. I decided I'd bring the Biography with me into the World to Come. My ancestors deserved that much. I was about to retrieve it from our starsloop, but Julio held me. Afsasat could go nova at any moment, he said. And . . . he wanted to sever us from the past. I disagreed."

Betsy started shaking again as the moment became clear in her mind. She remembered his exhausted, pleading eyes, his unruly black beard.

"Did you forget what they did?" Julio had said. "Did you erase that memory too? The Horde, the progeny of the human race, stole our children! And you want to bring their history with us? We decided we wouldn't allow that. The Biography has to be destroyed."

"I know what we decided, Julio!" she said. "But I can't let all those people die!"

"They're already dead, Betsy!"

"I can't believe you just said that." Her face grew hot. "They're not dead! They once lived within us! They gave us our lives, and we owe them our memories!"

"I don't feel that way at all."

"Julio, how can you abandon them so easily?"

"They led us to this place of death and horror. I sever myself from the past for that reason alone."

And in the end, it was she who had abandoned him.

She swallowed down her tears as the Twirlovers squealed and beckoned her to continue.

"I told Julio I wanted to wander the ship alone, and instead I snuck off to fetch the Biography. Maybe he knew where I was going. I'll never know. I reached my starsloop and was ready to return when I heard the alarm. Afsasat was collapsing. One minute to nova. Not enough time to return safely. I panicked. I had to save the Biography, all those lives, from destruction. Nothing else mattered. I powered up my ship and fled."

For weeks she had wondered, did Julio search the Eluder Ship for her? What did he feel when he realized she had left him? Like the thoughts of the boy in the film, she'd never know. He had entered a black hole, and nothing could cross that dark horizon.

The Twirlovers cried out, a piercing shriek. Perhaps they orgasmed together. Eventually, the second said, "What a dirty tale! So much abandonment. I feel defiled. A sinner! This is the kind of sharing you wanted, my beloved?"

"But in fetching her Biography she returned to her people!" the first said. "Don't you see? Isn't sharing so much more rewarding after a long absence?"

"You twist words easily, my bonded-one! Her story was . . . acceptable."

A large Perslop sloshed towards them. The creature was amber, a gelatinous three-limbed starfish with translucent skin and dozens of eyes like upturned brown bowls.

"Do you wish a comforting invocation?" the Perslop said. A slit tucked into one of its armpits burped open to reveal hundreds of tiny white teeth, and its warm breath reeked of dead seas. "I know rituals from a thousand faiths. Or, if you wish, you may teach me one." Its voice was like wind blowing over ruins.

"Blessings, smooth-skinned pleasure to behold!" the first Twirlover said. "We welcome a fourth to share!"

"No we do not!" the second Twirlover said.

"My flesh-love, please!" the first said. "Do not be rude." Then to the Perslop: "Instead of an invocation, my finely contoured friend. Will you share a story with us?"

"Incorrigible!" the second said, tumbling furiously.

With the moist end of one if its arms, the Perslop inched towards Betsy's wrist. The tip opened into a tripod of three small fingers, with diminutive brown eyes capping the end of each. The eyes wiggled nervously above the ancient film. "What is this?" it asked.

"It's her people's history!" the first said. "From six-thousand years ago!"

"Interesting," the Perslop said. "Your race hasn't changed much."

"That's a duck," Betsy said. "Extinct."

"So, that's you there?"

"No, that's a walrus. Also extinct."

"Then whose history did you say we are watching?"

"My race. They're at a zoo."

"A 'zoo?' " the Perslop said.

"A place that housed animals in cages."

"What for?"

"So they could observe them without danger to themselves," she said.

"Another act of separation!" the second Twirlover said. "Such a barbaric, dirty race!"

"Her filth notwithstanding, keeping something caged is not barbarism," the Perslop said, its moist arm dangling an hairsbreadth from Betsy's face. "Before the Horde destroyed my brothers, I used to travel with my colony to a fecal press, where we severed one of our limbs and tortured it in a cage until it released a small amount of feces. We then burned that feces as an offering to the Absent One. They were profoundly holy events. And I miss them very, very much."

The second Twirlover squeaked loudly three times.

"You see, my beloved?" the first said. "This is the joy you have missed by withdrawing from union all these years!"

On Betsy's wrist the film played on, men in white shorts and shirts playing handball. Women sitting on the sidelines bringing smoky cigarettes to their lips. The young boy, a few years older, standing on a porch, talking to a beautiful girl.

"You simplify my thoughts!" the second Twirlover said. "I take no joy in the suffering of others. If I did, I would find pleasure in the atrocities of the Horde. But those are stories I never wish to hear again. If I could, I would erase them from history like this creature erased this Biography from her genes!"

If only that were possible, Betsy thought. To rewrite history. If so, she'd go even further back, to the creation of the Horde, more than three hundred years ago. Humanity had been evolving rapidly for generations. They had augmented their consciousness to the point that the body became irrelevant. Flesh was now a temporary abode, while the mind was free to explore and play in infinite space. Epic works of art, science, and philosophy were commonplace. Physical suffering had been eradicated. It was a true Golden Age of humankind.

But the Hagzhi, a prideful, stoic and gargantuan species that had once peacefully abided humans, became fearful of humanity's growing power over matter and began to spread lies and sow seeds of mistrust. Later, the Hagzhi began to systematically exterminate humans as a way to prop up their own faltering galactic hegemonies. Humanity was nearly destroyed in the wars that followed, but after that tumult, humans vowed that they would never let such a catastrophe happen again. Through heroic feats of research they discovered the secret folds of negative time and learned the simple mystery behind the origins of consciousness. They learned how to, with a thought, create a sun. And with another, destroy it.

The Hagzhi race vanished from existence in a day. One hundred and seventy planets, moons, outposts and stations erased from the universe. Later, for no reason anyone could discern, other races vanished. Races which had never threatened humanity. The Onyx Horde, as this force came to be known, acted without cause or reason.

Not all humans accepted the rise to supra-consciousness. Not all humans wanted to change. The Horde slaughtered those who resisted. Those who hid were found, tortured, and killed. And there were those, like Betsy's ancestors, who had made a deal and were spared.

"Keep the Biography in your genes," the Horde had commanded her ancestors. "Keep your physical human form. Do this and you will not die."

And her ancestors agreed, and survived, even prospered, while the rest of the galaxy was ruined. When the other races discovered that there were humans who were spared the Horde's madness, that the Horde were the progeny of the human race, the long dormant seeds of doubt that the Hagzhi had planted re-sprouted, this time across the entire galaxy. Humans were slaughtered without remorse, and the Horde did not come to save them.

If I were given that choice now, Betsy thought. To live or die by their rules, I would have chosen death. I'd rather die than live under their darkness another instant.

On the film, a crowded beach. People swimming. Large umbrellas casting shadows. Wisps of cloud in the sky, all under a bright sun.

A young sun.

The Twirlovers stopped twirling. The Perslop leaned in closer to see.

"Such a young sun," the Perslop said. "Bright and warm. The sight fills me with sadness. No longer do such stars burn in the Milky Way. Here we orbit this dying star in a dead galaxy where only a few cinders burn in a quiescent sea. And all about the universe a hundred billion galaxies dangle forever beyond our reach. The Onyx Horde has sealed us forever from their glorious light. May their souls be stripped from eternity!"

On the film, a party. People laughing, dancing, hands on hips, forming a human train. Cone-shaped hats.

"What are they doing?" the Perslop asked.

"A party," Betsy said. "A new year's celebration."

"And why do they bounce up and down?"

"They're dancing."

"Do you remember, my soul-union," the first Twirlover said, "how we danced for three ascensions of the Hagic Moon with the birth of our tumble-litter?"

"I shall never forget!" the second said, squealing. "Our many tumblers, searching for their bond-sisters. How they merged and separated a thousand times before they joined the sisters to complete their soul!"

"May they find the path to the Glory Star that resides at the center of creation."

On the film, the blond boy in the corner staring into the camera eye. I'd always assumed that one day someone would look into the Biography and see me. But I'm the last, aren't I?

"Your children, are they dead?" the Perslop said to the Twirlovers.

"They were living on Ental," the second said. "It was obliterated by the Horde." A hiss like a distant wave crashing on an empty beach.

"I had nine offspring," the Perslop said. "Three died in the disastrous attempt to pass through the galaxy's transmatter shell. Three died of malnutrition. Two died in an experiment to create a new star."

"That's only eight," the first Twirlover said. "And the ninth?"

"Suicide."

On the film, an elderly couple in formal clothing sitting beside a bright window. Their bodies in silhouette. The woman, Bessie. The man, Oser. Betsy's oldest ancestors in the Biography. She and Julio had named their children after them. A boy and girl. Twins. She remembered their puffy, newborn faces, their eyes hungry for life.

She and Julio and her children had been living on the temperate moon of Aeoschloch with one hundred other Biography-carrying humans, far from the wars and the suspicions of the other races. And one morning, as the swirling black eye of the gas giant Ur rose above the distant hills, as she was breast-feeding her twin children, she was swept away.

She could not see or hear or sense anything, even her own screams, but she felt a presence probing her, scanning her, reading and rereading the Biography within her as if it were the most important thing in the universe. And she knew this presence, remembered it from the Biography and the memories within.

The Onyx Horde.

Then the Horde spit her and a hundred other humans out over the sandy coastline. Some people did not rise from the cold beach. Their eyes stared life-less into the starless sky. Some had organs missing or were merged with others into horrible grotesqueries. Some went mad. Some had reappeared in the ocean and drowned. And the children, all the pre-pubescent ones, had vanished. The Horde had taken them. Every one.

Oser and Bessie, two months old, barely enough time to open their eyes and learn their parents' faces. Gone.

The seventy surviving colonists were wrecked, devastated. Should they have more children? No, they decided, the Horde could just as easily take them again. Should they try to forget and live out their lives on this backwater moon? No, how could they ever find joy again, knowing that the Horde could come again at any time? Then the colonists heard about Afsasat, the Eluder Ship being built there and a possible way to escape the Horde forever.

And so it was decided. The colonists would end their history on their own terms. They would attempt to enter the World to Come, but without the Biography inside of them. They would excise it from their genes, shedding themselves from the thing which the Horde seemed so desperately to desire. Shedding themselves of humanity's sordid history. It would be, in their own small way, revenge.

But they'd have to get to Afsasat first. The Eluder Ship was being constructed in a quadrant of space that was rumored to be tolerant of humans. But the colonists would have to navigate through large quadrants of dangerous space. So they traveled in many ships, by multiple circuitous and zigzagging routes. Betsy and Julio arrived safely. When Betsy walked around the ship, looking for other humans, she found none. They were the last two.

And now, on this second Eluder Ship, there was only her.

Outside the windows, lightning the size of a hundred dead planets forked across Maera's surface. The star looked ancient, tired, ready to sleep forever. The aliens throughout the chamber paused to stare up at the star.

Her wrist flickered like the star outside. On the film, the mustachioed man. The woman with the beautiful black hair. Another party. A different day. A cake with five flames. Eyes reflecting candlelight. The boy, blowing the flames out. Smoke and applause. Silent cheer.

"You said you wanted a story," the Perslop said, "Well I have one. A few weeks ago I confronted a group of wandering Ergs. One told me that he'd captured a human—"

Betsy started in her seat.

"The Erg said the human was an ugly, repulsive thing," the Perslop continued. "With dark hair covering most of its carbuncle head, and liquid leaking from its odious eyes. It pleaded for its life. And the Erg, a compassionate being, decided ultimately to let it go. But afterward he became terribly distraught. He said he'd missed his opportunity to destroy a creature which had caused so much of the galaxy's pain. For a long time I considered this Erg's position.

"I once had a vast starship. I found a bore-worm nibbling in my refuse berth. I believed in the sanctity of all life, and decided to let it live. Six weeks later, my ship was infested with bore-worms, and no one would dock with me for fear of having their hulls eaten. I had to incinerate my ship. You see, I let one worm live, and thousands returned to ruin me. Is it not the same with humans? If we let one live, do we not give them the chance to destroy us again? I told the Erg that he did the righteous thing, but I truly did not—do not—believe it myself."

The Twirlovers chirped quietly.

"Where did he find this human?" she blurted. "How many weeks ago was this?" Dark hair covering its head? she thought. Julio, is he speaking of you?

The first Twirlover said, "Please, tell us more, beloved! This is wonderful!"

"What more is there to tell?" the Perslop said. "We may be reborn in a new universe, but if we carry that worm along with us, do we not risk infestation again?"

Betsy stared into the Perslop's tripod eye-cups. It knows, she thought. It knows what I am. Then she remembered the aeroform creature studying her and the Whidus staring at her and the Twirlovers' odd behavior around her.

They all know, she thought. Every one of them knows!

"Do not fear, human," the Perslop said. "I'll not kill you. I define myself by being what you are not. I let you live even though every pulse of my hearts says you should be squashed between my arms like vermin."

Betsy stared at the Perslop, shivering. Weakly, she said, "Was your story about the human true?"

Outside, a brilliant solar flare leaped from Maera and grew angrily out into space. The Daughter, shedding her last vestiges of life. Soon now.

The Perslop gestured to her screen. "Is your story true? Is not history filled with lies and obfuscations?"

On the screen, a beach, waves crashing silently. Umbrellas casting large shadows. A beautiful young woman smiling shyly at the camera. The future wife of the boy. A burning ball of light in the sky. Everyone watched the screen.

"So beautiful," the Perslop said. "And gone forever . . . "

Silence. Even the Twirlovers went still.

"Please!" she said. "Tell me! Was it true?"

"Why?" the Perslop said. "Why should I tell you? Why do you deserve an answer?"

She took a deep breath. "Because someone I love might still be alive," she said. "To me, that's everything."

The alarm trilled, startling her. "Gravitational collapse imminent, beloveds! Please take your positions inside your transitional shells!"

"No!" she cried. "Not yet!"

The Perslop began to move away.

"Wait!" she screamed. "Please tell me!"

The Perslop paused but did not turn back. "I am the last of my kind," the Perslop said. "I came over here to tell you that you are not."

The Twirlovers shrieked and suddenly merged. They tumbled madly, yelping, barking, while the Perslop left for its transitional shell.

Ninety seconds to collapse.

Maera flickered and angry waves rippled across its surface, but Betsy could not summon the will to close her shell. On her viewscreen, the park, the blond-haired boy skipping, scaring away pigeons. Dappled sunlight. A breeze through trees. A dead pigeon on the dirt. The boy, stopping, staring. Staring.

Suddenly, she understood why the boy stared at the bird for so long.

This is the first time you knew death! she thought. You knew the bird would never rise again. And you knew that one day you'd fall too, that everything falls! That's why you gave these films to your son. You wanted him to remember you, forever!

Seventy-five seconds.

The Perslop had been right, she thought. I could be polluting the new universe with this history.

Sixty-five seconds.

But all those lives, erased? I can't kill you, great-great grandfather. You are the first. Without you, we would be nothing. My ancestors, without all of you, I am nothing.

Sixty seconds.

The fourteen billion-year history of this universe had already unfolded. But for the World to Come, the story had yet to be written. Maybe the World to Come was a lie, but then again, maybe there was new life on the other side of the event horizon. Maybe they truly had been doing this forever and ever. A flower gone to seed.

She jumped out of her transitional shell, took off her grandmother's computer from her wrist, and placed it inside the shell. Then she pressed the button to seal it inside.

She'd send the Biography, its mammoth history, with its eons of joys and sorrows, through Maera. She hoped that in the next universe, humanity would be different. Better. What every parent wishes for her children.

"Goodbye," she said.

The Twirlovers still tumbled together in the air beside her, as wild as a radioactive atom. The alarm continued to wail. "Get in your shells!" she screamed. But they ignored her.

Twenty seconds.

She ran to the rear of the chamber and leaped into an escape pod. She pressed the emergency activator and in an instant she was hurtling away from the Eluder Ship at a large fraction of the speed of light. In the window behind her, Maera blinked twice, like two eyes closing, then began to fade. The star shrunk to half its size, and a moment later the sky filled with white light. The ship bleated a thousand warnings as Betsy closed her eyes.

"I'm coming, Julio. I'm coming for you."

She had watched the ancient film so often that it still played in her mind, projecting on the back of her eyes like a movie screen. The boy in the park, running, laughing. Falling. Scuffing his knee. Father picking him up, kissing him, comforting him. Above them, a sun.

A young sun.

ABOUT THE CONTRIBUTORS

Ann VanderMeer is the founder of the award-winning Buzzcity Press and currently serves as the Editor-in-Chief for *Weird Tales*, for which she has received a Hugo award. Ann has partnered with her husband, author Jeff VanderMeer, on such editing projects as the World Fantasy Award-winning *Leviathan* series, *The Thackery T. Lambshead Pocket Guide to Eccentric & Discredited Diseases*, *The New Weird*, *Steampunk*, and *Fast Ships, Black Sails*. Her latest book is *The Kosher Guide to Imaginary Animals*. She is also known for teaching writing workshops, including Clarion, Odyssey, and Shared Worlds as well conducting creativity seminars for such varied audiences as the state of Arizona and Blizzard Entertainment. http://www.weirdtalesmagazine.com

Rachel Pollack is the author of thirty-one books of fiction, non-fiction, and poetry. Her novel *Godmother Night* won the World Fantasy Award, while *Unquenchable Fire* won the Arthur C. Clarke Award. Her non-fiction work centers on Tarot, Kabbalah, and related subjects. Her book *78 Degrees of Wisdom* has been in print continuously since 1980 and is often called "the Bible of Tarot readers." Rachel's work is published all over the world, in fourteen languages. Rachel is also a visual artist, creator of *The Shining Tribe Tarot*. Her most recent book of fiction is *The Tarot of Perfection*, a collection of short stories.

Eliot Fintushel makes his living as a writer and as an itinerant solo performer. He won the National Endowment for the Arts' Solo Performer Award twice. Fintushel has performed solo shows at The National Theater and thousands of venues, including once, for a party of diplomats, under the anti-aircraft gun of a German ship in New York Harbor. He has published about fifty short stories, mostly in *Asimov's*, and the novel *Breakfast With the Ones You Love* (Random House.) He was a contributing editor for *Tricycle: The Buddhist Review*, until he lost his oneness. He performs with the Imaginists Theatre Collective.

Rose Lemberg was born on the outskirts of the former Hapsburg Empire. She received her PhD from UC Berkeley, and now works as a professor of Nostalgic and Marginal Studies somewhere in the Midwest. Her office is a cavern without windows. When nobody's watching, the walls glint with diamonds or perhaps tears, and fiddlers dance inside the books. Rose's short fiction has appeared in *Strange Horizons* and *Fantasy Magazine*, and her poetry in *Abyss and Apex* and *Goblin Fruit*, as well as other venues. She edits *Stone Telling*, a new magazine of boundary-crossing poetry.

Theodora Goss was born in Hungary and spent her childhood in various European countries before her family moved to the United States. Although she grew up on the classics of English literature, her writing has been influenced by an Eastern European literary tradition in which the boundaries between realism and the fantastic are often ambiguous. Her publications include the short story collection *In the Forest of Forgetting* (2006); *Interfictions* (2007), a short story anthology coedited with Delia Sherman; and *Voices from Fairyland* (2008), a poetry anthology with critical essays and a selection of her own poems. Her short stories and poems have won the World Fantasy and Rhysling Awards. Visit her website at www.theodoragoss.com.

Poems and short stories by **Sonya Taaffe** have won the Rhysling Award, been shortlisted for the SLF Fountain Award and the Dwarf Stars Award, and been reprinted in *The Year's Best Fantasy and Horror, The Alchemy of Stars: Rhysling Award Winners Showcase, The Best of Not One of Us*, and *Trochu divné kusy 3*; a selection can be found in *Postcards from the Province of Hyphens* and *Singing Innocence and Experience* (Prime Books). She holds master's degrees in Classics from Brandeis and Yale and named a Kuiper belt object last year. "The Dybbuk in Love" is dedicated to Bernice Madinek Glixman (1923–1997). Thanks to Michael Zoosman for Menachem.

Michael Blumlein is the author of three novels, *The Movement of Mountains; X, Y;* and *The Healer*, as well as the award-winning story collection, *The Brains of Rats*. He wrote the screenplay for the widely acclaimed independent film, *Decodings*, and has also written for the stage. His novel, *X,Y*, was made into a feature-length movie. He has recently completed a new novel, *The Domino Master*, the first book in the multi-volume Bonebreaker Chronicles.

Jonathon Sullivan, MD, PhD sees patients, teaches, and conducts research in the Department of Emergency Medicine at Detroit Receiving Hospital-Wayne State University, a Level I Trauma center. His fiction has appeared in several anthologies and has often been featured on Escape Pod. Currently he devotes most of his time to research on brain resuscitation after cardiac arrest and trauma—a field not entirely dissimilar to the animation of *golems*—but he hopes to return to writing more SF soon. He lives in an old house with his wife, Marilyn, and a demented cat, Smeagol.

Jane Yolen, often called "the Hans Christian Andersen of America," is the author of over three hundred books that range from rhymed picture books and baby board books, through middle grade fiction, poetry collections, nonfiction, and up to novels and story collections for young adults and adults. Her books and stories have won an assortment of awards—two Nebulas, a World Fantasy Award, a Caldecott, the Golden Kite Award, three Mythopoeic awards, two Christopher Medals, a nomination for the National Book Award, the World Fantasy Association's Lifetime Achievement Award, and the Jewish Book Award, among others. Five colleges and universities have given her honorary doctorates. Visit her website at: www.janeyolen.com.

Dr. Elana Gomel is a Senior Lecturer at the Department of English and American Studies, Tel-Aviv University, Israel, which she chaired for two years. She is the author of four books: *Bloodscripts: Writing the Violent Subject, We and You: Being a Russian in Israel, The Pilgrim Soul,* and *Postmodern Science Fiction and Temporal Imagination.* She has published numerous articles in academic journals in the U.S. and UK on subjects ranging from Charles Dickens to science fiction and narrative theory. Her fantasy story "In the Moment" won the second place in the 2009 Short Story Competition of the British Fantasy Society.

Ben Burgis is a philosophy professor at the University of Ulsan in Korea, and a low-residency Creative Writing student at the Stonecoast MFA program at the University of Southern Maine. He went to Clarion West in 2006, and his stories have appeared in *Flytrap, Podcastle,* and *Diet Soap.* He received his PhD in Philosophy from the University of Miami, which is a different way of saying that he spent his late twenties living by the beach, sipping mojitos and thinking about semantic paradoxes, thus earning the right to obnoxiously correct people who call him "Mr. Burgis." He blogs at benburgis.livejournal.com.

Benjamin Rosenbaum lives near Basel, Switzerland, with his wife Esther and their eerily clever children, Aviva and Noah. Benjamin's stories have appeared in *Nature, Harper's, F&SF, Asimov's, McSweeney's, Strange Horizons,* and a collection, *The Ant King and Other Stories,* from Small Beer Press, and have been translated into fourteen languages. He has been a party clown, a synagogue president, a computer game designer, and can cook a mean risotto. More at http://benjaminrosenbaum.com

Lavie Tidhar grew up on a *kibbutz* in Israel and has lived variously in South Africa, the UK, Asia and the remote island-nation of Vanuatu in the South Pacific. Lavie's first novel, *The Bookman,* was published in January 2010 in a UK edition, and will be published in the U.S. in October 2010. Lavie's other works include novellas *An Occupation of Angels, Cloud Permutations,* and *Gorel & The Pot-Bellied God,* linked-story collection *Hebrew Punk,* and a collaborative novel *The Tel Aviv Dossier* with Nir Yaniv.

Bestselling author **Neil Gaiman** has long been one of the top writers in modern comics, as well as writing books for readers of all ages. He is listed in the *Dictionary of Literary Biography* as one of the top ten living post-modern writers, and is a prolific creator of works of prose, poetry, film, journalism, comics, song lyrics, and drama. Some of his notable works include *The Sandman* comic book series, *Stardust, American Gods, Coraline,* and *The Graveyard Book.* Gaiman's writing has won numerous awards, including World Fantasy, Hugo, Nebula, IHG, and Bram Stoker, as well as the 2009 Newbery Medal. Gaiman's official Web site, www.neilgaiman.com, now has more than one million unique visitors each month, and his online journal is syndicated to thousands of blog readers every day.

Peter S. Beagle originally proclaimed he would be a writer at age ten. Subsequent events have proven him either prescient or even more stubborn than hitherto suspected. Today, thanks to classic works such as *The Last Unicorn, Tamsin,* and *The Innkeeper's Song,* he is acknowledged as one of America's greatest fantasy authors. In addition to stories and novels he has written numerous teleplays and screenplays, including the animated versions of *The Lord of the Rings* and *The Last Unicorn,* plus the "Sarek" episode of *Star Trek: The Next Generation.* He is also a poet, lyricist, and singer/songwriter. In 2007, Beagle won the Hugo and Nebula Awards for his original novelette, "Two Hearts." For more details on Peter's career and upcoming titles, see either www.peterbeagle.com or www.conlanpress.com

Max Sparber began blogging in 2000, at first editing an online poetry magazine, *Doggerel Weekly,* that specialized in bawdy themes and black humor. This later turned into *Bawd,* a personal blog exploring the same themes. Since then, Max has started a number of blogs detailing a variety of projects, including horror makeup, his work as a playwright, the culture of the cocktail, and supernaturally themed music. Lately, Max has been redacting all these projects into a single blog: sparberfans.blogspot.com. Max has written more than a dozen plays, many of them appearing at Omaha's Blue Barn Theatre, where Max had his first play produced.

Tamar Yellin is the author of *The Genizah at the House of Shepher* (St Martin's Press), *Kafka in Brontëland* (Toby Press), and *Tales of the Ten Lost Tribes* (St Martin's Press). She received the Sami Rohr Prize for emerging Jewish writers in 2007. She has a website at www.tamaryellin.com.

Glen Hirshberg's novels include *The Book of Bunk: A Fairy Tale of the Federal Writers' Project* (Earthling, 2010), and *The Snowman's Children* (Carroll & Graf,

2002). Both of his story collections, *American Morons* (Earthling, 2006) and *The Two Sams* (Carroll & Graf, 2003) received the International Horror Guild Award and were selected by *Locus* as a best book of the year. He won the 2008 Shirley Jackson Award for his novella, *The Janus Tree*. With Dennis Etchison and Peter Atkins, he cofounded the Rolling Darkness Revue, a traveling ghost story performance troupe. He teaches writing and the teaching of writing at Cal State San Bernardino.

Alex Irvine's most recent novels are *Buyout*, *The Narrows*, and *Transformers: Exodus*. He also is the author of nonfiction books including *The Vertigo Encyclopedia* and *John Winchester's Journal*, as well as comic series *Daredevil Noir* and *Hellstorm, Son of Satan: Equinox*. His short fiction is collected in *Unintended Consequences* and *Pictures from an Expedition*.

Michael Chabon has been called "one of the most celebrated writers of his generation" and is winner of the Pulitzer Prize for his third novel, *The Adventures of Kavalier & Clay* (2000). His most recent novel *The Yiddish Policemen's Union* (2007) won the Hugo, Sidewise, and Nebula Awards. After earning a graduate degree in creative writing from the University of California at Irvine, Chabon's first novel, *The Mysteries of Pittsburgh* (1988) made him a literary celebrity. His second novel, *Wonder Boys* (1995), was made into a popular film. He has also published collections of short stories, written for the screen, and penned a novel for young readers (*Summerland*, 2006). Chabon is married to writer Ayelet Waldman.

Matthew Kressel's fiction and non-fiction has appeared or is forthcoming in such publications as *Clarkesworld Magazine*, *Beneath Ceaseless Skies*, *Interzone*, *Fantasy Magazine*, *Weird Tales*, *Electric Velocipede*, *Apex Magazine*, and the anthologies *Naked City* and *Hatter Bones*. In 2003, he started the speculative fiction and poetry magazine *Sybil's Garage*. He is also the publisher of *Paper Cities, An Anthology of Urban Fantasy*, which won the 2009 World Fantasy Award for best anthology of the year. He has been a member of Altered Fluid, a Manhattan-based writers group, since 2003. His website is www.matthewkressel.net.

PUBLICATION HISTORY AND COPYRIGHTS

Rachel Pollack, "Burning Beard" © 2007. *Interfictions*, ed. Theodora Goss & Delia Sherman (Interstitial Arts Foundation). Reprinted by permission of the author.

Benjamin Rosenbaum, "Biographical Notes to 'A Discourse on the Nature of Causality, with Air-Planes' by Benjamin Rosenbaum" © 2004. *All-Star Zeppelin Adventure Stories,* October 2004. Reprinted by permission of the author.

Max Sparber, "Eliyahu ha-Navi" © 2000. *Strange Horizons,* September 2000. Reprinted by permission of the author.

Jonathon Sullivan, "Niels Bohr and the Sleeping Dane" © 2005. *Strange Horizons,* July 2005. Reprinted by permission of the author.

Sonya Taaffe, "The Dybbuk in Love" © 2007. *The Dybbuk in Love* (Prime Books). Reprinted by permission of the author.

Lavie Tidhar, "Alienation and Love in the Hebrew Alphabet" © 2005. *Chizine,* April-June 2005. Reprinted by permission of the author.

Tamar Yellin, "Reuben" © 2005. *Maggid: A Journal of Jewish Literature,* 2005. Reprinted by permission of the author.

Jane Yolen, and Adam Stemple, "The Tsar's Dragons" © 2009. *The Dragon Book: Magical Tales from the Masters of Modern Fantasy,* ed. Jack Dann & Gardner Dozois (Ace). Reprinted by permission of the author.